THE
DARKEST
PART
OF THE
WOODS

RAMSEY
CAMPBELL

TOR®

A TOM DOHERTY ASSOCIATES BOOK
New York

This is a work of fiction. All the characters and events portrayed in this book are
either products of the author's imagination or are used fictitiously.

THE DARKEST PART OF THE WOODS

Copyright © 2002 by Ramsey Campbell

Originally published in Great Britain by PS Publishing, Ltd., Harrogate

A Tor Book
Published by Tom Doherty Associates, LLC
175 Fifth Avenue
New York, NY 10010

www.tor.com

Tor® is a registered trademark of Tom Doherty Associates, LLC.

ISBN 0-765-34682-6
EAN 976-0765-34682-7
Library of Congress Catalog Card Number: 2003055983

First U. S. Edition: October 2003
First mass market edition: October 2004

Printed in the United States of America

0 9 8 7 6 5 4 3 2 1

For Angus,
another reason to open a bottle

Acknowledgments

Like so much of my stuff, this would never exist without Jenny. A section was written while I had a fulltime job at Borders Books in Cheshire Oaks, and I'm grateful to Mary Foss and Mark Graham for arranging my hours to let me write every day, as one must. Jane and Polly Byron advised me on Severn Valley elements, not least the masque. Poppy Z. Brite, Angela and Tony Heslop, Jeannie and Geoff Woodbridge, and Angus Mackenzie all know how they helped.

Contents

CONTENTS

THE
DARKEST
PART
OF THE
WOODS

I

The Mound in the Dark

HEATHER was scanning into the computer a book that smelled of all its centuries when Randall answered the phone. She looked up to find him holding a finger to his faint smile as if hushing himself until she was ready for him. His bushy brows were raised high, and as their gazes met, his wide pale blue eyes gave in to a blink. "An American lady is asking for you," he said.

She picked up the flat almost weightless receiver from his amiably strewn desk. "Heather Price."

"Heather . . ."

Her mother's voice sounded both determined and exhausted. "What's happened?" Heather said.

"Your father's out. Six of them have gone into the woods." Her phone demonstrated its mobility with an outburst of vicious static and subtracted a few syllables from "I'm driving over there now."

"Do you want me to as well?"

"I wish you would. The more of us there are—" The completion of her thought was lost in a chorus of static, after which a tattered version of her voice said "We'll find each other."

"I have to leave early," Heather told Randall, who was gripping his lowered chin and rubbing it with a thumb while he eyed a fluorescent tube that went some way towards bringing the rafters up to date. When his head lifted as his gaze descended, unsure how concerned it was entitled to look, she said "I have to leave now. Could you scan those last few pages for me?"

"I'll be more than glad."

She squeezed his surprised arm with both hands on the way to grabbing her handbag and coat from the stand behind her desk. She let herself out of the gate in the stout oaken counter and hurried between the massive tables surrounded by students at books and computer terminals. Three lecturers discussing cricket passed her abreast in the echoing vaulted sandstone corridor before she ran out of the towering front doors of the university, under an arch two feet thick, to the car park.

The air was edged with a late October chill. As she hastened to her car, past saplings crystalline with spiders' beaded webs, she felt as if the thinnest glaze of ice were fitting itself to her cheeks and forehead. The long lofty Gothic façade and its high pointed windows had acquired a glitter reminiscent of frost. When she started her Civic, the engine produced a cloud worthy of any of the bonfires due next week.

The main streets of Brichester were already clogged with traffic. She was wishing she had headed for the motorway by the time she reached the foot of Mercy Hill. As she drove up through its ribs of terraced streets, past the hospital that overlooked a graveyard, she remembered how her father used to drive her and Sylvia to the top when they were little—how he'd urged them to see as far as they could. The memory made her release a long slow breath that blurred the windscreen, unless the blurring was in her eyes. A mist was coating the lights of Brichester with luminous fur, while to the west, beyond the river Severn reddened by a low gigantic sun, Wales glimmered like a scattering of white-hot ash. To the east the motorway shone white and red, and at the eastern limit of her vision the Cotswold hills were a mass of humps in assorted shades of grey. Ahead to the north she saw a brownish mass that looked small enough to grasp with one hand. She drove faster towards it and the new bypass.

She heard lorries before the unkempt hedges of the old Goodmanswood road let her see them. As soon as she sped onto the bypass, vehicles big enough for families to inhabit blocked her view. At least they were no longer using Goodmanswood as a route between the motorway and Sharpness on the Severn, but they prevented her from seeing the woods until she was almost alongside. Without warning the lorry in front of her veered into the right-hand lane, causing another behemoth to gasp and bray, and she saw the woods stretching ahead to the left of the road, their leaves all the colours of old paper, shiny as scales in the gathering dimness. As the lorries roared onward, past a new roadsign that had acquired a greenish tinge, she swung her car into a lay-by. She fished her flashlight from behind her seat and ducked out of the car.

The clamour of traffic blotted out any sounds among the trees. There was movement in the woods, but none of it was alive. Whenever headlights swung around the curve beyond the lay-by, rank after rank of trees flared up, as lattices of shadow trawled the dimness. She could hardly get lost in less than a square mile of woods when the bypass was making so much noise, but she hoped that wouldn't cover up any sounds of her family. She stepped off the concrete of the lay-by onto soft slippery leaf-strewn earth.

Beam after headlight beam solidified by mist preceded her between the trees. Her shadow kept springing up in front of her, caged by tree-trunks, while unexpectedly chill shadows of trees glided over her back. Before long the beams fell short of her, but she didn't need to use the flashlight yet; she had only to head for the sunset that tinged the highest leaves crimson as though the world was yielding up blood to the sky. Perhaps the dimmest stretch of the headlights was still visible beyond her, producing an impression of thin movements that dodged between the trees. The traffic noise was muffled now, but a backward glance showed her a shuttling of lights. "Mother?" she tried calling, and raised her voice. "Anyone?"

She thought she heard a distant pair of syllables respond from the direction of the sinking glow. She followed as straight a route as she could towards it through the wooden maze, around humps of scaly earth. Moist air that tasted of fog and decay caught in her throat as she called "If you can hear me, give a shout" and switched the flashlight on.

She hoped it would show where she was. While its beam illuminated her way, it persisted in starting thin shapes out of concealment behind the trees, the kind of sight she could imagine troubling her as a child. She tried standing still and listening for sounds other than the drip of condensation around her in the dimness. She could no longer hear the bypass. "Where are you?" she called, because she felt observed.

"Heather."

So Margo was the watcher, wherever she was. Unsure what she could see ahead, Heather switched the flashlight off. The underbelly of the sky lurched at her, lowering itself on countless legs—at least, that was how it might have seemed to her before she'd grown up. She narrowed her eyes to make them work. Just close enough for her to believe the spectacle was real, trees glowed in the midst of the crowded dimness. "Is the light you?" she shouted.

"We're here."

Of course, the search had found its object, and the glow was of flashlights. As she followed her light towards it, a multitude of thin glistening shapes stepped out from behind their companions and shadows hitched themselves across the chaos of fallen leaves. She'd hurried some hundreds of yards before she was certain she could see lights converging on her goal. Another few strides and she was able to make out a uniformed nurse from the Arbour. He reached the clearing in the middle of the woods as she did.

The clearing was perhaps a hundred yards wide. Her father and five other people were posed on a ring of bricks far too low to be described as a wall. It took Heather a moment to recognise it from her childhood. The six appeared to be precisely equidistant on it, and staring at the shallow mound it encircled. They looked transfixed by the convergence of lights that united their shadows like a huge six-legged insect on the mound.

Her mother stood just outside the ring of bricks, directly in front of Heather's father, hugging herself with her arms folded over the artist's apron she wore in the studio. Her small face was more wrinkled than ever around lips pursed pale and greenish eyes that might have been determined not to blink until he acknowledged her. "I've just this instant got here," she told Heather, apparently to explain her lack of effect, and redoubled her frown at him. "Come off there, Lennox. You're working everyone up."

When this produced no result she turned her little body but not her head towards their daughter. "Look who's here. Look, she's here to help take you back. Look."

"Yes, do come with us, dad. You don't want to stay out here when it's getting dark."

His gaze didn't shift from the mound. He was clasping his left wrist with his right hand behind his back as if recalling how it felt to be a professor. As he leaned forward an inch into a flashlight beam, the furrows etched across his wide forehead and down his long loose face appeared to deepen while his brows and shock of hair grew even whiter. Either he'd neglected to comb his hair or the woods had dishevelled it, and Heather couldn't tell how much of their brightness his large blue eyes owed to a resolution not to look confused. She was swallowing a sudden taste of grief when he muttered "Where's the other?"

"I'm not understanding you, Lennox."

"The one who came last. Sister Twig."

"Are you talking about Sylvia? She's somewhere in America. It was Heather who stayed, and you won't even look at her."

"It's all right, mummy. I understand why dad wants Sylvia," Heather was quick to say. "Only why are you here, dad? You don't need to come here any more."

His gaze drifted towards her and grew unexpectedly sad. She wasn't sure he was responding to her until he said "Why are any of us, Heather?"

"I can't say," she admitted, hoping fiercely that he'd reverted to his old self. "Can you?"

"Didn't you hear?"

A flashlight must have shifted, which was why the trees beyond him appeared to edge attentively forward. "Hear what?" Margo demanded impatiently. "You're the lecturer."

He clapped his hands, a sound that rattled through the woods. With delight or incredulity he declared "They never heard."

Heather made herself relax before her innards tightened too much. All of his fellow patients had burst out laughing—a woman whose fingers were clasped prayerfully together so hard they gleamed white, a man apparently unable to prevent his head from ducking from side to side, a woman digging her fingertips into her cheeks as though to support her protuberant eyes, a man whose fists had spent minutes in beginning to open towards the mound, another poised in a crouch that seemed on the point of dropping him to his knees. Four male nurses from the Arbour who had been attempting to persuade them off the bricks fell silent as the five turned just their heads to Lennox. He glanced at each of them, a smile trembling on his broad thick lips. "Maybe," he said at last, "his mouth's full."

Not all of his companions were happy to greet this with laughter, but the woman with clasped hands and the crouched man made up for the rest. "Well, okay," Lennox said when they eventually subsided. "We may as well go."

He gestured to include Heather and Margo and the nurses in his invitation as he stepped off the bricks. He'd barely started across the clearing when the other patients followed him. "Fair enough, that's the way," Heather heard a nurse murmur to his colleagues. "Just stay close."

She saw the flashlight beams jerk among the trees, casting a net of shadows over Lennox and his followers. "Thanks, Heather," Margo said and gave her a shaky hug. "I don't know what I'd do without you."

"You'd do pretty amazingly," Heather assured her, "as if that's news to anyone."

Margo kept hold of her. "My car's at the Arbour. Shall I drive you back to yours?"

"You don't want to be walking alone in the woods now it's dark," Heather understood aloud. As they reached the edge of the clearing she took Margo's arm and glanced back. She might have turned her flashlight beam that way if she had been by herself. Instead she shone it forward, illuminating her mother's route, and saw how the nurses appeared to be using their lights to herd the patients between the scaly columns in the dark. There was nothing behind her that she hadn't already seen, she reflected. Three decades must have exposed more of the ring of bricks, that was all. When she and Sylvia were children they had called it the path that led to itself.

2

The Rumour of a Book

HERE comes a casualty of progress," Randall said and at once seemed not to know if he should have.

Heather looked up from comparing two imperfect copies of *A Description of a Journey through the English Shires on Foot and Horseback*. Sam was limping across the room, apparently unaware of the admiring glances of several students, most of them female. His long serious face and the stubbornly inquisitive expression that was seldom absent from his deep blue eyes reminded Heather of her father, Sam's grandfather. She had to assume Randall meant to ingratiate himself by commenting "You're hobbling well."

"I'd stand a chance in a cripple competition, you mean."

"I didn't say that." Perhaps suspecting he'd appeared to come too close to doing so, Randall added "Was it worth it?"

"Was what?"

"Was your protest worth going to hospital over?"

"You sound like my dad."

"I hope that's acceptable, then."

Sam planted his elbows on the counter. "I don't know why you'd want to," he said, and stared at him.

Heather marked her place in both books and stood up. "Time we were on our way. These won't come to any harm from being a day older."

"I'll drive if you like," said Sam.

"Will you be taking the bypass?" Randall enquired.

Sam turned his back. "Just because we tried to stop them cutting down the trees," he threw over his shoulder, "doesn't mean it isn't there."

"I'll see you in the morning, Randall." Heather restrained herself to saying only that until the door Sam limped to hold open for her had closed behind them. "Now what was all that about?" she said low enough not to echo in the sandstone corridor.

"Me being a stool."

"You aren't, and if you were it wouldn't be an excuse, so what was the problem?"

"I'll go and apologise if you like."

"You'd only confuse him. Leave it for now. That doesn't mean you shouldn't apologise to me."

"Sorry, mum."

He lowered his head and widened his eyes at her from under his brows like the little boy she didn't think he'd quite stopped being, and she hid an affectionate smile. "Stop that," she said. "Just remember I have to work with him. Any objections?"

"How would I know? I don't know him. Am I going to?"

"Maybe if you visit me at work. I hope I haven't just seen how you'll treat any man I'm friendly with."

"Such as who?"

"I wasn't thinking of anyone. You're the only man in my life at the moment."

Sam closed the massive door out of the university. "I'll drive you to the Arbour and then I can go home and finish making dinner."

"I haven't left you much to finish," Heather said, though it was far more than his father, Terry, would have undertaken.

"Grandma will drive you home, won't she? If you're late do you mind if I eat and come back to Andy and Dinah's?"

"Be careful driving," Heather said, "be careful whatever you're doing," and wondered if she would ever be able to relinquish being so much of a mother.

He let them into the Civic with her keys and sent the car into the traffic more immediately than she would have risked, and drove through several amber traffic lights that she would have found too stern a caution. Mist was shortening the streets of increasingly small houses that bunched together on both sides of the road through Lower Brichester. The town petered out with a scattering of bungalows, beyond which the road met the motorway on the far side of fields spread with tattered tarpaulins composed of last night's rain. Less than five minutes later—more if Heather had been driving—the car swung off the motorway onto the Goodmanswood bypass, and in another five it swerved across the road into the grounds of the Arbour.

The private hospital stood at the end of a lazily winding drive. Originally a broad three-storey house built by a landowner, it had grown six new ground-floor rooms behind itself. A minibus was backing onto the gravel in front of the left-hand bay window, beyond which a man had thrust his fingers in his ears while the bus reiterated in a high sharp voice "Beware vehicle reversing." Sam halted the car and ducked out of reach of the kiss she aimed at him. As the car veered away with a stony screech, Margo hurried out of the wide front entrance. "There you are," she said as if she had begun to doubt the possibility. "Dr Lowe is ready for us."

The tall minutely stooped doctor turned from murmuring to the receptionist at her desk between the feet of a pair of curved staircases. He used a fingertip to separate a tuft of his greying hair from an arm of the silver spectacles that looked too flimsy for his broad round face. "Shall we go along to my office?" he said, holding out his palms well short of Heather's and Margo's backs to guide the women into a brief corridor.

Two pastel abstracts that might have started life as landscapes flanked his door, and Margo dealt them each an unfavourable blink. The office into which he bowed the women seemed both fat and dark with the leather of several chairs and with the bindings of dozens of nearly identical volumes shelved to the right of an extensive pine desk, an impression scarcely relieved by the view of the twilit lawn staked out by a few trees more solid than the misty woods across the bypass beyond the high wall. Dr Lowe indicated a couch and sat on the nearest chair rather than behind the desk. "I don't know if anyone thanked you for helping yesterday," he said, "but let me start by thanking you both. I believe you were instrumental in persuading Lennox to come back to us."

"I don't know if we did that, did we, Heather?"

Heather didn't immediately respond, having only just recalled that the man she'd seen watching the minibus had been among her father's companions in the woods. The memory felt more like a fading dream. "I don't," she said.

"But if we hadn't been around there mightn't have been enough people to cope."

"I won't deny there could have been a problem," Dr Lowe admitted. "We'll be discussing patterns of staffing next week."

"And maybe hiring some extra staff?"

"As you're aware, we don't have problems of containment as a rule."

"So why did you yesterday? You aren't someone else who blames Lennox for everything."

"Someone other than whom, can I ask?"

"It seems like half of Goodmanswood sometimes, doesn't it, Heather?"

"Quite a few people at least."

Margo sniffed at the revision. "I'd say more than that think he's responsible for everything that happened in the woods."

"It does appear to be the case," the doctor said, "that Mr Price was the instigator. He asked reception to look for something he told her he'd mislaid, some book he needed to consult. It was just a diversion. He wouldn't name the book."

"I wasn't talking about yesterday. I meant the reason we came to England in the first place," Margo said with some bitterness. "And incidentally, he's still Dr Price. The university wouldn't take that away from him."

"Dr Price, I should have said, of course. I'm certain anyone who knows the facts appreciates what he did. It's tragic that he should have been one of the victims of the very threat he identified. The sad truth is pioneers are often misunderstood." Having paused to observe that she was to some extent mollified, Dr Lowe said "The problem, as my colleagues and I see it—"

"You've had your heads together over Lennox."

"We had a conference this morning, since you were coming in."

"So you could give us your final decision."

"Hardly final. I'm of the view that nothing is when it comes to the mind. But it does appear that our other casualties of the sixties— Would that have been when you were born, Miss Price?"

"Mrs Harvey," Heather felt compelled to say, though she no longer was. "I was a couple of years old."

"And her sister was born two years later. Why?"

"In case the family dynamics are relevant. I was about to say the others seem to look to Dr Price to lead. They see him as the man who knows."

"Knows what?" Heather might have said, but Margo did.

"If we could establish that we might be on the way to helping them instead of merely containing them. They keep it very much among themselves, whatever they think. It's as much of a secret from the other patients as from us. I'm not suggesting it has any reality, only that it might give us more of an insight into this persistent mental state. Meanwhile Dr Price is the one who directs them."

"He brought them all back here last night," Margo said.

"He did, but only after he'd led them out. It isn't an incident we'd care to see repeated. Apart from stretching the staff too thin, any of his group might have come to harm on the road."

"So you suggest. . . ."

"One proposal was to split them up by transferring them to separate facilities. Of course there aren't any within a good few miles."

"You'd have a whole lot of upheaval for nothing. Don't you realise—"

"I do, Mrs Price. It was one of our newer people who proposed it. I've been here long enough to know your husband and the others would just make their way back to the Arbour."

Heather remembered the last time Lennox had, Margo's midnight phone call wakening eight-year-old Sam, her father's expression when she'd next visited him, a secretive justified look. "If that's not your solution," Margo said to Dr Lowe, "what is?"

"I believe we may have to try stronger medication."

"So you can have him more docile," she said, and rubbed the corner of one eye with a folded forefinger. "So there'll be even less of him."

"I do assure you if there were some viable alternative I'd be inclined to favour it."

"Have you found out what set him off yesterday?" Heather hoped aloud.

"Thus far that's one more piece of information we can't persuade him to share."

"I wonder if he might tell me or mother."

"Since when has he told us anything like that, Heather? I don't know any longer if it's him or the medication that's shutting up so much."

"By all means give it a try," Dr Lowe said. "I'll take you to him."

Margo was the last to stand, so slowly that the couch might have been uttering its weary creak on her behalf. Once they were all in the corridor, however, her stride took on some impatience. "Is Dr," the doctor said, increasing his stoop towards the receptionist, "is Lennox still in his room?"

"He hasn't come down, doctor."

Dr Lowe led the Prices along the corridor above the one that contained his office. Two watercolours that might have involved a glance at mountains faced each other across the passage, and he knocked at a door beside the less specific of the pair. When that brought no response he eased the door open. Heather's father was sitting on the end of the bed, his back to the pale greens and blues of the simply furnished room. His forearms rested on the windowsill, holding him in such a low crouch he might have been trying to hide from the woods, which were dim and blurred except for lights that swarmed up the outermost trunks to vanish under the glistening foliage. "Lennox, we've come to see you," Margo called.

Heather was dismayed to find she couldn't breathe until he moved. He pushed himself away from the sill and twisted on the bed, swinging his legs across it, thumping the wall with his shoulders and perhaps with the back of his head. Though Margo winced, he greeted them brightly enough. "Come and sit. Room for everyone."

Margo took Heather by the elbow to propel her forward as if overcoming some reluctance, Heather wasn't certain whose. When the doctor followed them, Lennox narrowed one eye at him. "You're not the family," he said, then shrugged, rubbing his shoulders against the wall, as Dr Lowe shut himself in. "I guess you can't do much."

"It isn't like you to antagonise people," Margo said, stretching out a hand that stopped short of touching him. "You've always been polite."

"Frankie's the last thing you need to be nervous about. We're old friends, aren't we, doc?"

"I'd like to think so."

"He's going to up your medication if you don't behave yourself."

"Well, Mrs Price, I'm not sure I quite said—"

"That's okay, doc. Fine with me. I can use some sleep." Before Heather could decide if his sounding so American was intended as a joke, he patted the bed hard enough to make the mattress resonate.

"I'll start believing I'm not polite, sure enough, unless you all sit down," he said. "Let your momma have the chair and you sit next to me. Space on the bed for you too, doc, if you're joining the party."

"I'll stand if it won't disturb you."

"Takes a whole lot more than that. Maybe you've noticed."

Heather sat within arm's length of him, though his vitality was somewhat disconcerting; she didn't know how long it might last or what its source might be. He grasped his knees to hitch himself around on the corner of the bed and gaze expectantly at her. "How are things shaping up?" he said.

"Much the same, which is fine."

"Is it?" He looked disappointed and then resigned, and seemed to feel bound to explain to the doctor "She's always been the cheerful one. Gets on with life and never complains." He cocked his head at Margo, who was sitting between and opposite them, her short legs drawn up beneath a chair with its back to the dressing-table mirror. "We haven't seen our grandson for a while, have we?"

"I'll tell Sam you were asking after him," Heather said, since Margo only shook her head. "I expect he'd like to come and visit if you want him to."

"Better do it soon," Lennox said, she wasn't sure to whom, then focused once more on her. "How are you making out at the university? You work there now, don't you?"

"I have for, oh, ages," she told him, not glancing at Margo in case that brought either of them to tears. "I'm in the historical archive now."

"I knew that," he said, remembering or convincing himself. "I could use a trip there. Will that be all right, Frankie?"

"Let's see how you progress."

"Forget it. Nothing there I can't . . ." He turned to the window, beyond which insubstantial luminous shapes were scurrying up the trees across the bypass, and his movement released a faint musty smell that reminded Heather of the depths of the woods. "They can't have that book," he muttered.

"Tell me the title and I'll search for you," Heather offered.

He expelled a breath that, having misted the window, appeared to be absorbed by the woods, and then he peered at her faint reflection among the trees. "It'll turn up," he told her or himself, and raised his voice. "Did you see anything last night?"

The question made her feel oddly forgetful. "You and the people you took with you," she said, and felt as though she was reiterating Dr Lowe's version of events. "Why did you go out there?" she had to ask.

"I don't think that's for you, Heather."

"I've had to cope with some things in my life," she protested, manufacturing a laugh. "Let's see if I can cope with this."

"Don't feel slighted. Try not to think any less of yourself."

She resented his condescension, which she couldn't even grasp, and yet he sounded so like the father she hardly remembered having that she was unable to speak. She saw Margo sharing her feelings, and it was Dr Lowe who intervened. "It's been coming for a while, hasn't it, Lennox?"

"You could say that. Why," Lennox said in what might have been genuine surprise and delight, "you did."

"I'm saying you've been growing restless for some time."

Lennox's enthusiasm faded. "More like ever since I was shut in here."

"It's been more apparent these last few months."

"Is that how long? Means more to you than me."

"Can you say what's been disturbing you?"

"Try looking in the trees."

"I know," Margo said, sounding determined as much as inspired. "You mean the people who lived in them to try to stop the bypass. Sam was one."

"When did you see them, dad? They were half a mile away up the road."

"They were on the radio, weren't they," Margo said, "and in the papers."

Lennox met Heather's reflected gaze, and his eyes seemed to glint from the dark of the woods. "Maybe you're the one who'll get it, Heather."

"They've been trying to build the bypass all year," she was prompted to say. "Was it just that they were taking some of your view?"

"Last night did you want to see they hadn't done too much damage?" Margo suggested.

Lennox crouched towards the window. Heather saw the woods brighten and grow insect-legged with shadows that merged with the depths steeped in fog and darkness as two pairs of headlamp beams were dipped. "You've tired me enough now," he said. "Maybe I'll even sleep."

"We'll come and see you again soon," Margo said as Dr Lowe opened the door.

"And I expect Sam will," said Heather.

Lennox's reflection was swallowed by a blur composed of his breath and the woods. He spoke so low she had to strain to hear him. "Wait till it's all of us."

3

A Meeting in the Forest

THE rotund crewcut boy halfway through his teens wore a
T-shirt over a shirt over a sweater. The T-shirt made it clear what
he would ask before he did. First he wandered through the shop, using
a finger and thumb to pluck from the shelves a very few paperbacks, at
whose covers he gazed before turning them over as if that might
transform them into something more attractive. Having returned a last
disappointment to its place and his hands to the pockets of his faded
piebald jeans, he confronted Sam across the counter. "Got any *Star
Wars* videos?"

"We don't sell videos, sorry."

"How about model kits?"

"Not those either."

"Comics?"

Sam was beginning to feel like one confronted with an unsympa-
thetic audience. "We're for books."

The angry rash at the corners of the boy's mouth appeared to drag
them down. "What's Worlds Unlimited supposed to mean, then? I
don't see any *Star Wars* books."

"That's because you can buy those anywhere," Andy was anxious
he should know.

"Can't be a sci-fi shop without them."

"We're more science fiction," Dinah told him as Andy winced at the abbreviation. "And fantasy and even horror."

The boy was almost out of the shop when he delivered his verdict. "Old people's stuff."

Andy sat down at the coffee table between the counter and the shelves, so hard that the middle-aged armchair was audibly distressed. "Twenty-three," he said, sweeping a lock of blonde hair back from his lightly ruled high forehead and trapping all his tresses in a rubber band at the nape of his neck, "and ready for recycling."

"Gives me and Sam another year," said Dinah, pensively pinching the chin of her small oval face. "Seriously, maybe he just meant a lot of the writers are dead."

"Their books weren't last time I read them."

Sam was about to concur when Andy, as he often had when they were at university and indeed at school, switched positions. "Anyway, there goes someone else who didn't buy a book."

"Quite a few have today," Sam pointed out.

"Less than half. We're selling more on the net than we do over the counter. Most of my dad's collection has gone."

Sam had discovered that local jobs of any worth and permanence were hard for even English literature graduates to find, but he said "Say if you can't afford me any more."

"I need you both. Imagine me sitting in here all day with nobody to talk to about books."

"That's what the customers want with their coffee." Sam heard himself making Dinah redundant too, and changed the subject hastily. "You were saying last night I could go early to visit my grandfather."

"I hadn't forgotten. The hash hasn't screwed up my memory yet. Go ahead."

Sam fetched his ankle-length Oxfam overcoat from the less than horizontal row of hooks outside the dauntingly basic toilet, and was limping streetward when Dinah turned from arranging magazines in the window. "I haven't had a chance to say sorry, Sam."

"I didn't think you needed to."

"I was wrong last night. You couldn't have done any more to stop them cutting down the trees when you were hurt. It's not as if I did anything at all. I expect I would have if I'd known you then."

Until last night Sam had assumed she and Andy were living together. Though she lived in the same faded Victorian house, Andy was sharing his bed with a man. Sam had been the only one to decline Andy's Moroccan hashish pipe, which had provoked Dinah to suggest that his having abandoned the protest had been another failure of nerve. He'd already gathered that arguing was her way of getting close to people, but he hadn't said much in his own defence, because he felt that in some way he'd broken faith with the woods. "Wish you had," he told Dinah awkwardly, and made his escape from the shop.

His green Volkswagen was parked on rubbly ground behind Worlds Unlimited and a takeaway whose rear emitted fumes and an outburst of Cantonese chatter. Having indulged in a fit of coughing, the car found its way out between two Victorian family houses that seemed to be competing over how many students they could accommodate. In less than a minute he was passing the university, where the students crossing the lawns already looked young to him. He remembered feeling unengaged last year by anything he read or wrote, however much his work pleased his tutors, as if some unidentified aspect of him had yet to be enlivened. His vigil at the edge of the woods had seemed potentially far more fulfilling—still did, so that he had to remind himself that he was on his way to visit his grandfather, not the woods.

Ten minutes took him out of Brichester and along the motorway to the bypass, beyond which the woods appeared to bristle with stillness beneath a stretch of low white clouds that resembled an elaborate skeleton the length of the horizon. The trees extended shadows to finger the car as he sped through the gap in the safety barrier and across the bypass to the Arbour. A shiver overtook him, though the afternoon was hot enough for several patients and two male nurses to be sitting in the grounds. One patient was lying on a recliner midway between the hospital and the gates. As Sam cruised past he saw it was his grandfather.

Sam parked between a Bentley and a minibus and hobbled across the grass. He wasn't sure if Lennox was asleep; his eyes might be shut or only nearly. His right arm was propped on its elbow, while the hand seemed to be mimicking the shape of a tree across the road. Sam tiptoed lopsidedly to gaze down at the long slack wrinkled face, and was disconcerted to imagine that he was seeing himself in his seventies. At that moment Lennox squeezed his lips together at the pain of flexing his upheld hand, and his eyes flickered open. Though he seemed to be peering past Sam, he murmured "It's Sam, isn't it? You look uncomfortable."

Sam hoped that referred to his injury. "Just my ankle," he said.

"Here's a place." Lennox sat abruptly up and patted the recliner. "So you won't have been getting about too much with that."

"I should have been coming to see you more often before."

"So long as it counts now," Lennox said, half turning his head away from the woods as Sam sat beside him. "Care to start off with a promise?"

Sam found his directness as unsettling as the proposal, but felt bound to say "If you like."

"Answer me a question when I ask it and I'll tell you some things."

"Go ahead." When Lennox only cocked his head towards the woods as though listening, Sam had to assume he was meant to prompt him. "How are you?" was the most he felt able to risk.

"Conscious."

"Well, good." He hoped to be able to leave it at that, but Lennox gazed in open disappointment at him. "Isn't it?" Sam said.

"Of what should be the question."

"Of what?"

"Of the dark there wouldn't be any light without. The dark that's above all this and under it too." As though the relevance ought to be obvious he added "Do you use drugs?"

"I tried pot the first year I was at university. Too scary for me."

"What scared you?"

"Felt as if I might see things I wouldn't be able to handle."

"Once you see you go on seeing."

Sam took that for agreement, and felt he had to respond. "You mean since you touched that stuff in the woods."

"Most of forty years." Lennox met Sam's dismay at this with a wry grin. "Tell me what you think you know about it," he said.

"You came to England to research it. You were, you're an authority on mass hallucination. You taught courses on the psychology of popular delusion."

"Sounds like I must have been damn sure of myself."

"You wrote a book about it. If you haven't got a copy here I can bring you one."

"I'm touched. I'll be telling Heather she should be proud of how she brought you up, or you can tell her yourself, but don't waste your time with that book." Lennox cocked his head at a wryer angle still and said "Remind me what I was up to in your town."

"A professor at the university read your book and wrote to you about all the stuff people were seeing in the woods. And then didn't he die, so you got his job as well?"

"Are we talking about old Longman? That's who brought me, sure enough. What did everyone think I was doing here again?"

"Trying to find out why people were hallucinating about the woods."

"Was that what they were doing? And was I a success?"

Sam was unable to judge if he was being mocked. "You traced it to some lichen," he said. "If you, if anyone even touched it it got to them."

"I'll bet I came up with the solution too."

"Some trees that had mutated because it grew on them, maybe they'd even produced it somehow, they had to be destroyed."

As Lennox leaned towards him, Sam was startled by a cold smell of decay until he saw the woods stir—there must be a wind. "How many?" Lennox said.

"About a dozen in the middle of the woods. A lot less than were cut down for the bypass."

"And that was the end of it, was it, except for me and my friends in here that your professor told me about in the first place."

Sam wasn't sure if he meant in the Arbour or in his head, towards which he'd raised his contorted hand. "Some scientists took away samples but those broke down before they could get them anywhere, so it was never analysed."

"Bad medicine anyway," Lennox muttered, "trying to deal with the symptom instead of the cause."

"I don't think I understand."

"You said you'd answer a question."

Sam wondered if this was being offered as some kind of an answer. "If I can."

"Heather told me you hurt yourself falling out of your tree-house, but what made you fall?"

"I was nearly asleep."

"How far up were you, twenty feet? Trying to get closer to something?"

"Trying to stay clear of the bailiffs."

Lennox grimaced with impatience. "Why did you fall?"

At the edge of Sam's vision the woods appeared to flex themselves. Another wind must have stirred them, since the smell of decay had revived, though they weren't moving when he glanced across the bypass. "I thought someone had got onto the platform with me," he said.

"Who?"

Lennox's eagerness made Sam wary of disturbing him. "I don't know," he said, truthfully enough. "It was just me falling asleep."

Certainly the incident resembled a dream he could barely recall, although the closeness of the woods appeared to help. He'd been sitting on the platform with his back against the tree-trunk, watching the sunset sink into the trees before he crawled into his sleeping bag. At first the sight of darkness rising from the forest had only reminded him that the nights were beginning to lengthen, and then he'd felt as if a presence vaster than the woods was advancing towards him across the changed landscape—as if the night sky or the blackness of which it was the merest scrap was descending into the woods. He'd closed his eyes to fend off the dizziness the impression brought with it, only to imagine the presence had shrunk and was perching next to him. He'd flinched away so violently he had toppled off the platform. Before his eyes were fully open he'd had a dreamy notion that the night would bear him up. Then the ground had struck his right foot like an enormous hammer hardly muffled by its covering of last year's leaves, and as the rest of him fell over he'd heard and felt his ankle snap. "I was just bloody clumsy," he said.

"Don't close your mind, Sammy." Lennox righted his head and turned it towards the forest while widening his eyes at Sam. "What can you see?" he urged.

There was no doubt now that a wind had risen. Leaves were flocking out of the woods to dance with their shadows on the bypass. "What am I supposed to?" Sam risked asking.

"I can't tell you. Trust your own experience." When Sam found nothing to say, not least because he felt too intensely watched, Lennox said "Go and look."

"Don't you want me to stay and talk to you?"

"There are better ways for a young buck to spend his time than listening to an old lunatic." Apparently this was meant to be overheard by a nurse, who frowned at him and wagged a finger at his choice of a word for himself." "Next time we'll have more to say to each other," Lennox told Sam.

As Sam stood up, his grandfather swung his legs onto the recliner and propped his cheek on the knuckles of one crooked hand as though in preparation for a spectacle. "Thank Heather for her efforts," he said. "I never answered any of her questions."

"Are you going to?"

Lennox stared into his face for so long that Sam had begun to wonder if this implied he should know the answer when his grandfather said "Selcouth."

"Will she know what that means?"

"Sooner or later," Lennox said, drawing his legs up towards his stomach.

Was he betraying that he was less able to cope than he'd pretended? He reminded Sam of a wizened fetus. "See you," Sam promised, and limped to his car. As he drove by the recliner he beeped his horn, but Lennox stayed expressionless and absolutely still except for his hair, which swayed in imitation of the woods that might have been all he was seeing.

As soon as Sam was through the gates the wind attacked the car. It must have changed direction, since it kept struggling to force him across the bypass while the trees at the edge of the road bent away from it, indicating or reaching for the depths of the woods. When he swung the car into the outer lane, large trucks sidled dangerously close to him. He was gripping the wheel so hard it bruised his fingers by the time he was able to make a U-turn to the lay-by alongside the woods.

His tree had been felled to help clear the space. It was only one of hundreds the protesters had failed to save while he was in hospital. No doubt they were protesting elsewhere now; few of them had been local. He couldn't blame them too much for the destruction when he'd been unable to prevent it himself. He wasn't even certain any longer how it might have affected the environment. He wasn't here only in response to his grandfather's suggestion; he thought a walk in the woods might help him remember what else he had seen from his tree. He'd glimpsed movement at twilight, he seemed to recall now— movement at or rather, to have been visible, presumably above the middle of the woods.

The moment he climbed out of the shivering Volkswagen, the wind did its utmost to frogmarch him away from the road. It felt as if the woods were panting to suck him in. He'd limped only a few steps across the earth that was shivery with leaves when the trees set about demonstrating how profound a refuge they offered. A stench of petrol followed him for a hundred yards or so, but the traffic was already being shouted down by the wind in the treetops. He didn't need to be able to hear the bypass; so long as he kept the sun to his left he would be heading for his goal.

He tried not to glance directly at the sun. Dazzling himself with it only made him feel there was more to the woods than he was able to identify, though of course it was the sun itself that peered now and then through the treetops, the sun or clouds that the wind swept onwards before he had time to confront them. Ahead of him, above the tapestry of fallen leaves, the colonnades of tree-trunks held as still as their topmost branches were frantic. Now and then a tree swayed with a long slow creak, and once that was answered by another in the depths of the woods, as if great birds or reptiles were calling to each other. Apart from that he heard nothing but the wind and the muffled bursts of traffic noise it carried intermittently to him, playing such a game with the apparent location of the bypass that he turned more than once to reassure himself where it was.

Before long it was hidden by trees, and the traffic was inaudible. Straining his ears only made him imagine that he could almost hear a huge voice muttering under cover of the wind. He still had hours of daylight, and how could he get lost so near the town in less than a square mile of forest? The notion seemed unworthy of the show the trees were putting on for him, the highest branches contorting themselves into shapes he wouldn't have dreamed they could take, leaves fluttering or gliding through the air in patterns too elaborate for his mind to grasp, then fitting themselves into the mosaic of decay that was the forest floor. Some stirred as if they weren't entirely dead. Each one that settled gave him a sense that a design was another minute step closer to completion, but he was more intent on the dance of leaves in the air. Was that related to whatever sight he'd glimpsed above the middle of the woods? The leaves were most hectic between the trees at the limit of his vision, where they swarmed like insects caught up in some nervous ritual. At that distance the air looked solid with them. He limped fast towards them, and was within perhaps fifty yards of them when they swayed like a dancer's veil and parted, sailing up swiftly as ash above a bonfire. He could have imagined they were returning to their trees as he saw he'd arrived at his goal.

He was at the edge of the clearing that had once been surrounded by infected trees. He knew how far he must have walked to it, though he had no sense at all of the time he'd taken. He couldn't recall his journey through the woods or anything he'd seen on the way. Somehow the sun had moved ahead of him to flare white between misshapen treetops. It made him feel as though cataracts of light were gathering on his eyes, so that he could barely distinguish a low mound as wide as a small house within a lower ring of mossy brick. Then two trees parted like the opposite of a prayer and seemed to focus on the mound all the light the sun contained.

The top of the mound was scaly with lichen. Though the patch was no larger than a man, a shape it rather suggested, it was iridescent with so many colours Sam couldn't begin to number or to name them. He limped between the gesticulating trees and stepped into the open. At once the glittering mass stirred and then surged into the air. It was a multitude of insects that swooped and darted in patterns so intricate he was robbed of thought and breath.

He didn't move until they veered towards him. As he stumbled backwards, part of his mind urged him to stand his ground, to see them clearly. Then the trees across the clearing swayed together, covering much of the sun, and the swarm soared back over the mound and into the depths of the woods. As he lost sight of them he thought they were shining brighter yet with colours he'd never seen, even in dreams. The withdrawal of so much light had left him virtually blind, and he shut his eyes and covered them with his hands. He was watching whiteness linger on the insides of his eyelids when a twig snapped close to him.

It needn't be a footstep—the wind was fierce enough to break more than a twig—but it had sounded closer to the mound than the trees were. His eyes sprang open, to see little except blankness. The treetops had revealed the sun again, and he thought he smelled the mound, warm earth and something sweeter. Then his eyes began to work, and he saw a figure advancing through the dazzle past the mound. For the moment he couldn't see its face. Its hands were outstretched to him as though to draw him forward, and above either hand an insect brighter than the sun was hovering.

4

The Author of the Book

NEARLY time to go," Heather called, and thought she should have left off the first word. When Sam didn't respond she went up past her mother's lithograph of an impossible tree whose branches were only as real as the spaces between them. He was no longer in the bathroom, where the mirror was recovering from blindness while the shower prepared its next drip. She twisted the tap shut and straightened his towel on the rail, then as a second thought dropped the towel in the washing basket on her way to knocking on his bedroom door. "Ready for the road?"

Surely he hadn't gone back to bed. She knocked again and eased the door open. He was at the window, and might have been ignoring the mess his room continued to be: the dwarfish hi-fi piled with naked compact discs on which headphones were resting, the bed not so much made as more or less draped with its quilt, the computer desk scattered with floppies, its chair wearing yesterday's clothes over some from the day before that. She could see nothing beyond the window for him to watch, just the woods a quarter of a mile away across the common. "If you're coming into town with me I'm about to head off," she said. "No point in using two cars when we don't need to."

Sam wiped his breath off the pane as though waving to the trees, and Heather saw a wind make them return the gesture as he backed away from the window. "No point," he apparently agreed.

"Who rang last night when I was in bed?"

"Dad, to see if I'm all right for Sunday." A faint smile like a shrug of his squeezed-together lips followed that, and a raising of eyebrows that rediscovered furrows in his high forehead. "I'll go out with him if it makes him happy," Sam said.

She wondered if the prospect of herself and Terry being almost as polite as strangers to each other in the house they all used to share was causing Sam to seem more withdrawn than usual. "I'm sure it will," she said, and left him to lock the house while she roused the car.

The Civic was keeping his Volkswagen company on the flagstones Terry had insisted on having laid in front of the large semi-detached house Margo had made their wedding present, herself moving into an apartment across Goodmanswood. Though Woodland Close contained no trees, a few gnarled brownish leaves were scuttling along the pavement. Cars chirped as drivers put their alarms to sleep while an early-risen vacuum cleaner bumbled like a fly unable to find an exit from the community centre, formerly a school. A third house on her side of the street was for sale. As soon as Sam was strapped in she drove onto the road.

Two minutes' driving brought her abreast of the High Road, pedestrianised now that the bypass spared it so much traffic. Such traffic as remained had to take a narrower road between the oldest cottages, and she wouldn't have been surprised if Sam had pointed out the contradiction yet again. Instead he was so quiet that she broke the silence once she was past all the schoolbound children she had to watch out for. "So where did you get to after you went to the Arbour?"

At first he seemed too preoccupied with the oncoming woods to answer. The bark of the tree-trunks was outlined by shadow black as soil, as if the trees had been disinterred overnight. "Just drove," he said with a frown that looked oddly like a struggle to remember, "and walked."

"Did visiting your grandfather upset you, Sam?"

"Maybe."

He turned to gaze past her into the woods, ranks of trees marching backwards as if to reconfigure a secret pattern, though the depths of the forest appeared not to move. She refrained from disturbing him again until they were past the Arbour, where she glimpsed her father at his window, holding the curtains wide with both hands. Abruptly Sam muttered "He said you asked him something in the woods. You never told me what you found there."

Her answer hardly seemed worth the effort of recalling. "I'm sure I did. Just your grandfather and some of the others."

"And you helped bring them back, but did anything else happen?"

"I asked him a question, apparently."

"He says the answer's Selcouth."

"I've no idea what that means. I'll have to look it up."

She saw trees rear up in the mirror before shrinking under the sun; she saw a truck lurching from lane to lane beside them, although there was no wind. For a change the motorway came as a relief; it gave her more of a reason to concentrate and leave behind the glimpse of Lennox at his window. She sensed Sam's impatience, presumably with her speed—it could hardly have to do with the word she needed to research.

Beyond the city streets mined with children bound for school, the university brandished its towers at the graveyard crown of Mercy Hill. She drove past the campus into the dilapidated Victorian streets that had become the student quarter. As she wondered unhappily whether Sam would ever be able to walk without a limp they came in sight of Worlds Unlimited, and she gasped on his behalf. His colleagues were on the pavement outside the shop, and so was most of the glass of the window.

Blonde long-haired Andy trudged to the car. "Has much been taken?" Heather said.

"Just about nothing. They didn't even care enough for books to steal them."

"Chucked a few about and did some other things with them," Dinah said, wrinkling her nose, an action that involved her whole small oval face.

"Police been?" said Sam, climbing with some awkwardness out of the car.

"We've called them," Andy told him. "We can't clear up till they come in case there are prints."

"I'll leave you to it, shall I?" Heather felt a little guilty for saying. "I'll pick you up after work, Sam, if I don't see you there."

So now she had another worry to add to the pile, she thought as she drove off: whether he would be forced to quit this job before he found something more permanent. That took its place on top of the question of what he was going to do with his life, not to mention whether he shouldn't have decided that by now, though was any of the problem how she herself had clung to the first steady job she could find? These thoughts and a gang of their friends kept up with her as she parked the car and made her way across the sunlit frost-bleached campus.

The echoes of her footsteps dulled as she left the sandstone corridor. All the computer terminals on the library tables were showing fog. She dropped her handbag on her desk and headed for the reference section; though she could have looked the word up on the computer, she still preferred to hold a book.

selcouth (sel-couth) strange, marvellous, wonderful. [from OE *seldan* seldom, *cuth* known]

More than one dictionary said approximately this, but it didn't seem much help. "Seldom known," she heard herself murmuring. She bore the fattest dictionary away from a table back to its weight-conscious relatives, then on an impulse continued down the aisle of shelves to find her father's book.

Lennox Price's *The Mechanics of Delusion* was leaning against a stout Freudian tome on a shelf higher than her head. She climbed down from a stumpy ladder and turned to the date label. Quite a few people had borrowed the book in the sixties and early seventies, when her father's research in the woods had made headlines, but since then the book had seldom left the shelf. It began with a history of popular delusions, brought up to date by an account of myths then prevalent about drugs. The bulk of it related fringe beliefs to ones more widely held and demonstrated their interdependence, while the final pages compared skepticism with the beliefs it sought to overturn and showed they were products of the same psychological mechanism. The book reminded her how keen his mind used to be, and revived memories that distressed her—his bouts of walking up and down the house as though desperate to leave behind some intolerable contents of his brain, his sudden bursts of introverted mirth, his demands for absolute silence that might be expected to last for hours while he appeared to listen for some sound outside the house, his staring at toddler Sylvia as if he couldn't quite recognise her and must do so . . . Heather shelved *The Mechanics of Delusion* and made for the art books.

Two volumes were called just Margo Price, a catalogue of her London retrospective in the eighties and a coffee-table book representing her work up to five years ago. Since then she'd concentrated on carving sculptures from deadwood she found on the edge of the forest outside Goodmanswood—the construction of the bypass had provided her with plenty of material—but Heather liked her paintings best, one in particular. She lifted the catalogue down and rested its spine on the edge of a shelf. The glossy pages fell open at Margo's Arizona paintings, desert landscapes relieved only by solitary flowers under an almost shadowless sun. Heather turned pages until she reached *The*

Light through the Thorns, the first canvas Margo had painted after committing Lennox to the Arbour.

It showed an arch of thorns so thickly entangled that only minute stars of light as spiky as the prickles managed to struggle through, but the longer one gazed at them, the more the thorns appeared to be partly an illusion. Did some of them rather consist of slivers of sky and a distant greenish horizon? When seven-year-old Heather had asked what was there her mother had told her it was whatever she could see. Perhaps the enigma helped explain why it was Margo's most reproduced painting, available as a poster, but sometimes it made Heather feel close to glimpsing a peace too profound to be expressed in words. Just now she seemed unable to grasp that impression. She returned the collection to the shelf and found herself heading for the folklore books.

Someone had replaced Sylvia's with the pages facing outward. Heather almost managed to suppress the thought that it was hiding like its author. Sylvia didn't need to stay home when Heather had chosen to, and it wasn't as if she didn't keep in touch, even if her letters had grown less frequent recently—none for months since a card from Mexico, where she was apparently researching a new book. Heather opened *The Secret Woods: Sylvan Myths* at random, to be confronted by a Chinese folk-tale about a boy who climbed trees in search of birds' eggs and found a nest of baby birds, headless yet alive. The image, or her reading it where she couldn't see most of the room, disturbed her more than made any sense. Snorting with impatience at herself, she took the volume and her flock of echoes to her desk.

The book contained stories she liked, but she seemed to have forgotten where they were. The preface pointed out that woods had been regarded as secret places ever since stories were recorded. They were the locations of many fairy tales, though the chapter on Germany opened with a Bavarian tradition that if you walked through certain forests at night with a baby on your back, by the time you emerged from the woods the child would have been replaced by something whose ancient voice would croak in your ear. As for America, here was a Burkittsville legend of a misshapen cottage said to have been visible from a woodland road—a cottage that shrank as travellers approached it, then grew as they tried to flee. Heather looked up Britain and was met by a Derbyshire tale about a woodwose, a satyr that emerged from a wood on Midsummer Eve in the guise of some local youth, whose betrothed it then seduced. In other versions it appeared as a brother who bedded his sister or a father who did so to his daughter. Heather had begun to wonder why she was continuing to read—perhaps in an attempt to demonstrate that not all Sylvia's interests were so dark—when someone came into the room.

She was a slim young woman in denim dungarees and a black polo neck, with a large dilapidated canvas bag dangling from one shoulder. Perhaps she wasn't quite so young, to judge by the traces of grey that were apparent in her carelessly cropped reddish hair as she turned to close the door. "We aren't really open until nine," Heather said, but wasn't about to make an issue of it. She was leafing through *The Secret Woods* when she heard footsteps approach the counter. "May I help?" she said, not quite looking up.

"Hey."

The voice was American. If the word was an answer, Heather didn't understand it. *The Secret Woods* had just turned up a spread of fairy tales. She splayed one hand on the pages and glanced vainly about for a bookmark. "I'll be with you in just a few moments," she said.

"You've always been with me, Heather."

Heather raised her slow astonished head to see large dark eyes opening wide to her, thin pink lips growing pale with the vigour of their smile, a small snub nose widening its nostrils as if scenting her. She stood up so fast her chair struck Randall's desk with a clatter whose echoes sounded like the fall of a branch through a tangle of boughs. "Sylvia," she cried.

5

The Return

WHEN Heather raised the flap in the massive counter it seemed to have grown almost weightless. She might have imagined that the substance of the oak had been transformed if she hadn't realised her sister was lifting it too. As they embraced, it fell with a thud like the stroke of an axe, cueing a team of smaller blades among the shelves. Heather hugged her sister with a fierceness meant to counteract her not having recognised Sylvia at once—because of the accent, she told herself—only to feel the waist of Sylvia's dungarees collapse inwards. She wasn't much less thin than sticks. All Heather's years of big sisterhood surged over her, and she clutched Sylvia as if she might never again let her stray. At last she controlled herself enough to take Sylvia by the shoulders and gaze into her eyes, which appeared to be brimming with memories too. "What have you been doing to yourself?" Heather demanded.

Sylvia tilted her smiling head. "Do you mean with?"

"I mean to. What have you been eating, or haven't you?"

"There wasn't much choice for veggies in Mexico."

"You're still a herbivore, then."

"Still eating like a wild thing, right."

"I wish you were. We'll have to see you do."

"You're still my old sister sure enough." Sylvia stepped back, breaking her sister's hold, as echoes and Randall came into the library. "Listen, am I keeping you from work?"

"If you do I'll take the day off. I'll take however long we need to catch up. Randall, this is my baby sister Sylvie."

"They must be delivering them fully grown these days," he remarked, then planted the back of his hand on his lips like a reproving slap while he cleared his throat. "Delightful to meet you."

"It's been years since she's been home," Heather told him. "I expect we won't stop talking while we've got any breath left."

He set his hoary bulging briefcase on his desk and scratched his eyebrows with a sandpapery sound. "I'll cover if you want to slip away. Our assistants should be here soon."

"Maybe we'll take a long lunch. You can sit with me now and we'll talk while I resurrect some old books, Sylvie."

"Sounds like magic."

"Which I'm guessing you still like."

"Ever since you used to read to me."

"We're both too old for stories, do you think? What I'm doing now is just technology."

Sylvia followed her behind the counter as Randall held up the flap, and then she pointed with all her fingers. "What are you doing with my book?"

"I was just glancing through it."

"For what?"

"Nothing in particular," Heather said, surprised by the urgency of the question. "I thought I'd read it since I hadn't for a while, that's all."

"You know what that means then, don't you?"

"I'm not sure I do."

"That you sensed I was coming, of course," Sylvia said, and trailed her fingertips across the tales of seduction in the woods before closing the book. "Did you say you're going to resurrect it?"

"No, only because it isn't old enough. The books I'm putting on the computer are a lot older." Heather sat in front of the machine but didn't switch it on. "Do you mind if I ask . . ."

"Anything."

"You know I don't mean this in any nasty way, but what's brought you back so suddenly?"

"I never felt good about leaving you to cope. Maybe you looked after me so much when we were kids I ended up thinking of you as the caring one."

"I try to be. I don't complain much, do I, Randall?"

He looked away from his computer screen, his face red as if he'd been caught eavesdropping. "Never that I've noticed."

"He's being kind, but anyway we're talking about you, Sylvie."

"I guess I felt I ought to use how I'd learned to research at university, and maybe I wanted to write a book like dad."

"You're still apologising. All I asked was why you've come back now."

"I felt I was needed. Aren't I?"

"Don't wonder," Heather said, hugging her until she was rewarded with a bony embrace.

"I was thinking more of dad. You and mom wrote some of how he's been, but how is he now?"

"His mind's been more active these past few months."

"Are you pleased?"

"I meant he's been mostly disturbed. He's asked after you more than once."

"Maybe he sensed like you did I was planning to come home, or maybe he made me."

"If either."

Sylvia looked disappointed for as long as it took her to blink. "How about mom?"

"She's doing well. She has an exhibition coming up in London. Haven't you been in touch?"

"Not since I got back to England yesterday. I wanted to see you first. We were always closest, weren't we?" Hardly waiting for Heather to smile at that, she said "Shall I call her now?"

"I think you should. Use my phone."

Sylvia leaned one elbow on her book and held the receiver away from her face so that Heather heard the shrill pulse. It repeated itself six and a half times before Margo said not altogether patiently "Hello?"

"Guess who this is."

"I'm afraid I couldn't say. If you're calling from America it's quite early here. I'm just at a crucial point in a piece I'm carving. If you'd like to leave me your name and number—"

"Heather didn't know at first either."

They heard a silence like the absence of a gasp, and then "Sylvia? Is that really you?"

"If it isn't someone must be using my body."

"You sound so far away."

"I'm not though, am I, Heather?"

For an instant Heather was tempted to join in the teasing, but didn't want to feel as young as her sister kept seeming. "Not any longer," she said.

"Are you there with her at work, Sylvia?"

"Stopping her doing it, right. Being all kinds of distraction."

"Why didn't you tell us you were coming home?"

"I didn't want you worrying where I was if I got delayed. It wasn't easy coming where I came from."

"All that matters is you're home. Stay there and I'll pick you up and we'll still be talking when it's dark."

"I thought you said you were in the middle of something important."

"Nothing's as important as you. It can wait a day. It's only a piece of wood with a mind of its own. I'll be there in half an hour or so. Don't you dare go far. Don't you let her, Heather."

"We won't," they said in chorus, at which they laughed so much that Randall ventured to join in. As they subsided and Sylvia replaced the phone, Heather admitted "I want to hear all about Mexico and wherever else you've been, but I really ought to get on with some work."

"I won't stop you." Sylvia brandished *The Secret Woods* as she hoisted the flap in the counter just enough to sidle thinly through. "I'll put myself away," she said.

"You can tell me all about your adventures later."

"Later, right." Sylvia glanced back as she moved into the shadow of bookshelves. Her voice sounded both multiplied and muffled by wood as she said "I may have to save it till the book's done."

6

Behind the Houses

WHEN Sam had hobbled slowly up one aisle of shelves and halfway down another as though in search of some book he couldn't name, Heather went to him. "I shouldn't be too long now," she murmured. "How's the shop?"

"We had to get the window boarded up till a friend of Andy's dad can put in some glass tomorrow, so now nobody can see what we sell."

"Didn't you have any customers today?"

"That many," he said, splaying the fingers of his left fist twice while he reached past her for a book that lay on top of several upright ones. "Doesn't mean they all bought anything."

"So long as some did," Heather said, thrown by the sight of *The Secret Woods* in his hand. "Strange you should pick that up."

"What's strange about it?"

"Not so loud, Sam. You'll soon see."

"Will I want to?"

"I'm sure you will. Wait till you see why we're waiting," she murmured, and returned to her desk.

She saw him lower himself into a seat, apparently not noticing that he was opposite a more than pretty girl about his age, and frown over the book. She couldn't help wondering how he would greet Sylvia.

On catching sight of her, Margo had released a cry of mingled delight and dismay that had made all the students raise their heads like club members scenting an intruder. She'd stood on tiptoe to give Sylvia a hug across the counter as a foretaste of the one she'd delivered as soon as the flap was out of their way. "Don't you ever stay away so long again," she'd whispered, and not much less fiercely "Look what happens to you when you do." At once she'd been abashed, not only by her words. "Sorry. This isn't like me usually. Just years catching up with me. We're on our way now," she'd told everyone in the library. "Are you coming, Heather? Too much work, poor girl. Then we'll pick you up for lunch."

They'd eaten in Peace & Beans, the vegetarian restaurant on the far side of the campus, but Sylvia had consumed nowhere near enough to satisfy her mother. "We're going to have to feed you up," Margo had declared, poking around in her vegetable moussaka as though hoping some meat might have sneaked into it. While she'd done most of the talking, to Heather she'd said only "Isn't he?" and "Isn't she?" and "Didn't I?" and more of the same kind of punctuation. She'd proposed that Sylvia should stay at Heather's, where there was more room—Heather would have made the offer herself if she'd had the chance. Holding Sylvia's thin cold hands, she'd assured her she could stay for as long as they were sisters, and had made that her cue to return belatedly to work while Margo took Sylvia into town to buy her clothes. Heather wasn't about to resent that—she'd had presents from Margo herself, really quite a few of them. All she wanted now was for as many of her family as possible to be together.

She thought more than two young students were chattering and giggling in the corridor until the American voices outdistanced their echoes. Margo held the door open for Sylvia, who was loaded with three large shopping bags. "Sam," Margo called and put a quick though jokey finger to her lips. "Do you know who this is?" she asked in a whisper that would have reached the limits of a bigger room.

Sam leaned his hands on two pages of *The Secret Woods* and raised himself into a crouch. "Where did I see her before?" he wondered aloud.

"Let's get reacquainted outside, shall we?" Heather said and left Nick and Sarita to staff the desk for the evening.

Sam started when she touched his arm to move him. Once they were all in the corridor and the door was shut, Margo said not quite impatiently enough to leave affection behind "It's your aunt Sylvia."

"I know," Sam said, and turned to Sylvia. "I was just looking at you."

"Well, don't be shy of each other," Margo cried.

Aunt and nephew performed a hug that struck Heather as, at least on Sam's part, awkward. As they separated Sylvia asked him "When were you looking?"

"You're on your book I was reading."

"Heather was as well. Seems like it has a new lease of life."

"I feel as if we all have," said Margo. "She must have brought it with her, mustn't she, Heather?"

"I don't know who else could have."

Sylvia took Sam's arm. "I'm going to be rooming with you if that's all right with you," she said.

"Can't see how it couldn't be."

Perhaps it was his apparent confusion that inspired her to say "You've raised yourself a real knight, Heather. Remember when you told me one lived behind the house?"

"I can't say I do."

"When I was little and I asked who Goodman was and why it was his wood."

"I still don't remember."

"Now, girls," Margo protested, "you aren't going to start arguing as soon as you're back together."

"I think I rather grew out of knights. I'll be happy if Sam's just a good person," Heather said, and hurried Margo and Sylvia past his embarrassment, out of the door he was holding open.

A dusk that she could taste was settling over the campus, rousing floodlights in their burrows at the foot of the sandstone façade. "You'll have had enough of me for one day," Margo said to whoever might have. "Somebody call me tomorrow and we'll fix a date for dinner very soon."

"Can I visit dad tomorrow?" Sylvia said.

"So long as you don't let him know in advance that you're here," Margo said, apparently no more certain than Heather if the question had expressed eagerness or nervousness, "otherwise he'll never be able to sleep."

She left Sylvia with another hug and restrained herself to a single backward glance. As Heather's party made for the Civic, Sylvia nodded at Sam's limp. "The wounded knight," she mused. "Mom was telling me how you hurt yourself fighting for the trees."

"Fell out of one, that's all."

"I doubt it's anything like all, Sam."

He was silent as a tree-stump until Heather took out her keys. "Shall I drive so you can talk?" he suggested.

"Girls in the front, boys in the back," Sylvia said at once.

Heather was silent while she drove through the evening migration. Indeed, nobody spoke until most of Brichester had withdrawn over the horizon and the woods loomed ahead like a storm cloud fallen to earth, its eastern edge flickering with headlights on the bypass. Abruptly Sylvia said "When were you last in the woods, Sam?"

He took so long to reply that Heather almost urged him to speak up. "Must have been yesterday," he said.

"You didn't say you'd been there," Heather objected.

"Grandad wanted me to."

"In that case it was kind of you. Will you have much to tell him?"

"I don't know what he'd want to hear."

"The truth, I should think, unless there's anything that might distress him."

"Don't a lot of things?"

She would have had to lean sideways to observe Sam's face. Ahead the interior of the woods was fluttering with elongated shadows, and she caught herself wondering how that might appear to Lennox—as though a vast dark shape was flexing all its legs? Perhaps it was this sight that prompted Sylvia to ask "What do you think we'd find in there now?"

"Whatever's usually there," Heather said.

"And what's that, Heather?"

"The sort of things woods generally have in them."

"Are you saying that because you read my book?"

"I'm saying it because it's just a wood."

At the limit of her headlamp beams a lorry shuddered half out of the inside lane. "Have there been many accidents along here?" Sylvia said.

"More than there used to be before they widened it," Sam told her. "The workmen had some with their equipment when they were. They kept saying someone in the woods was distracting them. Wouldn't you know they said it was us."

Sylvia peered into the oncoming forest, and Heather resisted imagining how it might look to their father, as if the dark or something else as vast was stalking many-legged under cover of the trees. Her sister seemed entranced by whatever she was seeing, until she demanded "Is that him?"

Heather gripped the wheel as the car threatened to veer. "Who? Where?"

"Dad."

Of course, the Arbour was in sight on the opposite side of the bypass. A man was standing in the gateway, back-lit by the floodlights of the hospital, and lowering from his mouth a trail of smoke. "He'll be a nurse," Heather said.

"Where's dad's room?"

"Upstairs at the front."

Sylvia covered her face and made herself as small as she could without removing her seatbelt. The car had rounded the curve towards Goodmanswood, and the trees had put out the lights of the Arbour, before she lowered her hands and sat up. "Mom said I shouldn't disturb his sleep."

As Heather turned onto the Goodmanswood road the woods and their mass of shadows continued to sidle alongside until the first crooked line of small ungainly cottages intervened. Once the houses had grown larger and newer the High Road sailed by, keeping its shops and scattering of restaurants alight for almost nobody just now. A side street bulky with pairs of houses brought the Prices to Woodland Close, where several little girls with coats over pale blue ballet costumes were being escorted by parents into the community centre. "Did you ever go to that school, Sam?" Sylvia said.

"It wasn't one by the time I started."

"There was so much to see out of the windows I don't know how often the teachers had to tell me not to look."

Presumably she had been looking at the woods. Heather parked on the flagstones outside the house and heard the dogged rhythm of a piano underlining the voice of a ballet teacher: "All be trees." Sam took charge of the bags of shopping while Sylvia hoisted her shoulder bag, and it was only then that Heather thought to ask "Where's your luggage?"

"I left it in London till I knew I had a place to stay."

"How could you think you wouldn't have?"

"Maybe I thought you might feel I'd been away for so long I'd turned into a stranger."

"You're no stranger than you used to be, Sylvie."

"I'll take that as a compliment, shall I? I can't tell you how it feels to be home."

Heather thought Sylvia's eyes must be unfocused by emotion, since she appeared to be gazing not so much at as through the house. Sam had barely opened the front door when Sylvia stepped over the threshold. As the keypad of the alarm ceased beeping under his fingertips she advanced to hang her shoulder bag over the end of the banister, then stretched her arms wide, embracing everything she saw.

"That's where the trees came," she said, pointing to the corner where the staircase met the wall.

"We still have one every Christmas," Heather said.

"Here's where I used to lean my bike till mom got tired of the marks on the carpet," Sylvia said, and pushed doors open. "Here's where we watched too much television if you believed mom, except she thought any was too much. What's this room now, just somewhere to sit and read? We did a lot of that too, Sam, only it was our playroom as well. This is still the dining-room, I bet, and I know where the kitchen is. How about my room?"

"You can have, it's the guest room now. It used to be dad's study."

Sylvia scampered upstairs so fast she almost neglected to grab her bag. "That's where we used to hang our schoolbags when we came home," she remembered. "Who's in my room now?"

"Right now, nobody," Heather said, since that was how the question had sounded. "It's Sam's room."

"I hope you'll let me come in sometimes, Sam, for old times' sake."

As Heather opened the door of the guest room she heard dogs start to bark nearby. The room was still recognisable as a study. The reference books and filing cabinet full of their father's papers had been transferred to the university, but Margo had left his desk and its chair as though they might one day summon him back. Heather found herself willing Sylvia to like the rest of the room, the plump green quilt, the fat green pillows, the wallpaper patterned with leaves, but her sister went straight to the desk. She sat on the chair, dropping her bag next to it, then interwove her fingers to prop her chin. "You don't know how much I appreciate this, Heather."

If she was talking to any extent about the view the window shared with Sam's, Heather had to assume she meant how it would look in daylight. Just now all that she could see through the reflection of the room was the dim common stretching beyond her seven-foot garden fence to the dark woods. Sam planted the shopping bags on the quilt and told her "I can make dinner if you like."

Heather moved to stand beside her sister. "Shall we leave you to—" The barking of dogs made her lean towards the window, and she interrupted herself. "What was that?"

At once it wasn't there. It must have been a trick of light, a head-lamp beam so fleeting she hadn't perceived it as such—had seemed to see only a dark shape not unlike a man but as long as a man's shadow in the depths of winter, gliding swiftly as a snake towards the woods. At the moment when its pace would have brought it to the trees, she imagined she saw the darkness thicken beyond all of them. "Just my eyes," she said. Then, somewhere close, children began to scream.

7

The Sticky Man

WHEN Sylvia pushed up the lower half of the window, a scent drifted into the room. It must be some kind of night blossom that Heather didn't recognise. Lurking beneath the sweet almost cloying odour was another smell, of decay or growth or a marriage of the two. At once it withdrew into the night, and there was nothing to distract her from the screams, which were coming from the direction of the old school. She leaned across the corner of the desk to crane out of the window and shivered, because the night had grown much colder since she'd entered the house. Before she could see anything except the deserted schoolyard and the boxes of darkness that were back gardens, Sylvia was out of the swivel chair like a dervish. "Better go and look," she declared.

She left the house so fast that Heather could only follow. Sam was on the stairs when Heather reached the front door. "Do you need me as well?" he seemed not to hope.

She didn't know whether any of them would be more than a hindrance. "See what you can do to tempt your aunt instead," she advised him, and shut the door.

She was hugging herself to fend off the cold, and its absence was a shock. It must have been emanating from the common. The screams were subsiding, or the children had been taken indoors, or both. Sylvia dodged through the old iron schoolyard gates as Heather's friend Jessica flustered out of the house opposite. "Jessica," Heather called, hurrying to catch up with her at the gates. "Is it Rosemary?"

If possible Jessica was even more dishevelled than usual, her red hair that always looked windswept sprouting more random curls than ever, her thick-lensed thin-framed spectacles in danger of sliding off her token nose and down her broad face. She was wearing a voluminous dark green dress and a plastic apron printed with bunches of cherries big as apples and spattered with traces of whatever dinner she'd been preparing. "She'd never make a noise like that unless something was terribly wrong," she said.

It wasn't clear whether that meant she thought one of the distressed children was indeed her granddaughter. Heather followed her into the entrance corridor as the nearby dogs stopped prompting one another. It was smaller than it had seemed in her childhood. Several pensioners in artists' smocks had emerged from a classroom to stare along it, past posters for flower arranging and wine appreciation and bookbinding as a hobby, towards the double doors of the former assembly hall. Sylvia opened the doors to reveal a huddle of small timid ballerinas, one of whom bolted towards Jessica. "Rosemary," Jessica cried. "Was that you giving me a fright?"

"It was Willow and Laurel trying to scare us," her granddaughter said, clinging to as much of Jessica's waist as she could encompass.

Two girls were isolated on the far side of the wide high stony room. "Isn't anyone looking after them?" Jessica protested.

"Their mummies aren't here yet."

"We'll take care of them, won't we, Heather?" Sylvia said, and hurried to them.

The ballet teacher and the pianist, two tall middle-aged women whose makeup had begun to fray around the eyes, were doing their nervous best to calm the other children. "Who are you, please?" the ballet teacher called in the high sharp voice Heather had overheard telling the ballerinas to be trees.

"She's a friend of mine from just along the road," said Jessica.

"And this is my sister," Heather said more protectively than she'd known she was about to speak.

"They can help till the parents arrive," Jessica said with some briskness.

"You're trees like me," Sylvia was telling the girls. "Let me guess. You have to be Willow."

The girl, who was even slimmer and more big-eyed than her friend, shook her head, trailing long blonde locks over her bare shoulders. "She is."

"Call strike one against me, then. I bet you're both nine years old."

"She's eight and a quarter and I nearly am."

"Gee, two strikes. They're real little maidens though, aren't they, Heather? Just like we were at their age."

"Sometimes."

The girls were too fascinated by Sylvia's accent to spare Heather more than a simultaneous blink or apparently to notice they were shivering. "Haven't you anything to put on?" Heather said.

"Our coats are in the cloakroom," said Willow.

"Then we'd better go and get them. It's all right to do that, isn't it?"

The women in charge both had the grace to nod. Heather bustled the girls to the cloakroom next to the entrance to the building. It smelled of the wood of all the coat-hooks. Though the smell reminded her of childhood—of herself and Sylvia making as much noise as the rest of the children crowded into the doorless room—it seemed older and more oppressive than she would have expected. As Willow and Laurel wriggled into their padded multicoloured coats, Sylvia said "What will your teacher tell your parents, do you think?"

"She'll say we frightened Lucy," Willow said.

"And Gwyn," Laurel added as if that might be a reason for sly pride.

"We told them if they came in the yard they'd see the man."

"Which man?" Sylvia asked, more eagerly than Heather thought appropriate.

The girls glanced sideways at each other, and Willow said almost too low to be heard "The sticky man."

Sylvia moved closer to her, and Heather felt she also had to. "Why do you call him that?" Sylvia murmured.

"You can see he is," Laurel said as warily as her friend.

"And he's so thin he can put all his arm through the railings."

"And if you touched his hand you'd get honey on yours."

"Honey or whatever it is."

"Then you'd try not to lick your fingers but you would."

Heather was opening her mouth to suggest they'd covered the subject enough when Sylvia said "What else is he like?"

"Sometimes his eyes are all green," Laurel confided.

"And when you see them next they'll have got bigger," said Willow.

"But now they're all brown and wrinkled."

"They've got wrinkles around them, you mean?"

"Not around them," Willow little more than whispered. "In them."

"And he smells of sweets," said Laurel.

So did the cloakroom. Of course it would when children still used it, Heather told herself as Willow objected "Sometimes he does, and sometimes it's flowers."

"That's quite a tale," Heather said. "Did you make it up between you?"

It wasn't just being met with mute impatience that took her aback, it was that some of it was Sylvia's. "What's his face like?" Sylvia said.

"Sylvie, I really—"

"All scrunched up," said Willow.

"Like an old tree with crawlies on it," said her friend.

"No wonder the other children made such a fuss if you told them all that," Heather commented.

"We didn't," Willow said.

"Not all, then. Some would be too much."

"We didn't have to. He was there."

"You saw him," Heather said, audibly meaning the opposite.

"You don't need to."

"You can hear him talking," Willow explained.

"Then may I ask," Heather said more pompously than she was able to control, "what he's supposed to sound like?"

"Like trees."

"Like when you hear them when you're in bed," Laurel added.

Heather could have done without imagining that the smells of wood and sweetness had grown stronger, and she started at a loud creak and a squeal behind her. The entrance door had admitted two women. "Laurel's in the cloakroom, Mrs Bennett," the ballet teacher called. "So's Willow, Mrs Palmer."

Heather always tried to like people, and so she did her best not to take against the two women in expensive trousers and fat sweaters who marched into the corridor as though eager for a reason to complain. Their chubby petulant faces were newly made up and lipsticked, and their perfumes blotted out any other smell. "Are they in disgrace?" said the woman with the larger and redder mouth.

"I'm rather afraid so, Mrs Palmer."

Mrs Palmer planted her legs apart and gripped her hips, apparently as aids to glaring at her daughter. "What's she been up to now?"

"Telling you someone was hanging around at the back of the building, did you say, Gwyn?"

"Someone nasty," said the child she addressed. "Someone horrible."

"Only he wasn't really," another girl, presumably Lucy, said.

"They just kept saying he was hiding and we'd see him in a minute," Gwyn remembered with a nervous giggle, "like anyone could hide behind a railing."

"It's Laurel and Willow who are nasty and horrible," small-mouthed Mrs Bennett said.

"They've made up one story too many this time," Mrs Palmer agreed, scowling harder at them.

"They're a sight too fond of upsetting people with their nonsense."

"They nearly made us crash last night coming back from Brichester, going on about somebody running behind the trees."

"Don't you worry, girls," Mrs Bennett told the ballerinas in the hall. "You won't be seeing them here again."

Laurel began at once to weep. When Willow looked uncertain whether to join in, Mrs Palmer told her furiously "And you won't be going to the hair salon tomorrow either."

Both girls burst into sobs and cowered as the women stalked forward to drag them away. "Do you know what people are going to say if you keep making up stories like that?" Mrs Bennett demanded. "They'll say you're on drugs."

"The kind that drove people mad round here before you were born," said Mrs Palmer, and frowned at Sylvia. "Are you waiting for someone in particular?"

"We just came over to see what the trouble was."

"Came over from America?" Mrs Bennett said, not quite in disbelief.

"We can do without Americans telling us how to bring up our children. That's when things started going wrong, Dr Spock and all the rest of them."

"Came over from my house just up the road," Heather had been waiting for the chance to say. "Jessica knows me."

This failed to impress either of the women. "Well, I hope you found out what you wanted to," Mrs Palmer was insincere enough to tell Sylvia.

"I'm starting."

Both women stared at that but didn't speak. They had dragged their woebegone daughters to the exit when Mrs Bennett offered a parting remark. "I didn't think you looked like mothers."

"I wouldn't want to if it meant looking like them," Heather murmured, and gave them time to slam themselves and their children into a car before she called "We'll be off then, Jessica."

"Thank you for helping," the ballet teacher said.

"Yes, thank you," said the pianist.

Their gratitude seemed less than wholehearted, but Heather was preoccupied. As she preceded Sylvia along the pavement, through a lingering chilly scent the women must have left behind, she said "Do you think someone ought to be looking behind what the girls were saying?"

"Willow and Laurel? I think you should always look behind things."

"I just wonder if it's too simple to dismiss what they said as made up. Didn't some of it sound like trying to talk about child abuse?"

At first Sylvia merely gazed at her. "Heather, sometimes your mind is really small."

"I don't think it's small-minded to care about children. And while we're talking about them, I should be a bit more careful how you question them, even if you are researching another book."

Of course, she thought at once, Sylvia had come home mostly for their father, which was why Sylvia said "I wouldn't want you to believe I'm here just to research." They left the glow of a streetlamp behind for the shadows outside Heather's house, and darkness seemed to well up from Sylvia's eyes, veiling her face.

8

Forgotten Dreams

HEATHER was in no hurry to emerge from a dense sleep featureless as fog when she became aware that she and Sam were no longer alone in the house. As she remembered the other was Sylvia she made to turn over in bed, hoping she could fit herself back into the sleep that the thought of restoring her family rendered even more peaceful, and then she found she was unable to move. The sheet between her and the quilt was pinning her down, trapping her on her back, arms pressed against her sides, as though a cocoon had enveloped her while she slept. A weight had joined her on the bed.

She splayed her fingers on the mattress and opened her eyes a crack. Sylvia was sitting on the far end of the bed, arms folded, head tilted to watch her sister. She wore a black dress long and loose enough to conceal most of her gauntness. Whatever expression she bore was swept away by a welcoming smile. "Hey, you're awake at last," she said.

Heather sat up against the padded headboard. "Why, have you been here long?"

"Pretty much since the sun came up. I don't sleep a whole lot."

A glance at the clock that was using her bedside novel as a plinth showed Heather it was nearly ten, which meant Sylvia must have been sitting there for hours. "What have you been doing?" Heather felt compelled to ask.

"Remembering."

"Much in particular?"

"When we used to share a room."

"Gosh, I couldn't tell you when I last thought about that."

"Remember how we'd tell each other stories while we were going to sleep?"

"It was like dreaming out loud, wasn't it? All the things we were going to do when we grew up. You had a phase when you were going to be an airline pilot and give us all free trips around the world. And I was going to be a doctor or a scientist and cure dad."

"Something could change him. Nobody can stay the same for ever." Sylvia stood up as though the notion had jerked her to her feet like the puppet she was thin enough to be. "When will we see him?" she said.

"As soon as you like once we're ready."

"I've been ready for a while. Is Sam coming with us?"

"You'll have to ask him."

"Okay, I will."

Heather hadn't meant immediately, but Sylvia almost ran to the door. She had one foot on the landing when she said "I don't suppose you'd want to share a room again."

"I've got out of the habit since Sam's father decided Goodmanswood was too small for him."

"Nowhere's small unless your mind is. Hasn't there been anyone since him?"

"Sam's enough of a man in my life just now."

"I can imagine. I meant share a room with me."

"I think we've outgrown that, don't you? Is there something you don't like about your room?"

"Couldn't be improved. I just don't think you can ever grow out of hearing stories in the dark."

Had she been proposing to tell Heather some, or was she nervous of being alone with them at night? Before Heather could ask, Sylvia knocked on Sam's door, provoking the kind of unwelcoming mumble Heather expected, since he had Saturday off work. Nevertheless his aunt ventured into the room, and Heather heard them murmuring. "I'll be in the bathroom," she called.

It had acquired a very few items of Sylvia's: a toothbrush, a hairbrush crested with a comb, a zippered plastic bag. Heather took her time in the shower, but when she stepped out of the bath Sam and her sister were still talking. Steam had gathered on the mirror, to reveal that someone had been sketching with a fingernail on the glass; a circle and a tree-stump or a tower. She didn't think the artist had any future to speak of. She cleared the quarter of the mirror occupied by the sketch, and then the rest of the glass.

"I don't know about anyone else," she called as she emerged from the bathroom, "but I'm having a bite to eat."

She was halfway through a bowl of Sticky Rotters when she heard Sam's door open, and Sylvia hurried down to join her. "I couldn't persuade him to come with us," she said.

"I expect he felt you should have dad to yourself."

"You'll be there, won't you?"

"If you don't just want me to drive you and stay out of the way while you get reacquainted."

"I don't. I want you to hear everything," Sylvia said, and shook her head at an offer of breakfast. "I'll wait while you finish."

"Coffee?"

"The smell's enough to put me on edge right now," Sylvia said, demonstrating with a squeal of chair-legs on linoleum as the phone rang.

Heather leaned her chair backwards and lifted the receiver down from the wall. "Heather Price."

"Margo of that line. How's the family now it's back together?"

"How you'd want it to be."

"So long as you do as well."

"I can't see what else I'd want, except for you to be here too."

"Me and one other," Margo said, and with a cheerfulness that sounded only slightly determined "I'm used to having my own place and my own hours that don't disturb anyone else. It's enough to know I'm welcome when I want to be."

"You know that's whenever. Would you like a word with Sylvie?"

"I'll have one before I leave you in peace. I wanted to let you know I've been speaking to the Arbour. Lennox didn't sleep much last night, apparently. Neither did I, oddly enough. The piece I'm working on is giving me too many ideas."

"I slept like a log myself. Like a piece of wood with no ideas."

"Well, you were always the placid one. Anyway, I wanted to find out if you were likely to disturb him. Not you, Heather, I know you never could."

Heather had to make an effort not to feel dismissed as predictable to the point of dullness. "You're talking about Sylvie."

"Not in herself, just her showing up, but his doctor's sure it will do Lennox good to see her when he's been asking after her so much."

"Is the doctor going to tell him she's coming?"

"He thinks she may as well show up unannounced. Is she with you?"

"Yes, and wondering what we're saying about you, aren't you, Sylvie?"

Sylvia responded only by accepting the receiver. "I'm good," she told Margo, and "Like I'm back where I should never have left" and "Anxious to see him. Anxious how he'll take me . . . " She was continuing along these lines when Sam padded not quite evenly downstairs. Apart from being barefoot, he was wearing yesterday's clothes. "Didn't you have a shower?" Heather enquired.

"I will. I was going to make breakfast if anybody wants some."

"Those who did have had it, thanks, Sam. But listen, I'm sure your aunt won't mind seeing you in your dressing-gown and nothing else."

That was his normal morning attire on his days off work, but he looked so embarrassed that Heather changed the subject as Sylvia hung up the phone. "Who was drawing on the bathroom mirror?"

For a moment Sylvia and Sam regarded her with a blankness so identical it looked like a shared secret, and then Sam said "Sorry. Me."

"No need to be sorry, but what was it about?"

"Couldn't tell you. I was half asleep. Who was talking in the night and woke me up?"

Sylvia resumed her blank look. Since she appeared to be set in her silence, Heather said "What do you think you heard?"

"Someone."

"Saying what?"

"I didn't understand what it was muttering on about. It stopped when I got up."

"I expect you dreamed it."

"Like I dreamed the stuff I was trying to see what it looked like on the mirror."

"As long as that's settled," Sylvia said, "do you think we could leave pretty soon?"

"We can now," Heather told her, and immediately wondered how their father would react to Sylvia. That was far more important than speculating about the length of time Sylvia might have sat with her on the bed. There was no point in brooding over that—no reason to think it had been Sylvia's voice Sam had imagined he heard in the dark.

9

In a Ring

AS soon as Heather drove through the gateway she saw Lennox.
Of several patients in folding chairs on the lawn, he was the closest to the gates. She couldn't tell whether he and his fellow inmates
were watching the road or the woods, which had trapped a morning
mist, though the November sky was clear. All six twisted in their seats
to observe her progress up the drive. So much of a reaction made her
tense, so that she was glad to see nurses in the grounds and Dr Lowe in
the front entrance of the Arbour.

He was polishing his glasses. Without them his round face looked
unprotected, not as competent as he would surely have preferred to
appear. He held the glasses up as though to focus on some aspect of
the woods, then emitted a gasp he might have wanted nobody to hear,
and breathed on a lens that he rubbed afresh with a large sky-blue
handkerchief. As Heather parked in front of a bay window he donned
the glasses, clearing grey hair out of the way of their arms with his
forefingers, and approached the car. Even when the Prices climbed out
he remained in a welcoming stoop. "You'll be the long-awaited
event," he told Sylvia.

Lennox and the others had adopted various gnarled postures to face
her. "Did you tell him we were coming?" Heather murmured.

"Just that he might be visited, but he seemed to know that. I won't be far away."

Presumably that was to reassure Sylvia. Heather was aware of little except her sister's nervousness as they crossed the lawn. The seated patients had turned to watch Lennox, who seemed almost to sprout upwards from his chair. He swung it aside and dropped it on the grass as he advanced on Sylvia, hands outstretched as if to measure her girth. "I told you she wouldn't let us down," he cried.

Sylvia took his hands, and they gazed into each other's eyes as if sharing a secret or trying to discover one. "How did you know I was coming?" she said.

"Because you were called."

Heather could only assume her sister was pretending that answered the question. "You haven't changed. You're more the same," Lennox said. "You've only grown where it counts."

He passed a hand over the crown of her head in a gesture not unlike a benediction before wrapping his arms around her, loosely enough to suggest that he feared she might snap. The seated patients cheered and stamped so loudly they would have been audible in the forest, which appeared to respond by withdrawing its mist not quite far enough to unveil a rank of dripping shapes. "You see how you're appreciated," Lennox said. "You as well, Heather."

As the stamping faltered and the cheers ran out of breath, the nearest man wheezed, "Introduce us."

"This is Vernon, girls. He used to be a naturalist. Still is when there are flowers in the grounds."

"They're what took me to the woods, the rarities," the man said with uneasy pride.

"And that's Delia. Her mother used to take her walking there every Sunday."

Delia clapped her fingers to her cheeks as if her protuberant eyes needed support. "Carried on after she was dead and buried."

"You did," Heather felt it was advisable to say, "not your mother."

"Her or something that kept looking like her."

Heather regretted having spoken, not least because Lennox gave Delia a smile that might have greeted a witty remark. "And that's Phyllis next to Delia," he said. "Phyllis used to pick mushrooms in the woods about this time of year."

"You are what you eat," Phyllis declared and used her greyish tongue to trace increasingly unappetising shapes around her lips.

"I'm Timothy," said the man beside her, his head swaying from side to side. "I always knew there were rare birds in the woods. I could just never photograph them."

"Something flies round the woods, but it isn't birds," his neighbour said. "Too big. Sometimes it's under the branches and sometimes up above, with a face. I'm Nigel," he added with no apparent sense of incongruity.

"It's Lennox who sees furthest into the woods," said Delia, tugging at the skin beneath her eyes.

"So far. Will you give me some time with my family now?" he said, and made for the hospital building.

Heather was glad to leave his companions behind. Not only had they all been victims in the sixties of the mutated lichen, but now she realised they had formed the party he'd recently led into the woods. He ushered the sisters up the left-hand staircase to his room, which was so warm it felt impatient for midsummer. He raised the window a hand's breadth, apparently as far as it would move. As a smell of fog and rotting vegetation found its way into the room he sat on the foot of the bed and beckoned Sylvia to join him. "Space for you as well, Heather," he said.

There barely was. "I'm not a sylph like her," she said. "I'll have the stool."

"So long as it doesn't make you feel like the dunce. That's where teachers used to sit children who were slow on the uptake."

"I did know that," Heather said, less sure of the relevance.

"Sure enough, you're the reader." Perhaps that was meant less than positively, since he added "You have to concentrate on what's important. I've finished with most of my memories now, but I remember you before you were born. I remember when you were conceived, Sylvia."

"Gee."

"Do you know what I saw then?"

"I don't."

"Everything that has to be."

When he turned to gaze into the blurred shifting noonday twilight under the trees, Heather tried to reclaim his attention. "What else do you remember about us?"

"I saw you come out of your mother. I saw your sister do it with her eyes open, she was so ready to see."

"I don't suppose you remember that, Sylvie."

"Maybe I will."

Heather assumed that was intended to appeal somehow to Lennox. "No need to be jealous, Heather," he said.

"I'm not."

As though to placate her he said "I remember how you were always taking her into the woods when you were children."

"Hardly always, and only when she asked."

"And your mother thought they'd been made safe." He might have been addressing the restless undefined depths of the forest as he enquired "So what are you going to do for me?"

It was Sylvia who risked asking "What do you need?"

"Let's see if your sister can tell us."

Heather took this for an attempt to include her, but couldn't find much of a response. "I'll let you," she said.

"The history of the woods."

"I can find that in your library, can't I, Heather?"

"Only what happened since anyone kept records," Lennox said. "Still, there'll be something before the manifestation that brought us here."

"Manifestation," Heather said as a query or a challenge.

"That's okay, Heather. We don't expect you to understand all at once."

She wasn't going to ask who else he thought he was speaking for besides himself. "Only don't give it too much time," he said. "We don't want you having to absorb it all in one go."

She didn't know she was about to blurt "Like you did, you mean."

"I haven't yet. There are changes on the horizon."

The only visible horizon was formed by treetops, but that wasn't why she made herself say "Tell us about them."

"In here," he said, tapping his forehead as if ascribing madness to someone else, "and out there, if there's any difference."

"I think there is, don't you, Sylvie?"

"Not once the woods get in," their father said. "Do you honestly suppose you could touch them and nothing would come of it?"

He had to mean the felling that had made way for the bypass. She was wondering whether to argue with him, and hoping that Sylvia would, when he stretched an arm in her direction before bending it towards the window as though to include her in an embrace. "Look out there," he said. "Tell us what you see."

"Trees."

She did: sunlit rows of them dripping like an army of the drowned, and more blurred ranks behind them—trees of the kind Sam had fallen from. For an instant the grey formless depths of the woods appeared to quiver as though considering what shape to adopt. "That's all," she said.

She wouldn't have been surprised to hear disappointment in his voice, but it was quite neutral as he said only "Sylvia."

Sylvia leaned towards the gap under the sash. The smell of leaves acrawl with fog surged into the room, and Heather glimpsed a secretive movement the width of the forest. She couldn't help holding her breath until Sylvia spoke. "I don't know yet."

"That's the way. You will," Lennox said, and pushed himself to his feet by dragging the sash down. "I think that's enough for one day. I'll walk out with you," he said, and smiled rather wistfully at the doubts Heather was unable to conceal. "Only to your car."

Dr Lowe met them at the foot of the stairs. "How was the visit?"

"I think we've made a good start," Lennox said.

"I'd say so," said Sylvia, and Heather felt bound to produce a murmur of agreement.

"And where are we bound now?" the doctor said with heavy casualness.

"Me, back where I was." Lennox stood away from the car as the sisters climbed in. "Come again soon," he told them, "for a check on progress."

He paced the car as it coasted along the drive, then made for his chair. Heather glanced towards him as she reached the gateway, and almost neglected to brake. As she regained control before the vehicle could lurch onto the bypass, the woods seemed to gather their dank depths and inch towards her. She forced herself to concentrate on the headlong traffic, and almost managed to put her last sight of the hospital grounds out of her mind. Lennox and the others were sitting in a circle, just as they'd stood in the centre of the forest. The memory seemed no more real than an old dream, and she could neither grasp it nor rid herself of it. She couldn't be sure, nor could she deny, that the circle of seats on the lawn was exactly the size of the ring of bricks deep in the woods.

10

A View of the Future

A peal of bells roused Sam. Though the church was behind him in
Goodmanswood, the wind that the trees across the common
were exerting themselves to snatch made the bells sound as though
they were deep in the forest, misshapen too and clogged with moss.
He knew he was hearing a tape so worn it had ceased to bear much
resemblance to bells, but he was disconcerted to realise he didn't know
how long he had been seated at his desk.

He ought to be on the move soon. A glance at his fat black wristwatch showed him that his father was already a few minutes late. He
wouldn't be loitering at the desk, where the computer screen displayed a faint reflection of his face with little of a mouth and less for
eyes, if he hadn't risen earlier than he ordinarily did on his days off
work. He'd felt a need to look out of the window, not that there was
much to be certain he was seeing. It didn't help him remember why
the knees of his trousers had been stained with mud the last time he'd
come home from the woods.

The glassy light of a sky laced with fast thin whitish clouds showed
treetops flaking like dead skin in the wind. The sun was caught in a
dance of branches that seemed constantly about to sway in unison.
The far edge of the common was crowded with shadows bent on

clawing the ground into the woods. Of course it was the wind and not the shadows that kept urging the grass towards them in waves, but he couldn't shake off the notion that there were more elongated spindly shadows than trees bordering the forest to cast them. He hadn't been able to locate the source of the impression when the doorbell rang.

Once he heard his father's voice he made himself leave the window. Sylvia had let his father in. Though he would have combed it before leaving the car, his black irredeemably wavy hair was tousled by the wind, and so was the pale blue silk scarf that adorned his throat within the collar of his dark blue shirt. He glanced up the stairs, and his comfortably overfed face sent Sam a wink. "Morning, old chap. I'm just meeting your delightful guest."

"She's my aunt."

"Sylvia." Sam's father appeared to recoil as he stepped back for a more comprehensive look. "I don't know if you'll remember me," he said. "I'm Terry Harvey, your nephew's old man."

"Heather told me we were expecting you."

"I hope that didn't sound too ominous."

"Just as neutral as could be."

If his father and Sylvia were flirting, Sam couldn't help feeling uneasy, but then her presence in the house had that effect on him. He limped downstairs as his father said "How does it feel to come back to a village when you've seen so much of the world?"

"Everything that's part of me is here."

"Sorry, I didn't mean to suggest . . . That's to say, I know this is your home."

"Maybe you should check with Heather."

"You know he doesn't need to, Sylvie," Sam's mother called from the kitchen.

"Apologies if I assumed too much," Sam's father nonetheless said. "I thought I'd grown out of that habit."

Sam took another step down, only for his father to break the awkward silence. "I was really just saying how much of life you must have seen before you decided to come home."

"Some of us didn't feel we had the choice," Sam's mother said as though she didn't care if she was heard.

"Is that maybe a shade unreasonable? I wasn't thinking about you."

"Hardly the first time."

"I was thinking of this young fellow," he said, and to Sylvia "I keep telling him he ought to find out how much more there is to life than here and the town up the road. So where are we heading today, Sam?"

"Can we go into town for lunch?"

"That gets my vote, only another time you might want to come down to me. Stay chez Harvey any Saturday night by all means. Fridays too if you like."

"Not London, Brichester. I promised Andy I'd check the shop if I was round that way."

"If we're really only going up the road, anyone else who wants feeding is welcome to join us."

"No, you go and be uninhibited," Sam's mother said, he couldn't tell how slyly. "This is the boys' day."

His father's glossy black Rover had refrained from invading the personal space of the Civic and the Volkswagen on the paving in front of the house. A swarm of contorted parchment-coloured leaves came scuttling along the road, and one shaped like a reptile's claw swooped towards Sam as he shut himself in the Rover. The car was gliding out of Woodland Close when his father said "So was I making as much of your aunt as everyone seemed to believe?"

"I didn't."

"That's because you aren't a woman. How's the girlfriend situation?"

"Nobody just now."

"Well, remember if there's anything you want to consult me about I'm as close as your phone." As Sam assured himself that wasn't meant to treat him like a client, his father said "And what are you making of Sylvia?"

"I'm trying to get used to having her around."

"Lucky you, or is it?"

"It's strange with someone else in the house."

"I wish it weren't," his father said, and cleared his throat of a hint of wistfulness. "Anyway, we aren't talking about me."

"I wish we were."

"We did explain the situation to you at the time, me and your mother."

"You can use longer words now."

"It was simply when the firm moved out of Brichester it was either tag along with them or start again with people I didn't particularly like and at less of a salary into the bargain. I know you understood why your mother felt she had to stay. I thought you understood me too."

"I didn't say I didn't."

"It made sense for you to stay with her when Margo could help look after you, and we tried to make sure you saw enough of me. That doesn't stop me feeling guilty, all the same."

"Why would you want to feel that?"

"I don't want it at all," Sam's father retorted, only to admit "Perhaps I do if I'm honest. Perhaps I don't need to. We'll have to see how you grow up."

That sounded like a threat to engineer the process. Apparently concluding he'd said enough for the moment, he inserted a compact disc of Beethoven symphonies into the player as the car left Goodmanswood behind. The music had barely announced itself with a flurry of notes when he turned it lower than the wind. "Sorry I was late, by the way. I nearly did a silly on the bypass."

Sam wasn't merely watching but feeling the woods crowd towards him. He was less than fully aware of being expected to ask "What was that?"

"Tried to dodge something that wasn't there."

"What?" Sam demanded.

"It must have been the shadow of a tree or a lot of them. I thought it was someone running in front of the car at first, as if anyone could stretch across the whole road."

"How could just a shadow make you late?"

"Because I braked before I tried to take avoiding action. I nearly had a pair of trucks up my nether regions, and after that I needed a few minutes in a lay-by to recuperate."

"I still don't get it," Sam said uneasily. "It couldn't have been a shadow when the sun isn't behind the woods yet."

"There are trees on this side of the road as well, old fellow. As a matter of fact I think it was here," Sam's father said, nodding at the trees that staked out the grounds of the Arbour.

Sam tried and failed to see how any of those trees could have cast a shadow across the bypass, even when the sun was lower. He felt as though the depths of the forest or something they concealed were effortlessly pacing the car. He couldn't think for the Beethoven, which kept repeating itself louder like someone shouting at a deaf person or a foreigner while the treetops seemed to describe shapes more sinuous and patterns more complex than any music. He couldn't grasp how long it took the car to pass the woods. He saw them shrink in the mirror as the motorway glittered with traffic ahead, but he felt as if they were dwindling only to reveal more of themselves, to increase themselves somehow. They remained a hovering restless many-limbed presence in his mind and at his back as the motorway reeled Brichester towards him. He was indifferent to the sight of the university towering over streets of repetitive houses until his father said "You'll need to tell me where we're meant to go, old chap."

That was Worlds Unlimited, which Sam realised now had been the first destination he could think of. "Past the, right," he said. "I don't mean right, I mean right, straight on. Right now, right here." He felt as if he was playing a video game on the monitor that was the windscreen, and clumsily too. "Along, right, no, just along. Here."

He could see without leaving his seat that the new shop window was intact, but he hobbled to check the door was locked. Beyond the window the display of books seemed to consist of little more than lumps of paper. "I can't say I'm surprised you don't want to hang round in a seedy district like this," his father remarked as Sam returned to the car.

Sam saw a page of last night's newspaper dodging from doorway to doorway like a messenger outdistanced by its message while two beer bottles clashed in the gutter. "Onward then, is it?" his father said.

"May as well."

"Where do you suggest?"

"The pub."

"I like a mystery as much as the next man, but I wouldn't mind knowing which."

"Go back. We have to go back."

They had indeed already passed the Scholars' Rest, which might have been the only one Sam could bring to mind. Beneath a jauntily sagging slate roof the squat sandstone building faced the university campus, where isolated saplings were practising moves. Each window of the pub held a swelling like a great blind eye. Once across the thick doorstep worn convex by centuries of feet and through the small stout door, Sam was reminded that the dim low-timbered interior was lined with old books. He let his father buy him a pint of Witch's Brew, the strongest ale, and downed a quarter of it, then another. Having observed this with a mixture of admiration and amusement, his father said "Are we eating here as well?"

"There's food."

"I did spot that. Let's see what's tempting," his father said, opening an unnecessarily giant menu that bore a cartoon of a mortarboard. "Lecturer's Lasagne. Student's Salad. Graduate's Grill. Professor's Prawns. Co-ed's Chilli. Bursar's Burger. Vice-Chancellor's Veggies. Sophomore's Steak . . ."

"Lasagne sounds all right."

"Does it?" his father said as though he'd failed to make the humour sufficiently obvious. "Lasagne it is, then," he told the gowned barman, "and a Porter's Platter for me."

Sam had halved the remainder of his pint by the time the barman finished typing the order on a till that chirped like a bird. "Another before we sit down?" his father suggested.

"Do you want me to get it?"

"No, I want you to get around it." He gave Sam's immediately empty tankard only the briefest of frowns. "Everything's on me," he said.

Sam carried his second pint to a desk laid with sunlight that couldn't penetrate the empty inkwell. Whenever traffic or pedestrians passed outside, their distorted movements in the bloated windows made him feel as if he were viewing the street through someone else's eyes, too many of them. He tried peering at the contents of the shelves around him—children's novels older than himself, fifties self-help books, outdated histories, forgotten best-sellers—but the act of trying to distinguish ill-lit books seemed inexplicably ominous. "Looking for something special?" his father said.

"No."

"I'm sure you are even if it isn't here. You won't be angry if I admit I don't think it's that shop of yours."

"Maybe I don't either."

"Then shall we give your future a look?"

Sam's brain felt full of enough alcohol for any uninvited advice to float on. "If you want."

"I was rather hoping you might."

The arrival of lunch—a less than full but steaming dish of lasagne, and a platter laden with the bread and cheese and pickles ploughmen, not porters, were alleged to favour—was by no means the only reason why Sam failed to see ahead. He fed himself a mouthful of lasagne to gain time, and was taking at least as long as seemed justifiable with it when his father said "Maths was always my best subject, which is why I'm an accountant. English is yours, so can't you make it work for you?"

All at once the setting inspired Sam. "I will soon."

"I feel happier already. Any preview available?"

"I'll still be in books. I'll be a publisher."

"Well, nobody could accuse you of not being ambitious."

"I don't mean right away. I'll get a job in the industry and work my way up."

"That's the attitude. You know you'll have to move down my way to get anywhere. Have you told Heather?"

"Not till I've been for some interviews. I'm only telling you because you asked."

"I appreciate it, old chap. It's a secret, is it, till you say otherwise?"

"She's got enough changes in her life right now," Sam said, and tried to hold on to his vision. "So when I've been in publishing a few years I'll know when anyone is looking to put money into a new firm, and I'll have made enough of a name that they'll want me along. And I'll know who the writers are who are going to be hot, and we'll buy them in. Maybe I'll be one of them too. I feel like writing a book."

"If you can impress whoever interviews you as much as you've just impressed me I don't think you'll have many problems. Even if things don't work out exactly as you think, you'll be in a real job."

Sam bowed his head to meet a forkful of lasagne. "So is anything else hatching in there?" his father said.

"Where?"

"The old skull. The old brain."

Sam found the choice of words obscurely unnerving until his father said "I was just wondering if you had an idea for a book."

"A wood bigger than the world."

"A fantasy, you mean."

"Someone who lives in it, who's been born in it, tries to get to the end of it to see what else there is. He keeps climbing trees but he can never see anything else."

"What did some writer say, write what you know? You climbing that tree may come in useful after all." Sam's father took a sip of barely alcoholic lager and said "Does he have a name, your chap?"

The details of the book felt even more like dreaming aloud than Sam's thoughts about publishing had. "Bosky," he said.

"I'd say he'd stick in people's minds. Anything else you want to share about him?"

"He meets someone who leads him to the secret of the woods."

"A girl, would I be right?" When Sam found himself nodding his father said "And the secret is . . ."

"Stuff a wizard buried."

"Do you know what that is yet, or don't you want to say?"

Sam felt his brows tightening as if to hold in any response. "Keep it to yourself if you'd rather write it first," his father said. "Have you got a title?"

Sam's mind had another surprise for him. "*The Only Way Out is Down.*"

"You know, I think all this is worth celebrating. What do you say to champagne?"

"You're driving."

"Then we'll save it for the next time you're in London."

Sam was unable to envisage when that might be. "What's been happening there recently?" he said to compensate.

"They've opened a Thai round the corner from me I'll buy you dinner at next time you're down . . ." Sam's father described what sounded like at least a week's worth of attractions as a preamble to making no more of his successes at work than he apparently felt a man should. Almost whenever it seemed appropriate, Sam uttered expressions of interest or enthusiasm or admiration while finding the subjects almost as unreal as the future he'd invented. He felt closer to his tale of Bosky, but even that struck him as a retelling of a story he couldn't remember having been told. Eventually he became aware that his tankard was the focus of attention. "Another," his father said, "or shall we do something else with the rest of the day?"

A glance showed Sam that the street was competing with the interior of the pub for dimness. "Looks like there isn't any rest," he said.

"How about a stroll to walk off lunch? A fit man means a fit head. If you come to live near enough you can join my gym."

"Would you mind a lot if I went home? I didn't sleep all that much last night."

"I hope it was having so many ideas that kept you awake."

"Must have been," Sam said and stood up fast to abandon the topic.

Misshapen leaves pattered to meet him as he left the pub. They'd been blown from the saplings on the campus, but he could have imagined that the trees south of Goodmanswood had sent them to urge his return. Long before the forest swelled into view, amassing the dusk beyond the motorway, he felt it growing in his mind. As the car came abreast of the woods, it seemed to him that their depths were impenetrably lightless. Or could there be a room that was—a room where a figure was turning its head in the dark to follow the progress of the car? "Sam," his father said, and then "Tell me to be quiet if you're getting ideas for your book."

"Quiet," Sam said, though at the sound of his father's voice the woods had closed into themselves in some indefinable way and were pretending to be no more than woods. He rubbed his knees to erase a memory of damp earth. When the Arbour came in sight he saw his grandfather at the upstairs window, a silhouette intent on the view. Sam clenched his teeth so as not to speak—clenched them until the forest swept away the lights of the hospital. While it was visible he had been tempted to ask to be driven there, to find out whether Lennox was aware of a room in the woods.

II

A Hidden Price

RANDALL confined himself to clearing his throat for the benefit of whoever might take notice until a student marched to the
counter. "Excuse me?" she repeated, this time to him.

"Yes, of course. That's to say I'll just be . . ." When she drew a
breath and expelled it with quite as much force he waived the delay
and raised his bushy eyebrows to her. "How can I help?"

"Can you ask that lady to be a bit quieter?"

"I'm sure she isn't meaning to disturb you," he said loudly enough
for Sylvia to hear but without any visible effect on her. "I'll speak to
her," he added hastily, then glanced at Heather. "That's if—"

Heather sighed and stood up. "I will."

She hadn't reached the table on which books surrounded Sylvia's
notepad when Sylvia emitted yet another laugh not unlike a gasp.
"Sylvie," Heather murmured.

"Yes, come take a look. The more I read the more I find there is."

"Well done, only could you see about keeping some of your enjoy-
ment to yourself? I don't mean don't tell me. It's just that most of
these people are studying for essays if not exams."

"Like we did, and look how far we've come." Before Heather could decide if that and Sylvia's wide eyes hid any irony, Sylvia added "Of course I'll do what my big sister says. Sorry, anyone who's been having to listen to me."

"I expect they'll forgive you this once."

Most of the students nodded in at least some agreement, and Heather had taken a step away from the table when Sylvia said "See just this one thing while you're here."

Heather lowered her voice in the hope it would take Sylvia's down. "What is it, Sylvie?"

Sylvia pushed a bulky history of Roman Britain towards her and underlined a passage with a fingertip, and Heather remembered fingering stories as she read them aloud to her sister.

While the Roman advance left Stonehenge unscathed, there is evidence of the destruction of at least one Neolithic site of worship. This appears to have been a stone circle some fifteen miles north of the present boundary of Bristol. Later quotations from a contemporary account, now lost, suggest that the razing of the area subsequent to the demolition of the circle uncovered evidence of still earlier rites. The account apparently noted that such was the thoroughness of the demolition that the stones of the circle were reduced to dust, itself then cast into the River Severn. It remains unclear whether the Romans planted the area with trees, but it was forested by the seventh century, when a nearby settlement was named Godman's or Godmund's Wood.

"Ah," said Heather. "You're saying now we know who Goodman was."

"Do we?"

"An Anglo-Saxon by the sound of him."

"If that's how you read it. I thought the important part was this was the only stone circle the Romans didn't leave alone. Did you know the ice in the Ice Age stopped just a few miles north of Goodmanswood?"

"I think I learned that at school, but I don't see—" Heather became aware that students were gazing none too patiently at them. "I've lunch in half an hour," she murmured.

"I guess I can wait that long. I wouldn't want you making too much noise in here when I tell you something."

Heather didn't know whether the remark was simply an expression of pique, but it distracted her from the book she was scanning into the computer. The second time she glanced at her watch to confirm that it had yet to be one o'clock, Randall said "Slip away now if you want to. I'll hold the fort till we're relieved."

The sisters' breath manifested itself as they emerged into the late November air. Thin isolated trees and their very few leaves looked embedded in the ice sheet of the sky. Sylvia was silent as she led the way past clumps of scarfed students. "You've been busy," Heather eventually said.

"How do you mean?"

Heather could have meant Sylvia's research on their father's behalf, or her visiting Lennox more often than Heather did, or helping Margo to collect material to carve and generally helping her at the studio, or driving Sam to and from work in exchange for being lent his car. "I need to make up for all the time I've been away," Sylvia apparently answered herself.

"I understand," said Heather and at once was less sure, given Sylvia's odd brief smile, that she did.

Students and a few health-conscious oldsters occupied most of the rough bare tables in Peace & Beans, but a table for two had just been vacated by a pair of worthy dons. Sylvia saved the places while Heather brought over a trayful of falafel and Bombay potatoes and various items all called salads. "Do you want to eat first?" Sylvia said, producing her notepad from her canvas bag.

"Tell me what you think is interesting."

Sylvia splayed her fingers on the midriff of her loose denim overalls before leafing through the pad. "There's a reference around the time Arthur was supposed to have lived, and that's centuries earlier

than the place got its name. The Good Man was meant to guide anyone who got lost in the woods, especially at night."

"Sounds like a decent chap to meet."

Sylvia paused long enough to be discarding a response. "It's often
placatory, that kind of name. Up in Scotland Goodman's Croft is the
devil's ground, dad says."

"He'd mean that's what people deluded themselves into believing."

"Not any longer." Before Heather could decide if she wanted that
elucidated, Sylvia said "Actually, your book doesn't quite say the Good
Man guided people. It says he made them a path. You'd wonder how
he did and where it led, wouldn't you?"

"I wouldn't, no."

"Okay then, try this. In about the thirteenth century there were
stories of a Mr Goodman who wouldn't let wealthy travellers pass the
woods till they left something for the poor. Only I think the bit about
the poor may have been added for safety, because I found this as well."
Sylvia turned the page and read, " 'For some decades the route past
Goodman's Wood in Gloucestershire was avoided after dark for fear of
a man or other creature which was reputed to pursue the unwary
faster than a horse could gallop.' "

"What on earth is that from?"

"*Old English Traditions*, 1863," said Sylvia, underlining the attribu-
tion so vigorously that her fingernail scratched the page. "I hope you
don't think I'm making any of this up."

"I'm sure you aren't if you say you aren't, but I don't understand
why you're so pleased with it."

"Because it's been waiting for someone to put it together."

"You're pleased because you're the first person who has, you
mean."

"I don't know that I am," Sylvia admitted. "Here's something from
a midsummer masque that was performed in Gloucester:

'Come man and maid, come dance and sing!
But stray not into Goodman's ring,

Lest spirits of the air and earth

Play midwife at their sibling's birth,' "

she read, and gazed expectantly at Heather. "You know where that was, don't you, the ring?"

"I don't think we can be sure."

"You ought to read some of your books," Sylvia said and clasped her hands over her midriff as though to contain her impatience. "There's one called *A Description of a Journey through the English Shires on Foot and Horseback.*"

"I was scanning it the other day. I don't remember anything in it like that."

"Then you can't remember this," Sylvia said, enclosing a paragraph with her fingers and thumbs like a gate until Heather craned to read.

I have it from the indefatigable Mr. *Lyndsey*, who had it from a Grandam of the Shire, that in bygone Years the Traveller betwixt *Berkeley* and *Gloucester* might spy within the Woods West of the Roman Road the Crown of a Dwelling taller than the Trees and circular in Section. What Occurrence laid this Folly low, the Grandam would not tell.

"Don't say you don't know where that was," Sylvia said.

"Where you used to run off when I was supposed to be in charge of you, you mean."

"Our secret place."

"Only because mother would have been unhappy knowing we'd gone that far into the woods. It didn't matter that the place had been made safe."

"You liked it too," Sylvia insisted. "You liked pretending it was a circus ring with all sorts of strange animals. And sometimes it was a moat around a fairy castle, or the inside was the top of the highest mountain or an island that had just risen out of the sea after millions of years. Sometimes the ring was just a path we walked round and round and tried to see what was around us, only all you ever said was it made you dizzy. I never believed that was all."

Heather found it disconcerting to have forgotten most of that, and felt defensive as she pointed at the notepad. "Sylvie, what's all this for?"

"Dad wanted it, if you remember."

"Of course I do, but what use is it to him? How is it going to affect him?"

"He isn't getting high on it if that's what you're afraid of. It's more like it confirms what he thought."

"How can that be good, Sylvie?" Heather lowered her voice and thrust her head forward. "What's the point of letting him think what he imagines is true? That isn't going to bring him back."

"The doctor seems happy with how he is."

"That's only considering, isn't it? Dad came here to sort out a delusion and ended up its worst victim. Once he'd have said all these references you've found show how there was some kind of mass delusion over the centuries. I expect he'd have written a wonderful chapter about it, possibly even a book. Now all he's doing is storing it up inside his head, and how do we know what shape it's taking? Isn't there anything you might want to keep from him?"

That appeared to provoke a reaction, though none that Heather would have hoped for. Sylvia jerked a hand away from her midriff and pressed her fingers to her lips and stood up so abruptly the chair tottered on her behalf. As it clattered to a standstill she vanished into the toilets that exhibited above their entrance a plaque carved with leeks. Heather gave several diners who'd witnessed the incident a grin that tried not to look too perplexed while she considered following her sister. She was gathering their bags when Sylvia reappeared, her forehead glistening with traces of water she'd splashed on her face. Heather dabbed them away with a paper napkin as Sylvia sat down, gazing steadily at her. "What's wrong?" Heather said.

"Why does anything have to be wrong?"

"I don't know if it has to, but it looks as if it was."

"I'm okay now. I hope you're going to eat some more, otherwise I'll feel guilty for dragging you here."

"You didn't. I'll have some more if you do."

"I may in a while. Right now I'm wondering what I may end up eating."

"Sorry, you're saying you've had enough of being vegetarian?"

"I don't know if I have or not. I should think you'd know how it is."

At last Heather grasped what her sister's gaze was willing her to realise. Her mouth fell open, she had no idea in what shape. "Sylvie, you're saying . . ."

"There's going to be another price."

That would have been how it sounded to anyone who overheard, but not to Heather. "With a capital P," she cried.

"I expect he'll need one of those, or she will."

Heather felt as if the entire restaurant had brightened—as if her face might be capable of lighting it up. "So you didn't just bring yourself home."

"Right, I've got a passenger."

"When did you know?"

"Not long. No need to whisper, Heather. Soon everyone's going to realise."

Nevertheless Heather kept her voice low. "Does the father?"

"I don't see any reason."

"He won't be entering the picture, then."

"He's already in it as much as he's going to be."

"Does he have a name at least?"

"Sure, and he'll be keeping it. I don't need to take it from him. Are you saying you want it?"

"Not if you'd rather I didn't have it."

"Let's try not to keep things from each other except that one." Sylvia stared at the laden table and rubbed her lips hard with her knuckles. "Do you mind if we make a move? I've looked at enough food for a while. Pretty soon I guess I'll start eating for two and then I won't have much choice."

Heather took her elbow to guide her between the tables. The sisters' breaths turned to mist as they stepped out of the restaurant, and she wished Sylvia had worn a coat instead of a denim jacket. At least she should have clothes for every season now that her three cases of luggage had been delivered. Heather was ushering her towards the refuge of the university, though not so fast it might make her ill, when Sylvia said "How do you think mom will take it?"

"I'm sure she'll be as delighted as I am. She was when Sam was the news."

"You were married though, weren't you? You had a husband to show her."

"I don't think she's ever been that old-fashioned. Not too many people are these days."

"I don't want to get her agitated when she's exhibiting next week. Do you think we should leave telling her till she's finished meeting her public?"

"All right, it can be our secret," Heather said, reaching for Sylvia's hand. It was colder than she liked, and thin as twigs. "It'll be like old times," said Heather.

"Here's to their return," Sylvia said and gripped her hand until Heather felt her sister's bones.

12

More Than a Shadow

THE Tottenham Gallery was on Tottenham Court Road. Though
the thoroughfare was almost as busy as Oxford Street at one end
and Euston Road at the other, Heather had the impression that it was
being visited by trees. As she followed Margo up the shallow concrete
steps to the plate-glass doors, a second car with a Christmas tree
strapped to its roof passed in the midst of the traffic, while in the window of an electronics shop at least a dozen televisions were displaying
a tree in a snowstorm as though they were ornaments that had just
been stirred up. Even the top of the Post Office Tower above the roofs
resembled a tree-stump elevated towards the frostily glittering sky.
Through the tall wide knee-high window of the gallery Heather saw
a gratifying crowd of people bunched in front of Margo's paintings or
gathered around her glassed-in carvings. A few viewers had brought
their glasses of champagne onto the steps for the duration of a ciga-
rette. Heather did her best to overhear comments on the exhibition,
but nobody seemed to be talking about it; one slim young woman in
a long dress as black as herself was wholly occupied in fingering a
whine out of the rim of her glass. Heather thought the doorman, a
bulk in evening dress but with a bouncer's shaven head and studiedly
neutral flattened face, might have intervened on behalf of the glass

instead of halting Margo with a thick upraised palm. "May I see your invitation, madam?" he said in not too much of an East End accent.

"Lucinda didn't send any," Margo said. "I'm Margo Price."

"That's the artist."

"The girl of the moment, that's me."

His immediate response was to render his face still more noncommittal before opening the left-hand door for her. Sam was letting his mother and Sylvia precede him when the doorman treated them to the sight of his palm. "Can you show me your invitations?" he said.

"They're my family," Margo told him. "They're with me."

"Sorry, madam, but it's one guest per invited person. That's because of the numbers they're expecting to attend."

"I'm glad to hear I'm doing so well, and I know you're only doing your job, but this is ridiculous. Where's Lucinda?"

As the smokers grew hushed with interest in Margo or in the argument, Sam said "I can see your exhibition next time I visit dad. I expect he'll want to see it anyway. I'll take the train and meet you all back home."

"That's kind, Sam, but it doesn't solve the problem," Heather said, thinking yet again that he hadn't been so restless on a journey since he was a small child. "There'd still be one too many."

"That can be me," Sylvia said at once. "I'll come down when Sam does."

"You're both very thoughtful."

Heather was wondering if Margo had concealed any hurt in that, and reminding herself not to ask after Sylvia's condition until they were alone, when both doors were opened at arms' length by a woman more middle-aged than her ankle-length backless silver-scaled dress and carelessly cropped ash-blonde hair were designed to make her appear. "Margo dearest," she cried. "Why are you hovering out there? Come and raise a glass to yourself."

"Not unless my family can too, Lucinda. Apparently they aren't allowed in without tickets."

"Most emphatically they are. Did I forget to tell you they were imminent, George? Apologies to all."

"No problem, Mrs Hunt," the doorman said with a butler's discreet cough. "Can't think of everything."

"File in, do," Lucinda Hunt urged. "Nobody's more welcome. Quick, while there's bubbly."

She strode flashing like a collection of knives through the crowd to a table bearing flutes of champagne and tumblers of orange juice. "Anyone not tippling?" she enquired.

"I'm not much," Heather said.

"You're a great deal," Margo protested. "All my family is."

"I'll take an orange juice," Sylvia said.

"Aren't you going to help me celebrate when Heather's driving?"

"I feel like I'm still travelling when I've been on the road."

"At least someone isn't going to make it look as if I'm drinking more than my guests," Margo commented, for Sam had already picked up and half emptied a flute.

Heather waited to be handed one and strolled after Sylvia to murmur in her ear "Is that all that's wrong, what you said?"

"I had to give mom some kind of explanation. You ought to know why I'm staying clear of alcohol."

"Just trying to look after my sister."

"You don't need to here. It's almost like being back inside mom."

While Heather wouldn't have phrased it quite in those terms, she supposed her experience wasn't altogether unlike Sylvia's. The first room of the exhibition was so full of familiar images—even the original of the impossible tree in her hall—that she found it felt positively comfortable. The next room represented Margo's English period, and the third contained all that year's work. Heather made for that one, only to frown at herself—surely only at herself.

She'd seen most of the pieces in Margo's studio, and had thought them her mother's best work: carvings that conveyed a sense of the infinite contained within the small, a quality Heather loved in the paintings. Now the carvings looked like no more than they used to be, pieces of deadwood whose shape Margo had elaborated, perhaps over-elaborated. Heather told herself she was exhausted by driving and, worse, by parking. She was circling one sculpture after another in an increasingly anxious solitary dance when a woman said "She's lost it, hasn't she?"

She was frowning delicately at Margo's latest piece. Her thin pale long-chinned face was framed by a pair of dangling ringlets that pre-tended to have escaped from the mass of black curls packed on her scalp. "I didn't mind some of her earlier product," her companion admitted, his mouth almost hidden by the upper portion of a clump of reddish hair that would have covered his raw pate.

"Her Escher period, you mean."

"But now here she is trying to get up to the same tricks."

"Bad planning on someone's part to let us see how she repeats herself."

"That's called having a theme," Heather said, loudly enough that everyone in the room stared at her. She was allotted several polite smiles when the woman with the ringlets told her "No, it's called run-ning out of ideas."

"And not having many in the first place," said the man with the compensatory beard.

Heather wasn't sure what she might have retorted on her mother's behalf if she hadn't seen Lucinda Hunt leading Margo and a Metro-politan Television crew into the room. "Shall we give the star a corner to herself?" Lucinda suggested to the spectators. "No need to hush, though."

She was so intent on ushering her party to the chosen spot that she didn't notice until too late that she had virtually emptied the room. "Would some of you like to sound as lively as that in here?" she shouted from the doorway.

Only Sam and Sylvia responded. "Can you chatter?" she not so much asked as told them and Heather.

"What do you want us to say?" Sam pleaded.

"Whatever you think, of course," Margo called across the room.

He began to wander from exhibit to exhibit as the interviewer, a slight but intense young woman with blonde hair as long and as broad as her back, thrust at Margo a microphone twice the size of her hand. "Go," she said, a signal to the cameraman rather than a dismissal. "Holly Newsome talking to Margo Price for *Arts After Dark*. Margo, what do you want your exhibition to say to us?"

"Come and look."

"And anyone who does, what will they find?"

"Just about all I've done that I'd want to be known for."

"This is your choice of your work, then."

"Mine and Lucinda Hunt's. She particularly wanted to include my recent pieces when she saw them in the studio."

The gallery owner reacted by gesturing the Prices to break their silence. "What do you think of it, Sylvie?" Heather blurted as Holly Newsome said "You wouldn't have included them yourself."

"Certainly I would. The last time I felt this inspired was when I'd just come to England."

"I wouldn't have missed seeing what mom thought was impor- tant," Sylvia said.

"Don't forget to look in the mirror, then. Any favourites?"

"I've always liked *The Light through the Thorns*."

"Me too. How about the pieces in this room?"

"Looks as if mom's on the way to something new."

"It's a voyage of discovery, my work," Margo was saying. "I'm still discovering what's in my wood."

Sylvia muffled a laugh and caged her stomach with her fingers. "We haven't heard from Sam yet."

He made little haste to rejoin the sisters as Holly Newsome said "What do you want your audience to take away from your work?"

"They needn't be that far from it. They can always take some home."

The interviewer looked faintly pained, and Heather did her best to provide a distraction by asking "Which do you like, Sam?"

"The one in our hall," he mumbled, shuffling his feet as though eager to return there.

"If an artist could explain what she does," Margo was saying, "she wouldn't need to paint or carve it or whatever her thing is."

"Any last words?"

"Just they should come and see for themselves."

"Margo Price, thank you." The interviewer lowered her club of a microphone and turned to the cameraman. "Let's have some noddies."

As he began to film her nodding as though to encourage what her interviewee had finished saying, Margo hurried over to Lucinda Hunt. "Was I as inarticulate as I thought?"

"She was super, wasn't she, you people? You were all your audience expects, Margo. They'd only resent being told what to think."

"We were proud of you," Heather told Margo as Holly Newsome beckoned the cameraman to photograph the contents of the nearest glass case. Margo was beginning to appear ready to accept some praise when the interviewer said "Is something wrong here, Lucinda? What's this?"

Margo and Heather reached the exhibit before Lucinda did. A tapering black stain that resembled an extension of the spiky shadow of the foot-high carving had trickled across the white plinth. "That shouldn't happen," Margo declared. "It never has before. I treated that wood the way I always do."

"I'll fetch the key," Lucinda said, striding to her office. Heather stooped to the glass, telling herself she couldn't have glimpsed movement in the miniature labyrinth of contorted scrawny branches and elaborately drilled trunk. She had distinguished only lurking shadows when Lucinda returned, jangling a few small keys on an extravagantly large ring. She twisted one in the side of the plinth and hoisted the glass as half a dozen spectators drifted into the room. Margo picked up the carving and turned it over.

Hers was the first cry. As her fingers recoiled, dropping the sculpture to shatter on the plinth, two women screamed and fled into the next room. The underside of the carving glistened like the belly of a snail, but that wasn't why Margo had let it fall. The base had been covered with small twitching objects, too many for Heather to begin to count as they swarmed down the plinth. They must be some species of beetle, she thought, but she had no time to make out their darkly glinting colours or their shapes. For an instant she imagined they were massing into an elaborate pattern on the floor. Then, with more eagerness than they had shown for the exhibition, three visitors surged forward to trample the swarm into less than pulp.

13

Unseen Company

HEATHER was unlocking her front door when Jessica reached the gates at her ungainly version of a run. "I brought the papers from the shop," she panted, "in case you hadn't seen them."

"I've seen a few. Come in," said Heather as their breath on the night air turned orange with the streetlight.

"I will for just a minute. I'm in the middle of making cakes for the shop and then I have to run back."

She was more dishevelled than ever, with flour in her unruly hair and on the backs of her hands. The way she and her husband Joe ran the corner shop struck Heather as disorganised to the point of extravagance, but it seemed to work for them. "Here I am," she called into the house, "and Jessica."

Sam and Sylvia emerged from the kitchen along with a spicy smell. "Dinner's nearly fixed," Sylvia said.

"I'm just showing Heather what the papers said about your strange event."

"Which was that?" Sylvia said, crossing her wrists in front of her midriff.

"Your mother's uninvited patrons."

"The insects," Heather explained, since Sylvia's face stayed blank, only for Sam to look worse than confused. "Can I hang onto the papers till mother's seen them, Jessica? She's coming round for dinner."

"They're yours or hers, whoever wants them. Buy some cakes from us sometime. Is this the celebrity now?"

The sound of heels clacking on the path terminated in the briefest ring of the doorbell. The new arrival was indeed Margo in an old coat thrown over last night's spangled evening dress. "Have we acquired another member of the family?" she said.

Heather had to tell herself that referred to Jessica, who said "I just brought some of your publicity round because I don't think you usually read these papers."

"Forgive me, Jessica. I wasn't expecting so many people, that was all. We must get together soon and catch up on news."

"I'd enjoy that. I'll be on my way, then," Jessica said, but stopped short of the door. "Did you hear about the Finches next to the old school? They found a buyer for their house."

"Good," Heather assumed she ought to say.

"Well, only till they had a survey done. Apparently they'd noticed a bit of a smell in the back bedroom but couldn't see where it was coming from. The surveyor pulled out a wardrobe and its whole behind was a mass of fungus."

"Nasty. Will they be able to sell?"

"They hope so once they find out where the damp gets in. Makes you want to go and look behind everything in case you've got an unwanted guest, as you might say," Jessica said, and let herself out of the house.

Margo draped her coat over the end of the banister and grimaced at the tabloids. "Lord, do I want to know what those rags have been writing about me?"

"Let's take them in the kitchen so we can all look," Heather said, and separated the papers on the table. Jessica had used a ballpoint to mark a headline inside each with a blotchy cross. **THE PAINTER DIDN'T TWIG . . . SHE'S STUMPED BY HER ART . . .**

**ARTIST BRANCHES OUT TOO FAR . . . LITERALLY
LOUSY ART SHOW . . . THIS BUGS ME, SAYS
ARTIST . . .** "I never even spoke to them," Margo complained.

"Everyone knows that paper makes stuff up," said Sam.

"As if I'm not frazzled enough about my other pieces. I know we
couldn't find anything wrong with them last night, but that one
looked all right when I was working on it."

"Maybe all this publicity will bring you more custom," Heather
tried to comfort her.

"To see the insect lady's crazy art, you mean."

"Nobody's crazy here." As Sylvia turned to the cooker, her luminous reflection executed a pirouette in the dim garden, beyond which
the bare woods had set countless claws in the black sky. "Is it time for
me to serve yet?" she said.

"I'll help," said Sam.

"Looks as if we're surplus to requirements," Heather told Margo.
"Come through and I'll open the wine you like."

It was a Chablis that brought out all the flavours of Sam's fish soup
and appeared to do Sylvia's vegetable alternative no harm either.
Margo murmured her appreciation, of which she had plenty in reserve
for Heather's beef bourguignon. She'd lingered over several mouth-
fuls when Heather began to wonder why she was so unusually taci-
turn. She had just decided that Margo was preoccupied with
appearing on *Arts After Dark* that night when Margo said "Has someone got a surprise for me?"

If Sylvia revealed her secret now, it would surely rob Margo's television interview of the significance she deserved to feel it had. "What
makes you say that?" Heather risked asking.

"Just a feeling. Are you the one, Sam? Is it you?"

He seemed in no hurry to finish his mouthful, which apparently
required the aid of half a glass of Syrah to send it down. "Me what?"
he then said.

"Is that why you're trying to look innocent? You aren't engaged, are you? Don't tell me you're married and nobody knows."

"I won't. I'm not. There's nothing."

"You're just looking forward to seeing her on television," Heather said, "aren't you, Sam?"

"Everyone is."

"There's something else," Margo insisted, peering not much less than accusingly at him.

Heather was unable to glance at Sylvia for fear that they might burst out laughing at the misapprehension. When she heard Sylvia's lips opening she held her breath. "Why does there have to be?" Sylvia said.

"If I can't be right about my family I can't be right about anything."

"Of course you're right about us," Heather said at once. "We'd never lie to you."

"Only tonight you come first, mom. Forget about us for a while."

"Think about yourself. We all are."

"And lots of others will be," said Sam.

"Did I look presentable?" Margo said, and Heather knew the subject was changed at last. She and Sylvia kept up the topic all the way through dessert of how impressively Margo had conducted herself and how others had failed themselves, and then it was time to adjourn to the sitting-room, glasses in hand.

An earlier programme must have overrun. A gay soap opera was ten minutes later than it should have been in coming to an end, or rather to anything but. Margo sighed impatiently and tutted at herself and took sips of wine so tiny they might have been designed to exhibit her restraint. An announcer's voice synopsised the next episode over the closing credits, which were followed by a trailer for a series about the history of child abuse before an electronic fanfare and an onslaught of split-second computer graphics heralded *Arts After Dark*. The title flew apart in fragments to reveal Holly Newsome and three other people seated on minimal metal chairs in front of a curve of some material the colour of dense fog. "On tonight's *Arts After Dark*," Holly New-some was saying, "we chat online with the Ephemeralists, who exhibit only on the Internet. We look at transgressiveness in cinema—which country's movies break the most taboos and are there any left to break? We listen to a piece by a composer whose music you can hear by touching the notes on the score—she hates all the performances her work has been given and says musicians are history. But first, a major retrospective by the American expatriate painter and sculptor Margo Price opened today in the wake of some last-minute publicity. I talked to the artist at the private view."

"What does she mean by last-minute?" Margo demanded as the presenter turned to watch herself and Margo on a screen.

"Nothing much, I should think. Remember she said major," Heather said, and was shushed.

The presenter had left in nearly all her questions and interpolated the odd apparently responsive nod as well, although the interview began with Margo's exhortation: "Come and look." She talked about renewed inspiration and continuing discovery and the intuitive pro-cess she recommended, while her family's voices could be heard in the background, though not their words; they were even visible in a cou-ple of shots. As she concluded by saying "They should come and see for themselves" Margo raised her glass, only to roll it the width of her forehead. "Well, that was a poor performance."

"It wasn't at all," Heather protested, but Margo interrupted her. "Why are they showing that?"

Last night's camera had zoomed in on the broken carving. While she was glad the insects had gone, Heather would have welcomed a chance to see what they had been. The close-up turned into a still that remained on the monitor Holly Newsome turned away from to say "The image from Margo Price's exhibition that most people will have seen. Here to discuss the exhibition are Dougie Leaver, media critic of the *Beacon,* Maria Perez, art historian, and Abdul Kidd, Reader in Pop-ular Culture at Birmingham University."

"See, you're popular," Heather said.

"Depends how it's meant," Margo told her as Holly Newsome said "How significant do we think that image is?"

Dougie Leaver rested his hands on his even larger stomach and unfolded some of his chins. "I think it'll be what everyone remembers best."

Maria Perez lifted one bare bony arm to sweep back her long wavy hair, which resembled a cascade of oil. Her thin face looked ready to peck him as she said "If your paper has anything to do with it."

Abdul Kidd wrapped a fist in his other hand and inclined his top half in her direction without quite facing her. "In general the public has already made its mind up about contemporary art, and the media only confirms that, not tells them what to think."

Heather was wincing at his misuse of language as Holly Newsome asked him "Is it your observation they're in favour of Margo Price?"

"Last time I looked they seemed to be."

"You can see her on quite a few people's walls still," Maria Perez said.

"That's just one poster though, isn't it?" Dougie Leaver commented, pinching a handful of his chins.

"Sometimes one poster can be enough to root an artist in the popular consciousness."

"For how long?" Dougie Leaver presumably wanted to know.

"It's a dangerous game, trying to predict reputations. Yesterday can be tomorrow in the arts."

"Price is part and parcel of a yesterday we're better off without."

"You'll tell us which," said Abdul Kidd.

"The druggy sixties. You can see that in the kind of tricks she likes to play with what you think you're seeing. Hear it in the way she talks, as well."

Holly Newsome tried to intervene. "I don't think you should—"

"I'm not saying she takes drugs. I'm not even saying she wants to appeal to people who do, but she said the kind of thing they all say about having to take a voyage of discovery and not being able to explain it to anyone who hasn't."

"I'd place her in an earlier tradition," said Maria Perez, "of illusionism if not of actual trompe l'oeil."

Holly Newsome turned to her. "And how important do you think she is to that tradition?"

"I don't think the exhibition shows us anything we haven't already seen. I felt she was trying to recapture her inspiration of the sixties as she said she was but only managing to repeat herself. But I think we'd seen the effects she was attempting before she ever started."

Heather felt her face grow hot with anger and embarrassment even before Leaver said "You'd wonder where her inspiration back there came from."

"Abdul?" Holly Newsome invited with some haste.

"I quite enjoy a wallow in nostalgia now and then. I'd recommend anyone who does and who's passing to go in for a look."

"Particularly anyone who ever had flowers in their hair," Holly Newsome said. "Otherwise I think the consensus, and I'm speaking for the majority of people who were at the gallery last night, is that Margo Price has had a good try at resurrection but doesn't quite succeed in bringing the past back to life."

"I'd say the piece we saw falling to bits sums it up," said Dougie Leaver.

"And now from the past to the future," Holly Newsome almost interrupted, and faced the monitor again. "This may look like an ordinary music score, but composer Ellen Ogunduwe—"

Heather had prepared a comment to make as soon as the television was switched off. "I shouldn't think anyone who knows about art will care what that Leaver man thinks, or a programme that has him on it either."

"It's kind of you to say so," Margo said in a voice that sounded squashed flat. "Does anyone want to say anything else kind?"

"They're just people who get paid to carp."

Sam came to Heather's aid. "To crap, you mean."

"I'll bet a whole lot fewer people have heard of them than they have of you, mom."

"I think," said Heather, "if you ring Lucinda you'll find they don't represent the majority at all."

"I guess I'll wait till she calls me. I'm not going to ask any of you what you really thought of the exhibition, because I know you'd feel bound to praise it. Don't be insulted if I ask you to excuse me. I believe I can use a quiet stroll home."

"You mustn't go till you've cheered up," Sylvia said.

"In that case you'd have to make up a bed for me."

"Of course we will," said Heather.

"I appreciate it, Heather. I appreciate all of you. I'd just like to be by myself for a while if you'll let me. I'll be fine, so don't worry."

"Don't you want to hear my news first?" Sylvia said.

"I don't know. Do I?"

"I think you might," Heather said. "I think it calls for another bottle as well."

She was in the kitchen, lifting out of the refrigerator a bottle of Margo's favourite she had kept in reserve, when she heard Margo say "Do I get a hint while I'm waiting?"

"There's someone else here with us," said Sylvia. "Someone you can't see."

Heather wished she hadn't put it that way, suggesting that the revelation was about to be overheard. She shut the refrigerator and made for the hall. Perhaps it was the impression left by Sylvia's words that caused her to glance over her shoulder as though she'd belatedly become aware of something odd about the view at which she hadn't even glanced. Looming over the fence at the end of the garden was the silhouette of a head.

She would have dropped the bottle if she hadn't clutched it with both hands. She set it on the table, an action that felt like a bid to hold reality together, and urged herself to the window. She couldn't really be seeing a presence: the fence was seven feet high. Perhaps the shape above it was a mass of branches, in which case the objects crawling dimly on it must be leaves, the explanation why its outline was so restless. How could a tree appear to have strayed so close to the house? She was leaning her hands on the chill tiles under the window, and making an effort to scoff at the notion that the shape was about to grow some kind of face, when she grasped that she would be better able to distinguish it if the kitchen was dark. For a moment her hands felt frozen to the tiles, and then she pushed herself away and lunged for the switch.

"Have you got lost?" Margo called. "I won't know what the surprise is till you come back."

"I'm just . . ." Heather closed out the light from the hall and kept hold of the door as she turned to the window. She sucked in a breath and came close to laughing out loud at herself. There was nothing at the fence. Beyond it she could just discern the bristling darkness that was the edge of the woods, and a faintly luminous low cloud that seemed to sink into the depths of the forest as she watched. Perspective must have created the illusion—of course the cloud was only sailing away—and another trick of perspective had let her mistake it for a head. "Here I come," she called, grabbing the bottle. She'd had enough of being troubled by the woods. They had nothing to do with the secret Sylvia was about to share with Margo and Sam.

14

A Sunday Gossip

HEATHER was wakened by a gentle knock at her door. "Are you on your way to being up yet?" Margo said, easing it open. "We're all ready for breakfast."

"What time is it?" A second blink confirmed the bedside clock was holding up its hands at ten past ten. "That's what comes of talking till whenever we did," Heather said. "Give me a few minutes and I'll make something for everyone."

"I've fixed breakfast. It's been a while since I've done that for anyone besides myself."

Heather smelled bacon fried as crisp as Margo always cooked it, as the English seldom did. The aroma lingered after Margo went downstairs. Heather lay in bed for half a minute, listening to Sunday bells that sounded loud yet muffled. If she let herself she could feel like a child in her mother's house, with as few responsibilities as she chose to have. She sighed not too wistfully and headed for the bathroom.

Margo's was the voice she heard most often as she performed an abbreviated morning ritual. Last night Margo had shed at Sylvia's news the tears she'd managed to keep to herself over *Arts After Dark*. She'd hugged Sylvia and Heather and reproached them fiercely for not telling her before, and had taken some persuading that Sam hadn't known too. He'd already looked uncomfortable, and once the women had started crying and laughing together he'd retreated to his room. If Sylvia had been readying herself to be asked more than she was prepared to reveal, that hadn't taken place; perhaps Margo was too delighted that more than Sylvia had come home.

"Here's the rest of the family," Margo announced as Heather reached the kitchen. "All of us that are here, I ought to say." That silenced her while she ladled bacon and scrambled eggs onto plates, and then she said "Have you told your father the good news?"

"You don't think I'd tell him before I told you. There's no chance it might upset him," Sylvia didn't quite acknowledge asking.

"I don't see how it could, even with him as he is. We may be old but we were never too conventional. We used to have quite a sexy time together until—" Margo looked towards the woods rather than at anyone and summed up with a cough whatever she might have added. "Sorry, Sam. I'm embarrassing you again."

Heather thought it chivalrous of him to say "I don't know why you said again."

"I'll tell dad this afternoon," Sylvia said.

"Will you be telling him a name?" Margo was eager to learn.

"I believe I've come up with one for it, yes."

"Don't think me peculiar, but promise you'll never call your baby an it, will you? That's like wishing they won't be a person. I've always thought it was bad luck." Margo waited to see something like agreement before saying "So are we going to hear the name?"

"Nathaniel."

"Nathaniel Price," Heather sampled aloud. "Nat Price. Natty Price. I'm sure he can live with those if he's a he. Did you get it from anywhere in particular, Sylvie?"

"It came to me in the night."

"Suppose," Margo said, "our new person's a girl?"

"Natalie."

"You certainly know what you want," Margo declared, though for a moment, and for no identifiable reason, Heather wasn't sure her sister did.

Once breakfast was finished Margo stood up. "I'd better stir my old sticks. I want to go by Jessica's before she sells all the Sunday papers."

"I'll walk along with you," Heather said.

"I could use a walk too," said Sylvia.

"I'll stay and wash up," Sam told them.

"I hope Natty turns out as thoughtful as you," Margo said and embarrassed him with a protracted vigorous hug.

Outside the air tasted of frost. The street was silent except for a thin shrill scraping on glass. Overnight the windows of every parked car had grown as blank and pale as the sky while the windows of the houses had turned white around their edges. The women were half-way to the shop when Sylvia said "Mom, what didn't you want Sam to hear?"

Margo glanced around them. They'd left the man with the scraper well behind, and the pavements were deserted apart from the occasional sentinel tree. Nevertheless she responded with some wariness. "About what?"

"You were telling us about you and dad."

"Well, yes, I was. I did."

"You were going to say more and then you stopped because of Sam."

"I was thinking of you as well." Margo halted on the corner of the street that led into Goodmanswood and to the shop. "I didn't want you thinking I could possibly be blaming you," she said.

"For what?"

"The last time your father and I . . ." Margo held her hands apart and moved the fingertips as though to trace something invisible between them. "It was when you were conceived," she said, lower still.

"I don't know why I'd ever blame myself for that."

Heather didn't want to ask the question that felt like an additional chill in the air, but Sylvia did. "Why was it the last time?"

"Because that was when he started being how he is."

"He didn't hurt you," Heather wanted to be assured.

"Never physically. He just went away from me."

"Went where?" asked Sylvia.

"Into himself, where he is now." Margo glanced at her in case that was sufficient and saw it was not. "We thought he'd left all that behind," she said. "It was two years since he'd gone in the woods and been affected by that devilish stuff. He wasn't even taking tranquillisers any more, it was so long since he'd felt any effects. And then it all came back, and worse."

"What did, mom?"

Heather thought Sylvia was being too childishly inquisitive, but their mother said "He started talking, not to me or for me to hear. He wasn't looking at me either or anywhere in the room. He might have been trying to see through the wall, the way he looked—no, maybe that's not fair, maybe trying not to see. I couldn't understand a word he said, but there was a whole lot of it. And afterwards he said he couldn't remember a thing. Anything, mind you," she added with some bitterness.

Heather's mind produced a glimpse of her father's face looming above Margo's inverted one while he stared towards the woods as if the bedroom wall had ceased to be. She rid herself of the image by realising how anyone who saw the three of them would think they'd stopped for an everyday gossip. "It couldn't have been his fault, could it?" she risked saying.

"I never said it was, especially not to him. He didn't need much persuading to move to the hospital. Come on," Margo said, determined either to dismiss the subject or to confront whatever lay ahead, "let's take a look at my press."

Beyond a mutually supportive pair of five-foot shelves against which sat faint shadows of the legend stencilled on the window—

J's & J's—Jessica was serving an old man with as much conversation as groceries while her husband Joe, his bulk done up in an ageing overcoat and his head kept warm by a shabby woollen hat, sang mangled carols to their granddaughter, who was perched on a stool behind the counter and crayoning on a pad.

"We three things of Orient are,

Bearing cash we head for the bar . . ."

"They're kings and they travel afar," eight-year-old Rosemary protested with a mixture of amusement and exasperation.

"See if you know this one, then," he said and sang in a hoarse baritone that managed to land on most of the notes:

"The holly and the ivy,

When they are both full grown,

Of all the trees that are in the wood—

Why, it's our local star," he said, belatedly abandoning the melody. "We saw you on the telly last night, Margo. No such thing as bad publicity, isn't that what they tell us? What can we do for you, Margo and Heather and can this really be the youngest come home to roost?"

"Have you brought her to show her off, Margo?" Jessica said, counting change onto her customer's palm.

"Happy to, and Heather as well, but I wanted to see what the Sundays are saying about me."

"You may as well read them here," Joe said. "We don't want you paying for anything you don't like."

Heather had to remember to breathe while Margo found her name. **MARGO PRICE RETROSPECTIVE INTRICATE BUT INSUBSTANTIAL.** Margo released a sound related both to a grunt and a muffled laugh, and Heather didn't know if she should touch her. She confined herself to skimming the review until Margo tidied the newspaper and spread out the next one. All the reviews lived up to their titles: **DEPTHS BUT LITTLE DEPTH, A TYRANNY OF DETAIL, A REPETITIVE RETROSPECTIVE, LOST IN THE WOOD . . .** Margo uttered no further sound on the way to returning all the newspapers to their unread state. "Well, that's that," she said. "Poor Lucinda."

"Poorer you," said Sylvia, taking her hand.

Heather was reaching for the other one when Margo said "I don't think I'm poor at all."

"Not while you have a family you aren't," Jessica agreed.

"You shouldn't let it matter what people think of you," said Joe.

"Except all the ones who like your work," Heather was quick to add.

"You know what I figure you did wrong?" Sylvia said. "You shouldn't have taken your new work to London. You should have made people come and see it in your studio. Remember that's where Lucinda saw it and liked it so much. Maybe it loses its power if it's taken away because it's a part of the place."

Nobody except the eight-year-old had anything to say to that. "Part of the woods," she corrected.

"Sylvia was always the imaginative one," Margo told Joe and Jessica. "Mind you, you've good reason to be a little strange just now," she said to Sylvia. "I know I was sometimes when you were on the way."

She put a hand over her mouth and gazed big-eyed at Sylvia. She was miming the question of whether she should make it absolutely clear why the reviews hadn't troubled her when the bell above the shop door clanged as though to start a round, announcing two women and a good deal of perfume. "Good morning," they said to Jessica and Joe. "Hello, Rosemary."

"When are Willow and Laurel coming back to ballet lessons?" the little girl said.

"When they learn not to tell stories," Mrs Bennett said and pressed her lips together without managing to pale her small red mouth.

"In other words never," Mrs Palmer said with a glossy crimson grimace.

"I like stories."

"Not the kind they tell," Mrs Bennett said.

She and Willow's mother were turning to the shopkeepers when

Rosemary said "You needn't have taken them away. People still tell stories. Gwyn and Lucy do."

"Only because our little brats did," said Mrs Palmer. "I'll have a *Sunday Beacon*, please, Jessica."

"They're different stories."

"A *Beacon* for me as well."

"What stories are those?" said Sylvia.

"About the man who comes to the railings."

"They sound like the same old nonsense to me," Mrs Palmer said and pouted at having betrayed she was listening.

"They're not. They're new ones. Lucy says he's getting so thin he'll be able to come through the railings soon, and they're only this wide," Rosemary said, holding up one palm. "And Gwyn says bits keep falling off him and you can see them running across the common if you look."

"Have you?" said Sylvia.

"We don't go in the yard any more. I'm glad grandma and grandad live on the other side of the road."

"I should think so," Mrs Bennett declared and let fly an impatient sound. "I don't mean being scared, you've no reason to be that. I mean not going looking for things nobody ever saw."

"Nobody but druggies," Mrs Palmer said.

"There's been a few of those round here, so just you make sure you and your friends never start."

"I wouldn't be surprised if there were a few in that lot who tried to stop the bypass."

"So long as they know they aren't welcome round here."

Both women had their backs to the Prices but kept their voices raised to compensate, while Joe and Jessica struggled to hide their discomfort. Margo watched the women pay for their tabloids and waited until they turned around before she said "Excuse me, were you talking about anybody in particular?"

Mrs Bennett stared at her for so long it would have appeared to be a substitute for speech if she hadn't remarked "You were on television."

Mrs Palmer gazed over the Prices' heads. "Anyone who thinks we were talking about them knows if we were."

"You can tell about some people just by looking at them," Mrs Bennett said, seeming to observe some absence in the air above Sylvia's head.

"Don't you believe it," Margo said and began to laugh, then coughed and waved a hand in front of her face. "Come along, girls. I'm getting a bit stifled, aren't you? A treat to see you, Joe and Jessica. We must do it more often."

"You know our hours," Joe said.

That didn't strike Heather as exactly inviting, but perhaps he was doing his best to stay neutral. She and Sylvia followed Margo out, to be overtaken by the women, who sailed past on a wake of perfume and set about muttering together before they were quite out of earshot. Margo watched them vanish into adjoining houses guarded by imitation gas lamps. "You know," she said, "I believe those two silly cattle may have meant me."

The sisters gazed after her as she marched away, head held even higher as she passed the ersatz gas lamps, and then Sylvia said "One more revelation to go."

"And that's . . ."

"I mean, one more parent to tell."

"Do you want me to come with you?"

"I don't always need my big sister," Sylvia said, giving her a smile that was prepared to be apologetic. "I can cope with dad. If he's ever going to be in the mood for the news it ought to be now. After all, it's nearly Christmas."

15

A Wooden Visitor

HEATHER was reading a newspaper column entitled *Always A Price* when someone opened the front gate. The coverage of Margo's exhibition had reminded the columnist that throughout her student days she'd had Margo's best-known poster on her wall. A rummage in her attic had failed to locate the poster, and the rest of the column consisted of memories prompted by items she'd found. "Buy a new one if it means that much to you," Heather muttered, and then her frown deepened. By the sound of it, whoever was on her path was using more legs than anyone ought to have.

She sent herself into the hall, which wasn't sufficiently dim even so late in the afternoon for her to bother switching on the light, and pulled the front door open. She was expecting to see a person with a stick, not Sam grasping a small fir-tree by its slender trunk. "Sam," she cried, more exasperated with him than she'd felt for years. "How far have you had to hobble with that?"

He let go for a moment and rubbed his forehead, staining it faintly green. "Not far."

"I know it was time we got one, but I could have driven if you'd said."

"I didn't know I was getting it," he told her, grabbing the tree as it lurched towards her. "I just saw it and I thought it would do for us."

"Of course it will. How much did it cost?"

He responded only with a shrug that clattered branches at her—he must think he was too old to be repaid. He could have an extra Christmas present, Heather decided as she said "Prop it up there while I dust off the tub."

The plastic bucket dressed in Christmas wrapping paper spent most of the year in the cupboard under the stairs, along with fairy lights and decorations awaiting resurrection. As Heather stood the bucket in the hall, the tree leaned around the open front door, its branches scraping the frosted glass. "Can't wait to get in," she remarked. "You can give it a hand, Sam."

He limped along the hall with it as though he and the sapling were caught in a clumsy arms'-length dance, and inserted the spidery roots into the bucket so that Heather could wedge the trunk with lumps of brick. "Did they dig it out of whatever it was in for you to carry home?" she said as the phone began to ring.

He looked bemused, presumably by which to answer. "Could you get that while I see this stays where it is?" she said.

Two uneven steps took him to the extension opposite the stairs. "Hello . . . Oh, hi . . . Not yet . . . I'll ask. When are we expecting my aunt home?"

"Any time, I should think. Who'd like to know?"

"It's Margo."

As Heather stood up she must have brushed against the tree, which shivered not unlike a reflection in water and at once grew still. She took the receiver from Sam's cold hand as he made for the stairs. "I was just reading about you," she informed her mother.

"I'm not going to let myself care."

"You can if you like. It was quite a decent piece about how the columnist was looking for one of your posters."

"I expect they'll find it if they really want it, but I genuinely mean

I don't care what people say about me any more, not when your sister's given me so much to look forward to."

"I'm glad. Anyway, you want her."

"I want both of you, Heather. Always have, and now I've got you both. So yes, I would like a word."

"She's still at the Arbour unless she's on her way back. How urgent is it?"

"I'm not sure. Somebody was trying to reach her. They recognised her on *Arts After Dark* and that's why they called me."

"Did you give them my number?"

"I did, and now I don't know if I should have. She seemed more than a little odd."

"Where does she know Sylvie from?"

"America, apparently."

"I expect there's no reason to worry. You won't have given her my address, will you?"

"I should hope not. I'm not quite that incompetent yet, I flatter myself."

"You aren't incompetent at all, and I don't believe you ever will be," Heather said. She hadn't taken her hand away from hanging the receiver up when the phone rang.

She must have jumped, because the longest branches of the sapling groped at the air. She retrieved the phone with a clatter of plastic. "Hello?"

There was silence except for a stealthy creak of branches. As she opened her mouth to repeat herself, the receiver emitted the dialling tone. "I must be losing my charm, Sam," she called up the stairs to no response. She was turning away from the phone when it summoned her back.

She knew of no reason not to sound welcoming. "Yes, hello?"

"Did you just speak?" a high quick female Californian voice demanded.

"I did. I said yes, hello."

"Before that," the voice said, higher and quicker.

"If you rang off without saying anything just now that was me saying hello then too."

"Who am I talking to?"

That was said in a tone Heather might very well have used. "Heather Price," she said with what struck her as exceptional patience, "and you're . . ."

"Merilee. Are you supposed to be English?"

"More than supposed. Can I ask what you actually want?"

"I'm looking for someone whose mother said I should call the number I thought I called twice."

"You did that all right, to speak to my sister."

"You wouldn't be trying to kid me."

"I can't imagine why."

"Your sister wrote *The Secret Woods*."

"Indeed she did."

"I don't see how she could have ended up with an English sister."

"Because she is too."

"Hold it right there. Her mother doesn't sound any more English than Sylvia, so how did you get to be?"

"Just by being born."

"Some trick."

Heather managed a laugh, if only so as not to feel she was being wished out of existence. "Yes, well, I don't think any of us has much control over how we see the light. Anyway," she said with a hint of bitterness she would have hoped not to feel, "you want my sister."

"You're still saying that's who she is. Okay then, put her on."

"She isn't here at the moment."

"Hey, why am I not surprised."

Heather had to exert a good deal of control not to plant the receiver on the hook instead of saying "Shall I ask her to call you?"

"You want me to give you my number because you're her sister."

"That sums it up, yes."

"Sure, like I'd give you my number just for saying you are," Merilee said, and was gone with a click and an insect buzz.

"Let's hope she's the only person like that Sylvie knows," Heather called up the stairs as she replaced the receiver. When Sam didn't respond she headed for the kitchen, until the shrilling of the phone seemed to clutch at her neck.

Its summons failed to tempt Sam out of his room. As she tramped to grab the receiver the tree flexed several branches while its shadow, almost hidden in the corner behind it, waved its feelers. "Heather Price," she declared.

"It's only me again."

"No only about it, mummy. You're more than a welcome alternative to the last call."

"Why?" Margo said with a nervousness Heather wouldn't have wanted or expected to cause. "Who was it?"

"The woman you rang about. Merilee, her name is, though I still don't know what her connection is with Sylvie. Mind you, she wouldn't be persuaded I could have anything to do with Sylvie or you either."

"I told you she was odd." Margo's brusqueness might have been rebuking Heather for seeking needless reassurance. "Anyway, never mind her," Margo said. "She'll keep. I've just had the Arbour asking if I know where Sylvia and Lennox are."

Heather kept a twinge of panic to herself by asking "Where are they meant to be?"

"Apparently he was so pleased to hear we're due for another grandchild that he wanted to go out and celebrate, but they don't know where."

"I thought he couldn't drink with his medication."

"I'm told he said a soft drink would be enough of a celebration, and Sylvia promised to see that was all he drank. You know how persuasive she can be."

Heather wasn't sure if Margo was suggesting Sylvia had persuaded

Lennox or the hospital staff. "Only she said they'd be an hour," Margo said, "and they've been more than two. It'll soon be dark."

"Then I expect that means they're nearly back."

"I wish you'd gone with her to see him."

"She didn't want me to."

"You're still her elder sister. I don't like to think of her driving in her condition. I never used to."

"I'm sure she'll be careful. She was about drinking at the gallery, remember. I'll have her call you the moment she comes home, that's if she doesn't call you from the Arbour."

"I guess she could be trying right now. I'd better leave you in peace. Sorry if anything sounded as if I was criticising you. I can't help worrying about my family, that's all."

"I shouldn't think there's any need at the moment, mummy," Heather said rather than admit that peace was hardly the state in which Margo was leaving her. Once they'd said goodbye she held the receiver as though its drone might prove soothing, then realised she could be blocking a call. She hung up and sent herself kitchenwards.

At first glance through the window she thought the night was closer than it should be, but the darkness of the horizon beyond the fence was mostly composed of the woods. She picked up a bunch of celery, and one stalk snapped like a twig damaged by a footfall. As a rule she enjoyed chopping celery—found its crunches satisfying—but now the sensation penetrated her nerves. Perhaps that came of straining to hear the car Sam had lent Sylvia. But the sound that made her drop the knife, scattering greenish vegetable segments, was yet again the clamour of the phone.

The tree rattled its branches as she sprinted to seize the receiver. "Hello? Yes?"

"Heather."

Her mother's voice was so subdued that Heather was afraid to ask "What now?"

"They've found the car."

"Found it," Heather said, and not much less stupidly "Who has?"

"One of the nurses. It wasn't far away." Before that could seem at all reassuring Margo said "It's by the woods, and there's no sign of Sylvia or Lennox."

16

Out of the Mound

THEY were in the woods—Heather was sure of that much. As the Civic sped onto the bypass she did her best to watch for them among the trees. A shrunken sun that resembled a blank lens embedded in the grey sky more than a source of any light kept peering through the treetops, reminding her that soon they would blot it out. The entire forest was moving because the car was, tall thin scaly twisted shapes dodging out from behind one another and hiding again only to reappear. She could have imagined that the dimmest and most distant shapes weren't parading quite as they should, but told herself it didn't matter. "Let me know if you see anything," she said.

Sam poked his face forward. "Anything," he repeated.

"You know what I mean." If it was a joke, not that his tone owned up to the possibility, she didn't appreciate it. "If you see them," she said.

"They're all I'm looking for."

His voice was so flat he might have been asking a question or trying to persuade himself. Before she could decide how or whether to respond, the Arbour sailed into view. The floodlights in the grounds had been switched on, pointing the shadows of the scattered trees across the lawn as if the woods were urging them to join the forest darkness. As the car swung up the drive, Margo hurried out of the building. She took a pace forward and raised her outstretched hands, and then her face dulled as she saw there was no passenger but Sam. "Shouldn't one of you have stayed home," she began objecting well before Heather left the car, "in case someone tries to call?"

"We thought we might be needed to help search."

"I thought I might, but half the nurses are looking for them. Surely they've noticed it's getting dark."

Sam limped around the car. "Why do you think they went in there?"

"For a walk. Why would anyone? It isn't Lennox by himself or with the other patients. He has Sylvia with him this time," Margo appealed to Dr Lowe as he emerged from the hospital.

"I'm sure they'll be looking after each other." While his round face didn't quite presume to smile, his eyes were concerned but encouraging. "I don't need to tell you how delighted he was at the news. He came to find me with it, and I really think he's found a focus outside himself." As though he had enthusiasm to spare the doctor added "By the way, I didn't know you were an artist till I saw your television spot the other night. You might like to know I'll be buying one of your books."

"Thank you," Margo said, having waited to be sure he'd finished.

"Perhaps you could—" He'd barely started miming a signature on the air when his finger jerked up to point at the woods. "I think there's someone now."

Heather was already gazing at the woods until her eyes ached. The mass of trees and vaguer trees looked as still as a painting of itself—so still that it felt like some kind of pretence. For an instant she thought a tree deep in the dimness had betrayed itself, and then she understood that she'd glimpsed a figure dodging around it. "It's Lennox," Margo cried.

Heather saw him advance past three trees before sidling right with his back to another three as a preamble to pacing forward. "It's just him," Margo protested. "Where's Sylvia?"

She shouted the question as she ran across the grass, Heather and Sam following. She hadn't reached the gates when a lull in the traffic made her raise her voice again. "Lennox, stop that and listen to me. What have you done with Sylvia?"

Though she cupped her hands around her mouth, he didn't immediately look up. He was intent on the floor of the woods, presumably on whatever pattern he thought he was describing. When he raised his head, it seemed that might be the whole of his response, unless dodging behind a clump of trees was the rest of it. He couldn't be doing so out of guilt, since he reappeared almost at once and zigzagged forward several paces. "Where's Sylvie?" Heather shouted as Margo called even more fiercely "Where's Sylvia?"

At that moment Heather made out his face. He looked as if he scarcely recognised her or Margo—as if his consciousness was trapped in the dim scaly cage of the forest. Nevertheless he might have been answering the question when he stretched his arms wide and turned his palms up to indicate the entire woods. "Don't you shrug at me, Lennox Price," Margo cried and stalked into the road.

She would have been in the path of a truck, which she apparently expected to brake for her, if Sam hadn't wrapped his arms around her waist and pulled her backwards. The truck raced by with a blare of its horn and a flaring of its headlights, and Margo gave her grandson a studiedly dignified look. "You can let go of me now, thank you," she said. "I'm not your grandfather."

"Let's cross now while it's safe," Heather intervened.

Both Sam and Margo regarded her as though she was failing to appreciate their ages, especially when she grabbed their hands. As they stepped over the knee-high metal barrier that divided the concrete strip along the middle of the bypass, she saw that the metal was greenish with some kind of growth. The three of them had to straddle the barrier while a pair of cars speeding abreast honked at the party or at each other, and she felt Margo wobble, if that wasn't her impatience to reach Lennox. Headlamp beams fluttered over the outermost trees, and shadows seemed to trawl the empty depths of the forest for Sylvia. Margo tugged at Heather's hand to urge her across the road, into the dark.

The woods appeared to have reserved some illumination to themselves. The dim sky that was cracked with branches retained only a faint glow, but the elaborate tapestry of dead leaves underfoot was managing to seem more luminous. Given time, Heather might have been able to discern the shape of every leaf and the pattern they composed, but she was hearing Margo's low intense voice. "Stop that nonsense now and talk to me. Where's our daughter?"

Lennox had halted as the three entered the forest, and was watching them as though he had a secret he was eager to reveal, but only extended his arms again, perhaps to help him keep his balance now that he was still. "Don't do that," Margo cried. "I said talk."

"What do you want to hear? There's plenty if you listen."

"Lennox, try and concentrate," Dr Lowe said, kicking up leaves as he hurried between the trees. "Do you remember who took you out this afternoon?"

"Certainly I do," Heather's father said with heavy dignity. "I remember everything."

"So you'll remember when you last saw her."

"It needed to be dark."

Margo gripped his upper arms hard. "Lennox, if you don't give us a straight answer—"

"Nothing's straight here. You could start by knowing that."

"You'd better be with me. Don't you care you've lost Sylvia?"

"She's anything but lost. She'd never say she was."

Margo held her husband at arms' length and did her best to scrutinise his face. "So where did you leave her? Can't you see it's nearly dark?"

"More than that where she is."

A smell of earth and decay seemed to surge out of the thick dusk as though all the trees had stirred their roots to creep imperceptibly closer. Margo released Lennox and lifted her hands, which were on the way to turning into claws. "What do you mean? What have you done to her?"

"To her, nothing," he said, looking hurt. "For her, everything I could."

"Can you be specific?" Dr Lowe prompted.

"I always have been. I wouldn't have progressed very far in the world if I hadn't, would I?"

"About your daughter."

"I gave her a bottle like we used to, Margo. See, there's something I remember."

"Maybe you remember I never wanted to. I always wished she would feed from me like Heather did." Margo was making this clear not just to him, and visibly resented the time it took. "What do you mean, you gave her a bottle?" she demanded.

"Remember we'd put something extra in to help her sleep when her dreams kept waking her up."

"You're saying you got her drunk? And left her where?"

"That's right, it was alcohol we used to give her," he said as if that sufficed for a reply, and turned to the doctor. "I may as well confess I haven't been taking my pills the last few days. You might want to realise how easy it is for someone to look as if they're swallowing them. I kept them in case they came in useful, and they did."

"You're saying you gave some to Sylvia," Margo said tonelessly.

"A few. I didn't tell her, you understand." He seemed to find that more than reasonable, and Heather was aware, as she'd tried for years not to be, how out of reach his mind had grown. "I was trying to make it easier for her," he said with some pique.

"What?" Margo said, less a word than an agonised gasp.

"You can ask her."

Heather twisted around to follow his stare. The ground or the leaves it had yet to absorb slithered beneath her feet. At first she saw only trees dimmed by trees that led her gaze into bristling darkness, and then the outline of a trunk some hundreds of yards distant appeared to waver before sprouting a shape that lurched away from it—a figure that began to follow a route not much less intricate than the one Lennox had pursued. She saw that the figure was Sylvia just as her sister stumbled, clutching at a tree so hard the crack of bark resounded through the woods.

As Sylvia paced forward so uncertainly she might almost have been recalling how to walk, the women ran to her. Margo bruised Heather's arm twice in supporting herself but relinquished it to sprint the last few yards. She took Sylvia by an elbow and slipped her other arm around her daughter's waist and peered into her face. She uttered a low cry and glared between the unmoved trees at Lennox. "What did he do to you?"

Sam contributed an embarrassed cough before his grandfather protested "Why did you get up, Sylvia? I was sure you understood. Selcouth."

Heather took hold of Sylvia's free arm with both hands. Her sister's face was stained with mud or tears or both. Her eyes appeared to be unsure how to focus, and she smelled of exposed earth. Her mouth took long enough to open for Heather to grow apprehensive, but all she said was "I don't seem to be able to hear very well."

"Selcouth," Lennox repeated at the top of his voice.

It sounded as much like a summons as an explanation. For a breath Heather felt that the woods were poised to reveal a secret—that it was dark enough for them to stop pretending. A lorry roared along the bypass, swinging shadows of trees across the ground as though a huge barred gate had opened in the elaborate decaying patchwork, and she helped lead Sylvia towards the light. "Let's go where you can sit down," she murmured.

Sylvia stumbled forward as the men turned to the barred glow of the Arbour, Sam looking unsure which group to join and staying between them, Dr Lowe remaining close to Lennox. The only sound in the woods was the shifting of leaves and twigs underfoot until Lennox said to the doctor "So much for your medication."

"I'm not sure I understand."

"I thought it was meant to be soporific."

"Only in the sense of making you calm enough to sleep."

"I wish you'd made that clear," Lennox said, and glanced over his shoulder. "Sorry about that, Sylvia. I'd have tried to find something else to give you if I'd known."

When Sylvia didn't answer, perhaps because she was still deafened, Margo cried "How dare you talk to her after you gave her drugs? Your own daughter. I've been praying you'd get better but I won't any more. You've gone beyond ever coming back to us."

"You got that right. You'll have to catch me up."

"Just you keep your distance."

For a moment Margo's voice was entangled among the trees as though they had taken her rebuke personally. Lennox responded, if at all, by turning to the doctor. "What do you think the stuff that grew in here till they destroyed it all was for?"

"For."

"Is there an echo in here? It wouldn't be the first time I've heard one in these woods, or something like one." He cocked his head at the trees and the mass of darkness that seemed to be emerging from them as much as cloaking them. He might have been sharing his comments with the forest or even feeling prompted to say "Try again. What would the lichen have been for?"

"To be part of the ecology like everything else, presumably," Dr Lowe said, as much to Sam as to Lennox.

"He hasn't got it, has he, Sylvia?"

"She isn't speaking to you," Margo declared almost before Sylvia failed to answer, "and she doesn't want to hear you raving either."

"She won't. I'm not. Try and learn while you're in here. It'll help," he said, gesturing beyond the women as though to invoke the aid of the darkness growing vaster at their backs. "It was meant to make us ready, don't you understand? To prepare our minds."

He'd halted at the edge of the trees and looked reluctant to pass beyond them. As Sylvia faltered, Margo shouted at him "Don't stand in our way."

Dr Lowe grabbed his arm as the headlights of a truck found them. Once the truck had rumbled by and the men had stepped over the metal barrier, Margo and Heather escorted Sylvia across the road. Heather had no time to give in to an impression that they were leaving more than trees behind, and forgot it as she reached the gates. The men had stopped at the near end of the drive as if their elongated shadows had tethered them to the woods. The gravel turned Lennox's shadow scaly as a tree-trunk and Sam's too—Heather didn't care about the doctor's. As Sylvia was led into the grounds the doctor said "I should let them know they can call off the search."

Lennox wandered to a recliner that had been left on the grass. "I'll just sit here for a while."

"Sylvia needs to sit more than you do," Margo objected, "and she doesn't want to sit with you."

Apparently Sylvia did, or didn't mind, since she wobbled towards the recliner. Margo sat her on the far end from Lennox and planted herself between them with a furious grimace at him. "You'll all be staying here while I resolve things, will you?" Dr Lowe said, and hurried across the lawn.

Margo sat forward to gaze unhappily into Sylvia's face, then peered closer. "My God," she cried, "what's that? Is that why you can't hear?"

Heather only glimpsed that the orifices of her sister's ears were black not just with shadow before Margo snatched a handkerchief out of her diminutive handbag and wet a corner of the pastel fabric, which she pushed gently into Sylvia's left ear. Some of the material she dislodged slithered down Sylvia's cheek and spattered the recliner. Margo examined the corner of the handkerchief and turned on Lennox. "What did you do to her?" she demanded. "It's mud."

Though Margo's voice was low with rage, Sylvia nodded and stuck out her blackened tongue to rub mud off it with her fingertips. "That's what it is, sure enough."

Her apparent lack of emotion aggravated Margo's fury. "Answer me," she almost spat at Lennox.

"You can, can't you, Sylvia? You can tell her why it had to be."

Sylvia was still cleaning her tongue, and her blurred response sounded childlike. "I don't know if I know."

"That'll be the drugs I gave you, sorry. Remember what we heard."

Margo presented her back to him, hunching up one shoulder to emphasise her aversion. "Come along, Sylvia. Let's go inside where it's more pleasant."

Sylvia used her hands to brush the midriff of her denim overalls, which were stained with earth as much as with shadows. "I'm trying to remember," she protested, more childishly than ever.

"The grave . . ."

"Whose grave?" Margo cried. "You're making me wish it was yours, Lennox."

"Mine," said Sylvia.

"You're telling us he . . ." Margo said as if her mouth would scarcely work.

"Finish it, dad," Sylvia begged.

"The grave shall be a cradle," he said, and stared not much less than imploringly at her.

Sylvia fingered her tongue and scrutinised the result before flicking away the grains of soil. "I'm sorry, I don't get it."

"Be glad you don't. You'd be as crazy as your father," Margo said and slipped an arm around her. "Come away from him."

"Don't do this, Sylvia," he pleaded. "You're making me forget. Help me remember."

"How?" Sylvia asked in much the same tone, and a tear found a path down her muddy cheek.

"She's going nowhere with you," Margo said, hugging Sylvia to her.

"Then you'll excuse me if I go by myself."

His sudden assumption of dignity seemed ponderous, so that his surging forward out of a crouch took Heather unawares. He was striding fast towards the gates before she called "Dad, wait"—for what, she couldn't think. She wasted another second in gesturing Sam to follow, and one more in saying "Quick." Lennox was nearly at the bypass when they sprinted after him.

He heard them, and ran through the gateway as if trying to imitate his elongated prancing shadow. When Heather heard the thunder she thought at first it was coming from the woods. She could almost have imagined that the darkness the trees were using to hold themselves still was owning up to its nature. Then she realised what she was hearing. "Dad," she nearly screamed.

He didn't falter; if anything, he put on speed. As he dashed into the road, the lights of the oncoming lorry turned him incandescent and the giant trumpet of the horn seemed to greet him. It only arrested him. He was standing in the road, his torso contorted towards the vehicle and his arms outstretched in a parody of an embrace, when he was flung with a sound like the thump of a vast drum across the metal barrier, as though he was being offered to the forest. His luminousness went out, and he sprawled at the edge of the trees. As the lorry groaned and panted to a halt it ploughed into the hedge beyond the Arbour, and Heather began to tremble with more than the chill of the December night. For a heartbeat she was convinced that the snapping of twigs came from the shape that lay twisted on the far side of the road. It twitched once and then was as still as the woods.

17

A Yuletide Rite

CHRISTMAS Eve might have been peaceful except for the wind from the woods. Whenever it revived, Heather saw them flex their multitude of bared claws, and couldn't help bracing herself yet again before its chill reached across the common. It seemed to carry a smell of turned earth, but perhaps that was rising from the churchyard, where the wind set the few leaves that still clung to the infrequent trees chattering like flattened desiccated birds and sent a flight of them scuttling and scraping among the headstones. It did its best to dislodge Margo's headscarf while it flapped the priest's black robe and fluttered Sylvia's voluminous overcoat as if the garment was being kicked from within. One of the undertaker's men smoothed down a troubled tuft of hair, whose roots didn't quite match its black- ness, as he and his colleagues stooped to ease the coffin out of the hearse. Margo was the first to pace after them, holding Sam by the arm. Heather followed, staying close beside Sylvia as Terry did in case she needed support, into the church.

While it was Victorian, the architect had done his utmost to render it Norman. It seemed to Heather to be overgrown with leaves: masses of them carved on the thick arches of the doorway and windows, arrangements of them concealing the roots of the stout round pillars and encircling their capitals beneath the heavy reddish vaulted roof. Later someone had undertaken to relieve the austerity by replacing the plain windows with stained glass, most of which included images of leaves. Heather was unnecessarily aware of all this, and felt that her grief was staying out of reach, hovering over her like a cloud laden with unshed rain. She trudged past the couple of dozen pews, which were less than a third occupied, and waited while Sam limped aside to let Margo sidle along the left-hand front pew. As Heather joined her she enquired none too quietly "Do they have to be here?"

"They ought to be, shouldn't they?" Sylvia murmured.

Most of the congregation were from the university, even if retired, but scattered among them Heather saw five patients from the Arbour—the five to whom Lennox had introduced her and Sylvia. They appeared to have tried to position themselves in a circle, which was less undermined than emphasised by the presence of two male nurses and Dr Lowe. He nodded gravely to the Prices as they turned towards the altar.

The undertaker's men were lowering the coffin onto the stand, so soundlessly that Heather was confused to find herself thinking how still the forest could be. She watched the priest climb the steps of the pulpit with a slowness that gave him the appearance of being elevated by the half-inflated balloon of his roundish pale bland wrinkled face. He inserted his plump fingers between one another on top of the wooden-leafed pulpit and inclined his balding head, then raised it and his soft bedside voice. "We are gathered here to remember Lennox Weaver Price. Tributes will be paid by some of his former colleagues at the University of Brichester, where he was respected both for his teaching and his research . . ."

"Before he tried to bury his own daughter alive," Margo muttered.

Sylvia reached across Heather to take their mother's hand. "Don't, mom."

"Maybe it's me that oughtn't to have come."

"You know you should," Sylvia said, and slipped past Heather to sit between her and Margo. "You'd feel worse if you stayed away. He couldn't help what he did."

"Don't tell me that. Anybody could, especially when it's their own child."

"No, mom. You have to believe me. I was there, remember."

All the same, it wasn't clear how much she had forgotten or preferred not to recall. Heather hadn't even been able to judge when the drugs had worn off. For days after their father's death Sylvia had seemed hardly to know where she was or what she felt. Margo had done her almost unrelenting best to ensure Sylvia at least felt protected, and hadn't concealed her relief when Sylvia had refused anybody else's counselling. She'd told the police only that Lennox had drugged her and that she was certain he must have thought she was dead when he'd buried her—why he'd done so, she couldn't say. The police had found the shallow hole he'd dug within the exposed foundations in the depths of the woods, and the coroner had accepted Sylvia's version of events. Now, however, Margo said "You won't convince me."

"Then I won't try any more. Just listen to what we all have to say about him."

Having lapsed into silence, the priest was observing their dispute. His expression suggested he was understudying any one of several stained-glass images of Christ in the windows. "Shall I continue?" he said.

Margo barely held her hands out, not bothering to turn up their palms, and it was left to Sylvia to tell him "You should."

"Professor Dyson, former vice-chancellor of the university, will now share with us his memories of Dr Price."

The professor came with a pair of sticks. He took some time to arrive at the pulpit, and not much less to be assisted into it by the priest, all of which was insignificant compared with the period he spent remembering Lennox with, it seemed to Heather, almost as many wheezing breaths as phrases. He praised her father's professionalism and the results he'd achieved with students, then hitched himself down from the pulpit and along the aisle. At last the sounds of wood on stone ended, but only until the priest announced Dr Bowman, who was accompanied by a solitary stick. She had a good deal to say in favour of *The Mechanics of Delusion* and its author's commitment to research before she returned to her pew. Heather didn't know to what extent the hollow bony clicks of wood on stone were making her uneasy and how much was her anticipation of the next speech. The edge of the pew felt moist as new wood, presumably because her grasp on it was, as the priest said "And now Sylvia Price will speak for the family."

"You don't have to say anything," Margo muttered.

"I want to, mom."

"You want to put yourself through this in your state?"

"Especially in that."

Margo frowned into her eyes, then released her in something like despair. "I shouldn't stop you if it means so much to you," she murmured. "Just be careful, that's all I ask."

It wasn't clear whether she meant Sylvia to take care what she said or of herself. At least a scan at the hospital on Mercy Hill had confirmed the baby was unharmed. Heather massaged her sister's shoulders as they went by. Sylvia grasped the sides of the pulpit as she ascended the steps, her long voluminous dress matching the priest's robe for blackness. She moved her hands to the leafy front edge of the pulpit as though exploring an aspect of the wood. Her fingertips ranged back and forth like branches swaying in a wind as she spoke.

"I guess most people who know our family would think I never really knew my father, even less than my sister did. I was pretty young when he went away, but we used to go and see him, and usually he'd ask how I was getting on. Sometimes he'd want to hear everything I'd done since we last met, and I'd feel like I couldn't tell him enough to satisfy him. I think he always wanted to be the father he wasn't allowed to be."

Heather thought their mother might have felt accused, and laid a hand on Margo's stiff unyielding brittle arm. "Anyway, I grew up and went away myself," Sylvia said. "I can tell you I was trying to be like him, like everything I admired about him. Maybe one reason I came home this time was I thought I'd managed. I believe he wanted me to know he thought I had."

For a moment Heather took her pause to mean she was keeping a memory to herself, and then she heard the interruption, a repeated scratch of something like a fingernail. It came from the direction of the coffin—from the window beyond it, where a leaf or a large insect was twitching next to Christ's left foot. Heather saw the oddly symmetrical leaf detach itself from the pane against the outside of which it had been held by the wind. It vanished into the clouded gloom that appeared to be draining colour from the image in the glass.

"I know some people say he tried to harm me at the end," said Sylvia. "The papers did. All I can say is maybe nobody alive knows what he meant to do. Wait, that isn't all," she said as Margo gave signs of being unable to stay quiet. "That last day he was more like the father he wished he could be and I did than I'd ever seen him. If anyone hasn't heard I'm pregnant, well, I am, and I think knowing that let him be everything he could be. That's how I want to remember him, as my baby's grandfather. He saw one grandchild, and I only wish he could see another."

As Margo emitted a muted sniff, Heather had the surely unworthy notion that in some way Sylvia had won. Sam restrained himself to looking embarrassed as his aunt took three steps down from the pulpit, so measured that Heather could almost have imagined she was being guided by the child inside her. Heather saw Terry wonder if he should move to offer Sylvia his arm, but it wasn't her state that made Sylvia falter. A voice had said "He did."

The bench slithered beneath Heather's hands as she twisted round. Nearly the whole of the congregation was staring at Timothy, the man who was convinced rare species inhabited the woods. Only his fellow patients continued to watch Sylvia, who spoke so low she might not have wanted an answer. "What do you mean?"

Timothy's head seemed determined to nod at the same time as it shook. "He could see deep into you," he said.

"Into everyone, you mean."

"Into his own most of all. He told us once that nothing sees like blood."

This was too much for Margo, who retorted "Blood didn't mean much to him at the end."

"It must have," Timothy insisted. "He said nothing mattered more than who you made. The closer you were the more you'd understand."

The priest cleared his throat with some vehemence. "If I can remind everyone where we are and why . . ."

"Let's talk later," Sylvia said to Timothy.

"The later the better," Margo mumbled, and waited for Sylvia to rejoin her. "Why do you want to talk to them?" she demanded under some of her breath.

"Because they knew dad. They must have spent more time with him than I ever did."

Margo seemed to think this deserved either no response or only one best left unsaid. She made a show of concentrating on the priest as he invited the mourners to reflect on the occasion or pray in silence. Heather was delving into herself for more of a sense of her father than she was able to resurrect—perhaps it was the presence of his fellow inmates at her back that enveloped her mind in the notion of following him into the woods—when the priest broke the hush with a last few words. As the undertaker's men stepped forward to heft the coffin, a taped soprano began to sing "I know that my redeemer liveth." With a kind of defiance, and to nobody in particular, Margo explained "He used to say Handel was one of his favourite things about England."

Heather was reminded instead of the professor who'd invited Lennox to study the effects of the forest, only to succumb to Alzheimer's and lose himself in the woods, in whose midst he had starved to death. A cold wind that smelled of earth came to meet the coffin and the Prices as they emerged from the church. Margo glanced back, visibly about to tell Sylvia to button up her coat if she hadn't already been doing so. The five from the Arbour had turned to face the coffin as it passed, and now Heather heard them—not only them, she reminded herself— shuffling in pursuit. The wind raised the hair on the heads of all the undertaker's men as they paced towards the side of the churchyard nearest to the woods. The late afternoon sky was as sombrely clouded as it had looked through the windows; Heather could have imagined that the restless bony mass of the forest was dragging darkness to earth. The four men in black halted by a gravestone that gleamed white as a child's first tooth. While they deposited the coffin on a platform in the open grave, the priest folded his hands as if tacitly inviting prayer and stood behind the stone that bore Lennox's name and dates. When nobody else gave any sign of making a move, Sylvia lifted a pinch of earth from beside the grave and scattered it along the coffin lid.

Heather refrained from wondering if Sylvia was reminded of having been buried herself. She stooped to snatch up a handful of earth and cast it on the coffin. Margo grabbed a handful and shook her hand free of it over the lid, and once Sam and Terry had imitated her, the other mourners did. The quintet from the Arbour stepped forward in a circle to drop simultaneous portions of earth that seemed to provoke a muffled creak, no doubt carried out of the forest by the wind. Heather saw Margo consider objecting to their gesture, only to rub her mouth with her fingertips as the coffin began to sink into the grave. At that moment the five turned to gaze at the woods.

Heather thought she saw the woods respond. She saw the treetops opposite the churchyard writhe and grow spindly as insect legs with the effort of producing a light they held up. Just as it became too intense to face, she identified it as the sun, creeping from behind the dark grey sky-wide bank of cloud. The cloud and the woods squeezed it small, concentrating the light until it resembled an impossibly protracted flash of lightning, relentless and chill. The wind had dropped as though frozen by the light or seized by the thousands of filaments of shadow that had come alive, stretching themselves across the deserted common towards the churchyard. The only sound was the faint hum of the mechanism that was lowering the coffin into the grave, which had deepened with blackness. Before the coffin could touch bottom, a shape fluttered into the graveyard.

It slithered over the turf, humping up grublike whenever it reached a headstone, and appeared to vanish into the open grave. When Heather squinted towards the light, whatever had cast the shadow had disappeared. Of course that made sense. If she felt vibration underfoot, heading for the forest and immediately gone, that must be an effect of the mechanism of the platform. If she'd seemed not so much to hear as feel a muffled voice or voices, no doubt they belonged to some of the quintet, all of whom were gazing at the sky. It was Sylvia, however, who said either eagerly or nervously "What was that?"

Heather rubbed her stiffened hands together and felt as if she was ridding them of a glaze of ice. The five were shivering and grinning through the mist of their breaths. She was about to declare that it had been nothing but a shadow when Timothy said "It was birds. Many birds."

"I thought it was the face I used to see," said Nigel. "The face that flies."

"I saw a face, but it was crawling on the ground," Delia said, tugging at her eyes from beneath.

"And growing," Phyllis added, clasping her hands together so hard they shivered more than ever.

"It's nearly his time, then," Vernon said as best he could for shaking.

Dr Lowe gestured to the nurses to help him intervene, but Sylvia was faster. "Say whose."

"The one your father kept telling us about."

"The one that told Lennox his name."

"Gave him his name and a lot more you need—"

Neither Timothy nor Nigel nor Vernon waited for one another to say any of this, and the women's impatience with them was too great to let them finish. Delia and Phyllis drew breath in chorus and bellowed "Sel—"

Margo clapped her hands so fiercely that she winced. "That's enough. The end," she said as if she were rebuking children, Sylvia included. "Whatever Lennox did, he's gone now. Show him some respect and let him rest."

The five covered their mouths, and might have appeared chastened if Timothy hadn't proved unable to contain a snort of mirth. "He just went all right, true enough."

"We heard him go," Phyllis said behind her hand.

"But there won't be much rest for him," spluttered Vernon.

"Nothing rests in the woods," Nigel mumbled.

If Delia had anything to add, Terry headed her off. "Look, that really is more than enough," he said, his face reddening with every phrase. "You ought to be able to have some sense of the occasion, otherwise you shouldn't be here at all. It never hurts to know when to be quiet," he appealed to the doctor.

"Come away now, Sylvia," Margo said. "You'll have had your fill of burials, I should think."

At once she looked upset by her own choice of words, which had made Heather feel a little sick. Sylvia moved away from the inmates of the Arbour and supported herself on Sam's arm. "Okay, I'm finished here," she said.

The lowering mechanism had quieted, having placed the coffin. As Heather linked arms with Margo and turned away from the grave, a wind followed them. This time it brought no smell of earth, only a few distant bars of *Silent Night*. It had always been Heather's favourite carol, and she was letting it recall to her how childhood Christmases had felt when she wondered who could be singing in the woods. The wind must be confusing her sense of direction, just as it began to distort the voices. In a moment she could no longer hear them, but in that moment the high voices sounded as much like birds as children. They sounded almost as if they were mocking both the similarities and the carol.

18

The Uprooted

WHEN Heather heard Sam cross the landing to the bathroom she waited to be sure that the oven almost full of turkey fired itself up, and then she went upstairs to tap on the bathroom door. "Sam?" she murmured, and had to say more loudly "Sam?"

"What?" he demanded in a voice that sounded not much less than drowned.

"Happy Christmas, to begin with."

A few seconds passed before he slid back the bolt. "Happy Christmas," he offered as an apology.

"You look as if you've dressed for the event."

She was referring not to his unclothed top half that he'd edged around the door but to the moustache and beard of foam he'd donned. "Why are we whispering?" he whispered, licking not just his lips but the foam around them.

"Don't do that. You'll put yourself off my Christmas dinner," she said and reached to clean his nervous lips with a thumb. "No need to wake Sylvie. I was wondering if I could use your computer while I have a few minutes to myself and look something up on the net."

"I'll have to put you online," he said, not much short of a complaint, and shut the door in order to emerge wrapped from the waist down in a pink bath-towel.

"You could tell me the password if you wanted to save yourself trouble."

He didn't respond before switching on the computer and typing a word she had the grace not to read, glimpsing only that it began with **f** and **o** and had an **e** in it as well. "There's the web for you," he said as the modem began burbling to itself.

His room was the mess she expected: the hi-fi piled with overlapping compact discs and crowned with headphones, the computer that appeared to have borne a litter of floppies, the office chair in front of it, dressed in a selection of his clothes as though understudying Sam— and yet she had an odd notion that the room wasn't quite as chaotic as it appeared, that it was rather too reminiscent of her previous sight of it. Beyond the common, beneath a sky the colour of thin ice over black water, the bones of the forest were twitching in a wind. She sat forward on the cluttered chair and pulled down a search engine from Sam's menu of favourites and typed Selcouth in the narrow rectangular space.

She had no idea what she might be calling up. She wasn't expecting to be shown more than a dozen sites, even if some of them were repetitions. *Websters Dictionary 1913, p. 1384 . . . Game of Obscure Words . . . Financial Services, Portland, Oregon . . . Word of the Week . . .* She was about to follow up a lead to Middle English verse when the last retrieved site scrolled into view.

Aleister Crowley, Peter Grace, Roland Franklyn, and John Strong were among those who regarded Nathaniel Selcouth as the most far-seeing . . .

As frequently happened, the search engine displayed just the start of the opening sentence to be found on the site. Heather closed her hand around the mouse and rested her forefinger on the left button. The name Nathaniel had to be a coincidence, or might Lennox have mentioned it to her sister? She clicked the button hard rather than waste time on wondering. The incomplete sentence that was printed in bright blue turned black, and the bottom margin of the window set about filling with blue from left to right as if the essence of the sentence was concentrating itself there. Though it was in no hurry to finish, she did her best to keep her attention on the screen, but eventually she had to rid herself of the impression that someone had come to the edge of the forest to watch her. There was nothing to be seen except the skeletal gestures of the trees and the message the computer sent her. *Connection timed out,* it said.

She backed up to click on the sentence, which had stayed blackened. The blue band had crawled less than a third of the length of the window when the computer declared *The page cannot be displayed* and suggested she open the home page of the server. That brought her the same message, and so she clicked once more on the charred sentence. The blue band had scarcely commenced oozing like a chemical into its tube when the window turned utterly blank. At that moment the woods dragged down a vague pale shape from the sky to merge with them and then swell forward out of them. It was Sam's reflection as he stooped to gaze over her shoulder. "What did you do?" he said in a tone he might have used on someone younger than himself.

"Just looked for something that seemed not to want me to find it."

"I've never seen that happen before. Would you like me to try?"

"You might want to get dressed first," Heather said, since he was still sporting the towel, though apparently unaware of a chill that had come to the window. "I'll have a last shot," she said and backed up, to discover that the listing for Selcouth had vanished. "Never mind. I'll look it up when I get back to work."

Sam turned away from the view of the forest as they heard a door open. "Are we having Christmas yet?" Sylvia called.

She'd asked that every Christmas morning when they were little.

The memory and a sense of more loss than she could quite define brought tears to Heather's eyes. "A happy one," she promised. "Even happier now you're up."

"Then I'd better stay that way. Do I get to give my nephew a seasonal kiss?" Sylvia said and ventured into the room, her voluminous bathrobe flapping, only to retreat at once. "Sorry, I didn't realise you weren't decent."

"He's not far off it, do you think? You may as well get used to that kind of sight now you're a mother. Worse than that to come, Sylvie."

"I'll be making coffee if anyone else wants some," Sylvia said.

Heather gave Sam's thin shoulders and pale ribbed torso and proudly hairy chest a further glance that reminded her of when they had been thinner still and entirely innocent of hair. He looked so uncomfortable that she left him to it and closed the door. "I'll keep you and the turkey company," she told her sister.

A piny smell met her on the stairs, and she thought how things would have started growing as the nights began to shrink. Sylvia was filling the percolator while she gazed at the livid cracks in the sky that were the crest of the woods. "Are you through in the kitchen," she said, "or can I help?"

"There's a few vegetables to be dealt with and then we won't have mother doing her best to be helpful and getting in the way."

"Let me fix the potatoes. I always liked scraping them."

If the earth on them didn't rouse unpleasant memories, Heather wasn't about to do so. She confined herself to washing the sprouts and dropping them into a saucepan with a sound that used to make her and Sylvia giggle, more uncontrollably when Margo had asked why. The bubbling of the percolator was completing the trio of sounds when Sylvia said "Want to promise me something?"

"I can't think why not."

"Don't let me tease Natty. Tell me if I ever start."

Heather looked for Sylvia's reflection but could see only the woods not quite hiding beyond the hedge. "Could anyone have mentioned that name to you recently?"

"Such as who?"

"I was wondering about dad."

"Maybe. I can't remember. If he did it's something he gave me I can keep," Sylvia said, and without a pause "So will you promise?"

"Why should I need to stop you teasing anyone?"

"I've been lying awake thinking what a bitch I used to be."

"Oh, Sylvie, you should have come and talked to me instead of being by yourself. When were you ever one of those?"

"I was to you when we were kids."

"It couldn't have been very serious, because I don't remember."

"I'm only starting. I've been remembering when we were in the woods."

"Everything comes back to them, does it?"

"I think we do," Sylvia admitted, lifting her head as if the claws of the forest had indicated it should rise. "Remember when I used to say we had to hit the ground with sticks."

"Vaguely," Heather said. "Were we playing at being primitive? The first people in Goodmanswood, and we thought they'd drum on the earth."

"The earth inside the foundations. We didn't just hit it, we did that and then we ran away."

"That's children for you."

"Screaming."

"I think that was mostly you being little. I can hardly remember."

With gathering impatience Sylvia said "Then maybe you remember the quiet place."

"You'll have to remind me."

"Where we used to watch the shadows moving all around us but where we were it was as still as the trees are now."

Presumably she'd glanced out of the window to check, though Heather hadn't noticed; the treetops were indeed so motionless they might have been supporting the sky while draining it of colour. "It must have been very sheltered," Heather heard herself say.

"It wasn't, Heather. It was the same place, inside the foundations. You have to remember."

Heather felt more as though she was striving to recall a dream from many years ago when Sylvia said "And the black pool we threw sticks in and hoped nothing pulled them down or got wakened by them. That was on top of the mound when it started to fall in one time, and then we were too scared to go back."

"Let's say so if you like, but haven't we strayed from your point?"

"Which you think was . . ."

"You were calling yourself a bitch."

"Wasn't I one when I showed you how to hide from mom?"

"Sounds as if I must have been as well, and I was older."

"You remember what we did, then."

"I think I remember trying to be the quietest thing there was. We haven't had snow round here for years."

"It's the way the world's changing. What made you think of that?"

"Don't say there's something you've forgotten, how we used to try and walk like snow falling."

"You did, but I tried to do it like dead leaves. I'd feel them settling on the earth and starting to turn into it, and that's how I wanted to go. That was the beginning, I think."

"Of what?" Heather could find no excuse not to ask.

"Of learning what you can do in the woods."

"Nothing much that I can bring to mind."

"I thought you were remembering how we hid from mom."

"You mean when we were playing on the common and sometimes we'd sneak into the woods so she wouldn't see us when it was time to go home."

"Right," Sylvia said eagerly, "and do you remember how close we were to the edge of the woods? You'd have thought she would have been able to see us from the back gate."

"Maybe she did."

"You aren't remembering. You're trying not to."

"Honestly, Sylvie, I don't see the point of digging all—"

"Can't you remember how it felt?"

Heather didn't know if she was being accused of inability or reluctance. "It's been most of forty years."

"For some people that's less than a breath." Sylvia clenched her fists, apparently unaware that they were blackened with earth. "They're still inside us," she insisted, "the children we were. We just get bigger around them."

"I think there's a little more to it."

"In the end there isn't, Heather. They're the depths of us. Just let yourself feel."

"I've done quite a lot of that in my time."

"No need to feel lonely any more," Sylvia said, perhaps having taken Heather's remark as an accusation. "I meant remember what I used to tell you to do."

"Strange how much of that you did though you were younger."

"Maybe that means I saw clearer. Remember what I said about the trees."

"I expect we both used to imagine things. It's part of being little."

"We're all little compared with some," Sylvia said, and stretched her earthy hands towards her sister. "Tell me you remember how we had to be like the trees that were so thin you could see in front of them and behind them both at once."

Heather felt as if she was in danger of dreaming while awake, which failed to appeal to her. "I never—"

"You did when I got you to understand it wasn't how they looked but how they felt. Don't you remember feeling so thin you could hide behind a twig? You kept being afraid it was like dying, but it was only like we weren't there, just the woods."

Abruptly Heather saw Margo shouting their names across the common as she made a number of tentative zigzag advances towards the trees, opening and closing her hands and clutching her breasts with them. The sisters had never hidden from her after that, having seen how upset she was—so upset they had been afraid to reveal themselves until she'd returned to the house. Or had Heather been most afraid of finding herself unable to grow visible? If so it had only been a child-ish fear, she told herself as the doorbell rang.

She hurried to answer it, leaving any memories behind. The hall smelled more like the depths of a wood than the site of a single tree. "Mum, you're early," she declared.

"Not too, I hope," Margo said, miming readiness to leave.

"Never that. Come in out of the chill," Heather urged, for the icy air appeared to be stealing their breaths.

Margo unburdened herself of a carrier bagful of presents like a tribute to the tree before shedding her winter coat over the post of the banisters to reveal the dress she'd worn at her private view. "Have you heard from the gallery lately?" Heather was prompted to ask.

"Lucinda was suggesting I could find another way of doing what I do, so I've treated myself to a video camera."

Heather might have sought to discover what Margo was leaving unsaid if Sylvia hadn't called "Get some coffee, mom. We've had ours."

Heather was disconcerted to realise she couldn't remember when, as though reminiscing had engulfed any other awareness. "Happy Christmas to us all," Margo was saying. "Come down, Sam, if three girls aren't too much for you."

He'd swapped the towel for trousers and one of the very few Worlds Unlimited sweaters in existence, but looked embarrassed by her flirtatiousness, though she was too intent on hastening to Sylvia to notice. "How are you feeling?" she murmured, seizing Sylvia's hands.

"Kind of guilty."

"Who's been making you feel that way?"

"Me, all by myself."

"I hope you know you'll never be that again while any of us are around." Margo waited until this provoked a wistful smile. "What about?" she said.

"How we hid from you in the trees when we were supposed to come home at night."

"Then you're not the only one who should feel guilty, are you? Your big sister was meant to be looking after you." Before Heather could react more than inwardly, Margo said "Anyway, you're both forgiven. I should have known you knew your way around the woods and never got lost and always stayed away from where that poisonous stuff grew, because I'd asked you to. I'll be like that soon if I've anything to do with it."

"Like what?" Heather had to learn.

"At home in the woods. I'm going to explore everything about them. That's why I bought the camera."

"I'll walk with you if you like," Sylvia said.

"No need, dear. I'll be finding my way gradually. Don't worry, you won't lose me."

"I meant I'd quite like a few walks in the woods."

"Would you mind very much if they weren't with me for the moment? I make my best work when I'm by myself. I expect someone will keep you company if that's what you're looking for."

Sam had joined them and was pouring coffee into his Fight For Foliage mug. "Me if you want," he blurted, and seemed instantly confused.

"Sylvie," Heather said, and felt too committed to her question to suppress it. "Why would you want to go back there?"

"Heather, we all love you and wouldn't change anything about you," Margo said, "so don't feel hurt if I say you were never the most imaginative member of the family. Sylvia will tell me if I'm wrong, but I assume she wants to reclaim the place for herself."

When Sylvia nodded slowly twice as though her midriff was tugging her head down, Heather left the decision to her. "Shall we come back to today?" Heather said. "I wouldn't mind opening my presents."

They finished their coffee before heading for the front room, where Heather popped a bottle of something akin to champagne and filled four glasses with dwindling fizz. Once Margo's was topped up she rose with studied dignity to her feet. "Age gets to start," she said on the way to retrieving her packages.

She'd bought Sylvia a capacious dress and Heather one more fitting, and so expensive a shirt for Sam it could almost have been designed as a rebuke to his clothes sense. He seemed abashed by handing out the presents he'd been able to afford—a history of art for Margo, a vegetarian cookbook for Heather, a book on Severn Valley legends for Sylvia. "It's second-hand but I thought you'd like it because it's quite rare," he said.

"I don't think we even have it in the library," said Heather.

Sylvia's gifts to the women were delicate necklaces composed of seeds, while Sam's package proved to be a wooden box as black as a shadow. "That's for your secrets," she told him.

Heather's parcels were small enough to have sat overnight on the tree rather than beneath. As she recovered them from the branches, the irregular flickering of fairy lights brought feelers that were shadows groping around the tree-trunk. She wasn't sure whether the parcels were slightly damp, but rubbed them with her handkerchief in preparation for delivering them. Everyone had silver earrings, since Sam had taken to adorning his left ear. His ring was plain, while Margo's and Sylvia's pairs bore tiny leaves. "Now we're even more alike," Margo remarked as Heather made for the kitchen to monitor dinner.

Nothing was playing hide and seek with her behind the tree except a many-legged insect shadow. All the same, on her way back she knelt and switched off the fairy lights at the socket on the skirting board, to prove to her presumably drunken self that she had the power to extinguish the appearance. The tree seemed poised to lurch at her—because she was looking up at it, of course, which let her see that it was slightly tilted towards her. She removed bricks from the plastic bucket and took hold of the rough spiky trunk to return it to the vertical. At once her grasp was full of the swarming of insects.

She didn't cry out or even recoil very far. She stood up quite carefully and strode to open the front door with the hand she wasn't staring at to convince herself it was bare, empty, clean. "Have we got another visitor?" Margo called.

"I'm just—" Heather didn't want to explain until she'd finished. She pushed the door wide and hurried shivering to unplug the lights and grab the tree with both hands. Though not even a hint of movement was visible, the trunk felt frantic with swarming—felt as though it was about to hatch. As she heaved at it, trembling with the effort or with the chill that had closed around her like a sudden fog, the roots snagged in the bucket somehow. She could have imagined they were determined to cling to their nest. She was opening her mouth to ask Sam to come and help when the tree sprang out of the bucket, waving its roots.

It took her only six breathless steps to carry it out of the house, but in those seconds she thought it writhed in her grip—thought it felt less like wood than like soft scaly flesh. She didn't just let go of it but flung it away from her. It fell against the house with a diffused thump, jingling its decorations like a jester's bells. "Was that you? Are you all right?" Margo cried.

"No," Heather called, "yes," which was no more uncertain than she felt. She was making herself reach to strip the tree of its lights when Margo and the others came to find her. "What on earth are you doing?" Margo demanded.

"Something's living in the tree. One of you, Sam, bring out the bucket and the rest of it as well."

"What's living?" Sylvia asked with an odd wide-eyed frown.

"I don't know exactly. I don't care. All I know is I don't want it in the house," Heather said, shivering more than ever as she unwound the flex budding with lights. "Get the bucket and the bricks, Sam."

Margo waited until he was in the house before she murmured "I didn't mean you had no imagination at all, you know. No need to go mad to prove you have."

For a moment Heather thought she had nothing but anger with which to respond, and then she found a reason to jab a finger at the tree. "I'm not imagining that, am I? You can see that too."

"You aren't imagining we can see what?"

"Something's grown on here," Heather insisted, using a fingernail to extract a dull truncated chime from a silver globe that anyone could see was greenish.

"I shouldn't be surprised. We've had some of those since Sylvia was born. Don't catch cold, Heather, and especially not Sylvia. Come inside."

"Not till I know what's coming in with me." Heather did her best to conquer her shivering as she examined every bulb and every inch of the flex before carrying the plastic vine of lights to the cupboard under the stairs. "Hurry up and take those out," she told Sam and watched to be certain he loaded all the bricks into the bucket while she stored the lights in their box. She followed him out with the carton for the rest of the decorations. "Don't touch those," she not much less than shouted at the sight of Margo lifting off the tinsel globes, "please."

"Then I won't do anything," Margo said, but observed Heather's scrutiny of all the globes, most of which she risked returning to the carton, leaving in place six that looked faintly coated with moss. "Is that the end of it now?" Margo hoped aloud. "Can we get back to Christmas?"

"I don't want any of this near the house," Heather said and seized the handle of the bucket. "Someone help me take it out the back."

She wasn't only loath to touch the tree. She wanted one of her family to experience at least a hint of what she'd encountered. Sylvia was making to lift it when Margo said "You take it, Sam."

"Be careful what you're touching," Heather was impelled to say.

"It's just a tree," he said, but nevertheless held it at arms' length as he bore it around the house, its roots waving as though in search of somewhere to cling. As Heather dumped the bucket next to the dustbin he opened the gate onto the common and slung the tree into the long grass. He appeared to have felt nothing untoward. "Don't forget to bolt the gate," Heather told him.

Perhaps the cold had stilled whatever insects were lurking under the bark, and that was why Sam hadn't noticed them. The important point was that they hadn't escaped into the house. Heather managed to bury the incident deep in her mind well before dinner, abetted by her portion of another gushing bottle. Several more accompanied the meal while the day gave up its light, and another helped the Prices play charades once they'd agreed that pronunciation should be English.

The games ended when Margo dozed, which was the cue for Sylvia and Sam to take their presents to their rooms. Eventually she wakened to proclaim that it had been a far better Christmas day than she could have wished for. She refused to be escorted home. "This still isn't the kind of place where you need to be afraid at night," she said.

As Heather washed up the dinner things, belatedly aided by Sam, her attention kept straying to the back gate. Sam hadn't finished drying the plates when she wiped her hands on a towel in preparation for taking a flashlight from under the stairs. At least there was no sign in the cupboard of anything unwelcome, but she wanted to discover if the hidden contents of the tree had made themselves apparent. She followed her fading shadow away from the house and unbolted the gate. As she pulled it open she raised the flashlight beam.

At first she saw only her breaths hovering above the grass, and then far too little else. There was no trace of the tree except a flattened path through the grass. When she sent the beam rather less than steadily along it, the faintest edge of the light appeared to stir the nearest trees like the dim vanguard of a stealthily advancing multitude of bones.

She was feeling compelled to use the light to hold them still when Sam came to stand by her. His silence was almost as eloquent as the words he finally spoke. "It looks as if it dragged itself back where it came from."

19

The Reconfiguration

A man was leading Heather and Sylvia by their hands into the depths of the forest. His chant was lost amid the uproar of the trees, a vast creaking chorus that sounded like their failure to pretend to be composed of wood, hardly a deception they could maintain while clutching in unison with the same repeated gesture at the sky, which was darker than any night she would have hoped to see. Nevertheless there was light from the trees themselves, which appeared to be snaring from beyond the dark a glow too lurid to own up to any colour. The illumination focused on the object that rose from the earth in the midst of a clearing ahead. At first she thought it was the essence of the forest, though it was bare of branches and perfectly round, and then she saw it was a tower as cracked and stained as an old tree. The two windows that were visible were stuffed with soil. As the tower heaved itself up, or the ground sank to reveal more of it, the top window began to scatter earth down the scaly wall. Hands, or objects related to them, were groping into view. Her escorts urged her forward, calling out a name.

She didn't know whether she was wakened by her efforts to distinguish the denizen of the tower or to avoid seeing it. She only knew she was glad to be out of the dream and surrounded simply by the dimness of her room—except that more than the dream had roused her. Something was at the window.

She heard its enormous irregular breaths as it fumbled for a way in. Her lungs were stiffening around her own held breath before she grasped what it was. Strong winds had been forecast, but this was at least a gale. She mustn't be fully awake, because she heard it start to form itself into voices—Sam's and Sylvia's. She had to drag the quilt away from her face in order to convince herself that they were in the house.

A chill was waiting for her shoulders as she pushed herself up from the refuge of the bed and blinked in time with the colon of the bedside clock, which showed almost four in the morning. She located her slippers on the carpet by the bed and managed to insert her feet so as to stumble to the door. As she poked her hands into the twisted sleeves of her dressing-gown and captured the ends of the errant cord to tie it more or less at her waist, she heard Sylvia say "And pretty soon the rest of her caught up."

Heather felt sly for easing the door ajar, but less so once she saw that while both Sam's and Sylvia's rooms were open, no light was to be seen. She paced onto the landing and caught sight of her son and her sister. They were at his window, beyond which the dim woods were in the throes of a convulsion. The gale conveyed their creaking, a distant version of the sound in her dream. She was nearly in Sam's room when the intent silhouettes turned, though only for a moment. "Yes, come and see, Heather," Sylvia murmured. "You don't want to miss this. They won't be the same woods when the sun comes up."

"Why won't they?" Heather demanded, feeling as if she hadn't left her dream. "What will they be?"

"She means we've been watching the wind blow them down."

For an instant that felt like still being unable to waken, Heather wondered if Sylvia had indeed meant that or if Sam hoped she had. Then an onslaught shook the windows and she heard roof tiles smash nearby, and a second later the forest emitted an agonised creak. She couldn't judge which tree had fallen, although Sam and Sylvia were peering through the glass as if they could. "How long has that been happening?" she supposed she wanted to know.

"Hours at least. I guess we rather lost track of time, Sam."

"You're saying you've been up that long?"

"Sam didn't seem to mind."

Heather could see nothing in the violent gloomy antics of the trees to justify so much attention, let alone invading Sam's room, even if now she had done so herself. Another issue troubled her more, however. "What were you saying just before I came?" she said.

Sylvia hesitated. "You mightn't like to hear."

"I'd like it even less if I didn't hear it when it was in my house."

"It used to be my house too. I thought maybe it still was."

"You know it is, and your baby's, but shouldn't that mean you don't keep me in the dark?" That prompted her to add "Does anyone mind if I switch the light on?"

Another paroxysm shook the woods, and she appeared to glimpse the wake of the ferment racing across the common towards the houses. Nothing but the wind was in the grass, she told herself as she pressed the light-switch down. She saw the forest vanish into Sam's and Sylvia's reflections before they turned, blinking in unison. They looked so resentful she could have imagined she'd wakened them or interrupted them in the process of sharing a secret. "So enlighten me," she said.

The woods seemed to respond with a noise suggestive of an enormous rearrangement in the dark before Sylvia said "I was just telling Sam a story."

"In the dark?"

"That added to it, didn't it, Sam?"

He closed his eyes as though to relive some aspect of the experience while he muttered "Must have."

"Why don't we find out how it lives up to a bit of light?"

"I ought to say I've Sam to thank for it."

"It was in the book he gave you for Christmas," Heather guessed. "A legend, then."

"More than that. There's a chapter on incidents that are too recent to be legends."

"I'd have thought the process was pretty fast like just about everything else these days."

"It was in the thirties." As if revising the sentence aloud, Sylvia said "It was in our woods. A woman got lost for nearly a week."

The window shuddered, and Heather seemed to glimpse the entire forest raising itself towards the black depths of the sky. "What kind of person could do that?" she objected.

"She had a reputation for being strange if that's what you mean. Some people thought she was crazy but most of them said she was some kind of witch because she kept being seen near our ruins, walking round them and talking to someone nobody else could see. You realise they believed in witches round here right up till when they started being scared of drugs instead. I expect the stories about her were why nobody bothered searching for her."

"But you're saying she turned up."

"She came out on a Sunday. She was changed, wasn't she, Sam? That was the part that got to you."

"She looked as if she'd been praying so hard," Sam said, "nobody could move her hands apart."

"She couldn't have lived very long, then, or did they feed her for the rest of her life?"

"There wasn't much of that. She wouldn't let anyone feed her," said Sam.

"Then I expect there wouldn't be," Heather retorted, irritated by his speaking so quietly he might have feared to be overheard.

"Not because she wouldn't eat. She wasn't much older than me, but when she came out of the woods saying words nobody could understand her hands were an old woman's hands. And when the rest of her caught up she died."

"I believe starving makes you look as if you've aged. And who knows what else she may have been up to in the woods," Heather immediately regretted having said.

"Sylvia and me won't be, don't worry. We'll make sure we're always out before dark."

Heather was thrown by his revealing her anxiety, not least to her. "I wouldn't mind if you didn't go at all."

"You don't have to be frightened, Heather," Sylvia said.

"I'm not. I should have thought if anyone was you might be after that tale."

"Why would you want me to be?"

"Of course I don't," Heather protested, though her feelings seemed increasingly hard to grasp. "But I can't help thinking you're in danger of becoming obsessed with the woods."

"It's like mom says, I need to come to terms. You'd understand if you'd been there."

Heather glimpsed the treetops straining themselves skyward in the tumultuous night and imagined how Sylvia would have needed to heave herself up from the earth. "Anyway," said Sylvia, "I'll have Sam to keep an eye on how I go."

"Are you sure you'll have time, Sam?"

"I will now. Andy says he doesn't need me or Dinah so many days at the shop."

"Sounds as if you should start looking for a better job."

"There's nothing wrong with it. I don't like letting people down."

"You can always tell me if you get bored with me in the woods," Sylvia said.

"I won't be. There'll be lots of stuff to see. There are things I wouldn't mind seeing again."

Heather wasn't about to ask what; she felt uneasy enough. "I'm going to try and catch up on my sleep," she said.

"I'll watch a while longer. I can from my room if you're ready for bed, Sam."

"You can stay if you want. I haven't finished watching."

Heather tried to tell herself that wasn't further evidence of an obsession with the woods. Sylvia's might be understandable, but Sam's? Perhaps once she'd slept she would be better able to address that. "Turn out the light," Sylvia said as Heather reached the door, and she could find no justification for refusal that made sense. As she turned away she saw the treetops rise up as though to greet the silhouettes at the window.

20

The One That Called

ALEISTER Crowley, Peter Grace, Roland Franklyn and John Strong were among those who regarded Nathaniel Selcouth as the most far-seeing of their predecessors. Joseph Curwen is known to have visited England in search of Selcouth's journals but failed to locate them. As a young man Selcouth travelled the world extensively and met both Paracelsus and Agrippa in the early stages of his research. Anecdotes suggest he was impatient with them and with John Dee, who later consulted him. Selcouth is said to have commented that none of his contemporaries dared gaze into the dark, let alone beyond it, even Count Magnus "de la Gardie", whom he attempted without success to meet in Sweden. He spoke openly of having participated in witches' sabbaths in Europe and of gaining insight into necromancy from a study of the Broucolack, the vampires of the Greek volcanic island Santorini.

While he was born in London and spent his youth there, on his eventual return to England he built his final dwelling in woodland between Bristol and Gloucester, on a site he had identified as the focus of powerful occult forces. The large high building was perfectly round, and he declared it "rooted in the earth as any tree". Its shape was designed to allow observation of every aspect of the woods. His plan for his mature years is said to have been to create a messenger or servant that would mediate between him and the limits of the universe, both physical and spiritual. A series of experiments was only partially successful. Sightings of the results in or near the neighbouring village led to his arrest for witchcraft, and necromancy was added to the charge when it was discovered that he had transported his mother's corpse from London, apparently hoping to revive it. He was executed in 1567, and the bravest of the villagers tore down the round house. He remains one of the most mysterious English occult pioneers. Records of his birth have proved untraceable, Selcouth being the name he adopted to signify himself.

The website called itself the International Foundation for Occult Research. Heather didn't know if its initials were an attempt to make the organisation sound friendlier or an inadvertent sign of how humourless its members were. She was inclined to assume the latter, given the credulity the anonymous writer appeared to take for granted. Perhaps readers were expected to understand that the account didn't necessarily endorse Selcouth's beliefs, but Heather had her doubts. Nevertheless the site was helpful if it gave her an idea how Selcouth had become lodged in her father's head.

Lennox must have uncovered some hint of him while looking into the history of Goodmanswood. If that fell short of explaining why Selcouth had taken on such significance for him, at least it seemed clear that he'd communicated his obsession to his fellow patients at the Arbour. That wasn't all she'd hoped to learn by visiting the university this Sunday morning rather than wait to return to work in the new year, however. She'd wanted to find some way of confronting Sylvia with the morbidity of her obsession with the woods.

If Lennox had become aware of Selcouth here in the library, it would presumably have been in the occult section. Heather shut off the computer and ventured among the shelves, which cut off her echoes and shrank her footsteps. Such books as were indexed betrayed no trace of Selcouth, and her leafing through the others failed to reveal his presence either. If her father had found any reference in one of the volumes from the locked case—tomes originally restricted because of their content and then for their extreme rarity—she wasn't about to discover it. Not long after Lennox had been hospitalised, a Muslim student had been given access to the contents of the case, only to spray them with lighter fluid and set fire to them. Heather hadn't been sure how much she regretted the destruction of items she had never cared to open—the *Necronomicon*, the *Revelations of Glaaki*, *De Vermis Mysteriis*, and other titles as ominous—but she wished she had a chance to read them now, though perhaps not while she was on her own. The clunk of each book she returned to a shelf sounded wooden, while the smell of old paper reminded her of decaying vegetation. She couldn't pretend she wasn't glad to finish her search, even though it had turned up nothing. She collected her handbag from her desk and switched off the lights before locking the library and hastening down the shrill corridor.

Though the morning had been warm, the temperature outside came as not much less than a shock. Under a sky of a blue she wouldn't have expected to see for months it felt like spring, and inside her car it seemed close to summer. The trees around the university had stood up to last week's gales—indeed, there seemed to have been more upheaval in the forest behind Goodmanswood than anywhere else—and had been coaxed by the subsequent balmy days to let their buds appear. The world was changing, but the Sunday sound of bells reminded her of her childhood as she drove out of Brichester.

The edge of the forest was a tangle of fallen trees. Those that had sprawled onto the bypass had been cleared out of the way, though scattered twigs remained, snapping beneath the wheels with a sound and a sensation that put her in mind of treading on insects. As she drove past the Arbour she refrained from imagining how the gale and its aftermath had looked to her father's fellow patients. She rubbed at a pair of tears before accelerating away from the sight of her father's window, all too reminiscent of a frame emptied of an old photograph which had needed to vanish to make her realise how well loved it was. Then, through the confusion of entangled trees past which she was speeding, she glimpsed her mother.

She braked and peered into the mirror. Margo was examining a random arrangement of branches through the viewfinder of a camcorder. Heather reached to beep the horn and thought better of it, and wondered if she would only hinder Margo if she joined her. She was watching in the mirror as the trees closed around her mother when she almost lost control of the car, more so by clutching at the wheel. She'd seen that Margo was unaware not only of the vehicle but also of the presence at her back. It was Lennox, or a version of him.

The figure was crouching out of the shadows of a tree. It was thin as a giant withered spider or a spider's victim, and seemed to be twisted into the shape in which Lennox had given up his life. The next moment skewed trees intervened, cutting off Heather's view of the figure and of her mother.

She swerved into the first space she could find, almost running into the uprooted tree that had left the gap. She had no time to ensure her door was properly shut as a preamble to dashing the several hundred yards she'd had to put between her and her mother. Any breaths she might have used to call out to Margo were snatched by panic. A swaying lorry roared by on the far side of the otherwise deserted bypass as she clambered through a mass of leaning trees, which clawed at her with twigs and branches while bark shifted under her hands. By the time she was able to see her mother she'd made so much noise that Margo had abandoned filming to gaze in her direction, ignoring the presence at her own back.

Except that nothing was there apart from a bunch of branches sprouting low on a tree. Their shape was sufficiently reminiscent of Heather's final sight of Lennox to explain why she'd thought it was more similar, she told herself. Shadows that had aided the illusion must have moved on, and perhaps as she'd driven past the Arbour she had been reminded of the unrestrained comments that had brought the funeral to an end. She tried to finish off with a smile whatever expressions her face had been betraying as Margo said "Well, that was some entrance. What's the alarm?"

"I didn't want to lose you."

"Not much chance of that, I should think. I ought to know my way around at my age."

"I'm sure you do," Heather couldn't very well not say. "I was passing and I saw you but I had to carry on till I found somewhere to park. Am I interrupting?"

"I'm done for today," Margo said in a forgiving tone and held up the bagged camera. "You'll have to see what I've made. You'll be amazed how much this changes things."

Heather glanced at the clump of branches. Their outlines were absolutely precise under the bright clear sky, just as they'd looked when they had appeared to take her father's shape. For the merest instant she had the impression that the phenomenon had reproduced itself elsewhere, but scanning the area showed her only the web of trees. "How?" she said.

"Colours, perspectives, even what you can see and what you can't if you play with the exposure. I had it looking like the middle of the night before, and you couldn't be sure what was there."

"Is that good?"

"I'm certain it's better than anything I've been doing recently. It's giving me more ideas than I've had since whenever. Maybe I should come back in the middle of the night and see what I can make that look like."

"Do you think that would be—"

"Oh, Heather, don't take me so seriously," Margo said with a grin so wry she might have been sharing it not only with Heather. "I'm just trying to show you how many ideas I'm getting."

"I hope the rest are better than that one." Unless Heather's expression conveyed the response, she kept it to herself. "So long as it's working for you," she said aloud.

"You can buy shares in that, and I'll tell you one more thing—it's what Lennox would have wanted."

Heather kept her gaze on Margo's face and told herself there was nowhere else around them she need look. "I wouldn't have expected that to mean so much to you."

"Forgive me, Heather, I don't think you like me to say this, so let me try and put it positively. Maybe not having as much imagination as the rest of the family is one of your strengths."

"Then I'd better hang onto how I am," Heather said stiff-mouthed.

"That's right, don't you change. I'm sure none of us would want you to."

Heather did her best to meet that with a smile before ridding them of the subject. "Where are you parked?"

"At home."

"You're saying you've walked all this way through the woods?"

"I still can when I want to. It's only an hour's walk," Margo said, then glanced at her watch. "Well, okay, maybe I was more. Shows how many ideas it was giving me that I didn't notice."

"Would you like me to run you home?"

"That would make me happy. We can talk a while longer."

Heather went second so as to assist Margo over any difficulty, but of the two of them her mother appeared to be more at home in the woods. Heather saw the surrounding trees rearrange their positions without moving, as if in a slow secret dance. Whenever she held onto a tree to clamber over it she felt the bark shift or prepare to shift, and remembered how the Christmas tree had seemed to change in her grasp. She opened the passenger door for Margo before hurrying around the car to shut herself in and send it fast into the road. "So where were you coming from?" Margo said.

"Work. Well, not work, but the library."

"Good to hear you're so fond of your job," Margo said as if she didn't quite have time to attend to Heather's words. "Is your sister any nearer finding one yet?"

"Not that she's told me. I don't know if she's looking very hard."

"She'll have too much on her mind, I expect. You'll remember how it can be, and of course she has a book to work on."

Heather remembered staying at work until Sam's imminence had bundled her off to the hospital on Mercy Hill, but she could see no point in arguing. "She isn't costing too much to feed, is she?" Margo said.

"Not much at all."

"That sounds like too little when she's no longer just herself."

"I can't stand over her and shove it in her mouth. I could never make her do anything she didn't want to do."

"Maybe she's afraid of being too much of a burden on the household, what with Sam not having much of a job either. Don't tell her in case she feels obligated, but I'll help. Make whatever tempts her and a lot of it."

"Don't leave yourself short," Heather said, hoping she didn't sound jealous.

"You haven't told me yet why you were at work. Okay, before you correct me, not at work."

"I was trying to find out why dad kept saying Selcouth."

"And did you?"

"He was someone who used to live round here."

"That's all you discovered."

"No," Heather admitted and used a glance in Margo's direction to convince herself that only the depths of the woods were appearing to pace the car. "The story goes that he was some kind of, I suppose the term would be a black magician. You can still see the ruins of his house. That's where we found dad and the others the night he led them over the road."

"Will you be telling Sylvia?"

"Why, don't you think I should?"

"I can't see why I'd think that. It'll just be another reason for her to go in the woods."

Heather's dismay at realising this hadn't occurred to her must have been apparent, because Margo said more sharply "You haven't been trying to put her off again, have you?"

"I think I've given up."

"She'll be glad. You can respect her feelings even if you don't understand them."

"Fine, her feelings are her own affair, but I'm not so sure I like her involving Sam in them."

Margo turned a gaze on her that Heather could feel on her cheek. "Being sympathetic won't do him any harm."

"Maybe I'm afraid she'll ask too much of him."

"That wouldn't be like Sylvia, would it? I'd say she asks too little of any of us." Margo kept gazing at Heather, less intensely now. "Don't feel excluded because they've grown close," she said.

"I don't," Heather felt compelled to say as the forest hid behind the first houses of Goodmanswood. In a couple of minutes she halted the car in front of the tall broad house, once a magistrate's, of which Margo occupied the top half. "Want to come up and talk some more?" Margo said.

Just now Heather wasn't anxious to renew the confusion she'd experienced on visiting Margo's studio last week. Those of Margo's carvings that hadn't been included in the London exhibition were as vital as ever—far more so than anything in the retrospective had seemed. Heather had been unable to pin down an impression that the effect derived from some relationship between the shapes of the carvings and that of the forest visible over the roofs. "I'd better get back and see what they're up to," she said.

Before the words had finished escaping her she wished she had chosen them better. "I'll pass on your love," she added, squeezing Margo's hand as it supported her mother off the passenger seat and out of the car. Once she'd watched Margo withdraw into the house with a wave that looked either tentative or unfinished, she drove home.

Several houses along the route were caged with scaffolding while their roofs were repaired after the gale. Hers had needed only a few slates replacing, and Margo's had survived intact. Sometimes the oldest things were the strongest, she thought, hoping that was true of her mother. She coasted along Woodland Close to the accompaniment of distant church bells that sounded as though they were tumbling down a possibly bottomless hollow. She stopped the car outside her gate, then eased the door shut rather than slamming it as she climbed out. Half of the gate was open, and a woman was peering into the house.

Despite the heat, she wore a mousy overcoat that looked at the very least second-hand. Much of her black curly hair was sprouting from a pair of rubber bands placed rather less than symmetrically on either side of her head. Her hands were pressed against the glass as she peered into the living-room. The object resting on her insteps was not a dog but a shabby shoulder bag. "Hello?" Heather enquired as she unbolted the other half of the gate.

She had to step forward and repeat herself before the woman twisted her top half around, leaving grey handprints to fade from the pane. She looked younger than Heather, though her face was pale and creased as crumpled paper and not much less scrawny than its bones. "Nobody's home," she said in a high fast Californian voice.

"I am."

This earned Heather a scrutiny that narrowed the woman's left eye even more than the right. "I guess you could be her sister," she allowed at last. "You're a bit alike."

"Glad to hear it. I take it we've spoken before."

"I don't know about that," the woman said, and squeezed her left eye shut while staring at Heather from beneath her raised right eyebrow. "You don't sound too much like anyone I spoke to."

"Blame the phone. You're Merilee, aren't you?"

"Suppose I am?"

Heather chose to be amused rather than offended by her wariness. "Then you can more than suppose I'm Heather, Sylvie's sister."

"Whose?"

"We've been through this. Sylvie. Sylvia. Sylvia Price."

Merilee tried closing her right eye and widening the left before she admitted with some reluctance "Okay, so maybe we did speak. I have to be careful with people I don't know."

Heather wasn't about to ask why. She parked the Civic beside Sam's car while Merilee resumed pressing her hands against the window. Heather was only starting to climb out of the car when Merilee turned, palms squeaking across the glass. "Can I wait?"

"You might need not to be in a hurry."

"Well, I am. I have to fly back to the States tonight. It's the end of my vacation."

"You'll have left your luggage somewhere, then."

"Everything I have is safe," said Merilee as though Heather wanted to learn too much.

Heather inserted her key in the front door but didn't turn it. "Did Sylvia know you were coming?"

"Why would she have gone out if she had?"

Though Heather was tempted to answer that, it seemed more important to discover "So if you haven't been in touch with her, how did you know where to find us?"

"Asked."

"Asked . . ."

"People who know you. Seems like anyone round here does."

"You'd better come in," Heather said and was aware of sounding bent on hiding the visitor from the neighbours. She pushed the door open and saw a page from a message pad lying on the stairs. She was reaching for it when Merilee, having followed almost on her heels, demanded "Who's that about?"

Her wariness was so apparent that Heather felt bound to show her the note. *Sam's taken me walking*, it said. *You know where. Back while it's light.* Merilee performed the routine with her eyes as though to parody the unease Heather was experiencing, then grimaced. "I can't wait that long."

"Would you like to leave a message?"

"I didn't say I wouldn't wait."

Heather considered that she had, and didn't think Merilee was entitled to sound so resentful. She stepped over the bag Merilee had planted on the carpet and closed the front door. Hospitality required her to add "Come and sit down. I take it you've walked some way."

Merilee let her continue assuming that and trudged after her into the front room, where she glanced sharply about as if in search of some item either she or Heather couldn't see. She arranged herself in the exact centre of the couch, resting the bag against her toes and yanking her coat over a bony knee that had momentarily exposed itself. "Can I offer you something to drink?" Heather said.

"Water. I'll get it," Merilee told her, grabbing the bag.

She scrutinised the glass she was handed in the kitchen until Heather wouldn't have been astonished to receive it back unused and with some rebuke too. Merilee ran the cold tap for at least half a minute before chancing a third of a glassful, which she carried into the front room and set on the floor as a preamble to a detailed recreation of her previous ritual of seating herself. Heather sat opposite and did her best not to watch too closely, even when Merilee unzipped her bag a scant few inches and dug two gnawed fingers through the gap to extract a pillbox. Snapping off the plastic cap, she shook a piebald capsule onto her palm and zipped the pillbox into the bag before feeding herself just enough water to send the capsule down. This done, she gazed defiantly at Heather, who was searching for a neutral subject of conversation when Merilee said "Is she still better?"

It was instantly clear to Heather that she had to seem to know what she was being asked and to choose her words with extreme care despite the sudden tightness in her guts. "Why wouldn't she be?" she risked saying.

"She came back here."

"She did."

Merilee's left eye began to pucker, and Heather was afraid she'd revealed she understood the answer less than was expected. Her words must have passed the examination, since Merilee said "She was scared to."

"I don't know why she would be."

"It was something to do with her father, wasn't it? Were they, you know, too close?"

"How do you mean?"

Merilee appeared to take Heather's sharpness as an admission. "Did he mess with her when she was a kid? I never told her, but that's what screwed me up."

"I'm sorry," Heather barely had time to say before declaring "Our father wouldn't have harmed either of us. Even if he'd wanted to, and I don't believe for a moment that he did, he never had the chance."

"Then it was some other man back here."

Heather could find nothing more informed to ask than "Who you're saying did what?"

"Maybe just called her."

"And said . . ."

"She didn't tell me that. Seems like just hearing him scared her. She said once he was mixed up with all the stories in her head and kept turning himself into people in them."

"He didn't call her on the phone, then."

At once Heather feared she'd betrayed her ignorance, but Merilee was more amused than suspicious. "Why would she have committed herself over some guy just phoning her?"

"You're right, of course," Heather said, feeling as if she'd been punched in the stomach. "Do you mind my asking how you know all this?"

"Because we shared a room. She told me a lot more than she told our doctor."

Heather's skull was clamouring with thoughts and less than thoughts, and yet she couldn't think of a response. "So where is she?" Merilee demanded.

"Out walking with my son."

"I saw that. It said you knew where."

"With any luck, on their way home by now."

"You still aren't telling me where."

"That's true. There'd be no point."

Merilee met that by trying on various shapes of her eyes. When none of them provoked a response she exposed one unsunned arm a good deal too thin for its sleeve, then glared at Heather as though holding her responsible for the absence of a wristwatch. "How long have you kept me talking?"

"Not as long as it feels like," Heather couldn't refrain from saying.

"You don't know how it feels to anyone like me. You aren't the type." Even more accusingly Merilee said "How long?"

Her intensity forced Heather to glance at her own watch. "I'm afraid I didn't check when I met you," she said, willing the woman to leave her alone with her thoughts.

"You can say what time it is now, can't you?"

"Ten to three."

"That's too late." Merilee appeared to have forgotten how to sound other than distrustful when she admitted "I don't know how long I was outside. Long enough for the shadows to come round."

She meant moved around the house by the sun, Heather thought, only to realise that Merilee might not have. "Can I run you somewhere?" she said, not least to be rid of her visitor.

"I can walk," Merilee said and demonstrated, having grabbed her bag so fast she almost knocked over the remains of the water. "I know where the bus goes from to the train. You don't need to follow me."

Heather was merely seeing her to the front door. The encounter had left her so confused that it took the sight of Sylvia's note to suggest she ought to ask "Don't you want to leave a message at least?"

Merilee stared at the note as though it might tell her how secret anything she wrote would stay. She said nothing on her way to clawing at the latch, and remained silent as she hurried to the gate, from outside which she surveyed Woodland Close altogether too hard to be looking only for Sylvia. It wasn't clear to Heather what made Merilee trust her enough to whisper "Say if I can get better, anyone can."

Heather closed her fingers around the metal bars of the gate. Their solidity was by no means as reassuring as she needed it to be. She watched Merilee tramp away, her bunches of curls wagging like unkempt antennae, her bag thumping her right side with every step and eliciting a wince so automatic it looked like a tic. Once she was gone Heather shut herself in the house, wishing Sylvia and Sam home, then not just yet. The contradictory wishes switched themselves on and off in her skull like a faulty fluorescent tube, and felt as if they were buzzing like one. They were only making it more difficult to think what she could say to her sister.

21

The Steps to the Dark

PERHAPS it wouldn't be a novel but a book of fairy tales, Sam thought, and the tale of Bosky would be one of them—of how Bosky was born in the immeasurable woods and had to see beyond. Sam didn't think a novel would be capable of incorporating all the ideas that were coming to him; the screen was more than full of those he'd typed so far. There was a black and white timbered cottage whose sections appeared to bulge away from one another as though it was an illustration in a story book, only to curve inwards like an optical illusion and then rearrange themselves with the motion of foliage in a wind. He wasn't sure what would happen to anyone who strayed into that cottage, nor to whoever thought they were heading out of the forest towards a church that revealed itself as an autumn tree in exactly the shape of a steeple deep in the woods. Or they might encounter someone in the dusk whose face grew suddenly paler and larger and blurred while the wayfarer experienced a tickling as of insects on or under the skin. Elsewhere in the woods the wanderer might feel icy drips on the back of their hand and eventually glimpse a minute translucent globe sinking into their flesh—a drop that contained their own peering reflection or else a tiny face on its way to resembling theirs. Could all these be things Bosky took for granted?

Sam was unable to grasp what that would imply. It seemed more important to record the ideas, even if he had no inkling where they were coming from—the very act of making them appear onscreen felt like continuing to dream them. Now here was the notion that if you called a name in the depths of a forest it would bring the owner of the name to you, a fancy that felt as if he'd heard it somewhere. He was trying and failing to determine if that was the case while he typed when a movement drew his attention to the window.

Nothing appeared to have stirred. Beyond the common, where every blade of the long grass seemed fixed on demonstrating its individual stillness, the elongated skeleton that was the forest looked as implanted in the bare blue sky as in the earth. January shadows reached from the edge of the woods for the town, and Sam had a sudden impression that the trees or the shadows weren't quite as they should be. He was gazing at them, and feeling as if the mass of them had advanced to settle over his mind, when he heard a chirping on the windowsill.

So that was the movement he'd noticed: the arrival of an insect outside his window. He leaned across the desk, and the microscopic chirping rose to meet him. He barely glimpsed its source before it darted away. He fell back into his chair, growing less certain by the moment that he'd seen not an insect but a bird as multicoloured as a forest and smaller than a grasshopper, with its face averted from him. As the speck of it flew towards the woods and vanished, he heard a tapping behind him.

It was at the door, but the wooden sound made him feel surrounded by the forest—by the waking dream in which he hadn't realised he was so immersed. When he called "I'm here" he might have been attempting to convince himself.

"Would you like to be elsewhere?" Sylvia said.

"I might."

He heard the door inch open. "Is it okay for me to come in?" she murmured.

"There's nothing you can't see."

He didn't sense how close she was until her fingertips perched on his shoulders. "I didn't know you were busy," she said.

"I think it's gone for now."

She was silent while she read the screen, perhaps longer. "You'll be like me before you know it, Sam."

"Nothing wrong with that, is there?" he had to say.

"So long as Heather doesn't think so," said Sylvia and brought her musky perfume closer. "If you call someone in a wood they'll come to you—that's a really old belief. Maybe we should try."

Not only the fallen or leaning trees alongside the common put him in mind of the night of the gale, when he and Sylvia had watched the forest reshape itself in the violent dark. Once again he felt as though the woods were a secret they shared without understanding it, certainly in his case and, he suspected, hers too. "Who would you call?" he said.

"Nobody you couldn't bear to see. Nobody at all if you don't care for the idea, but I do feel like walking over there today. Would you want to walk with me?"

"I should," he said and shut down the computer. "You oughtn't to be in there alone."

He was saying that because she was pregnant, but he felt as if he could have meant more. The notion grew no clearer as he watched his aunt find a message pad on his cluttered desk and write his mother a note, which she let fall like a leaf on the stairs. After that he could only follow her out of the house.

They used the front door rather than leave the back gate open. As they made for the common from the end of Woodland Close, the low sun sank into the clutch of the forest. "It feels like the start of more than a year, doesn't it?" Sylvia said.

She was talking about the unseasonable warmth, Sam decided—the warmth that seemed to emanate from the woods because of the position of the sun. As they tramped through the long moist grass and its underlying secret chill, she rested a hand on his arm, so lightly that he couldn't tell whether she was supporting herself or guiding him. The trees were motionless as a painting of themselves, but were their shadows on the common almost imperceptibly shifting? It must be heat-haze, he reflected as he saw the appearance retreat into the forest, causing rank after rank of trees to flicker, only to insist they hadn't stirred. By the time he and his aunt reached the edge of the forest, the restlessness had hidden in its depths. "Ready?" Sylvia said.

They were at a gap between two leaning trees whose resemblance to the columns of an ancient ruined entrance was almost too considerable. Her question made him feel about to cross a threshold vaster than he could see. "For what?" he blurted.

"For me."

"Course I am." Honesty forced him to add "How do you think you'll be?"

"Not too embarrassing, we hope. You can always walk away if I get to be too much."

He had to acknowledge that he thought Margo or his mother might be better at handling Sylvia's emotions, but that was no excuse to let her down. "I won't do that," he said.

"Then I'm as ready as you are," his aunt said as though proposing a game, and held his arm while they passed through the entrance.

Stillness closed over them at once. It felt like being caught in the web of the innumerable shadows of the woods, except that he and Sylvia were moving freely forward, not enmeshing themselves more deeply in a web. Admittedly they were forced to follow a devious route by tangles of windblown branches, quite a few of which resembled bones that had been splintered and discoloured by some process of digestion. More than one fallen tree and its scattered branches came close to shaping an entire skeleton, though Sam found he preferred not to imagine those in the flesh. His thoughts rendered the forest oppressively present around him and in particular behind him. He glanced back to see that the common was more distant and less visible than he expected; he couldn't make out the houses at all. Sylvia gripped his arm as if to recall him or distract him. "Do you feel it too?" she said.

He didn't want to own up to any unease when she must surely be on edge. "How still it is, you mean."

"That's part of it."

If that was his cue to ask about the rest, he couldn't quite, but felt compelled to search for it around him. Could she have in mind the way the yielding of the ground underfoot suggested some medium other than earth and leaves? He would have liked to see more sky than was trapped in the nets of branches. Trees kept creeping into view, but only because he was moving, and nothing else as grey and scaly and as thin or even thinner was pretending to be the same as them. He was beginning to feel he'd encountered much or all of this at some time in the past, and might he have forgotten more? He felt less than eager to remember, instead peering about for creatures like the one he'd glimpsed on his windowsill, but the trees seemed to have only themselves to offer in the way of life. He recalled that while opposing the bypass he'd seen birds fly over the woods rather than alight in them, yet the bareness of the trees revealed nests in the treetops, even if they looked composed of bones and sprouting from the trees instead of built in them. Now that he'd noticed them he saw them everywhere overhead, greenish with decay or growth. He was limping to keep up with Sylvia's determined belly-heavy trudge when she said "We're close."

"What makes you say that?"

"Can you still not feel it?"

He hoped she didn't mean what he was trying not to feel—that the yielding of the forest floor reminded him of flesh. He needn't imagine that they were walking over a face the size of the woods, a flattened face that was holding its breath while they approached its mouth. A shiver overtook him as though his body was anxious to dislodge the clinging shadows, and Sylvia renewed her grip on his arm. "Whatever you're feeling is right," she murmured.

"I doubt it."

"Don't be scared. I'm not, so why should you be?"

"I didn't say I was."

"I never am when I'm in here. Sometimes I forget that when I'm away from it, that's all."

"You must have been . . ."

"Go on, Sam."

The words were as hard to find as to speak. "The last time you were here."

"Not even then."

"Because you were drugged, you mean."

"I wish he hadn't done that. The drugs just got in the way."

Sam would have preferred not to have to ask "Of what?"

"That's the point," his aunt said, impatient with him or with herself. "I can't remember. That must have been the drugs."

"But if you can't remember . . ."

"I know it was something extraordinary. I've held onto that much," Sylvia declared, and lowered her voice. "I feel as if it may be where my whole life has been leading, Sam."

She was speaking as if she might be overheard. She mustn't be as untroubled as she'd said, and he couldn't help staring about in the hope of not seeing a reason. The nearest trees were elevating nests towards the sky as though to trap something from it. Many of the lower branches were tipped with buds whose shapes seemed oddly wrong. Before he could start to imagine what they had in store, if indeed he wanted to, his aunt said "We're here."

That was loud enough to be addressing not only him. She tramped forward as if tugged by her bulky midriff. Beyond the trees ahead of her Sam saw the centre of the woods and in its midst the low wide ring of bricks. They and the mound within them were clear of the shadows of the trees, so that the forest seemed to be focusing the sunlight on them. To Sam the mound looked far too reminiscent of a grave, especially since it had nearly been Sylvia's. He was unnerved to see her march to it and announce "This is where I was."

Sam took his time over limping to stand by her, but thought of nothing to say except "You make it sound like it was something to be pleased about."

"Don't you think not being disturbed is a reason?"

"If you aren't that's good." His voice seemed dwarfed by the stillness that felt more than ever like a breath held by a vast lung. "I mean, you aren't," he said. "I see you aren't."

"There are worse places to come to yourself."

"You're talking about now."

He might have thought the stillness had entered her until she said "Then."

Maturity required him to ask "Do you want to tell me about it?"

"I do while I remember. Maybe two of us will have more chance to keep it in our heads. I'm certain I forget things that have happened in the woods once I leave."

Sam felt as though he was risking more than he could grasp by admitting "Me too."

"I was right to make you come with me then, wasn't I?"

He didn't know whether she meant that on his behalf or her own. "So what have you remembered?" he said with some haste.

"It felt like waking up."

"Remembering did."

She giggled, a tiny high sound that part of the woods seemed to echo. "Coming back to myself. I kept thinking I was camping out and he'd tucked me up for the night. I didn't feel too bad even when I realised what he'd really done."

"You were drugged."

She paused in pacing around the ring of bricks to look frustrated.

"Once I got my hands and face out I didn't mind lying there. I could see all the trees watching me. It was like being little again."

Sam glanced at the trees, whose impassiveness was nowhere close to reassuring. "You couldn't have been under long," he tried to reassure himself. "You wouldn't have been able to breathe."

"Unless there was something I could."

He understood she had to come to terms with what she'd undergone, but she seemed almost nostalgic for it. "If you say you didn't mind lying there," he objected, "what made you get up?"

His aunt leaned over the bricks, and the middle of her loose dress swelled. "I didn't want mom worrying where I was."

She sounded so distracted she might have been saying the first thing that entered her head—perhaps less than or not even the truth. Her midriff seemed to haul her closer to the mound before she lurched across the bricks. Sam limped fast to her, thinking she'd tripped, but she had only bent towards the earth. "Look," she whispered.

Her whisper brought the stillness closer. The light the clearing isolated was so intense that the mound appeared to shine with a blackness deeper than any night sky. Protruding from it was a tattered brownish object Sam took at first to be an elongated autumn leaf. He had to stoop as low as his aunt was crouching to distinguish that the marks on it weren't just wrinkles filled with soil. They were letters in a handwriting that looked centuries old. ∤ *Nathaniel*, they said.

Sam was staring in bewilderment at this and dismissing the possibility that it was a Biblical reference when Sylvia slipped her fingertips under the fragment to pick it up, only to let out a small cry. The scrap had crumbled into pieces so minute no writing was distinguishable on them, and Sam was immediately unsure it hadn't after all been a leaf. His aunt began to straighten up, rubbing brownish flakes off her hand. Then she lowered herself to one knee and dug her fingers into the soil. "There's something else."

Sam wasn't eager to see; the spectacle of her clawing at the mound was unsettling enough. When she desisted he wondered if she'd realised how she must look, until she said "Sam, fetch a stick."

Though her tone didn't quite suggest she was talking to a pet, he resented the words. Nevertheless he couldn't refuse her, not in her condition. He must already have noticed a fallen branch at the edge of the clearing, because he limped to it at once. "The champion with his staff," said Sylvia, taking it from him to poke and scrape at the earth. "I was right," she cried.

For a moment he thought she'd uncovered only an area of the foundations—a random stretch of blackened stone. Then she thrust the branch several inches into the earth, and with an effort further still. "Here," she said, half withdrawing the branch to angle it towards him. "See what you feel."

He felt close to fearful. Rather than infect her with that, he stepped onto the mound and grabbed the branch. The exposed slab was broken, he saw; there was a jagged gap about a foot wide and packed with earth, which Sylvia had been probing. He shoved the branch into it, only to encounter at a depth of several inches an obstruction so solid it jarred his arms. He worked the stick free of it and poked deeper, and found another obstacle an equal distance beneath. Leaning on the branch let him find a third. "You know what's there, don't you?" Sylvia said eagerly.

"Steps."

"How far do you think they go down?"

"I wouldn't know."

"We'll find out, won't we?"

Whatever expression that brought to his face made her giggle loud enough to be echoed somewhere nearby. "Not now. We'll need a flashlight and a spade," she said. "Better cover it now so nobody goes down before us. We don't want them taking away anything that's there."

She watched him extract the branch and use it to spread earth over the broken slab. Once he'd finished she improved on his work before treading on the earth to obscure any traces of their presence. The sight and sounds of her trampling on the mound dismayed him so much that he was retreating towards the trees, not that they seemed likely to offer any comfort, when she said "Stay a moment."

"What is it now?" he heard himself blurt, but no echo.

"Just making sure we don't forget." Having propped the branch against the nearest tree, she found a ballpoint in her pocket and wrote on the back of her hand a message she displayed to him: SPADE LIGHT WOODS. "Now even if we forget what it means we'll know what to do," she said, apparently under the impression this would please him. It didn't, and as he turned his back on the mound to escort her through the forest he felt sure he had already forgotten something else about the place. For no reason he could bring to mind, not that he was anxious to, he felt grateful to be unable to remember.

22

Secrets

HEATHER didn't know how long she had been sitting at Sam's window to watch for his and Sylvia's return when she glimpsed movement in the woods. As she leaned across the desk, bruising her elbows on the spaces she'd cleared amid the clutter, she saw the rest of Sylvia surface from behind a tree, followed by Sam. Trees confused her view, so that the pair appeared to be retreating rather than advancing, drawn back by the woods and a haze that set tree-trunks writhing around them. She had to peer so hard her eyes ached to be certain they were emerging from the woods, though not from the out-stretched shadows. Their own shadow hitched itself on four elongated legs across the common, its two heads nodding together, a spectacle Heather found so disagreeably fascinating that she failed to move away from the window until they were halfway to Woodland Close. She didn't want to be seen waiting for them—preparing to talk to her sister.

When she arrived in the kitchen she was expecting to hear a knock at the gate. She seemed to wait altogether too long for the rasp of a key in the front-door lock. They must be footsore, she told herself as Sam called "It's us."

"Us three," said Sylvia.

How long had she looked as though her midriff was on its way to consuming her? Perhaps her voluminous dress emphasised her pregnancy, or Merilee's visit had intensified Heather's sense of her sister, not a reason she cared for. "Coffee for anyone?" she said in an attempt to pretend everything was normal. "Oh, Sam, Andy rang and wants to see you. He wouldn't say why."

"I'll drive over to his, then."

"What did we need to remember?" Sylvia reached to detain him and gazed at smudged writing on the back of her hand. "There it is," she said. "Better write it down somewhere else."

Before Heather could ask what it was, Sylvia made with ungainly haste for her room. "I ought to be home for dinner," said Sam.

"Be careful driving," Heather said automatically. As soon as she heard the Volkswagen chug into the road she called to Sylvia "Were you having that coffee?"

"I was just going to lie down for a while."

"Do you mind if I come and talk?"

"Why would I ever mind?"

Heather thought there might be a reason now. If Sylvia didn't want coffee, she didn't either: her nerves were active enough. She had yet to decide what to say once she'd climbed the stairs. Sylvia was lying on the plump green quilt overlooked by leafy wallpaper, and for an instant Heather imagined her sister prostrate on a grassy bank in a wood. There was no question that her midriff was more prominent, but it would be in that position, Heather told herself. She sat at their father's old desk and turned her back on the trees, which were extending their spidery shadows towards the house as they clutched the sun. "Was it all you hoped," she said, "your walk?"

Sylvia closed her eyes as her lips considered smiling. "I believe so."

"You feel better for it, then."

"More complete."

"Sam looked after you, did he?"

Sylvia's hands moved apart on her stomach, and Heather saw the writing on the left hand was illegible, leaving the skin to look grubby or bruised. "I wouldn't want to do anything in there without him," Sylvia said.

"Good for Sam," Heather said with more enthusiasm than she felt. "So what was so important that you wrote it on yourself?"

Sylvia squeezed her eyes tight, and Heather didn't know if she was trying to hide from the question or remember. "Just a message," said Sylvia.

"Is it a secret?"

"Maybe till I've followed it up."

"Don't let me stop you coming to terms." When Sylvia's face accepted this without a trace of an expression, Heather took a preparatory breath. "I've got to apologise," she said.

"You shouldn't," said Sylvia, and let her sleepy gaze find Heather. "You've gone nowhere near upsetting me."

"I don't mean about now."

"Now or for a long while. As a matter of fact I can't remember when you last did. You needn't try so hard not to if it's a strain. Just tell me if having to be my big sister gets to be too much."

"I don't see how it could," Heather said, telling herself that included now. "The thing I have to apologise for, I forgot to give you a message."

"When was that?"

"The day we lost dad."

"Then I'm not surprised you forgot, and stop apologising. What was the message?"

"Someone you knew in America was trying to get in touch. Someone you shared a room with."

"Any more to it?"

"Merilee."

"Right," Sylvia said, her lids beginning to veil her eyes. "I remember her."

"I should think you would. She was here today looking for you."

Sylvia's eyes stopped just short of closing. "Is she coming back?"

"I imagine she's well on her way to the airport by now."

"She's been wanting to travel for a long time. She thinks everywhere in the States is either too fast or it's too slow. She's looking for somewhere with enough history that it feels stable to her."

"I don't care about her, Sylvie. I care about you."

"I hope she finds somewhere," Sylvia said with a hint of defiance, and continued to show little of her eyes. "Did you talk much?"

"Enough."

"So what did she say about me?"

"How you met and where you were." Sylvia's reduced gaze strayed past Heather, who wanted to launch herself from the chair and grab her sister's hands. Instead she protested "I thought we weren't going to have secrets from each other."

"Maybe nobody can share everything they are. Maybe they shouldn't." As Sylvia opened her eyes to see if the answer had satisfied Heather, she resembled a child playing a game. "I wouldn't have minded telling you," she said. "I think you can handle it if I have. I just didn't want mom worrying I'd started to end up like dad."

"Did you?"

Sylvia giggled so hard that Heather thought she heard a tiny fleeting echo at her back. "Come on," Sylvia said. "Have I been acting like him?"

"You both have a thing about the woods. I mean, he had and you have."

"You're saying it has to be the same thing."

"I don't know if you keep secrets, do I? All right, that isn't fair. I know what you're having to deal with, but that isn't why you were in hospital with that woman."

"No need to make it sound as if it was her fault. She had a whole lot of problems, that's all."

"I just don't like the idea of you sharing a room with someone like her."

Heather heard herself sounding jealous as well as concerned—perhaps that was why Sylvia risked a faint smile. "It's okay, Heather. You can't catch someone else's mental problems just by living with them, so I hear."

Both the smile and the remark angered Heather enough that she said "So what did you need to be cured of?"

"Nothing."

"That isn't . . ."

"Go on. You keep saying we shouldn't have secrets."

"You must have been in hospital for some reason."

"That isn't what you stopped saying."

"I was going to tell you your friend said there was a reason."

"I don't know why you'd believe her when you think she's such a crazy bitch."

"I didn't say that, did I? That doesn't sound like me."

"Only thought it."

Heather stood up so fast that Sylvia visibly held herself still in order not to react, even when Heather sat on the bed and began to stroke her sister's forehead. "All I'm getting at," Heather said, not that it was, "is you must have felt you needed help."

"I just needed to sort myself out, and hospital seemed like a good place."

"What needed sorting?"

"Material for my next book. Too much of it going round and round in my head while I was trying to earn a living with jobs. You're lucky not having to write."

"Are you working on it now?"

"My mind's full of Natty right now. I guess it will be till he appears, and after that, who knows."

"If he's anything like Sam he'll be your world for a while."

"I won't have a problem with that. Are you happy now?"

Heather would have liked to be able to lie. "Not altogether, Sylvie."

"Go on then," Sylvia cried and sat abruptly up. "Tell me what Merilee said, since you want to so much."

Her movement brought her midriff into contact with Heather's hand. The baby was as still as the forest where the night was taking shape. "I only want what's best for you," Heather said.

"So finish with Merilee."

"She said you heard somebody calling you home."

"You think I didn't?"

"I'll believe you if you say you did."

"You know I did," Sylvia said, gazing past her at the oncoming dark. "That's what made me come home."

"Then why did you need—"

"To put myself in the hospital? You know, sometimes I have to agree with mom that you could use a bit more imagination. Maybe if you thought you heard a voice that wouldn't stop till you did what it said you'd go on tranquillisers too."

"You're saying that's all."

"I had to tell them I was cured of all sorts of stuff before I could leave."

Heather wanted to believe that, and surely it must be the truth. Nevertheless she didn't know what she was opening her mouth to say when the doorbell rang. "Are you going to get that?" Sylvia said.

"Do you want me to?"

"It's your house."

"I'd better see who it is," Heather said and made for her room. She felt uncomfortably like a child with a guilty secret when she retreated from the window before murmuring "It's mother."

Sylvia headed her off at the top of the stairs. She held out her hands but stopped short of touching Heather, who had the odd irrational notion that the unborn child had intervened between them. "Are you going to tell her what we've been talking about?" Sylvia said.

A stranger would have thought her blank gaze meant she didn't care. "You haven't stored up any more surprises," Heather said with more lightness than she was expecting to discover in herself.

"If I have they'll be good ones."

"She won't find out otherwise, will she?"

"Not from me."

"She's been upset enough. Let's remind her she still has most of her family. Even more of one now," Heather amended, and led the way downstairs.

Margo was extending a finger to the bellpush. When she stepped back Heather thought she was recoiling until the smile Margo produced made it clear that she'd wanted more of a view of her daughters. "I feel better already," she said.

"Than what, mummy?"

Margo only blinked at that on the way to scrutinising Sylvia, and Heather felt doubly ignored. "How's Sylvia?" Margo said.

Since the question could have been addressed to either of her children, neither responded at once. It was both the silence and realising Sylvia was waiting for her to keep her word that made Heather blurt "Pretty well as she looks."

"Only pretty well?"

"I'm fine, mom. Just feel as if my insides are bigger than I am."

"That's exactly how I felt when I was having you. And how's Heather?"

Since her sister seemed unlikely to reply on her behalf, Heather said "Staying on top of things."

"And taking care of everyone as usual. That'll always be our Heather, won't it, Sylvia?"

"You bet."

Heather was feeling not so much complimented as sentenced when

Margo said "I'd sing a carol except it's too late, so do I get to sit and maybe talk?"

Once the three were seated facing one another in the front room she seemed content to draw breaths deep enough to pass for sighs. Even if they weren't designed to provoke a question, Heather hadn't stopped wanting an answer. "You were going to tell us why you needed cheering up," she said.

"Was I?"

This could have been an appeal to Sylvia, who admitted "I thought so too."

"You don't want to let an old lady's problems bother you."

"You're not old, and of course we do. We'll only worry more if you don't tell us. You don't want Sylvia doing that in her state."

Heather saw her sister resist glancing at her to be sure what state she had in mind. Both of them eyed Margo until she tried on a wry grin that didn't fit her words. "Everything's come to bits at the exhibition."

"What's anyone been saying now?" Heather demanded.

"No, I mean literally. The exhibition's finished, and when Lucinda and her people started moving my pieces they fell apart. The pieces, not the people."

As the attempt at humour made Heather's eyes feel big with moisture, Sylvia said "Was anything inside them?"

"Insects, you mean, like the ones I'm famous for now if I'm famous for anything. None that anyone could see, Lucinda said."

"So what's she going to do?" Heather said with more anger than she could contain.

"I've told her to junk it all. By the sound of it that's all it's worth."

"Aren't you at least going to take a look first?"

"I know it wouldn't mean anything to me, Heather."

Heather was too dismayed not to say "But it's years of your work."

"Years of learning what I should be doing instead, and now I am."

"That's one hundred percent positive of you, mom."

Heather was less persuaded that it wasn't unacknowledged desperation. "How much responsibility is Lucinda taking?"

"Her insurance company will be looking at the damage, but you can guess their argument will be the problem was in the wood and not the gallery. According to Lucinda it all looked as if it had rotted from within."

Sylvia clasped her hands over her stomach. She might have been taken to be praying if she hadn't said "They'll have heard about the insects."

"That'll be part of their argument for sure."

As the last to be positive, Heather had a try. "Nothing's gone wrong with your pictures, has it?"

"No, they'll be coming back to me. I'll still have them if nobody buys them, and remember I'm a video artist now. I'll have to show you the results soon, though nothing I make in the woods is anywhere near as important as our forthcoming event."

Sylvia crouched over the cage of her fingers. "Hear that, Natty?" she whispered. "Grandma's anxious to see you."

A sound not unlike a scratching of fingernails seemed to respond. At first Heather couldn't locate it, perhaps because she wasn't expecting to hear it so soon. As the key was withdrawn from the lock and the front door shut with a muted thud she called "Is that you, Sam?"

Since he was the only candidate, she couldn't blame him for answering with barely a syllable. "You weren't long at Andy's," she said.

"Long enough."

He was heading for his room when Margo called "Aren't you going to say hi to me?"

"Hi." He sounded willing to leave it at that, but relented and produced a dutiful smile as well as himself. "Hi," he said without much variation.

"What did Andy want?" Heather took the opportunity to ask.

A shrug and a terse laugh or at least an expulsion of breath let her guess the answer before he said "Just to tell me he's closing the shop. Closed it, actually. I don't know why he couldn't have told you instead of making me drive over."

"Never mind, Sam. More time for us to walk in the woods," Sylvia said.

"I expect Sam will be out looking for jobs," said Heather, not too heavily, she hoped. "I know Terry would want that too."

Perhaps her mentioning his father betrayed how concerned she was. Margo broke the awkward silence by saying "Can't Sam do both?"

"If he can't I expect you could walk with Sylvie."

The silence this provoked was longer still, apparently because Margo was choosing her words, though Heather didn't think much of her choice. "Don't try to make him less than he can be, Heather. We all ought to be doing everything we can to stay close."

She either took Heather's muteness for assent or ignored her inability to trust herself to speak. "Have you been back in there yet?" she asked Sylvia.

"We were today."

"How did you find it?"

"I feel like I could go in any time."

"That has to be nothing but good, doesn't it, Heather? We want her to be whole before she has to concentrate on being a mother."

From the size of her sister's midriff, Heather could have thought that would be sooner than it had any right to be. "I don't think I'll need to go back many more times," Sylvia said, "thanks to Sam."

"Thank you, Sam," Margo said, and aggravated his uneasiness by taking his hand. "So stop worrying about them, Heather. If I can you can."

Heather felt her lips open and was unable to predict what she would say. She had the impression this might be her last chance not to be alone with everything she'd learned from Merilee. She saw her sister splay her fingers on her midriff as though its occupant was threatened, and that swayed her. "I'll do my best," she said, and glimpsed the fleeting smile Sylvia gave her. It must be meant as gratitude, but she felt as if they were children again, hiding from their mother in the woods.

23

The Cells

"HAVE you remembered?" Sylvia said.

Sam had to separate her murmur from the other sounds of the forest. The notion of having to turn up a memory connected with the woods brought him unexpectedly close to panic. "How about you?" he said in an attempt to fend it off.

"I remembered when we were on the common."

"That's all right then," he said without the least idea whether it was.

"But you know why we're here too."

He raised the spade that kept letting him down as a walking-stick. "Not much we can use this for except digging."

"You know what, though."

He'd known as soon as he'd left the common, but could have done without referring aloud to the prospect while the wind that was invisibly at large in the woods made everything restless, the multitude of trees and shadows describing passes over one another that looked magical—that he could have imagined were designed to lure him and his aunt deeper into the forest. "Steps," he nevertheless said.

"They're our secret for now, but I'm looking forward to sharing whatever we find with the others, aren't you?"

"It's only a secret because we forgot it. How can you take that for granted?"

"I don't see what else we can do with it. There are stranger things in the world."

If she was about to tell him more of her tales, the possibility failed to appeal to him. "I believe you," he said quickly.

That silenced her, and she contented herself with holding onto his arm. The lack of conversation only aggravated his awareness of the sounds around them. Behind the cawing of branches as the trees tossed their spiky faceless heads, the huge irregular breaths of the forest resembled a blurred voice close to forming words. Sam dug the edge of the spade into the ground he was limping over, in case the act could drive away an impression of walking on a substance more alive than it appeared to be. When the clearing appeared beyond the trees, he didn't know if he was relieved that it would bring him into the open and the sensation perhaps to an end.

There was no question how the sight affected Sylvia. She strode forward, pulling at his arm, as the woods muttered around them and snatched at the sky. Yards short of the clearing she let go of him and hurried ahead, only to halt at the ring of bricks. "Someone's been here," she complained, and then her resentment faltered. "Or something has."

The glare of the unseasonably hot mid-morning sun caught at Sam's eyes as he ventured to join her. He had to blink and use his free hand as an eyeshade in order to see that the patch of the mound he remembered her tramping smooth had been not disturbed but altered. It had acquired a covering of leaves, an almost perfect square of them that appeared to contain an elaborate pattern. Before he could distinguish it, the leaves raised themselves in unison as though scenting the newcomers and swarmed off the mound, scuttling away to add themselves to the gestures of the woods. "They were just leaves," Sylvia said.

Sam peered across the clearing but could no longer identify the withered brownish fragments. He was in danger of growing entranced by the dance of trees and shadows, which looked cryptically ritualistic, when his aunt said "Ready to dig?"

He wasn't, but he didn't think he ever would be. "Here I go," he mumbled, and stepped over the bricks to clear earth off the surface under the mound. Sooner than he liked he finished exposing a stone slab, pallid where it wasn't blackened, about three feet square and lacking a large portion of one corner. He thrust the spade into the gap to the length of half the blade, and it fetched up against an obstruction that sent a shiver through his arms and then through him. "We'll never get through there," Sylvia protested. "You need to lift it up."

Sam dropped the spade and dug his fingers under the broken edge. Earth gritted beneath his nails as he hauled at the slab. An ache spread from his shoulders to his skull, and he felt as if the clamour of the trees was invading his consciousness. Either it or tension almost deafened him before he straightened up. "Won't move," he gasped.

"Let me help."

"You don't want to strain yourself." He was aware of sounding even more like Margo or his mother as he said "Think of the baby."

"Natty would want me to help," Sylvia said, and crouched as though urged by the presence she'd named. "Try again, Sam."

When she poked her fingers under the slab he had to come to her aid. He rammed the spade past the broken edge and leaned all his weight on the shaft. In a moment he felt Sylvia adding her efforts to his, and then the blade started to bend. "No use," he panted, so relieved that he even managed to feign frustration.

"Once more."

Her voice was so low that he could have imagined she was addressing somebody other than him, especially since she was gazing downward. So long as lifting the obstruction was beyond them it would do no harm to indulge her. He tramped the spade deeper and levered at the slab until the blurred sounds of the forest seemed to close around him as though the trees were leaning towards the mound and chorusing encouragement. He saw his aunt's arm begin to shiver with exertion, and opened his mouth to suggest they had tried hard enough. At that moment the slab reared up.

Perhaps the final effort had dislodged the earth that had been tamped around its edge, but it felt to Sam as though the slab was being raised from beneath. He would have let go of the spade if that mightn't have left his aunt supporting the slab. He fell to his knees as the spade pivoted almost horizontal and the slab balanced on its far edge for a moment before thudding against the height of the mound. The opening it had revealed was full of earth. Sam found the sight so ominous that it seemed he might reassure himself by saying "You couldn't have been here, could you? You couldn't have got through."

"I must have been close, though, and you know what I think?"

"What?" Sam would rather not have said.

"Suppose he didn't want to bury me? Suppose he just wanted me to go down there?"

How that could please her was beyond Sam, unless she was more like her father than anyone cared to admit. "Don't stop now," she pleaded. "Make a way for us."

He wanted to refuse but couldn't think of a reason; his mind was overwhelmed by a shapeless mass of sound, the voice of the forest. He began to dig in something of a frenzy, flinging earth onto the canted slab until Sylvia intervened. "We may want to put that back," she said.

His bad leg was eager to demonstrate new ways to ache from treading on the spade. His shoulders seemed bent on giving the leg more ideas while clamminess that felt mixed with grit was well on the way to covering the whole of him. He disinterred one step and then another, and saw how they wound downwards. The second was partly blocked by the rest of the slab. He only wished it had made further progress impossible, but most of the earth in the hole had lodged against it, leaving the route all too clear. He was gazing unhappily at the blackness into which the steps led when Sylvia ran down the two steps to hug him. "Well done, Sam."

When she smiled in his face he felt trapped—by her, by the narrow reddish passage that surrounded their calves, by the trees that creaked like a jaw in the process of rediscovering its use. The pressure of her swollen midriff against him brought him close to panic, as did her moist breath in his ear. He was suddenly terrified of being overtaken by an erection. "Will you go first?" she murmured.

At least that gave him an excuse to free himself and climb onto the mound. "I don't think either of us should."

"No need to be scared, Sam."

"I'm not," he said as a shiver—only an aftershock of his toil, he wanted to believe—travelled through him. "I just think we should have some more people with us."

"Think how long this may have been hidden. Don't you want us to be the first living people to see?"

"It mightn't be safe."

"Only one way to find out, and someone has to." A blink ended her disappointed look, and she produced a flashlight from a pocket of her loose denim overalls. "You could hold this while I go through," she said.

He saw there was no overcoming her determination. He tried to hold the flashlight steady while she planted her hands on the dis-coloured reddish walls and eased herself past the leaning chunk of the slab. She looked as though her midriff was dragging her through the gap. "Thanks," she said briskly as her swollen shadow wobbled down-ward, and held out a hand.

Sam passed her the flashlight and watched her descend, her free hand supporting her on the left wall. She didn't have to do this, he told himself. He'd tried his best to dissuade her, but she was more than old enough to know her own mind. Below her the light wavered as if betraying a nervousness she refused to admit, and then it shrank around the curve of the narrow passage, tugging her after it. Within seconds there was no trace of her except a faint illumination that van-ished into the depths. He couldn't even hear her footsteps for the triumphant roaring of the forest. He was about to call to her when she spoke. "Here's the first thing."

Perhaps it was only the subterranean passage that made her voice seem too low to be addressing him. "What?" he blurted, and heard the mound swallow the question.

"You'll have to see for yourself."

He felt his lips part well before they managed to pronounce "I'll need some light."

The darkness at the limit of his vision remained unrelieved long enough for him to wonder if she'd misunderstood him. Then a faint glow crept around the bend onto the dimmest of the steps. He was taking the light away from his aunt, he thought; he was leaving her and her baby in the dark. Disgust with himself sent him down the steps, pressing a hand against the rough damp wall as he edged past the fallen chunk of the slab. The surrounding trees seemed to crane to watch before they cleared the sky for the sun. Its light and their crowing dwindled as he hurried down to Sylvia, and he hadn't reached the glow of the flashlight when it began to withdraw from him. He took a breath to ask her to illuminate the steps, only to inhale a smell of something like decay but sweeter. By the time he expelled the worst of it he'd turned the curve, and her light was waiting for him.

Or rather, most of it was beyond a doorway off the steps. Just enough of it remained in the passage to show him that the wall above the doorway had at some time been blackened by a fire. It showed him his aunt's face too, intent on the room beyond the doorway. Nevertheless as he reached the step above her she swung the beam towards him, so that he barely glimpsed a shape huddled against the far wall of the room. He had a sudden uneasy suspicion that she was checking that he was who she expected. "I'm glad you decided to be brave," she said.

"Let's see, then," he urged, because having to imagine what was there might be even worse.

Sylvia shone the beam through the doorway at once. Sam had the impression that the darkness was refusing to give way until he saw that the walls and low ceiling and even the bare stone floor were charred. The room was sufficiently extensive that the light grew fainter by the time it touched the far wall. About midway along the stone curve the solitary contents of the room had shrunk into the angle of the wall and floor, perhaps in a vain attempt to escape the fire. Its arms and legs were bunched together as if it had been struggling to return to not having been born. It was merely a skeleton smaller than a man's, but any reassurance that might have offered was negated by its shape. Sam tried to tell himself that the bones had been distorted as well as darkened by the fire, but there were too many of them, by no means all familiar. The skull was the worst, because it was nearly human. Sam might have attempted to believe that it had somehow been robbed of a mouth by the fire, but that could hardly explain the eye sockets, which were more than twice the size they should have been in proportion to the skull.

Sylvia was watching him with an eagerness he didn't like at all. "What do you think it is?"

"Was," he corrected, and tried not to imagine meeting the creature in whatever flesh it might once have had. Could anyone have encountered it crawling on all fours up the steps, its huge eyes swelling out of the dark? Or would they have met it loping upright through the woods or peering around the trees? What expression would they have seen above the absence of a mouth? "We'll never know," he said, willing that to put a stop to his thoughts.

"Do you think it's what he wanted me to see?"

"How could it be?" Sam protested, and made himself turn away from the room to frown at her.

"You're right, there has to be more. Let's go find it," his aunt said and pointed the light down the steps.

Darkness rushed across the room and through the doorway to join the darkness at Sam's back. Just a few steps up would take him into daylight, but how could he abandon his pregnant aunt down here? Her condition was affecting her judgement, he thought—there could surely be no other explanation for her enthusiasm. He might have said as much, but the illumination had already ushered her around the bend below him. When he followed, it felt altogether too much like hurrying to outdistance the dark and the misshapen skeleton. As he caught up with the edge of the light it halted, and he was able to believe it was waiting for him until he saw that Sylvia had found another room.

She kept the light out of it until he ventured down to her, and so he was able to observe that the wall above the doorway was scorched. Anything beyond it must have burned, he told himself, but that didn't help him breathe as Sylvia sent the beam into the room. It was much like the first one: the same size and shape, and as blackened. Its occupant lurched forward from the far wall as the light discovered it, but only shadows were rousing themselves. Their prone source was dead and charred and fleshless, which offered little in the way of relief. If the remains of its face had been turned away Sam might have thought it had once been a child with an outsize head. Its long legs were drawn up almost to the elongated chin, and its hands were clenched on the ankles. All this made it seem dismayingly human, even if it had far more teeth than enough. Sam did his best to persuade himself that most of the round holes in the upper half of the skull could hardly have contained eyes, but he didn't know if any other possibility might be worse.

Sylvia had returned to watching him. He faced her in a rage that was both provoked by and attempting to overcome his dread. Before he could demand what she was looking for, she reached up to cross out his lips with a finger. "Did you hear it?" she whispered.

When she released his lips they almost didn't work. "What?" he barely said.

"Something further down."

"What?" he felt worse than stupid for repeating.

"Moving about," said Sylvia, aiming the flashlight down the steps as though to summon whatever was there.

"If there's anything it'll be rats."

She flashed him a reproachful grimace of the kind a child might give someone who'd attempted to rob them of a belief. "We'll find out," she said, and followed the light.

For a painful heartbeat the idea that it was about to discover or call forth something at large in the dark paralyzed Sam, and then the notion of her encountering that by herself sent him after her, into a luminous stone cell whose walls and ceiling he would have been able to touch—a cell that jerked downwards, dragging him deeper with each step his aunt took. A hint of decay and sweetness drifted up, one of the reasons he was holding his breath when the beam fell on another stretch of charred wall. Sylvia hurried down to send the light through the doorway below it, and he saw her mouth widen in shock.

He had to force himself to peer around the doorway. While the sight beyond it seemed to bear no immediate relation to his fears, it failed to do away with them. In the middle of another curved stone room stood a jagged black pile several feet high. At first he thought it had been composed of bodies or parts of bodies, and then he identi- fied the objects that resembled bones protruding from the mass as the spines of old—very old—books. He was taken aback to hear Sylvia murmur "That's awful."

"What is?" Sam responded, barely audibly.

"Can't you see?" she said with unexpected fierceness. "Just imagine how much knowledge may have been destroyed."

"Depends what kind, doesn't it?"

"No, it doesn't. If you don't have knowledge you have ignorance. I thought you were supposed to be working on a book."

That struck him as so inappropriate that he wondered how little sense she had of the situation they were in. If the contents of the books had been in any way connected with the creatures whose remains he'd seen, he was glad the volumes had been reduced to lumps of ash. He was about to say as much when Sylvia advanced into the room.

Darkness flooded down the steps and up them to close around Sam, but he wasn't anxious to follow her and feel even more trapped. He watched her stoop to the heap of ash and pull out remnants of bindings. "Of the embodiment of the spirit of a place," she intoned, "of the raising of the dead," and he realised she was reading titles or translating them aloud. None of the spines retained more than charred scraps of pages. Sam wished she wouldn't concentrate so much of the light on examining them, especially when he heard something dart out from the far side of the heap. His aunt swung the light after it in time to catch a whitish shape the size of a man's hand vanishing into a hole at the foot of the wall. "Like you were saying, just a rat," she said, turning herself and the beam towards the doorway with a smile he thought was intended to convince not only him. Then the beam jerked to one side of him, and he took her to have noticed something he couldn't see within the room until he heard a sound behind him.

It was a scratching, a scrabbling. It sounded as if the cause of it was digging something up, perhaps itself. It was below him, but in the confined space he couldn't judge how near it was. His aunt hurried forward, thrusting her midriff at him, to search with the light. Sam never knew what prompted him—desperation, disgust with his own passivity, a last attempt to protect her by at least intervening between her and whatever was to be encountered—to snatch the flashlight and thrust the beam into the dark. Once that was done he could only follow it down.

He felt by no means as much in control as he supposed he'd hoped. He was close to feeling that his aunt's bulky presence at his back was forcing him to descend. His limping shook the light, so that the narrow passage appeared to quake on his behalf. With every step he expected a face or less than one to lurch into view. The noises had ceased, but what might that imply? The sweetish decaying smell rose out of the dark as the beam lit another charred stretch of wall. Whatever was down there must have burned, he thought so furiously he almost announced it aloud. He stumbled down to the opening that presumably had once framed a door and jabbed the light into the blackness.

The occupant of the room was crouching just inside the doorway. When it floundered at him as though it had been awaiting his cue, it took Sam a moment that felt like the end of his life to realise that it had only been pushed forward by its shadow. At first all he saw while he recoiled was what appeared to be its fist-sized mouth, which seemed to widen as the light shook. Then he distinguished that the rest of the face would have been under it—that the round toothless orifice was on top of the small skull, which displayed no other sockets. Otherwise the body looked to have been quite human and scarcely as large as a child's. It must have tried to escape from the room—perhaps even to follow whoever had set the fire—before the flames had seared its bones black. He started when his aunt spoke. "Sad," she whispered. "Another one that didn't make it."

"Who'd want them to?"

She didn't answer immediately upon opening her mouth. His nerves were demanding he reduce the question to one word when she said "We still have to find that out, don't we?"

"No," he muttered—would have shouted if he hadn't been afraid that might draw some attention. He felt as though Sylvia and in particular her midriff were blocking his way back to daylight. When his response didn't move her he said not much more loudly or fiercely "Why, for Christ's sake?"

"Oh, Sam." As well as disappointment he thought he glimpsed a secret loneliness in her eyes. "I know you'll see," she said.

He was seeing the small body with its gaping cranium. He found himself striving to hold the light on it absolutely still rather than allow the dark to hide it while it was near him. Once he'd stayed immobile for some moments his aunt said "Are you going to carry on leading or shall I take over?"

He ached to say that the answer was neither. He couldn't even tell which was worse. The light wobbled half out of the room as he took one faltering pace downwards. "Go ahead, Sam. You can do it," his aunt said as if she was amused by his behaviour. That angered him so much it almost overpowered his panic, and he limped down fast into the twisting stony dark. No sound came to greet him, and only a hint of an odour suggestive of more than decomposition seemed to be lying in wait as the steps fell away at the edge of the light. Then they ended, so abruptly that he snatched away from the wall the hand that had been doing its best to steady him and doubled his grip on the flashlight. "What is it?" Sylvia demanded, resentful of his nervousness.

"I don't know yet," Sam protested, and forced himself to direct the beam into the rectangular hole below him. It was by no means as deep as shadows had made it appear. It had been exposed by the removal of a loose step that lay on its lower neighbour, the steps not having ended after all. They led to a doorway and, at the limit of the flashlight, were terminated by a blank wall. As he leaned towards the hole exposed by the step he willed it to be empty—to contain nothing that might tempt Sylvia to venture closer to the unlit room. He struggled not to react, but a grunt of dismay escaped him. "What is it?" Sylvia repeated, pressing her midriff against his spine in an attempt to crane over his shoulder.

It was a book not much smaller than the shallow cavity. Sam considered saying there was nothing but knew that wouldn't satisfy her. He ran limping down the steps as the walls capered about him and the doorway worked like a hungry mouth. He grabbed the heavy book and held it against his chest, though the black leather binding was cold as a reptile, a dead reptile that nonetheless felt capable of movement. He fled up to prevent Sylvia from descending more than a couple of steps to meet him and thrust the book into her hands. "That's all," he said wildly.

He was praying that his urgency together with the prize would send her out of the cellars, but she gave him a quizzical look. "What else is down there, Sam?"

"Nothing." He shouldn't have glanced back, he realised. "Isn't that enough?" he said, and managed to sound reproachful.

"Let's see," his aunt said, holding out one hand for the flashlight while she propped the book on the mound of her midriff.

He didn't want to relinquish control of the light—to lack even that meagre defence against anything behind him. When he handed it to Sylvia his mind did its utmost to observe his actions as distantly as possible. He watched her sink into a crouch and open the book on her lap, then train the light on the first page. "Sam," she breathed.

Her voice wasn't just appreciative, it was insisting that he look. He could tell she wouldn't move until he did, and so he bent his head over the page as she angled the volume towards him. The page was blank except for a very few words in a thick angular handwriting Sam took to be centuries old, though the black ink gleamed like an insect's carapace. *Nat. Selcouth, his Journall.* "That's great," he said, and altogether more sincerely "Had you better read the rest of it outside?"

"Seems like this might be the ideal place."

"You don't want the stone up there sliding down and shutting us in."

At once he wished he hadn't thought that, let alone said it with the darkness at his back, but his dread must be worthwhile if it communicated itself to Sylvia. She touched the corner of the page to turn it, then let it lie. "Could be you're right," she said, passing him the book as she rose slowly to her feet. "Will you look after it for me?"

"I'll do that," he said—surely little enough to undertake if it sped them on their way. He hugged the book to his chest and planted his other hand on the wall, which felt exactly as cold as the binding, while Sylvia took almost more time than he could bear over facing upwards. The light reeled around her, then steadied as she trod on the next higher step. Some illumination was reflected off the wall, and Sam risked a final backward glance into the dimness. Something had come to the doorway to watch.

Its hands were gripping both sides of the entrance. The fingers were at least twice as long as his, though thinner, and there were too

many on each hand. He could just distinguish that they were
encrusted with a substance that might have been lichen. He glimpsed
long arms reaching out of the darkness from a shape that he was pro-
foundly grateful to be unable to see in any detail, especially whatever
face might be found on its huge pale head. The sweetish odour drifted
up the steps, and Sam wondered if that was its breath. When he grew
aware of bruising his chest with the book he only clutched it harder,
to keep in any sound that might halt Sylvia. He had to turn his back
on the doorway in case she saw him looking and wanted to know
why—worse, insisting on finding out. As she climbed towards the daylight he followed almost close enough to trip her up—to send both of
them tumbling into the dark.

The curve of the passage intervened between him and the lowest
room, but that was no relief. His aunt seemed to be finding the climb
significantly more of a task than descent had been. His ears throbbed
with listening for any hint of pursuit, until he could scarcely hear.
Sylvia switched off the flashlight before he'd quite escaped the dark.
He limped quickly into the daylight, only to have to wait while she
sidled past the fallen chunk of stone. He hadn't emerged from the passage when she halted and looked down at him. "Block it after us, Sam."

He wouldn't have needed telling. He thrust the book at her and
dragged the stone fragment onto the mound, then planted his feet on
either side of the opening and dug his fingertips behind the upper
edge of the rest of the slab. It was too heavy to move. No, he was able
to wriggle his fingers further behind it, scraping off skin. His feet
wavered on the brink that was slippery with earth. He felt himself
falling, and hurled himself backwards, heaving the slab with him. It
tottered on its edge and then, just as he dodged, fell into place with a
stony crash that sent up a whiff of decay. As he manhandled the
remainder into the gap it had left, Sylvia handed him the spade. "Better cover it," she said.

He could think of plenty of reason, but he needed to know hers.
"What for?"

"We don't want anyone else seeing, do we?"

"Why not?"

"Because they wouldn't understand." In a tone close to wistful she added "I'm not sure you do."

She was right about that, he thought, and wondered if he should be glad. He began to fling spadefuls of earth on the slab as the trees pranced in celebration of their capture of the sun while their lengthening shadows clawed their way towards him. He didn't finish until the area that hid the steps was piled with earth. He flattened the patch before limping hastily after Sylvia to abandon the spade among the trees. If he was going to forget some or all of the day's events once he left the woods, part of his mind welcomed that. He thought he would prefer to be unaware of fearing that neither the slab nor the weight of earth could imprison the creature he'd glimpsed in the dark.

24

The Gift of Vision

RANDALL waited until Heather had finished printing out from the computer. Once he'd stroked his bushy eyebrows he used the forefinger to hold his tentative smile still. As she took hold of the page, which felt as unnaturally warm as the January day outside, he said "Something of interest?"

"There wouldn't be much point otherwise," Heather said with studied gentleness, "would there?"

"Sorry," he said hastily, blinking his pale blue eyes less wide. "I didn't mean to . . ."

"No, I am. Don't take any notice of me."

"I don't know how I'd stop doing that, supposing I wanted to." Having earned himself a fleeting smile, he said "May I see?"

Heather watched him read the page she'd printed from the International Foundation for Occult Research website. Eventually he said "I take it the point of interest is that it's local."

"Too much so."

That visibly took him aback. After a pause he said "So what use will you be making of it?"

She wished she knew. She'd lost patience with herself for not printing out the information when she had originally found it, but now she had it in her hands she wasn't sure why. She thought Margo would either dismiss it or take her to task for having sought it out, and wouldn't it simply aggravate Sylvia's obsession with the woods? She was trying mostly to convince herself by saying "As much as I can."

"I don't suppose this is really the place."

"For what, I'm sorry?"

A cough that stayed inside his lips appeared to be the whole of his answer until he went as far as murmuring "If you'd ever like to, ah . . ."

"I'm lost, Randall."

"I wondered, well, I mustn't presume."

"I haven't heard you do that yet."

"It was only that if you ever need someone to talk to, of course I realise you have your family, but someone other than them, though I'm sure you have many friends too . . ."

She'd lost nearly all of those once her father had betrayed his condition to them. Those who'd wanted to stay friends had been prevented by their parents, either for fear that she might have been infected by his state and infectious as well or that Lennox was dangerous. No doubt the association with drugs had lowered her status further. "You're here," she rounded off Randall's sentence for him.

"That's it, though as I say, perhaps here isn't ideal. If you ever felt like going out for a drink, or a meal if you'd rather, or by all means both . . ."

Just now she felt her life was undergoing all the changes she could cope with. "That's extremely kind of you, Randall," she said.

"Nothing to do with kindness. Please don't think that, especially if it means you'll say no."

"It must have something to do with it, since you're kind."

"Well, thank you, but it isn't only that. Not even largely." He turned as much of his back as seemed not unambiguously impolite towards the counter, where a student with her hair entwined in many colours was dumping an armful of medical books. "Is it best left for the moment?" he murmured.

"Thanks for understanding. If I ever need a confidant I'll know where to come."

It wasn't until his eyes grew studiedly blank that she realised he had been proposing they continue the discussion without an audience. She was searching for a response that he would neither misinterpret nor find embarrassing when the phone rang. "I'll deal with that," he declared as though it had rescued him.

"Thanks," Heather told the student, not only for the books, and heard Randall say "I'll see if she's about."

Though he wasn't looking at her, she could understand why he might prefer not to. "Is it for me?"

With a faint sigh at her having let herself be overheard he admitted "She's here now."

"Who is it?"

"Tommy Bennett."

Heather shrugged at failing to recognise the name and took the phone from Randall's carefully aloof grasp. "Hello?"

"It isn't Mrs Price, is it?"

She was being told that rather than asked, and by a woman's unfriendly voice too. "It used to be Miss and now it's Ms," she said. "Who did you say you were calling for?"

"The person I'm speaking to."

"On whose behalf," Heather said with decreasing patience.

"Mine and I should think quite a few other people's."

"But you're somebody's secretary."

"I'm nothing of the sort. I'm a beautician. You've started imagining things as well, have you?"

"I was given the name Tommy Bennett."

"That's me." After a silence in which her displeasure seemed to remain audible the woman said "Thomasina Bennett. Laurel's mother."

Heather remembered the small-mouthed woman, not least because each of Mrs Bennett's remarks sounded as though it was further shrinking her mouth. "We met at the old school in your road. Your sister was encouraging Laurel and her friend to tell more of their nasty stories."

Before Heather could take exception to that, a voice in the background tried to do so. "Mummy . . ."

"Never mind that now," Mrs Bennett said with enough force to be rebuking both of them. "Have you or any of your family been anywhere near our house?"

"I wouldn't know where that is."

"Pine Grove. The next along from your road. Have any of you been hanging round here?"

"I very much doubt it. I certainly haven't, and I'd like to know what makes you ask."

"Laurel saw one of you."

"I didn't say that, mummy."

A sound like thunder overwhelmed the handset, and it seemed that Mrs Bennett had blotted out any discussion with her hand until Heather was just able to hear "What are you saying you said, then?"

"I saw someone looking over our back wall."

"They couldn't do that unless they were standing on something." Before Heather could judge if this was an objection or another accusation Mrs Bennett protested "You said it looked like one of the Prices."

"It was the man."

"Which man?"

"The sticky man. The man out of the woods. He's got lots of fingers now, and crawlies all over them."

"That's quite enough. That's more than enough," Mrs Bennett said, and flattened her voice against Heather's ear. "I don't know if you heard any of that."

"Every word," Heather said as emotionlessly as she could.

"You see the sort of ideas someone's putting in her head now."

"I don't see who you're claiming is responsible."

Mrs Bennett emitted a noise too curt to be called a laugh. "Do you know what your family gets up to when you're at work?"

"Do I get the impression I'm about to be told?"

"Maybe you really don't know they've been in and out of the woods. Most people round here wouldn't let their children go anywhere near them."

"Since you're so well informed I should think you'd know my sister was almost killed in there last year. She's trying to come to terms with that, perhaps you'll understand."

"Sounds like she needs counselling or some kind of help."

"She needs whatever works for her," Heather retorted, furious at feeling compelled to respond.

"There must be something wrong with her if she has to go back where it happened. Just tell her to stay away from my house, and you may as well make that the rest of your family while you're about it. I don't want Laurel any more disturbed than she already is."

"Then I suggest you try looking for the culprit somewhere other than my family." Heather would have liked to end with that and with gently replacing the handset on its stand, but had a question that was starting to feel like a headache. "Before I get back to what I should be doing, who else were you calling on behalf of?"

"A lot of people. Pretty well everyone that knows where your son and your sister have been going, and that's a fair number, believe me." This sounded like a parting shot, but Mrs Bennett had an afterthought. "I thought I'd get more sense from you," she said. "I spoke to your sister first, but I wasn't expecting much."

All the protectiveness Heather had accumulated throughout her childhood surged through her, straightening her body like a sentry's. "Then let me give you the warning you tried to give me," she said. "Don't you dare disturb her any more."

After holding its breath for a couple of seconds the handset replied with a drone that, if she'd wanted to indulge her imagination, she could have found mocking rather than simply mechanical. As she restrained herself to dropping the receiver into place Randall more or less glanced at her. "Sorry," he mumbled.

"For what, for heaven's sake?"

"Forgive me for overhearing, but is this person threatening your family somehow?"

"With gossip by the sound of it. Words don't hurt if you don't let them," Heather promised herself as she slipped the printout into her bag and retrieved the phone. "She's just a silly woman with too much time to think and too little to think with. Small town, small mind," she said, and dialled home.

There was no reply, neither then nor the other times she tried during the rest of the afternoon. She managed to get on with her work and Randall without, she hoped, either inciting or rebuffing him. No doubt Mrs Bennett had sounded off to her daughter about Sylvia and Sam, which surely explained how they'd become mixed up with the rest of Laurel's fancies. Why, even Heather had momentarily convinced herself that she'd seen her father in the woods after his death. At Laurel's age she had been capable of imagining much more, though she had never been as fanciful as Laurel appeared to be.

None of this quite satisfied her as she drove out of Brichester, following lights onto the motorway surrounded by darkness. Alongside the bypass, shadows angled for the blackness of the forest. As she passed the Arbour and her father's unlit window, she couldn't help picturing how this might have looked to her father, shadows dragging a vast blackness out of the woods to swoop in pursuit of her car. She had to admit to welcoming the first glimpse of illumination through the trees, and was glad to reach the edge of Goodmanswood.

She opened her gates and parked in the paved garden and let herself into the house. "Hello?" she called, and then "What's that smell?"

She was beginning to wonder uneasily where Sylvia and Sam might be when her sister responded from upstairs "Dinner."

"Not that." Beneath the aroma of Indian spices lay a smell of something Heather hoped she wasn't going to be asked to put inside herself. "What else?" she shouted.

"Nothing bad."

Before Heather could be certain she was smelling earth and age, the odour vanished as though it had buried itself. She could live without knowing about it while she was anxious to learn "Where's Sam?"

"Here," Sam's faint voice said.

"Where's here?"

"With me."

Heather didn't know which door would open until Sam's did, revealing her sister. She felt as if Mrs Bennett's suspicions were threatening to infect her as she said "So what have you two been doing?"

"Nothing bad." Presumably Sylvia was grinning at the repetition and intending to look wry, but it gave her something of the appearance of a wicked child. "Reading," she said. "Reading to Sam."

"He used to like that as much as you did."

"He still does, don't you, Sam?" Sylvia rested her hands on her midriff and glanced over her shoulder to say "Maybe someone else appreciated it as well."

Sam's rejoinder was inaudible, at least to Heather. "What else has been happening?" she said.

Sylvia crossed to the top of the stairs. "You'll be pleased to hear I think I've finished using him as an escort."

While Heather was, she'd had Mrs Bennett in mind. "Why is that?"

"I believe it's finished between me and the woods."

"Then you're right, I'm pleased. Shall we talk down here so we don't have to shout at each other?"

"I don't think I was shouting, was I? I don't know why I would."

Heather heard defensiveness in that. She waited in the hall as Sylvia plodded heavily downstairs, followed at a distance and no more speedily by Sam. Once they were seated in the front room, Heather on the couch and the others facing her, she told Sam "I expect you'll be off on your travels now, then."

"Where to?"

"Anywhere you can get a job that appeals. It's time you saw a bit more of the world."

"Now you're sounding like dad."

"Nothing necessarily wrong with that, is there? We didn't disagree over much, you know. He felt he had to move away and I couldn't, that's all."

"What stopped you?"

"You know that," Heather said, thrown by what sounded like nervousness. "Family things."

"And maybe staying where your roots are?" Sylvia suggested.

Heather thought this so unhelpful it was close to disloyal. "You didn't answer my question," she said.

"I've been answering quite a few lately."

"From someone who lives not too far away, you mean. What did you say to her?"

"Nothing as terse as I wish now I'd said."

When she seemed happy to leave it at that Sam mumbled "You told her it wasn't just us she could see in the woods."

"Who else?" Heather demanded.

She might have felt nobody wanted her to know until Sylvia relented. "It wouldn't have been you, would it? Don't say you've forgotten mom."

"Why on earth did you tell Mrs Bennett she goes in there?"

"So she knows it's not just crazy Sylvia who wants to." Even more furiously she added "Sounds like it didn't work if she got in touch with you. Who does she think you're supposed to be?"

"Your big sister?" Heather said with all the gentleness she could find in herself.

"You mean that entitles people to tell you tales about me."

"I don't think she especially was, Sylvie. I felt she was blaming me just as much."

"For not keeping me away from her daughter, you mean."

"For being one of our family, more like. If you ask me, for reminding people of dad."

"They'd better stay reminded. He knew more than anyone, and he faced it too."

Rather than contradict that, Heather said "I know a few things as well, and I've had to face some."

"Okay, such as what?"

"Such as the name dad kept mentioning."

Sylvia widened her eyes as if she was seeing more to Heather. "How have you had to face that?"

"Not face it. Nothing to face, just to know," Heather said, opening her bag. "I found this on the net at work."

Sylvia's eyes stayed wide as she read the printout—Heather might have thought she'd forgotten how to blink. Her sister's face changed so gradually that Heather wasn't sure when her eyes began to gleam and the corners of her lips to raise themselves in a smile that looked close to smug. "Things must be coming together," she murmured. "It's about Nathaniel Selcouth, Sam."

"Oh."

The syllable was doing its best to be toneless but sounded like the escape of a breath he'd tried to hold. "I told you I'd been reading to him," said Sylvia.

"To Sam," Heather quite unnecessarily said.

"About your friend here." Sylvia shook the printout until it flapped with not much less than life. "We've got his book."

At once Heather knew what she'd smelled on entering the house, which made her not entirely want to learn "Where from?"

"Someone who doesn't need it any more, shall we say?" Sylvia said, and passed Sam the printout. "Look, this makes sense of some of it."

"Such as what?" Heather blurted.

"He can pass as swiftly through the earth as through the void between the spheres," said Sylvia, "being composed in equal parts of both."

Presumably she was quoting, given her reminiscent tone and the way she half closed her eyes, though that lent her a secretive appearance. "Who," Heather said with an attempt at a laugh, "this Selcouth character?"

"Not him, his experiment." Apparently Sylvia needed to slit her eyes further as an aid to adding "Yet he is fondest of the dark in which he was conceived."

Even reading the source of all this struck Heather as preferable. "Well, are you going to show me?"

Sylvia took so long to raise her eyelids that she might have been intent on something within them. She levered herself out of her chair but halted at the foot of the stairs. "You'll think I'm taking over," she said. "It's your room, Sam."

She stood aside to let him limp upstairs, then followed Heather, bumping her more than once with her midriff. She pressed against Heather's back as Sam fumbled with his doorknob, and Heather felt as if she was about to be offered the sensation of movement inside her sister. Then Sam moved away from the open door, leaving the room unlit, and she had to tell herself he wasn't afraid to enter his own room.

A lump of darkness lay in front of the computer on his desk. It looked blacker than anything else in the room—as black as the depths of the woods. It was just a book, and she confirmed this by slapping the light-switch down. Nothing but the blackness of the binding made the volume appear to stay darker than it should. Heather marched forward, wrinkling her nose at the oppressive smell of senile paper, and opened the book.

The cover gave a creak and a thump as if she'd raised a lid. The words it exposed made her draw in a breath she had virtually to spit out to rid herself of the smell. *Nat. Selcouth, his Journall*. Of course it was a coincidence—even less, perhaps, since Sylvia must have been as concerned to track the name down as she was—but hardly one she liked. "Where did you say you found this?"

"Don't worry, we didn't steal it," said Sylvia, lowering herself onto the edge of Sam's bed. "More like the opposite."

Heather might have turned the question on Sam, who'd ventured as far as the threshold of his room, if asking in front of her sister wouldn't have seemed distrustful. She turned the page, which felt disconcertingly vital, more like foliage or ancient skin.

I who am named for my Quallities shall here sette down the Historie of my Discoveries; that he who is to followe may carrie the Worke onwards.

That was the first line, and as much as she could concentrate on reading; the thick spiky handwriting seemed to gather like blackness somewhere behind her eyes. She picked up the journal to leaf through it and glimpsed a dim shape vaster than the woods raising itself out of the trees. She didn't need to look to know it was a reflection while she was preoccupied with the stifling smell of the book and with the feel of the binding, as cold and slippery as fallen leaves in winter but borrowing warmth from her hands. None of these was the reason why she almost threw the book down. She'd ceased turning the pages, not just to stop the letters swarming like insects across her vision but because she'd happened upon an illustration. *From life,* the inscription said.

Though it couldn't be, the drawing was dreadful enough. It showed a shape crouched in what must be a glade, suggested by a background of a few sketched trees. Above the naked childish body, which appeared to resemble cracked mossy bark and which was gripping the earth with unequal hands at the end of elongated arms, a head that looked painfully large for the extended neck was upturned to a sky displaying an elaborate pattern of stars. The wide mouth was baring far too many teeth in a grin that could have expressed delight or agony—the lack of eyes made it impossible to tell. The entire upper half of the head was honeycombed with sockets from which insects were streaming, unless those were eyes. A few of the sockets were inhabited by objects that apparently had still to achieve their final shape.

Heather shut the volume and restrained herself from dropping it on Sam's desk. She had no doubt that, whatever his background and the culture of his times, the man calling himself Selcouth must have been more deranged than her father. The smell that seemed to fill the room was enough to make her say "You won't be keeping this in here, will you?"

Sylvia held out her hands. When Heather reluctantly entrusted the journal to her, Sylvia clasped it to her stomach as if one might be a shield for the other. "It can live in my room," she said.

"Don't you think the university would be the proper place for it?"

"Not when you might have students who set fire to books," Sylvia said and managed to stand up while hugging the journal.

Heather watched her bear it to her room and heard the muffled thump as it settled on their father's desk. For the moment she could think of nothing to say except "Let's have dinner." At least that should tempt Sylvia and Sam away from their find for a while. Perhaps Heather had too much imagination after all, because just then she could think of no book she would less like to open again, ever in her life.

25

Nowhere But Home

SAM had no idea how long he'd been climbing the steps. He only knew he was unable to climb fast enough. He kept thinking he could hear or had just heard a voice calling him out of the dark. Now and then, as his hand groped over the curve of the wall, it encountered openings that were darker still, from which objects attempting to resemble hands reached out to help him on his way. He had an impression that they were somehow related to him. Either his eyes were changing or the darkness was growing less subterranean, since he was beginning to distinguish the edges of the steps. He very much hoped he wouldn't have to pass another cell and glimpse whatever made its home within. No, the steps were coming to an end above him. An aperture that put him in mind of a grave framed a sky black as burial except for a solitary constellation that looked in danger of flickering its last, and he knew the silhouette that loomed at the top of the steps was calling him towards that blackness. He found himself straining to name the constellation rather than recognise the silhouette's face. The Eye of the Void, he thought, or Night's Egg, but he was unable to stop trudging upwards. The stars appeared to merge with the shadowed face and glitter in its eyes for an instant before he awoke.

The silhouette above him was still calling him. As his body struggled to decide which way to retreat his gaze focused, and the outline against the daylight developed features. "Sylvia's here," she promised, then frowned at him. "What's wrong?"

"I didn't know where I was."

"With me."

"No, down some steps. Too many steps and too dark."

She gazed at him while her frown lingered over vanishing—she could have been miming comprehension on his behalf. "Perhaps it'll come to you," she eventually said.

"I'd rather it stayed away." The presence of her bulge above him had started to discomfort him, so that it was partly to hasten the end of their conversation that he said "Was I making a noise?"

"One I haven't often heard a man make."

"That's why you came in."

"It would have been, but somebody wants you."

By no means for the first time, Sam had a sense that talking to his aunt resembled descending a series of steps that weren't all where they should be. "Who does?"

"Mr Harvey. Your father."

Sam began to swing his legs out from beneath the quilt, only to realise he was naked. "Now, you mean?"

"He didn't sound like he was going away." For a moment she seemed arrested by her bulk, and then she bore it from the room. As Sam shrugged his way into his bathrobe and knotted the belt he heard her plod downstairs to announce "He was having some kind of a dream, but I think I've retrieved him."

When he took the phone from her it proved to be almost feverishly warm. "I'll be reading," she said, hauling herself upstairs.

"Are you there, old fellow?" his father's voice said against his ear.

"I must be."

"Busy with a dream, were you?"

"It was busy with me."

"Do I get to hear what it was about?"

"Nothing special," Sam said in the hope that would cause it to dissipate.

"Not the sort you need to stay in bed for, then."

"What sort's that?"

"Just change the subject if the girls can hear." When Sam could think of no reply his father said "Never mind, let me. Maybe we can bring a dream true for you."

"Which one?" Sam asked with an uneasiness that seemed to have been his companion for months.

"Remember what you told me in the pub before Christmas?"

That felt unnervingly distant both in time and space. "I'm not sure," Sam admitted.

"You won't have forgotten your wizard in the woods that were bigger than they ought to be and the chap who dug his secrets up, will you? What was the name again?"

Sam's lips moved before he knew what they would utter. "Selcouth?" he mumbled.

"That's another good one. Worth keeping in mind, I'd say. The one you told me was Bosky, though. See, it's lodged in the old man's head, and it didn't seem to go down at all badly with the girl I met last night at a party."

If Sam had been some use to his father's love life, that merely confused him further. "Who was she?" he supposed he had to ask.

"Fay Sheridan. She's in publishing. You never know, she might publish your book."

"You mean the one I'm never going to write."

"Didn't catch that, old fellow. You sound as if you're still a bit asleep. Are you going to be awake to drive to town?"

"Brichester? What for?"

"Not there, Sam. The real town, the one that makes things happen. Fay wants to meet you."

"I've got nothing to show her."

"Except the most important item."

Sam was unable to bring anything to mind except the old book Sylvia had acquired somewhere while he wasn't with her. "Which is that?" he heard himself blurt.

"Sam Harvey. Sam Price if you prefer," his father said with affectionate impatience. "Fay's looking for a new assistant. Her current chap is moving up the ladder in a few weeks. She likes her assistant to be new to publishing so she can give him her ideas. You'll never have a better chance to learn what you need to know from someone who wants to teach. Will you see her this afternoon?"

"Can't she wait?"

"You don't want that, Sam. Now I've talked you up we need to get you two together in a meeting soonest. Without promising too much, maybe she won't have to see anyone else."

"I'll need to call her," Sam said as if this might somehow release him.

"No you don't. I told her I'd call only if you couldn't make it. She's at Midas Books, just off Oxford Circus," his father said. "Ready for the address?"

Sam was about to discover aloud that he had no means of writing it down when he caught sight of a ballpoint lodged under the phone. He couldn't very well not use it to scrawl on his wrist the details his father dictated. For a moment the action felt capable of reviving a memory, but not while he was preoccupied with wondering when he'd last made a decision of his own. He seemed forever to be performing what one or other of his family required of him, and it scarcely helped to hear his father say not just "Good luck" but "Can I offer a piece of advice?"

"I expect you can."

"Just relax and be yourself. Fay's interested in you, so tell her all about yourself, especially your ambitions. She likes people that want to climb. She's happy to give them a hand up."

Sam was puzzling over how his father could appeal to her on that basis when he realised she might relish his father's ambition for him.

This seemed merely to confirm his status as a puppet, even before his father said "Can I have a promise in exchange for the advice?"

"What?"

"Nothing too unreasonable." Having sounded as though Sam's response was a minor injury, his father healed himself. "That's it, stay in control," he said. "Never agree to anything till you know what it is. I was only going to ask you to give me a call when you've seen Fay."

"I can do that," Sam told them both.

"That's all I ask," his father said, which was so unlike the truth that Sam didn't trust himself to pronounce more than half a goodbye. The receiver was still occupied when he dropped it on the hook and limped upstairs to the bathroom.

Usually shaving helped wake him up, but today it involved too much staring at a face that had no ideas to give him. He ended its act with the shower curtains and ducked under the shower, holding his left forearm more or less clear of the water. A few drops found his wrist and trickled down it, smudging the ink. That failed to render the address illegible, and in any case he hadn't forgotten that it was in All Souls Place. When he dabbed his wrist, having dried the rest of himself, some of the ink transferred itself to the towel, but the letters retained their shapes. He limped to his bedroom and donned clothes that had been good enough for the university and the bookshop, then rapped on his aunt's door. "If I'm not home for dinner tell mum I've had to go to London."

Perhaps his aunt had been reading her book; its ancient sweetish smell came with her to the door. "Your father's fixed you up with someone, then," she said.

"She works in publishing." His aunt could hardly be jealous, Sam told himself. "He thinks he's found me a job," he told her.

"And has he?"

"That's what I'm going to find out."

"We'll have to see how far you go," Sylvia said, clasping her midriff.

"Only Oxford Circus."

"It doesn't sound far, does it? What do you think?"

"I should be there in a couple of hours."

She glanced down before shaking her head as if she hadn't meant the questions for him. "Natty doesn't know."

Sam found this worse than embarrassing. "I'd better move," he said.

"He's anxious to leave us, isn't he? What shall we say to him?"

Sam told himself that she was only playing the kind of game expectant mothers played, but he had an uneasy sense of interrupting as he said "I'll see you."

"That's for sure," his aunt said, resting her hands on either side of her midriff as though to indicate she wasn't speaking solely for herself.

Sam limped downstairs and out of the house. Only the lowness of the sun and the length of the shadows demonstrated that it was still January: on the trees buds had started to unfurl. As he opened the gates and closed them after driving the Volkswagen onto the road, three neighbours whom he vaguely knew watched him from the corner of Pine Grove. All the way to the end of Woodland Close the car refused to do more than chug, giving them a generous amount of time to stare unfavourably at him. He was far less aware of them and of the streets around him than of the woods he would soon reach.

Perhaps that was at least partly the fault of the old book his aunt had insisted on reading to him. Its smell seemed to cling to his nostrils as its words clung to his mind. One passage in particular kept repeating itself in his head. "Lesser even than the task of summoning human vessels to receive the fruits of my studies is the calling of the void upon their minds, that they surrender to my forest all memory of the encounter . . ." This seemed to have some relevance Sam preferred not to acknowledge. He steered one-handed while he bared his inscribed wrist. "All Souls Place," he read aloud as if that might blot out the echoes of Sylvia and her book.

The last cottages fled backwards, exposing the woods. Under a sky that looked seared pale as bone the trees had acquired an elusive greenishness, which must be the beginnings of leaves but which reminded him more of mist and lichen. Strips of haze appeared unusually reluctant to drain into the roadway as he sped towards them, especially outside the Arbour, where he could have imagined something had produced the trail by creeping across the tarmac. Beyond it the tail end of a lorry quaked and grew gelatinous. As the woods swarmed past the car he was unable to rid himself of an impression that a presence composed of or otherwise hidden by all the trees was turning to keep him in view. "Surrender to my forest . . ." He might have thought that it wasn't Sylvia's voice he was hearing or that she was speaking on someone else's behalf. Once he was on the motorway his imagination would have to let him concentrate on driving, he tried to promise himself.

The trees swung away to his right at last, fitting themselves into the mirror above the oncoming motorway, and he felt as if they were shrinking in order to fasten the whole of their clawed tangled mass on his mind. "Surrender to my forest. . . ." Perhaps it was the repetition of the phrase that made the voice seem increasingly babyish. A tremor passed through the reflection of the woods, but he couldn't tell whether that was an effect of haze or a shudder of the mirror. Then the trees were blotted out by a lorry, its elongated trailer swaying as the cab towered over his back.

The driver was too busy not just talking to but gesturing with a mobile phone to brake as he herded Sam onto the motorway. Sam trod hard on the accelerator, but for a moment that felt like the end of his breath was sure he hadn't enough of a reserve of speed to outdistance the traffic the motorway unleashed at him. The coach he braved gave him an earful of its horn and swung into the middle lane well after it had finished growing too huge for his mirror. The quiet that followed it was relative at best, full of the muffled hum of tyres, and there was nothing like silence inside him, though the babyish voice had changed its refrain. "The calling of the void," it was repeating now.

"Dead Souls Place," Sam muttered. "Fay what's her name, I'll remember when I get there or she'll tell me. Minus Books." He was misspeaking the address on purpose so as not to be as boringly repetitive as the voice he was unable to outrun, but he could have blamed everything around him for distracting him. Even when he lowered the windscreen visor all the way it failed to blot out the sun, which ached in his eyes as though it was committed to forcing him to retreat. Whenever he tried to slow down, yet another lorry gained on him, swerving ahead of him at the last possible moment and blaring its horn as a bonus. He felt he wasn't driving so much as being driven, but to where? "Dead," he mumbled, "Fay however you spell it, some kind of book," and was pointed at by one of several children in the back of an overtaking Toyota, all of whom then turned to stare at him for talking to himself as he could imagine his grandfather might have. He didn't have to grope in his mind for the details when the address was on his wrist. He gripped the wheel with his right hand and shook his left forearm clear of its sleeve, then raised the arm towards his eyes. The Volkswagen wavered between the lines that marked the motorway lane and was wandering onto the hard shoulder before he clutched at the wheel with both hands. He glanced wildly up from his wrist to reassure himself he wasn't too close to the Toyota as its brake lights throbbed twice to herald the next junction, and then he glared hot-eyed at the ink on his wrist. Sweat had blurred it so much he couldn't distinguish a single letter. A random scattering of twigs, or rather the marks they and moisture might have left on him, would have made as much sense.

The Toyota veered up the slip road, and the children did their utmost to transform the faces they were presenting to him into objects he wouldn't have cared to meet in the dark. He was just too late to follow them off the motorway in search of a public phone, and could have imagined they were mocking his plight—they and the relentless lowness of the sun, the traffic swelling in the mirror, the utterance that felt embedded in his skull. "The calling of the void . . ." It could have been his aunt's voice imitating a child or the reverse.

He'd lost count of the number of times he had failed to quell the repetition by the time he came in sight of the next junction. At the end of the slip road an intersection showed him the Severn to the west, where it made the horizon look bared. He saw little between it and him except fields, and so he drove left along a road that set about winding to no immediately or even belatedly apparent purpose. It had to bring him more than grass verges and hedgerows that blocked his view, he did his best to think over the recital in his mind. For the first time in years he wished he'd kept his mobile phone; he didn't think its emissions could have rendered his brain any more useless. When he saw smoke at large in the sky ahead, he declared louder than the voice "It's a pub with a phone in it."

In fact it was a hotel, the Traveller's Haven, a broad two-storey building that had been Tudor or was now, with more black and white about it than any colour. Three limousines and dozens of cars were parked with some intemperance outside on the gravel, where Sam had to back the Volkswagen into hardly enough of a space. He wormed himself out of the car through the meagre gap its neighbour allowed him, and sprinted limping into the hotel.

Nobody was at the reception desk next to the wide oak staircase, nor was there any sign of a phone in the extensive panelled hall. A considerable uproar led him to the bar, a lengthy wooden room with an open fire blazing at the far end despite the weather. None of the drinkers appeared to welcome it, least of all a newlywed mopping her forehead with a lilac handkerchief that matched her silk dress. Some of the flowers sprouting from the expensive lapels of all the male guests appeared to be wilting in the heat. Sam felt out of place in far too many senses as he excused his way past a cluster of lilac brides-maids who were adding coins and noise to a fruit machine, and reached the bar.

The solitary barman, who seemed rather too sizeable for his shirt and tie and red-faced as a consequence, barely glanced at him. Sam peered about, for the moment hearing only the sounds of the bar, but

saw no phone. As soon as the barman spared him another blink, having
served several flowered men, Sam said "When you've a second . . ."

"Why, are you looking for a fight?"

The time Sam had to waste on understanding the joke made him
even more nervous than the comment had. "No, I mean a moment."

"I've got one of those now." When Sam didn't instantly respond
the barman demanded "What are you having to drink?"

"I'd better have something," Sam told him and himself. "Just a half.
Beer, that is, bitter, and can—"

"Guest?"

"I'm not staying here, no."

The barman stared as if only he was allowed to indulge in jokes,
though Sam hadn't been aware of cracking any. Once he'd finished
staring, the barman said "Guest pint. Are you having the guest pint?"

"Half of one. I was going to ask where the phone is."

The barman found a half-pint glass, apparently a substantial and
unwelcome task, and set about wiping it with a dish-cloth. Having
inspected it against the overhead light, he said "So are you?"

"Am I what?"

"Asking."

"Yes," Sam said in a voice that felt as though it had to fight its way
out of his nerves. "Where do you keep it, please?"

"Other end."

Sam peered along the bar but saw only a huddle of women emit-
ting hilarity and smoke. "Shall I go up there?"

"You won't get your drink if you do," the barman warned him,
hauling on a pump that bore a temporary sign for an ale called Witch's
Tit. "I'm serving this end now."

Sam watched the glass fill with a murky brownish liquid that put
him in mind of a pond. All at once the delay seemed welcome, or
would have done if it had helped him think. He paid for the ale and
struggled through the crowd while more of a struggle continued in
his skull. He sidled around the women at the end of the bar as another

grey cloud of laughter sailed up, and planted his glass on a shelf above the phone on the panelled wall. Clamminess that felt mixed with grit was well on the way to covering the whole of him. He couldn't think of his father's number.

He fed himself a mouthful that tasted as murky as it looked, then rubbed his forehead with the lukewarm glass. Even if he couldn't recall the number he could obtain it from Directory Enquiries, the number of the firm his father worked for, which was . . . whose name was . . . He didn't realise he'd groaned with frustration close to panic until the nearest woman draped over his shoulders a bare arm as extravagantly perfumed as it was freckled. It felt as though all the heat in the bar had put on flesh. "Not to your taste, sweetheart?" she said.

Sam almost managed not to recoil. "What?" he blurted.

"Thinks you're offering, Amanda," one of her friends said, and the others adopted various expressions while trying not to laugh too much.

"Not me, lover. Your teeny glass."

"It's fine," Sam lied and made a gesture of grabbing the phone. "I'm just . . ."

"Then we'll let you have your privacy, won't we, girls," Amanda said, supporting herself on Sam until she'd wobbled with some dignity to face them. "Just let us know when you want to be sociable," she told him.

His mother knew where his father worked, he thought, and squeezed his eyes shut while he strove to recall her number at the library. He'd phoned her there more than once, on . . . phoned her on . . . When he opened his eyes to focus his desperate glare he saw the barman ambling towards him. "Excuse me?" he called, and twice as loud "Excuse me?"

"Still not for you, Amanda," one of her friends said.

"Didn't sound too fond of his drink, Phil," another informed the barman.

Phil hadn't finished turning his unfriendly face towards him when Sam said "Have you got a directory?"

"They'll have one at Reception if they're there." With satisfaction no less total for its glumness the barman added "Which they weren't when somebody just went to look."

Sam imagined labouring through the crowd to no end and then back to the phone. He dialled Directory Enquiries instead, even though calling from the hotel meant he had to pay. "Brichester University," he told a woman up in Scotland, "the library," and was answered by a computerised voice barely shrill enough to be heard above the hubbub of the bar. He fed more coins into the thin-lipped orifice and dialled. The receiver was beginning to feel flabby with sweat when someone announced "University Library" as though he was determined to render the capitals audible.

"Is, is Heather Price there?" Sam said, covering his other ear.

"Not at present. Can I be of assistance?"

"Where is she?"

"May I ask who wants to know?"

"Sam. Her son. Where is she?"

"Hello, Sam. It's Randall. We've met across the counter," Randall said and was silent long enough to suggest he meant to add more than "She's gone for an early lunch."

"Can you get her?"

"She's out of the building, I'm afraid."

"When's she back?"

"Try calling in about an hour."

That sounded longer than a sleepless night would feel to Sam. He was straining to think of some response when Randall said "I've a feeling we got off on the wrong, I was going to say foot except I wouldn't want you to think I was making light of your injury, which I know you've borne with a good deal of fortitude. Your mother and I are friends, so by all means regard me as one if that appeals."

"Right," Sam said without knowing if it was, and let the receiver clatter onto its stand. He couldn't wait for his mother to return, but mightn't his father's number or the number of his firm be somewhere at home? Mightn't Sylvia be able to locate one or the other? Sam took hold of the receiver, then gave it up so shakily it rattled like a snake. He couldn't think of his own number. He couldn't even remember the address.

The heat and noise seemed to mass within him as his panic did. He felt like a child, very lost and very small. The one notion to which he was able to cling was that he knew his way home. As he stumbled away from the phone one of Amanda's party told the barman "He didn't care much for your special."

Amanda took a would-be steady step into Sam's path. "Want a bit of advice?" she said, and before he could limp out of her way "Next time you come out you want to wash first."

He didn't know if she was referring to the incomprehensible blur on his wrist or to how much he was sweating, not that the two could be separated. "Right," he said again, feeling as if all the words he'd learned as he grew up were deserting him, and limped and sidled and was scarcely able to restrain himself from fighting his way out of the room stuffed with hot flesh.

The car started at once, but that was no immediate relief. He accelerated dangerously along the rewinding road to the motorway, which was even more fraught with traffic. He had a moment of dry-mouthed panic at the thought of heading the wrong way on it—of being as incapable of reading the signboard at the intersection as he was of deciphering the sweaty mess on his wrist. He hadn't lost his homing instinct, however. When a gap large enough for him to brave let him join the race, he found the sun was behind him.

Its glare filled most of the mirror, back-lighting his wildly tousled hair above a forehead etched with apprehension. He felt as if his skull was being goaded onward by the lowering sun, aided by the protracted shadow that was dragging the car. He was disconcerted to be reassured by the sight of the forest ahead. It was close to home, he told himself. All it meant was that he could stop straining to remember.

In a very few miles the motorway abandoned him to the bypass.

He might have been shocked to realise how meagre a distance he'd ventured, but he was wondering what explanation he could give his family for having missed the interview. The woods were lying in wait for the sun, which had swung to his left, to fall into their upheld claws. As soon as the first trees blotted out the glare he felt less harassed, almost ready to think. He imagined how still the depths of the forest must be, and it felt like an offer of help. When he reached the first lay-by he steered the car into it and switched the engine off.

A lorry thundered by, its rear end veering back and forth. It was only far enough ahead to start to quiver with the heat when it was followed by a vehicle big enough to swallow it. Not only their noise distracted Sam: when they and others like them passed the Volkswagen it shook as though the heat was on the point of transforming its substance. He climbed out of the car and loitered by it until the dull din of traffic sent him into the woods.

He couldn't think yet, but he would once he reached stillness. Limping away from the road felt like repeating a step in a dance. The leaning trees uprooted by last year's gale helped ward off the murmur of Goodmanswood. The branches around him were tipped with growth, some of it hinting at the shapes it had in store, which looked less than familiar. Some looked capable of moving without the aid of a wind, but their immobility seemed to guarantee a greater peace deep in the forest, so that he hardly glanced at them or at the overgrown spiky constructions in the treetops. The trees stayed motionless as stalagmites holding up the pallid sky, and yet he felt as though they were about to shift in some indefinable way. He was limping so fast he couldn't judge whether he was hurrying towards the ability to remember or desperate to outrun a threat of remembering too much. He had no sense of how far he'd progressed—he might have been performing his ritual step for a few minutes or an unimaginable length of time—when he glimpsed more than brightness ahead.

It wasn't just sunlight in an open space. It was more solid, and performing a glittering dance. A few fast but reluctant unbalanced paces took him close enough to identify a swarm of insects. As he saw they were above the mound within the ring of bricks, he became aware of the forest all around him. It felt vaster and darker than the distance he must have walked or the time of day could explain. The insects were darting and swooping around one another, such a multitude of them that they were able to sketch a form as tall as a man before it fell into a crouch on top of the mound. Memories of his last visit to the clearing overwhelmed him, darkening his mind as if they were heaving up earth.

He'd cleared the steps under the mound. He and his aunt had ventured down past things he thought should never have lived, and he'd glimpsed one that was somehow still alive. He'd done his best to restore the mound to its state prior to their intrusion, but now that suggested an attempt to bury his memories of their descent and of finding Selcouth's journal. The memories felt poised to let another reach him, and not just of having encountered the insects before. As if they had scented his thought and were drawn by it, all the insects rose from the mound and flew at him.

They were across the clearing before he could retreat a pace. He was stumbling backwards when they streamed between the trees at the height of his head. As they passed through the network of shadows they continued to shine with colours he couldn't begin to name, colours he might have been dreaming rather than seeing. He'd backed less than a yard when his spine collided with a tree-trunk. The impact pinned him there as the swarm reached him.

He flailed at the oncoming mass with both hands. For a moment he thought he'd managed to ward it off as it swerved and danced back, creating pattern after intricate rapid pattern, towards the mound. He was on the point of grasping the impossible geometry the patterns implied when a single insect darted into his face. Though its wings, which were flickering almost too fast to be visible, were insect-like enough, the claws it stretched out to him might have been microscopic bunches of twigs, while its body and limbs appeared all too nearly human, despite their scaly covering that resembled iridescent moss. How could he distinguish all this when it was scarcely as long as his thumbnail? Yet he did, unless his mind was frantically inventing details to blind him to some reality. He was feeling pitifully grateful that he'd had no time to recognise its face, despite an impression of shimmering eyes and a mouth that opened to help them greet him, when the creature swelled up in his vision and vanished.

His hands jerked up to claw it out of his hair, though his finger-tips tingled with unwillingness, but it was beyond their reach. For the briefest instant—as long as he would have been able to bear the sensation—he felt it crawling within him, and then it seemed to expand, filling his skull with a darkness as cold and as immeasurable as space. Perhaps that was a memory of its origin; without question it unlocked memories—Sam's own. Now his hands were desperate to stop him seeing, but covering his eyes or even destroying them couldn't achieve that. He could only clutch at the air as if it contained forgetfulness.

He remembered straying into the glade months ago. He remembered the figure that had come to meet him—remembered her taking his hand to lead him to the mound. They'd undressed so slowly and wordlessly they might have been enacting some ritual. It had felt like a dream he was having while awake, but now it seemed more like a nightmare that wasn't about to finish. He hadn't recognised her then, and surely she couldn't have recognised him. As her long bare legs had closed around his waist, hauling him deeper into her, she had uttered just one word. At least, a voice had sounded in his ears or in his head, but perhaps it hadn't been Sylvia's. "Selcouth," the muffled voice had kept repeating. "Selcouth."

26

Parental Problems

AS Heather turned along Woodland Close she saw a man lurching to close her gate from within. He was swaying so much that she took him for a drunk. Another second's driving brought her close enough to recognise Sam. Of course only his limp was required to unbalance him when he was moving at such speed. She sounded her horn, and he glanced towards the sound. He had to be preoccupied, because he shut the gate hastily and blundered towards the house.

Perhaps he thought she was already home. Perhaps he was as anxious to tell her why he'd phoned her at work as she was eager to know. She left the car in the middle of the roadway and the door ajar as she ran to the gate. When her footsteps didn't make him turn from unlocking the front door, her voice outdid them for sharpness. "Sam."

She saw his shadow on the wooden panels shrink into itself, then bloom larger and paler as he floundered around to face her. "What?" he just about said.

"I don't know. You wanted me."

Was that gentle to the point of inaudibility? He looked as if he either hadn't heard or didn't understand. As she unlatched the gate and swung it wide she said "It was such a good day I went out for a lunchtime walk. I'm sorry I missed you."

"Doesn't matter."

"You sorted it out, then, whatever it was."

She would have thought he could take that as a question, but he was turning towards the house. "You aren't cold, are you?" Heather wondered, and went on as he shook his head "You can't be. Wait while I bring in the car."

She hoped he might at least close the gate behind her without being asked, and he did. She was out of the car before he could retreat into the house. "What was the matter, then?" she said, and when his face tightened "Is it still?"

"Just something dad wanted me to do."

"What kind of something?"

"Get a job."

"I think we'd all like that for you. Are we talking about a specific job?"

"Interview."

"Where?"

"Publishing."

"Well, don't overwork the suspense. How did it go?"

"Didn't."

"Oh dear, Sam, never mind. Did they tell you that or could you be underrating yourself as usual, do you think?"

"I mean I didn't."

"I'm sorry, Sam, you're saying you didn't . . ."

"Go."

A passing pair of neighbours she knew barely well enough to recognise as such glanced sharply at her when she raised her voice. "Why not?"

Sam jerked his left hand at her. She thought he was trying to ward off the question until she realised that the darkness on his wrist wasn't a shadow cast by nothing she could see, it was the remnant of a message. "I lost the address," he mumbled.

"Where did you get it from?"

"I told you, dad."

He hadn't quite, and his response suggested how confused he was. "Couldn't you get it from him again?" Heather more than wanted to know.

"That's why I called you." Sam's voice was growing raw with resentment of her questions or of the admissions he was being forced to make. "I forgot where he works."

"Hartley, Tracy and—"

"Harvey. The three adverbs, like you used to say. I know now. I forgot before."

The strolling neighbours glanced back as though in search of evidence that the surviving Prices were no more stable than Lennox had ended up. Nothing like that was wrong with Sam, Heather assured herself, but she'd had enough and a second helping of their scrutiny. "Let's continue inside," she murmured. "Why were you so worried about an interview?"

She assumed it was her interrogation that made him suddenly reluctant to move towards the house. "Who says I was?" he muttered.

"Mustn't that be why you couldn't remember where you were supposed to go?" When he frowned so unhappily his entire face seemed in danger of pinching inward she said "Of course it must. You'd be amazed what I've forgotten when I've too much on my mind. Go ahead, open the door while I unload the car."

She wondered if his limp was troubling him; certainly he took his time over reaching the house. When she followed with her handbag and a carrier of groceries he was edging the door open. He stepped into the hall and switched on the light, only to falter. Wasn't he used to the faint ancient smell that had taken up residence? She didn't want to grow used to it either, but she was about to urge him to move when she saw what he'd seen. Propped against the phone on the hall table was a note in Sylvia's handwriting.

All it said was *Gone to mum's,* though to begin with Sylvia had written *mom's,* so that the altered letter resembled an egg almost filling an upturned tube. If Sam's reaction didn't mean he'd wanted his aunt's presence to bring an end to Heather's questions, presumably he was glad she wouldn't hear them, if indeed he was sure which. "So had you better ring your father?" Heather said. "He may still be at work."

"Why?"

"Why should you ring him? To get the number of the publisher so you can let them know what went wrong."

"I remember."

"You remember . . ."

"Everything," Sam said, but closed his eyes and jerked his hands up, less in surrender than as though he was about to scratch at the container of his brain. She took him to be wishing her elsewhere, since he muttered "The publisher."

"Then I'll leave you to talk to them while I put away the shopping."

The kitchen light had finished flickering to life before she heard him lift the receiver. As she began to unpack the carrier he asked Directory Enquiries for the number of Midas Books. Heather set about rustling plastic and generally making a noise as if she didn't want to overhear what came of his dialling the number. She heard him ask for someone called Fay Sheridan and say "Oh, isn't she?" with some relief and "If you like" with none. Heather spent the long pause guessing that he'd been offered a word with Fay Sheridan's secretary, to whom he had to admit "It's Sam Harvey. I was supposed to see her today."

Heather busied herself with putting groceries away, but couldn't pretend she was making as much noise as she might have. When Sam said "I got lost" she willed him not to ruin his chances by owning up to all his forgetfulness. Pauses that her busyness was unable to rob of threat were followed by his saying "It got rubbed out" and "I couldn't remember any of it" and "It's all right, I should call her." With rather more animation than any of this had involved he said "Goodbye."

By now Heather had run out of items to unpack and was staring through the window. The reflection of the kitchen didn't quite disguise the appearance above the fence of the tangled scalp of a vast unseen head—of the treetops. She waited for Sam's footsteps to succeed the clatter of the receiver; she was hoping they would make for her rather than limp upstairs. When they stayed put and mum she called "How long did she have to wait for you?"

"I didn't say I'd be there. It wasn't definite."

"Let's hope she gives you another chance, then." Having waited for a reply, Heather pulled the door wide. Sam had picked up Sylvia's note and was staring at it. "Is something else wrong?" Heather said.

He must have begun to crumple the note, which unfolded like a misshapen blossom as he opened his hand. "What's his name," he said.

Despite its flatness, she assumed this was a question. "Natty, you mean?"

"Why would I mean that?" he said with a fierceness that took her aback. "We don't even know what it is."

"A boy or a girl, you mean." Her confusion made her ask "So is it the other parent you're wondering about?"

"Other, right. Mr Other." Presumably amusement was the reason Sam bared his teeth. "Are you expecting to meet him?" he demanded more than said.

"Somehow I don't think we will."

"What would you do if you did?"

"Welcome him if Sylvie does."

"You think you would," Sam said with undisguised disbelief. "You'd do that."

She couldn't have predicted his reaction; he sounded more like a father than a nephew. "Why, how would you deal with him?" she said.

"Christ knows how I'll have to."

"You won't, Sam. I'm sure he isn't going to turn up. Between ourselves, and we won't let it out of the family, will we, I don't even think he knows he's a father."

"Won't let it out of the family." When Sam had finished lingering over the repetition he said "Suppose he's realised?"

"I don't see how he can. He and Sylvie aren't in any kind of touch."

Sam's lips twitched and continued to grimace as he said "Don't you want to know his name at least?"

"Not if she doesn't want us to. It's my impression she'd rather forget him." As she spoke, Heather had an idea that explained altogether too much: could the father have been a patient at the hospital where Sylvia had shared a room with Merilee? Surely that couldn't affect Sylvia's child. It was partly to drive away the fear that Heather declared "The baby's all that matters. We don't need to know any more to look after it and its, let's say his for now, his mother."

She hoped Sam wouldn't disagree with that. She was less than reassured when the question that slowly opened his mouth proved to be "What have you forgotten?"

"I wouldn't remember, would I?" When the sally fell short of him and did little for her, she said "What are you trying to remind me of?"

"You said outside you'd forgotten stuff too. How do you know if you don't remember what it was?"

"I meant while I was a student, round about your age, come to think. Maybe it's something that runs in the family, we go a little strange when we're that age."

None of this appeared to hearten him. She was wondering whether she should try to take any of it back when she heard footsteps behind him. She saw him move his arm, which looked not much less stiff than a branch, to let Sylvia's note drift like a dead leaf onto the hall table. Though he didn't turn until the key had finished scraping in the lock and the front door had swung inward, she couldn't read his mask of a face. As his aunt leaned her swollen body against the door to shut it, he twisted swiftly around. "We were just talking about you," he said.

Sylvia raised her eyebrows slightly and the corners of her mouth. The expression made her look as her childhood self had looked— dreamily assured that all was well and ready to anticipate better—but her words were older, even second-hand. "Nothing bad, I hope."

"Maybe I don't know what is," said Sam.

"Nothing to do with any of us, can we say?"

He shrugged or writhed his shoulders, and Heather tried to put a stop to his embarrassment. "We were talking about our happy event," she told Sylvia. "What we really want to know is how you feel."

"Like I expect I'm supposed to."

"Well, good. Is it?"

"Like we could be seeing the one we're all waiting for any day now."

"He'll be a few months yet, Sylvie, or she will."

"Time doesn't seem to mean too much any more. Maybe that's because it doesn't to him."

With an affectionate laugh at the extravagance of that idea Heather said "You know he's a him or you want him to be?"

"Even these days I don't think we get a choice."

"It's just that we were wondering before."

"Were you, Sam?" Sylvia raised her eyebrows further while leaving her mouth as it was, and rested her hands on either side of her pro- truding burden as though to offer it to him. "What do you need to know?"

His shoulders moved again, convulsively. "Nothing," Heather would have predicted as his answer, and it was.

"Then we're together on that. I've got his name, and that's all I want."

She hadn't finished speaking when Heather realised she had some- how failed to be aware that they, Sam in particular, were well-nigh trapping Sylvia in the hall with the faint ancient smell that seemed almost to have been attracted by their conversation. "One thing I do

know," she said, "is you might like to sit down if you're anything like
I was."

She thought she was going to have to ask Sam to move, since
something—no doubt his embarrassment she'd failed to banish—
appeared to have paralysed him. Then he limped aside as if his restless
shoulders were operating the rest of him, and Sylvia plodded into the
front room to lower herself onto an armchair. Sam was taking his
discomfort upstairs when she said "We'll have something to look forward to tomorrow."

Sam's hand clenched on the banister, and it was left to Heather to
ask "What?"

"Mom, I keep telling myself I should call her mum now I'm back
where I came from, she's going to show us the videos she's made.
We're all invited."

"Then we'll all be there, won't we, Sam?"

Before Sam could perform more than a pair of nods that seemed to
force out a double mumble of resignation, the phone rang. Heather
saw his knuckles whiten on the banister, and he kept his back to her as
she picked up the receiver. "Hello?" she said with a tentativeness that
felt like timidity on his behalf.

"Is the new bookman home yet?"

"Hello, Terry," she said, as much for Sam's benefit as his. "He is but
he isn't."

"That doesn't sound like you, Heather. Do you feel like making
yourself clearer if it isn't too late in the day?"

"He didn't get as far as the interview."

Terry emitted a sound that could have passed for either a gasp or a
sigh before he demanded "Who stopped him?"

"Nobody that I'm aware of. He forgot where he was going. It can
happen."

"Not to me. How could he forget something that important, for
heaven's sake?"

"Too much pressure, do you think?"

"What pressure? He wasn't under any."

Sam had turned to gaze blank-faced not quite at her. "You can't say that," she said.

"I thought I just did. Is he there for me to speak to?"

"I'll see," Heather said as neutrally as she could manage.

She was holding the receiver towards Sam and miming a disinterested question when she heard Terry complain "It isn't always the man's fault, you know." She couldn't help thinking, however unreasonably, that he'd saved the comment until he thought she was unable to hear. "I didn't know I suggested it was," she said, having snatched the receiver back to her face. "I imagined you'd think he was taking after me as usual, and perhaps you'd even be right in this instance."

"I'm that more often than you'd like to admit."

It felt as though one of the arguments they'd succeeded in avoiding while they were together had grown harsher for being stored up. She thought Sam meant to rescue them from any more of it by limping downstairs and reaching for the phone. "It's me," he said, sounding less than entirely convinced.

Heather withdrew into the front room, where Sylvia whispered "So where did he end up?"

"I didn't ask."

Sylvia sat back as though to let the occupant of her midriff join her in overhearing Sam. "Just what mum said," he confessed. "I never got to London . . . If it's anyone's fault it's mine, all right? . . . I called when I got home but she'd gone . . . I will next week if you think I should . . . I've said I will . . . Mum?"

The receiver hit the table with a clunk. By the time Heather retrieved it Sam was limping doggedly to his room. His door closed as she said "What now?"

"I won't pretend I'm happy."

"Nobody's asking you," said Heather, and was tempted to pause before continuing, "to pretend. You don't think Sam is, surely."

"Happy or pretending?"

"Either."

"I wouldn't mind you seeming more concerned."

"I don't need to perform it to be it, and I hope you didn't overdo it to him."

"I went to quite a lot of trouble to set that interview up."

"I'm sorry if you think it was all for nothing."

"No, it was all for Sam."

The argument and its pointlessness were starting to exhaust her so much that she almost didn't care who won. "Shall we let him work it out for himself? We'll speak again sometime," she said without leaving a gap for an answer, and planted the receiver on its hook. When her silence didn't entice Sam onto the landing she made with some purposefulness for the front room.

Sylvia was so deep in her armchair she looked crushed into very little by her belly. "The main thing is he's home now, right?" she said.

"I suppose it must be," Heather said and shut the door. "I'll start dinner in a minute."

"Gosh, that's from the past."

"What is, Sylvie?"

"The way you're looking now."

"Which is . . ."

"Like a sister who wants to stand in for our mum and dad."

"I don't think I'm that ambitious, but can I ask you a question you don't have to answer if you don't want to, though I'd really like it if you did?"

"I don't see how I can say no yet."

"How did you meet Natty's father?"

"You're using his name. I like that," Sylvia said and smiled down at herself. "We like it, don't we?"

"You don't mind my asking."

"It's the kind of thing a sister trying to be a parent would want to know. We don't mind, do we?"

"Just a sister would." Heather was near to feeling excluded from the conversation. She sat opposite Sylvia in case that reclaimed her attention, but Sylvia didn't look up. "So am I going to hear how?" Heather said.

"We met in the right place at the right time. That's the closest to a fairy tale most people get, if they ever do."

"You didn't make it sound like one when you first told me about him."

"Depends which kind of fairy tale you're thinking of."

"Which are you?"

"I don't need to," Sylvia said and raised her eyes. "I'm living the truth."

"So tell me it. Don't be alone with it."

For a long breath Sylvia seemed to be gazing out of somewhere distant and dark, and then her gaze was attracted downwards. "I'm not alone," she murmured, "am I?"

"One more question," Heather managed to ask instead of pleading.

"We're listening."

"Where did you meet?"

"Closer to home than you'd think."

"Not—" Heather couldn't quite commit her fear to words, given its potential for offending Sylvia. Instead she tried "Not America, then."

Sylvia didn't speak until she'd regarded Heather with a sympathetic look not far short of pitying. "Not where you're thinking of."

Heather didn't care how American the father was so long as he hadn't been an inmate of the mental hospital, however unreasonable a prejudice that was. Of course, she thought, the baby must have been conceived in America, otherwise its growth would be too rapid, positively unnatural. She jumped up to deliver a hug that was intended to be both apologetic and accepting. "I'm glad we understand each other."

"Isn't that what sisters are meant to be for?" Having said that, Sylvia slipped out of Heather's embrace as though her midriff had tugged at her. "Do you mind if we lie down till dinner?"

Heather had to remind herself that she wasn't being referred to. "You get as much rest as you can," she urged. As she watched Sylvia plodding upstairs towards the insidious smell as reminiscent of dead wood as of old paper, she felt more excluded than ever. She almost felt she hadn't understood at all.

27

A Family Conference

HIS parents didn't know, Sam reminded himself yet again. That was the most important thing—that they never would. He and his aunt had done what they'd done, and there was no taking it back. They never would have done it if either of them had realised who the other was. Perhaps the relationship they hadn't recognised was theirs explained their instant attraction; if something else had caused them to perform, he never wanted to know. It was one of the nightmares he kept having while awake, the most immediate and real of which was that his mother would find out somehow. If she did, he could only flee to his car and drive away. It wouldn't matter if he had no idea where he was going so long as he never came back.

He'd almost reached home after failing to go for the interview when the prospect of confronting his mother had started to fill him with dread. He had been sure his guilt would be visible on his face, and had struggled to concoct another reason for it before he'd grasped that she was more than satisfied to worry about his problems with the interview, which she would also take to be causing any unease on his part—but the realisation freed his mind to wonder if Sylvia remembered as much as he did.

On her return from Margo's he thought she saw he'd learned

something. He'd kept feeling ill at ease with her ever since she'd come to stay, and that no longer seemed inexplicable, but the more he considered her behaviour towards him, the less certain he was how she felt about him. He had to discover how much she recalled, but not while there was the slightest chance that his mother might overhear, and so he'd spent a dinner that had felt prolonged almost beyond endurance in manufacturing conversation that had struck him as either suspiciously awkward and feeble or not nearly neutral enough. Once his mother and Sylvia had settled down to watch a television documentary about a female explorer whose discoveries had been claimed by better-known male Victorians, he'd taken that as an excuse to retreat to his room. Eventually he'd crawled into bed to wait until he was confident his mother was asleep. Now it was the darkest hour of the night, and he was beginning to think he would never be confident enough.

For a moment, or it might have been much longer, he grew unconscious of the dark and of the quilt that felt fattened by the mugginess even the night and the inch he'd left the window open seemed unable to dissipate. Something that resembled sleep kept snatching at his mind like this but came as no relief. All too often it was clammy with memories of thrusting himself deep into Sylvia, the earth of the mound gritting beneath his knees, the woods encircling him and looming over him like a multitude that had crept close to watch. The recollection threatened to swell him until guilt shrank him. Other images he found in the depths of his mind disturbed him in another way; they felt like someone else's memories, of a void that teemed with unseen life, a space so boundless it contained worlds beyond imagining. Once he glimpsed an eyeless form that glided from planet to planet and held each in its many-clawed wings while it absorbed the life-force of entire civilisations of creatures whose shapes he was grateful to be unable to distinguish. Once he saw a massive globe so dark no star could illuminate it, which roved in search of inhabited worlds, distorting them and their denizens before it engulfed them to the sound of countless pleas and screams lost in the void. Once, before he contrived to think his desperate way back to his room, he had to watch a member groping out of the limitless blackness to clutch at a whole solar system of planets, using appendages that nothing should possess, and lift its catch towards a face Sam barely managed not to discern in any detail, a presence whose glee felt like the end of all life. Now he was seeing only the woods, but all the trees were straining themselves skyward like antennae to capture some aspect of the source of these visions. He twitched himself awake before the impression had time to grow clearer, and then his breath caught in his dry throat. He could still hear the woods.

It was the wind, he told himself, though it sounded more like the irregular breaths of an entity that was trying to come to life. Even when Sam floundered onto his back and raised his head out of the darkness that the visions seemed to have lodged in his mind, it did. He widened his hot sluggish sticky eyes until his sight managed to separate the outlines of the contents of his room from the rest of the dimness, but the familiar disorder failed to ward off the notion that he was trapped in a dream or that the dream was real. He fumbled to dislodge the tangled sweaty quilt and sat on the edge of the bed, massaging some of an ache out of his leg, before limping to the window.

As he leaned across the desk to peer through the glass he felt as if the night had exhaled an unhealthily warm sweetish breath in his face. It was only a hint of the wind that set the treetops beyond the common groping for the darkness overhead that no amount of stars could relieve. The vast distant chorus sounded more like a secretive whisper now, but was that wholly outside the house? He eased the sash down until wood met wood, then raised his head and risked closing his eyes while he strained to hear.

There was a noise in the house. Perhaps it was the sound of someone, not necessarily as few as one, rather more than breathing in their sleep. He picked his unsteady way across the cluttered floor and took all the time he needed to edge the door silently open. As soon as it moved he heard somebody snoring with a discretion that bordered on elegance.

If it was his mother, he hoped she would keep it up. So long as he could hear she was asleep he would take the chance to venture into Sylvia's room, though he wasn't sure if he wanted to find her awake. When he stepped onto the landing he could tell it was his mother who was snoring. Something else was audible, if barely, in his aunt's room. Pressing an ear against an upper panel didn't let him identify it, and so he took hold of the unexpectedly warm doorknob with both hands to ease the door inward.

Perhaps the sound had come from the forest—her window was open wide—but he couldn't shake off a conviction that more than trees had been responsible for the furtive murmur. He sidled past the door and limped into the unlit room. His aunt was lying face up on the bed. So much of her was a dark lump that he could have imagined the mound on which she'd taken him had grown within her. It was his child, he thought, his child, but the concept seemed more than his mind could encompass. He was peering past the bulk of her, and had just succeeded in discerning that she was asleep, when he grew aware of being watched from somewhere in the darkness.

The only movement he could locate was on the far side of the common. He limped to the window with as much reluctance as stealth, and the smell of Selcouth's journal rose to meet him. Just now he preferred not to recall any of the passages Sylvia had read to him. As he ducked towards the gap beneath the sash, a wind intensified the ancient smell that could have been of the book or of the woods or both. At the same time the glimmering trees made a concerted gesture that might have heralded a revelation. He was struggling to grasp what he ought to understand when his sense of being watched returned. The watcher was behind him.

He twisted around, almost falling against his grandfather's desk as his bad leg threatened not to keep up. Though his aunt's eyes were closed, she was mouthing in her sleep. He couldn't deduce her words, and was glad of it while he was conscious of being observed, perhaps not with eyes, from somewhere darker than the room. There was no point in trying to deny that the watcher was in front of him, on the bed. The knowledge paralysed him, and then it sent him out so fast that the room appeared to stagger around him. He was forcing himself to linger until the door had been inched shut when he heard Sylvia mumble in her sleep. "Not yet, Natty," he thought she said, and "Not dark enough."

Whatever else she pronounced or came close to pronouncing was rendered unintelligible by the intervention of the door. Sam loitered only briefly before fleeing to his room and crawling into bed. No visions lay in wait for him. He was wondering uneasily whether they'd ceased because they or something related to them had succeeded in making a point when their absence let exhaustion catch up with him. For perhaps another second he was aware merely of the dark, and then not of that either.

No time at all seemed to pass before he was roused by a light someone was shining into the darkness to find him. She was calling to him. Once he began to understand her words they wrenched him further awake. "Are you staying down there all day?" she said.

At first he didn't know where he was or who. He forced his cumbersome eyelids open to see Sylvia looming over him. Her patient face appeared to be perched birdlike on top of her increased bulk. The light that was the sun beyond the window at her back showed Sam his room, but nevertheless he stammered "Down where?"

"In your lair." Presumably observing his confusion, she tried "In your bed."

"I couldn't sleep."

She gave that a smile of amused disbelief. There was no point in arguing when they had far more crucial issues to discuss. "What were you—what do you want?" he mumbled, still less than awake.

"Someone's come to see you."

His mind shrank from the possibility that she meant her child—their child, a notion that he wished the daylight could reveal to be a wild and grotesque dream. "Who?" he found himself able only to whisper.

"Can't you hear?"

She couldn't be inviting him to listen for the sounds he'd overheard in the night, he thought or tried to think. All the same, as he shoved himself upright against the pillow he felt as though he was recoiling, and not just from her. He had to drag his mind free of the idea to be capable of hearing voices downstairs, his mother's and a man's. "Who is it?" he had to ask.

"Mr Harvey, Mr Harvey."

He didn't know when he'd last been called that. If he'd had time he might have wondered whether he was even sure of his own name, but he was too busy wanting to learn "What's he saying?"

"Sounds a tad serious."

His father's voice had grown lower and more intense, and Sam didn't need to hear the words to guess the subject was himself. "I'll tell him you'll be on your way, shall I?" Sylvia said.

Sam heard his mother's voice sink to meet his father's, presumably in disagreement. He couldn't think when he might have a better opportunity to talk to Sylvia without the risk of being overheard. "Wait," he pleaded.

From turning away she swung completely around and back to him, so that he imagined her midriff or its tenant acting like the needle of a compass. "Yes, Sam?"

He took a breath only to have to swallow. It felt as though all the questions he might ask were shrinking into him. As Sylvia raised her eyebrows and parted her lips he managed to say "Will you tell me something?"

"Anything I know."

"When was the first time you saw me the age I am now?"

An expression that might have been some kind of smile flickered across her mouth before she said "Could be this very moment, couldn't it?"

"Grown up, I mean. When did you see me grown up?"

"Last year."

"When last year?"

"Are you asking for a date?"

The possibility that she was gently mocking him infuriated Sam. "No," he not much less than snarled, "I'm asking when was the first time we—got together."

"What would Heather say?"

That put him in mind of being found out by his mother, and made him blurt "In her library."

"Are you saying she's wrong?"

"Wouldn't you?"

He heard how accusing his tone had become, but couldn't think of any other way to sound, although disbelief was catching up with him—disbelief that they could be talking or rather not talking about what he fancied they were. He was struggling not to apologise or to concede the verbal game when Sylvia's expression owned up to itself. She contrived to look both suddenly aged and much younger as she murmured "What do you think you've remembered, Sam?"

"I don't just think, I know."

She glanced downwards, and he might have suspected that she was seeking instructions from the bulk of herself if he hadn't heard his parents arguing beneath her feet. Their voices seemed trapped by the floorboards—as trapped as he felt while he awaited his aunt's response. "Then do you think there could be a better time and place to talk about it?" she said.

"I want to now."

That wasn't just childish, it wasn't even true. It had been forced out of him by the realisation that until she'd spoken, his disbelief had remained a hope too secret to admit to himself. He could only watch as her face took its expression back. "So talk," she said.

He made his mouth open without the least idea what might emerge. If it hadn't been for recognising how stupid he must look, he might have clung to his silence. As it was, he faltered "Did I . . ."

"What, Sam?" she said with a hint of a smile.

"Did *we*. Did we . . ."

His harshness trailed off, but it had driven her smile into hiding. "Yes," she said blank-faced.

"You're saying," he stammered in a last attempt at incredulity, "you're saying we . . ."

"I'm saying only you and I know who the father is," said Sylvia, her gaze drifting inwards or downwards or both. "Except Natty will, of course."

That had to be years in the future, Sam told himself, and there was a far more immediate threat. "You won't tell anyone else, will you?" he pleaded.

"Wouldn't you want them to know?"

"Christ, what do you think?"

Her gaze took its time over finding him. The last expression he would have anticipated glimpsing in her eyes was hurt, and it made him more nervous still. "As the father likes," she said.

"Promise?"

"Nobody's going to learn who it was from me. There, will that let you sleep nights?"

Sam had to make an effort not to feel convicted of being a bad father. "Maybe nothing will," he muttered.

"If there's anything else I can do to help—" She must have sensed his inward wince, because she marched with some haughtiness to the door. "I'd better announce you," she said primly. "Mr Harvey must be wondering what's keeping you."

Even more disconcerting than her adoption of the role of a concerned relative was his sense that she thought it only reasonable and expected him to think so too. He didn't move until she began to plod downstairs, at which point he emerged from the refuge of the quilt and limped fast to grab his robe from the hook on the door, feeling painfully conscious of his nakedness. He'd just ventured onto the landing when his father called "Is that someone coming to life at last?"

"Something like that," Sam mumbled and dodged into the bathroom, where he was afraid he might be sick. Instead he had to watch his penis empty itself, his treacherous tube of flesh that had failed to recognise his aunt except as an irresistible partner. At least now her pregnancy stood between him and her attractiveness. Once he'd finished watching himself drip he was confronted by his face in the mirror. He couldn't think when he'd last seen anything that had less to say to him. When his meaninglessness sent him out of the room, his father called "Are you joining us now?"

"Depends who us is," Sam muttered, but seemed to have no other option than to trudge downstairs.

"I hope nobody thinks I'm unapproachable. You can tell me whatever you like."

His father had lowered his voice. For a dreadful moment Sam imagined that the invitation was addressed to Sylvia, and nearly lost his footing in his haste to limp downstairs. She and his mother were indeed with his father in the front room. His mother looked ready to defend Sam, but Sylvia's face was keeping its plans to itself. His father barely waited for Sam to enter the room before he said "Here you are, sit down. Let's feel at ease if we can."

Sam's mother gave that an askance blink suggesting she thought his father had forgotten whose house this was, then turned to Sylvia. "We'll leave them to talk, shall we?"

Sylvia was lowering herself beside Sam's father on the couch. "Isn't this for the whole family to hear?" she said as she settled her bulk or it settled on her.

"You won't mind that, will you, old chap? It can help to have someone with a different perspective around when you've a problem to solve."

"I don't see how."

"I wouldn't expect you to till we've given it a try," his father said with just a flash of sharpness. "Apologies to anyone if they've heard it all before, but off you go, Sam. Tell us exactly what happened yesterday, only do sit down first for heaven's sake. I'm always scared you'll topple over since you fell out of your tree."

Sam dropped himself into an armchair. "I told you."

"I want to hear it all from you. I didn't understand half what I heard on the phone."

"Then you couldn't have been listening properly," Sam's mother said.

"Let Sam talk."

His father said this with a trace of weariness she could have taken as quite an insult, and Sam felt compelled to respond before she did. "I lost my way, that's all."

"Give it some consideration, old chap. That won't be all you'll be telling Fay Sheridan, will it?"

"I don't know what to say except the truth."

"Nothing but the whole of it. That's what we're waiting to hear."

As Sam flinched inwardly at the prospect his father sat forward, clapping a hand on either thigh. "So where was the problem really? What are we going to tell Fay after she was expecting so much?"

"Maybe she shouldn't have been."

"Does anyone else think we're hearing the problem? You won't get far by underrating yourself, Sam. Everyone here thinks you are, don't they?"

"I don't believe anybody could overrate you, Sam," his mother said.

Sam was preoccupied with dreading that his aunt would join in, and she did. "There's more to him than most people realise."

That brought the whole truth close to escaping his lips. It felt as though an insect was writhing inside them. As he did his utmost to swallow, his father insisted "Nobody's asking more of you than you're capable of, old chap. Fay wouldn't be, so I don't understand why you're looking like that."

No doubt Sam's fear of knowing how he looked did his expression no favours, which might have been why his mother said "Terry, if you could just—"

"Anything except not find out what exactly happened so it can't again," Sam's father said and pointed his upturned hands at Sam. "I know one thing you didn't tell me."

Sam glimpsed secret amusement in his aunt's eyes—amusement that he was dismayed to realise she wanted him to share. He glanced hastily away but still felt watched, and by more watchers than he could see. He only just accomplished enough of a swallow to croak "What?"

"Where you got lost."

"On the way."

"You know, I believe I could have figured that out for myself. Where on it?"

"The second junction on the motorway."

"Second from where?"

"Home."

"You're saying what, ten miles from here?"

"More like fifteen."

"It's a deal. I'll give you fifteen," Sam's father said, then let his jaw drop in case the mirthless joke had lacked obviousness. "You won't ask Fay to accept you forgot where you were going so close to home and straight along the motorway as well. I'm sure nobody here can."

"I can," Sylvia said.

"You'll tell me how. What do you know about him that I don't and it looks as if his mother doesn't either?"

Sam saw his aunt part her lips with the tip of her tongue. He was fighting to draw a breath while he thought of an interruption when his father lost more patience. "Is he on drugs?"

"Are you, Sam?" his mother said as if the direct question was an offer she was making him.

"No."

"Then what?" his father demanded. "What do you need to tell us?"

Abruptly Sam had had enough. That aspect of the truth was more than he could be bothered keeping to himself. "I can't leave here," he said.

"Of course you can," his father protested, so immediately he hadn't time to sound impatient. "It'll be easier for you than it was for me."

"I never said it was easy for you, but you wanted to go, didn't you?"

"Are you saying you don't want to make anything of yourself?"

The question and indeed the entire argument seemed dwarfed into insignificance by the visions that had come to Sam in the night. "All I'm saying is that's you," he said, and in a desperate attempt to lessen the scrutiny he was enduring "It isn't us."

"Hold on, old chap, I think that's a bit much. You can't use these ladies as an excuse for hanging about. Your mother wants to stay near Margo, maybe your aunt does as well, and anyway you know why Sylvia wouldn't want to venture far just now. Only forgive me if I'm blunt, but that's got nothing to do with you, has it? There's no way you'll be involved, so there's no point in making it sound as if the family's the reason why you won't move yourself."

Sam gazed hot-eyed at him in a vain attempt to render himself unaware of Sylvia. "It's only you who's making out I did."

"So what reason are you giving us?"

"I told you, I can't leave. Something won't let me." As he spoke he grasped how true that was, which dismayed him so much he tried to take some of it back. "My mind," he said.

"Please promise me you won't say that to Fay Sheridan."

"You're talking as if this is all about this Fay woman," Sam's mother objected. "It seems to me it's about Sam."

"Let's leave Fay out of it by all means."

"I won't ask if your relationship with her has to do with more than Sam."

"You can. It has."

"And was he supposed to help that?"

"You're asking if I used him to attract her, is that what I'm hearing?"

"You'll hear what you choose to hear, Terry, and it wouldn't be the first or the dozenth time either."

Sam might have been grateful that their attention had wandered away from him if that hadn't left him more aware of Sylvia's. He sensed that he wasn't alone in finding the argument wholly irrelevant, beside some much greater point, and whose view was he sharing if not hers? "What's this got to do with anything?" he blurted.

His mother looked betrayed, his father justified. "Fair enough, you're the subject," his father said. "Tell us what you think the trouble is with your mind."

"When I tried to leave I nearly had a breakdown."

"That'll be a bit of an exaggeration, will it?"

"It won't, no. I couldn't remember where I was supposed to be going, I couldn't think at all. I couldn't do anything except come back."

He heard his aunt's lips emit a small moist sound. When he glanced at her, unable to predict what she might say, she was gazing at him as though he'd conveyed more than he knew. "All right, old chap, you're with the family," his father said. "What do we think he needs?"

"Understanding," said Sam's mother.

"To stay," Sylvia said almost as immediately.

"We can do better than that, can't we?" When nobody responded other than by staring, Sam's father said "Shall I tell you what I think is wrong with your noggin, Sam?"

"Not drugs," Sam's mother said at once.

"Of course not drugs. He says not and I believe him. I wouldn't think he'd go anywhere near those after what they did to his grandfather. No, Sam, I wonder if when you fell out of that tree you hurt more than your leg."

"I don't know."

"It's a possibility then, isn't it?" Sam's father asked the women. Since that received only a guarded assent from Sam's mother and none from Sylvia, he went on "Better find out what someone thinks who knows more about it than we do."

"Did you have anyone in mind?" Sam's mother said not much less than accusingly.

"I seem to recall you and Margo felt Lennox's doctor at the hospital was a good sort."

Though Sam's mother didn't quite grimace, Sam could tell she was distressed, whether by remembering how the doctor had failed to save Lennox or by the notion of sending her son to the Arbour. "Let's see if it happens again first," she said. "You'll be giving the interview another try next week, will you, Sam?"

He felt as though she'd missed the point only Sylvia had understood, but he said "I'll call dad's friend."

As her face restrained itself from showing her opinion of that, his father said "Can I ask you to undertake a bit more?"

"Depends if she wants me," Sam said, however dishonestly.

"I'll do my best on that front. What I'd like you to promise is that if you find you still have trouble leaving, you see the doctor."

"I'll see someone who knows about it."

"I expect that'll do." All the same, he let his gaze linger on Sam's face before sending himself to his feet with a slap of the thighs. "Well, if everyone will excuse me I ought to be on my way. Things to catch up with in town," he said, then grabbed Sam's hand to clasp it in both of his. "You'll be fine, old chap. Just tell yourself you will. We all have our days off mentally, don't we, girls, but there isn't much that won't fix in my experience. Remember you've got everyone in this room, Sam, and Margo too if you need her."

Sam felt that his father's touch and his intended meaning had both fallen short of him. When his father released him at last, Sam watched his parents make for the hall. As soon as they were out of the room he limped to close the door. He heard them murmuring outside the house, presumably about him, but that wasn't important now. He turned to Sylvia, who looked pinned down on the couch by her midriff. "You can't leave either, can you?"

"No." She said that as though the admission was a release, and yet he couldn't tell if the gleam deep in her eyes was of fear or delight or both, or even more that he might not want to learn. "None of us will," she said.

28

A Private View

"HERE'S all my family where I live at last," Margo cried. "I just wish you could all see what I have to show you and not just all but one."

She was bustling about the living-room of her apartment, which occupied the top floor of a large two-storey house on the eastern side of Goodmanswood. Like the largest space—her studio—the room faced the restless woods that appeared to be clawing darkness down from the night sky smudged by the glow of the intervening streets. Heather found the woods as distracting as Margo's behaviour, her hurrying to refill the glasses of champagne and Sylvia's of sparkling water between repeating offers of the trayfuls of hors d'oeuvres she'd prepared as if she was determined to transform the smallish room cluttered with venerable furniture into the location of her latest opening. "Sit down then, someone," she cried now. "You have a seat, Sylvia. I do believe you're bigger than yesterday."

As soon as Sylvia deposited herself on half of the couch, Sam limped to the farthest chair. "Are you going to be lonely over there, Sam?" Margo protested at once.

"No room for that," he said, largely to himself.

"Is he a tad nervous about the imminent event? Is that the trouble?"

"Hardly imminent yet," Heather said, having gathered that Margo meant the birth rather than tonight's show.

"You'd think it was, looking at her," said Margo, holding out a tray until Sylvia took a morsel in each hand. "I'm right, though, aren't I? Don't be afraid of our Sylvia, Sam. She's the same person she's always been. There'll just be more of her for a while."

While Heather thought Margo had identified one reason for his nervousness, she was certain that he didn't want attention drawn to it. As he performed an understated mime of not knowing where to rest his gaze, Margo turned to Sylvia. "Maybe when he's old enough or she is you'll be bringing Natty to see my new work somewhere else."

"I'm sure it'll be a different place."

Heather tried not to feel that Sylvia was sharing a secret with herself or at least not with the person she was supposed to be addressing. Had she felt that sometimes when they were little, perhaps in the woods? Before she could begin to grasp the memory, Margo said "I guess if we can all settle ourselves it'll be show time."

Sitting next to Sylvia, Heather felt dwarfed by some aspect of her. As Sylvia sent down the last of her handfuls of food to the source of the hunger, Margo switched on the video camera that was hooked up to the television. "It'll be bigger when it's finished," she said.

"What will?" Sam was apparently nervous of knowing.

"The image. When Lucinda exhibits it, I mean."

"Has she seen it yet?" said Heather.

"Heavens no. This is only the raw material in no kind of shape. I just wanted my family to see what I've made of the woods so far." As Margo crossed to the light switch she added "I hope I haven't got anyone expecting too much."

Heather didn't know what to expect. She seemed to glimpse the treetops across Goodmanswood raising themselves as though Margo had released them or alerted them by switching off the light. "Now it's dark," Sylvia said.

It was partly suspecting whom this was meant for that made Heather ask "Does it need to be?"

A silence gave her time to be uncertain who would answer. "Some of the footage is," Margo said.

She took hold of various items of furniture on the way to entrusting herself to the last available chair and picking up a remote control in either hand. The television responded first, displaying a carnivorous plant in the act of closing a beaded leaf on a fly already torpid from the effects of being snared. Though the film was speeded up, this only made the insect's feeble struggles look more desperate, while the inexorable movement of the vegetable mouth continued to appear gloating, positively conscious. Then, as Margo turned on the video camera, greyness flooded the screen like a sudden fog that momentarily hid the woods before they lurched into the room.

At least, their image did. The trees themselves and their elongated shadows were quite still. Heather deduced that they were in the depths of the forest, since there was no sound, no hint of a world beyond. The image wobbled and then stabilised as the camera began to zoom forward, appearing to pass through entrance after scaly wooden entrance on the way to some goal. The automatic focus kept wavering as if the trees were losing substance and then forming themselves afresh. As the zoom reached its limit, the clump of trees on which it settled lost all focus, swelling up like greyish tentacles or fingers full of poison, and a vague movement flickered across them. "What was that?" Heather felt delegated to ask.

"Me not getting it right first time," Margo said, presumably taking the question as a criticism. "Then I figured out I ought to use the manual focus," she explained over the next shot. It could have been of the same trees, but the zoom was even slower. As each pair of encrusted tree-trunks advanced to frame its progress they grew intensely clear, and Heather could have fancied they were taking hold of layers of her consciousness. The forest was silent except for the occasional creak of the camera as Margo filmed; it sounded more like wood than plastic. Heather was thinking she ought to find something to praise when, to the extreme left of the image, a shadow or a more solid presence dodged out of reach of the zoom. "What—" she was unable not to blurt.

"It must have been me," said Margo.

"I don't see how. You've gone beyond your shadow."

"Then it was something behind me and taller than me, except I'm sure it wasn't anything," Margo said and reversed the tape. "There, you see? It was nothing at all."

Heather could only assume the furtive movement had been the effect of a speck of dust or a transient flaw in the tape, since it didn't repeat itself. "I hope nobody's thinking this is how it will look when it's finished," Margo said. "This is just the raw material."

"What was in your mind?" Sylvia murmured.

"Making you look again. That's all my work can ever be about, isn't it?"

"Look for what?" Sam said uneasily.

"Keep watching and maybe you'll see."

Heather wondered if Margo wasn't sure. She saw her mother's shadow ensnared by trees, split into thin inhuman fragments and transformed into wood. The image had begun to spin, turning wholly over and righting itself, as the zoom advanced. Perhaps it was this disorientation that made her feel she kept missing glimpses of movement at the very edge of the image. If they had really been present, wouldn't Margo have seen them and reacted to them? Not necessarily, given the gathering twilight, which had Heather hoping Margo was close to the edge of the woods. That only showed how irrational she was letting herself become, since her mother had already returned safely from them. The camera lingered over yet another vertiginous zoom through the intricacies of the forest, drawing each layer of tree-trunks into focus and absorbing the dimness. The zoom had almost reached its limit when a clump of trees that filled the screen appeared to acknowledge it or Margo by bowing towards it and stretching out the tips of their branches. "How did you manage to achieve that?" Heather was anxious to know.

"Oh, it's full of tricks. I wouldn't be surprised if I haven't even used some of them yet. Camera tricks, I mean."

Heather thought Margo might as well have admitted she had no idea. "So that's all I've done so far," Margo said. "As I say, it won't look anything like that when it's finished, but what does anyone think?"

The footage had left Heather feeling she'd been in the woods for hours. She was trying to summon up a different comment, since the dim figures of her sister and her son had uttered none, when another image of the woods appeared on the screen, and then Margo did. "Well, look at me," Margo said. "I forgot I did that."

Heather thought she looked nervous, both on the screen and in its glow. She was wandering away between the trees and peering around at the gloom. She halted beside a stooped deformed tree as if she'd noticed something Heather was unable to distinguish. Then, so slowly that to begin with Heather couldn't be sure it was happening, Margo set about assuming the posture of the tree, raising her left shoulder in imitation of a fibrous swelling on the trunk, twisting her left arm into a shape Heather imagined would have been worse than painful so as to copy the position of a crippled branch, letting her right arm droop almost to the obscure mosaic of fallen leaves to emulate another. As she bent low, the camera inched down to follow her, and Sam turned a gasp into a whisper. "What's holding the camera?"

"A tree, I should think." When Margo's attempt at irony went unremarked she said impatiently "A tree, of course."

"But it moved."

"Obviously the camera slipped."

Heather found the spectacle it had captured disturbing enough in itself. Margo seemed determined to hold her pose until the night swallowed her up. "You can laugh if you want, anyone," she said from her chair without taking her own advice. "I want you to be honest about how you feel."

"How did you?" said Sylvia.

Margo gazed for some moments at her past self before declaring "Peaceful. Really peaceful."

Heather was watching her grow more lost in the dimness of the woods or in her sense of them—she'd begun to wonder what audience Margo had thought she was performing for or trying to placate by imitation—when a shiver that suggested an imminent transformation passed through Margo and the tree, and at once the screen turned blank. "The battery must have run down," Margo said.

That would explain the shiver as well, Heather told herself. "I'll put the light on, shall I?" she said.

It revealed her family blinking as if they had just wakened from a dream. Sam peered at the screen, apparently to make sure nothing further would manifest itself, and then he mumbled "When did you realise?"

"I'm sorry, what?" said Margo. "Realise what?"

"How long did you stay like that before you realised you weren't filming?"

"Don't laugh, but I really can't remember."

This visibly disturbed him—because, Heather concluded, he was becoming aware how age might affect his grandmother. "What were you after in the woods?" he said, barely aloud.

"I can't tell you that either. You know me. My work's about finding out if it's about anything, not knowing in advance. So is anyone going to risk an opinion of the footage so far?"

"I'd say it felt like the birth of something new," Sylvia said.

"Or something old," Sam muttered.

"As long as you're inspired, mummy," said Heather.

She didn't mean that to be patronising, but perhaps that was how it sounded. "I shouldn't have shown you," Margo said.

Heather hoped that wasn't aimed solely at her. "Who else if not us?"

"Nobody at all while I've nothing to show but work in progress. You won't know it when I've finished. Maybe you won't know me." Margo switched off the television and set the tape rewinding, then dug her fingernails into the arms of her chair and struggled to raise herself. "Give me a boost, someone," she said. "The old bones aren't what they were."

Sam limped across the room before anyone else could help and lifted Margo out of the chair by her elbows. She took some time over straightening up from a crouch. Of course she wasn't having to emerge from the posture she'd adopted in the woods, although her performance there might explain why she was stiff. "Thank you for coming," she said.

"We can stay longer if you like," Heather said.

"I've bored you long enough. I want to have another look and see what I can make of it."

"We don't mind watching it again," Heather said, however dismaying a repeat of Margo's mime would be.

"You mustn't think I'm being hostile if I ask you to leave me alone with it. I truly believe that's what I need."

"All right then," Heather said, though it was more a question to the others. If they didn't agree, they must want to believe they did. In either case, she seemed to have denied herself the opportunity to demur further. She confined herself to hugging Margo, and had to restrain her affection from growing too fierce; her mother felt stiff and frail as a bunch of old thin sticks, and more knobbly than Heather remembered, with knuckles that put her in mind of knots in wood. "We'll get together again very soon, won't we?" Heather managed to ask rather than plead.

"Of course we all will."

Margo insisted on making her way downstairs with them, though it was at least as laborious as Sylvia's. "Don't any of you worry about me," she said, waving a hand in front of her face to ward off either a smell of charred food from the ground-floor apartment or the humidity admitted by the front door. "I haven't nearly finished exploring."

Heather might have been happier if she had. Perhaps Sam and Sylvia felt the same—they were as silent as she was, at any rate. An intermittent wind set the hedges that boxed in the large discreet Victorian houses creaking and scraping their leaves together but failed to relieve the January heat that would have been premature even for April. The only other sounds were the footsteps of the Prices, isolated and diminished under the infinite dark. Sam's limp and Sylvia's plodding had brought them to the High Street, from which concrete bollards like standing stones or unnaturally regular tree-stumps barred traffic, when Sylvia said "Are you going to share your feelings with us?"

"Which?" Sam sounded forced to ask.

"Not yours right now, Sam."

"I'd have to ask which too," said Heather.

"Whichever you want us to hear about, but I was thinking of the show mom put on for us."

A wind awoke the scrawny trees that stood guard in front of the bright deserted shops, and bony shadows capered around the roots. "I don't think she made it just for us, did she?" Heather said.

"I believe you got that right, sure enough."

"So long as she doesn't make it too much for herself and loses more of her audience."

"Poor Heather," Sylvia said, and looked pitying. "You've no idea what we're talking about, have you?"

Heather was primed with a retort when Sam glanced hastily away from her. "Who's we?" she asked instead.

"The family, Heather."

"All right," Heather blurted as anger caught up with her. "If everyone knows so much more than me, you tell me some of it, Sam."

At once she was sorry for turning on him. He was looking anywhere except at her, as if they were surrounded by companions visible only to him. "Or you can, Sylvie," she said.

"Why don't you try? Tell us what you feel and you'll be right if you let yourself."

"I feel . . ." Heather had to quell an impression that Sylvia was prompting her to admit she felt both watched and hidden from. "I hope mother will finish in the woods soon and then we can all start to forget about them," she said.

"Not likely."

She didn't know who'd spoken in a whisper that barely owned up to itself; she seemed less to have heard it than to remember having heard. It made her feel more watched than ever, so that she couldn't help glancing behind her. There was no concealment in the paved street lit by display windows and white globular lamps—at least, the occasional benches would hide nothing larger than a child, and the saplings not even that. Those bore no relation to the woods outside the town, and there were no more bony shadows than there ought to be, nor did their twitching betray the presence of shapes too gaunt to live that were about to scuttle into view. She faced forward, only to be confronted by half a dozen trees, their shadows clutching at the pavement as though to help them or some aspect of them rear up. "Sometimes," she muttered before she knew she would, "I wish I hadn't been born here."

"Someone had to be."

Perhaps she wasn't hearing the high thin whisper, since neither Sam's face nor her sister's even hinted at having released it. If the imagination Heather was said to lack had determined to prove her accusers wrong, she would have preferred it to find another time and place. She held back from walking faster than Sam could limp and Sylvia plod, but when they turned the corner towards home she stifled a sigh of relief. She did her best to ignore the unquiet hedges and dimmer shrubs on the way to the corner shop.

The door of J's & J's was open, revealing Joe alone behind the counter. As the Prices came in sight he ceased speaking to three women, who swung round to follow his gaze. Apparently they recognised the Prices, though Heather barely knew them. "Has Jessica left you to it, Joe?" she called.

"She's at home."

His initial pause made Heather consider not enquiring and then ask "Anything wrong?"

"She's looking after the granddaughter."

"Rosemary's all right though, is she?"

The women appeared to feel expected to look hostile on his behalf. "She's been having nightmares about you," he admitted.

"What about me?"

"One of your family. I don't think it was you." He clearly wished they didn't have an audience. "Nightmares or seeing things, one of the two," he said with some defiance.

Heather stepped through the doorway. "Which things?" she was determined to hear.

"I couldn't tell you. You'd have to talk to Jessica. We found the child wandering out the back, it looked like in her sleep. We won't be leaving her in bed at home again if her parents even let her stay."

This sounded more accusing than confessional. "Was she in the woods?" Sylvia asked, having followed Heather into the shop.

"No." He stared at her as if to rebuke her interest—stared almost as hard as the women were staring—but couldn't quite sustain his harshness. "She'd have gone in if we hadn't woken her," he said. "I know you're not supposed to wake anyone that's walking in their sleep, but we didn't know she was till we did."

"So long as you kept her out of there," said a woman with a tin of cat food in her hand. "I wouldn't want a child going anywhere near."

"There's been a few too many seeing things round here just lately," said another, digging her fingers into a sliced white loaf.

"These last few months," the third said, inserting a humbug between lips wrinkled almost colourless.

None of them had looked away from Sylvia, who sighed. "Since I came home, are you saying?"

"Nobody was talking to you," the woman choking the loaf informed her.

"The town hasn't been the same since any of you came here," said her friend, absently scratching the label off the tin of cat food.

"Since someone started messing about in the woods," their companion added in a voice blurred and rendered hollow by the sweet that clicked against her teeth.

Joe was ready to protest, but Heather overtook him. "If you mean our father," she said with a calm she was far from experiencing, "he came here to help you. You already had the problem and he tried to sort it out."

"Ended up as part of it instead," declared the woman with the improvised toy drum.

"Till half the world knew all about it," agreed the strangler of bread.

"No wonder nobody round here can sell their houses," said their friend amid a further bout of clicking.

"Believe me," Heather took some pleasure in saying, "we wish you could."

At first Sylvia seemed willing to let that serve as her own riposte. She was on her way out of the shop when she remarked "Well, now we know what it feels like to be witches, Sam."

"I expect we'll see you soon, Joe," Heather said, and turned her back on the women to see Sam already limping homeward. Once she and Sylvia were out of earshot of the shop, Heather murmured "Did you need to bring up witches?"

"Seems like I must have since I did." Sylvia looked slyly amused by that or with anticipation. "I didn't tell you about the Goodmanswood witch yet, did I?" she said.

"No," said Heather, and even less enthusiastically "Get it over with."

"She lived in the cottage nearest to the woods. After Selcouth died she started spending most of her time in them until people saw her with, well, they said her familiar. Something like a child except it was too tall and thin and with hardly any face you'd want to call one. They got her arrested by the witch-finders, and she told them being in the woods had changed her. She'd grown another nipple—maybe that's where that idea originally came from. Only hers didn't stay in one place."

"Sounds as if a psychiatrist would have been in order."

"No, she showed them how it wandered all over her body. The story is she was glad they hanged her before she could change any further. They burned her cottage down and buried her at the crossroads in the High Street, but something's supposed to have dug her up and taken her back to the woods."

If all this came from the book Sam had bought his aunt for Christmas, Heather would have preferred him to have found Sylvia a different gift. He was opening their gate, having limped ahead as if to stay out of reach of the tale. Heather was about to follow him when she saw a youngish couple, presumably Rosemary's parents, hurrying along Jessica's front path. "I'll just see if Jessica wants a word," she said.

"Are you better off without me?"

"Never usually, but maybe till we find out . . ." When Sylvia tramped into their paved garden, Heather left her. "Jessica," she called.

Jessica was admitting the couple to her house. "Heather. I don't know if you ought—" She moved aside for the visitors and took a step onto her path. "She's in the front room," she told them. "I'll be there in a minute."

Heather didn't speak again until she was close enough to keep her voice low. "What happened? Is it our fault somehow?"

"Have you all been out?" Jessica asked, peering along the street at Sylvia and Sam.

"We've been at mother's watching her, her latest experiment."

"What was that?" said Jessica, more sharply than Heather liked.

"More of the art she brings out of the woods."

"You might want to let her know people have been talking."

"They do, don't they? And they've said . . ."

"You've all been seen going in and out of there all the time. Everyone except you at least," Jessica said and cocked her head towards a burst of comforting murmurs in the front room. "I'm not saying it is, but that could be why Rosemary imagined whatever she did."

"Is she getting over it?"

"She's stopped screaming. She started when we woke her. I know it's meant to be dangerous to."

The murmurs tailed off, and a small voice protested "I wasn't asleep."

"You must have been, Rosemary." Jessica gave Heather the sort of look adults shared about children as she confided "She said she was following somebody too tall for words."

"He was as tall as the sky," the little girl called past a renewed duet of murmuring, "but he kept being long instead like a shadow."

"If it was a shadow," Jessica said as if a problem had been solved, "it couldn't have had a face like you said."

"He did. It was like Mr Price."

Jessica backed into her hall. "Shall we discuss it another time, Heather?"

Heather saw that Jessica didn't want Rosemary further disturbed, but she couldn't help feeling cast out. She was risking a smile as she turned away when the little girl said louder than her parents' murmurs "He had a face and he talked to me."

Heather faltered and failed to keep a question to herself. "What did he say?"

"I'll speak to you again soon, Heather," Jessica told her. It might have been intended as a warning; the expression she withdrew into the house was disapproving enough. The next moment the door was shut, just not soon enough to prevent Heather from hearing the little girl's words. They had to be her answer to the question Heather would have given a good deal not to have asked. "My child," Rosemary said.

29

A Reading from the Dark

HEATHER lurched awake convinced she'd done something wrong. When she blinked away some of the dark that was glued to her eyes she managed to distinguish that the luminous twigs of the bedside clock showed a number of minutes past three in the morning. She might have drawn reassurance from the familiar charcoal sketch of the outlines of her room if a smell of hoary paper hadn't insinuated itself into the dimness. Though her next breath was free of the odour, she fumbled the quilt up to cover most of her face. Now she was alone with her sluggishly restless thoughts—with the memory of wanting to take an act back. She wished she had kept Rosemary's answer to herself.

Perhaps it was a fragment of some fairy tale the little girl had heard or read. Heather was perplexed only because it had disturbed both Sylvia and Sam. No doubt that was one more indication of the way his aunt's state was affecting him, and yet another development to be worried about, along with his apparent fear of leaving home that must betray how nervous he was of letting her or his father or himself down, and Margo's obsession with the woods that was becoming a little too reminiscent of Lennox's, and Sylvia's secret breakdown even if it had been treated, and her present condition, and the willingness of people Heather barely knew to blame her family for events they didn't even bother to define . . . Was there any aspect of her life she didn't need to fret about? Surely her work wouldn't turn on her, but as she let herself anticipate the day after tomorrow—texts to scan, muted queries from students, the masses of hushed books on the shelves, the sense of a past safely bound up for consultation—her job felt too much like a refuge, a denial of everything else in her life. Nevertheless allowing her mind to rest on it seemed to be her route back to sleep, and she was beginning to feel close to drowsing when she froze, as did her breath. There was a furtive sound in the house.

When she raised her head the night came to meet it. At first the only noise she could be sure of was the thumping of a heartbeat. Of course it was her own, though it sounded as if it belonged to the night. She eased herself upright against the pillow and held a long slow breath. In a moment she heard what had roused her. Sylvia was speaking in the next room.

She must be sharing confidences with Sam while she thought her sister was asleep. The notion almost sent Heather marching into Sylvia's room to demand what was so secret it had to wait for the dark. Instead she sneaked her legs out from beneath the quilt and took all the time stealth required. She didn't care how sly she felt—she wanted to hear.

She had just inched her door wide enough to let her out of the room when a muffled groan escaped Sam. What could Sylvia have said to distress him? His reaction hadn't prevented her from continuing to murmur as though she hadn't heard him. Anger at the insensitivity almost overcame Heather's resolve not to draw attention to herself, but she edged onto the landing without a sound. As she did so Sam groaned again, and she realised he was both in his own room and asleep.

Then whom was Sylvia addressing? For a panicky instant Heather was afraid to hear an answering voice, and then that Sylvia was talking to herself. Her speech hadn't quite the tone of a monologue, however;

it was more—Heather tiptoed a pace towards her sister's room and knew what she was overhearing. Sylvia was reading aloud.

She must be practising for when her child was old enough to listen, Heather told herself. Tiptoeing across the carpet gave her time to wonder what Sylvia was reading from, especially since no light was visible under the door. She had to press her ear against one unnecessarily warm upper panel before she was able to make out a word. As she covered her mouth and nose with one hand to silence her breath she heard Sylvia say "All shall be contained within a single form and give it life."

She was reading to her unborn child from Selcouth's journal. That would have been disturbing enough by itself, but Heather especially disliked the tone of meaningful affection her sister's voice had acquired for the duration of the sentence. Her unease was such that for some moments she failed to grasp why Sylvia had hushed. She must be aware that someone was outside the door.

Heather was reaching for the doorknob when the smell of ancient paper seeped out of the room. She didn't have to confront Sylvia now. For any number of reasons, some of which she preferred to leave undefined, it would be better to wait until daylight. She couldn't help it if her decision seemed like a retreat. She backed away as fast as stealth permitted and, having felt compelled to shut her door in fractions of an inch, sought refuge in her bed.

For altogether too long she was afraid of being followed into her room. What could Sylvia accuse her of? Trying to establish what was happening in the middle of the night in her own house? She was doing her best to prepare a response that wouldn't sound defensive when she heard Sylvia resume reading aloud. She strained her ears until they felt stuffed with her pulse, but could identify only one word. "Nathaniel," Sylvia murmured, and minutes later "Nathaniel."

The affection in her voice surely meant she was speaking to her child rather than reading the name from the book, but reassurance wasn't coming anywhere near Heather. As she heard her sister's murmur underlying her own breaths she grew desperate enough to try to feel that Sylvia was reading her to sleep. She had no idea how much time passed before unconsciousness took her, let alone before she was awakened by a presence in the room.

She felt as if she hadn't slept—as if she had been followed directly from Sylvia's room—but when her eyes sprang open she saw daylight and Sam. He knotted the cord of his bathrobe tighter around himself while she blinked stickily at him. "Have I overslept?" she mumbled.

"It's Sunday."

"I won't be late for work, then. Do you need me for something? Does Sylvie?"

He'd been ready to answer the first question, but the second pressed his lips together. He seemed uncertain how or where to look as he muttered "She's gone."

"Sorry, gone where?"

"Couldn't say."

"What did she tell you?" Heather said impatiently.

"Nothing. I was asleep when she went."

"Then how do you know?"

"You can see what she left."

"I will."

She had scarcely taken hold of the edge of the quilt when Sam limped out of the room, leaving her to reflect how much warier he was of glimpsing her undressed since Sylvia had moved in. She retrieved her robe from the hook on the door and groped into the sleeves, and tied the cord around her waist as she padded onto the landing. While Sam loitered at the top of the stairs she pushed Sylvia's door open, then sucked in a dismayed breath that tasted bitterly of paper. Her sister's three suitcases had been nesting on top of the wardrobe, but there was no sign of them.

Advancing into the room didn't help. The cases weren't hiding on the far side of the bed, and there was insufficient space beneath. If the room didn't feel wholly deserted, that was no comfort: the occupant was Selcouth's journal on the desk. She was overwhelmed by dislike of the secrecy of its contents, its binding as black as the carapace of a beetle, its indefinably rotten smell. She turned her back on it to find Sam watching her. Without giving her time to interpret his expression, he pointed down the stairs. "She left a note."

"Couldn't you have brought it up?" Heather protested, and would have steered him none too gently out of her way if he hadn't limped aside. A small square of paper so thoroughly inscribed that from the top of the stairs it looked almost as black as Selcouth's journal was drooping against the phone. The couple of seconds involved in running downstairs gave her too much of a chance to imagine Sylvia's message before it was in her hand. *Thanks for putting up with me and looking after me! Please don't think I'm being ungrateful or impulsive, but the book's taken me away again. No need to worry about Natty or me. You'll be seeing us soon. Wish I could have helped more. SXXX.* The handwriting of the last two sentences was so microscopic Heather might have concluded they were designed not to be read. Even so, they had left so little space for Sylvia's initial that the kisses had to compose themselves from the extended lower curve of the letter, as if they were pinning her symbol down or consuming it or both. Heather's thoughts snagged on the idea. Any moment she would have to consider the implications of the note, and she knew she would like them less and less. Her mind hadn't freed itself when the phone rang.

She snatched up the receiver, hoping it would have Sylvia's voice. "Hello?"

"Mrs Harvey? That's to say, Ms Price?"

"Either," she said, anxious to know why the man sounded familiar.

"It's Francis Lowe at the Arbour."

"Dr Lowe." She both wanted and was afraid to learn "Is my sister there?"

"Your sister. No, Mrs Price."

"You don't need to keep playing with my name. Why are you calling?" she said, experiencing dismay that came close to rendering him irrelevant as she reread Sylvia's note.

"I'm saying it's your mother. She's the Mrs Price who's here."

"Oh, I see. Sorry if I was . . ." Her growing sense of Sylvia's absence was robbing her of words, and she had to search for the right question to ask. "Why is she?"

"My apologies for bringing you bad news." Presumably his pause was intended to let Heather brace herself rather than demand what kind. "I'm afraid there's been an accident," he said. "She was in a collision with a car."

30

The Lowest Room

THAT was my house when I was just me," said Sylvia, gazing across the common. In the dimness before sunrise Woodland Close was back-lit by the streetlamps, but every window was dark. For a moment she hoped to see hers light up—hoped that, having found her note, Heather was hurrying upstairs to discover the suitcases hidden in the wardrobe and realise her sister couldn't have gone far. The window stayed unlit, while behind her the forest whispered and creaked and touched her neck with a clammy breath. Even if all that was only the wind, it felt as though the trees were eager to have her among them. "You'll be with me, won't you, Natty?" she murmured.

"Yes."

She didn't so much hear as feel his voice. It seemed to rise from a depth far greater than she could contain—from a darkness under the earth or beyond the thin faint sky—but it was her only companion. She had to leave her old home behind and everything it represented. She lifted one hand in a wave almost too small and tentative for her to be conscious of performing it, and turned to step into the forest, past a log that resembled a giant eyeless lizard with deformed unequal stumpy legs. As she set foot on the edge of the vast pattern of decaying leaves she felt the woods grow aware of her, and saw the trees flex themselves like antennae attuning themselves to her presence.

For as long as it took her to remember to breathe she couldn't move. She wouldn't have been surprised to see the log raise itself blindly but purposefully on its remains of legs to lead her or herd her between the trees. She did her best to think that would only be like one of the games she used to play by herself in the woods, since it had failed to appeal to her sister—the game of turning over a log to expose its hoard of insects that would swarm back into hiding for her to turn up again and again, though hadn't the teeming mass put her in mind less of insects than of fragments of discoloured bark? The poised stillness of the wooden reptile sent her stumbling into the woods as if she had to keep up with her swollen belly so as not to overbalance. She was digging in her handbag for the flashlight when she realised that although the trees had closed around her and overhead, she could see her way, just as earlier she had been able to read Selcouth's journal in the dimness of her room. "Are you doing that?" she wondered. "Are you changing me?"

"Yes."

She was more aware of his consciousness than of anything physical within herself. She had yet to feel movement in her womb. Sometimes, in the depths of the night, she felt she contained nothing except a darkness more intense than she imagined could be found even at the limits of the universe, and then she would become sensible of harbouring a mind besides her own. Since its conception she had gradually regained her memories of all her visits to the forest, a process that felt as if the creature with which she was sharing her body was adding its mind to hers or using hers. It couldn't harm her, she kept needing to think, without harming itself. "We'll look after each other, won't we?" she promised or pleaded or both.

"Yes."

The response was enough to send her plodding onwards, watching for signs of her father. Surely it must have been whatever was left of him that had given Rosemary the message. That was a reason for Sylvia to be here, and so was her pledge not to betray her and Sam's secret—she wouldn't have felt certain of suppressing it if she'd stayed with him and Heather. Besides, she had never been afraid of the woods; why should she start now? "It's a magic place, isn't it?" she murmured.

"Yes."

It appeared to be. The trees of the natural avenue down which she was advancing framed a vista that brightened as she watched, tree-trunks gleaming like silver pillars cracked by antiquity, fallen leaves composing a design as elaborate and many-coloured as the floor of an ancient temple. She thought dawn was responsible for the brightness until she glanced back. She hadn't realised she had already walked so far; she could barely distinguish the glow of the streetlamps, let alone the shapes of houses, and no other light was to be seen. Yet when she faced forward the glow of the woods renewed itself as though it had only been waiting for her to look. "Are you there?" she ventured to call, however softly.

"Yes."

"Not you this time, Natty. I know you are," she said, though the buried voice had seemed less precisely located than ever. "I meant my father."

She had a sense, too vague for definition, that he was near. If he was hiding behind any of the trees ahead he must have grown considerably thinner. She couldn't help hoping he wouldn't play the game she used to play among the trees with Heather. Perhaps it was thanks to the nervousness she was suddenly unable to ignore that she had a momentary impression of being accompanied, not under cover of the forest but beneath the ground she trod on—accompanied by a vast presence that had shrunk itself to pace her. When she twisted around, planting her feet wide to support the burden of herself, she saw only forest, not a hint of the town. She turned away for fear of losing her balance, and as her midriff carried her another step deeper into the woods she was informed "He's waiting."

"You can talk. You don't just answer. You're growing up fast," said Sylvia, telling herself she had really heard the words: she wasn't talking to herself as she roamed the forest—she hadn't gone the way so many people thought her father had. "Where is he?"

"Keep going."

She took that for an answer as well as a direction while she attempted to decide whether the voice sounded more like a child trying to imitate a man or the reverse. She was distracted from looking for signs of her father by a scent in the humid air. It was almost too faint to be distinguishable from fancy—it was subtle as the intimation of a mystery—and yet if it had been any more intense its sweetness would have overpowered her. "You can't smell that, can you?" she hardly knew why she asked.

"We can."

He must mean he was sharing her experience, she thought, and felt enlarged beyond words. "What is it, then?"

"Our season."

No ordinary child could use language like that. She was almost as proud of herself as of him. She wished someone else were there to admire his development; she hoped her father would be. The woods were brightening further as if to demonstrate they had nothing to hide, so that she hardly started when a butterfly she'd taken for an especially colourful patch of dead leaves fluttered up to hover a yard or so ahead. She had nearly reached it when it darted along the latest avenue she was following. Having swerved from tree to tree, on which it appeared to fit into the patterns and texture of bark, it hesitated until she was close before dodging onwards, trailing the scent she would have attributed to some seductive blossom. "Is it playing with us?" she whispered.

"Yes."

As he answered she gasped, but only with delight. Another patch of the floor of the woods had sailed up to join the first butterfly. They must be of the same species, however different their colours were, because they danced around each other as they led her down the avenue. She did her best to watch their antics while trying to identify where the next one would reveal itself. That made the entire decaying floor of the avenue seem about to come to life, but she could see no reason to be apprehensive. When another fragment of the shadowed tapestry proved capable of taking flight, she clapped her hands. "It's like . . ." she murmured. "What did it say in the journal?"

"All things shall be changed by the procedure of the dark, and all shall partake of its essence."

Except that nothing she was seeing could be called dark, she thought. Perhaps she had been thinking of another passage in the journal, but she was diverted from remembering by the spectacle of so many butterflies adding themselves to the dance. At least a dozen were leading her now, tantalising her with their hesitations and their scent, and she felt close to some revelation contained in the intricate patterns they were describing in the air. They were fluttering onwards almost too swiftly for her to match their pace, but her midriff no longer seemed to be weighing her down so much as bearing her through the forest, and she was able to focus her attention on the enigma of the rapid jagged insect dance. She fancied she had almost grasped its significance when the flock of butterflies flew apart in all directions and instantly vanished. Had they really turned on edge to reveal a lack of one dimension? She had no time to wonder, because she could see where they had brought her—where she'd tried to be unaware of heading ever since she had entered the woods. "I didn't know your father when I met him here," she whispered. "It just felt as if we were made for each other."

She couldn't pretend that her having failed to recognise Sam had caused her sudden nervousness, and only silence answered her. If her father had called her back where he'd tried to leave her—where Selcouth had lived and the child she hadn't realised she was naming after him had been conceived—why couldn't he show himself? She was beginning to feel he was caged by the trees or trapped within them. When she ventured towards the clearing it wasn't just in search of him; it was partly to reassure herself that she couldn't reach the buried steps—she had no spade, and could hardly be expected to dig without one. Then a gap between the trees gave her a clear view of the mound, and she hugged her midriff as though to protect both its contents and herself. The mound wasn't as Sam had left it. The earth above the steps had been dug up.

As she faltered, reluctant to approach the open space even though it seemed bright with more than the imminent dawn, the butterflies reappeared above the mound. Had they emerged from the disinterred passage? "Look, there are our friends," she murmured, not least to reassure herself. She was moving forward only to watch them, she tried to think. Then, behind or within the rapid dense intricate patterns, a figure looked out of the mound.

No sooner had it beckoned to her than it withdrew into the earth, but she was certain she had glimpsed her father's face. As she tramped into the clearing and stepped over the bricks onto the glistening upheaved soil she felt as if the heat had gathered within her, urging her to be quick. The butterflies sailed high like shards of a fire and were lost somewhere under the dim thick sky, but she was peering down the spiral of steps, above which the two chunks of the slab were propped. "Is that you?" she called.

"Yes."

The whisper was below her. It sounded as though he was finding it hard to produce any voice. "Where are you?" she called louder.

"Waiting."

"Will you be with me?"

"Of course."

She heard that he felt distrusted. How could she demand any further reassurance or abandon him down there in the dark? She took the flashlight out of her bag and followed its beam down the steps. The forest reared above her, and she felt as if it was urging her downwards—as if the effect of last year's gale had been to close the focus of the woods around her. When the mound cut off her view she tried to probe the secretive curve of the passage with the light. "Won't you let me see you?" she said.

"Come down first."

His voice was more stifled than ever, but then hers sounded trapped by the walls. Only the scent she had associated with the butterflies drifted up to meet her. She plodded down, supporting herself with her free hand on the clammy wall, until she came in sight of the doorway of the first charred room. She didn't have to shine the beam on the remains she remembered were there; just now she preferred to hurry past. As she came abreast of the doorway, however, she became aware of far too tall and scrawny a figure that stood in the depths of the room, watching her from the dark.

"All the way down," the voice murmured below her, and she was glad to obey, though once she was past the doorway she wished she had retreated instead. She could only flee downwards while the walls capered around her and the low ceiling appeared to jerk lower. At least there were no watchers in the other rooms. The solitary sound was her own tread, flattened and shrunken by the passage. It ceased as she reached the bottom of the steps and sent the beam into the lowest room.

It wasn't just charred bare; the floor was exposed earth. Nevertheless an attempt had been made to prepare it for her. Piled against the far wall was a long broad mound of fallen leaves at least a foot high. When she stepped forward, having used the beam to ascertain that the room was deserted, she didn't know whether she felt fulfilled or as exhausted as the flashlight was beginning to appear. She only knew she had to take her place on the bed of leaves, though she wouldn't have been altogether surprised if they had revealed their true nature by swarming into the air. They merely yielded while she lowered herself onto them and was rewarded by feeling bathed in the scent that had helped entice her down. She clutched her handbag to her as if she was clinging to all that was left of her life up to that moment, and laid the flashlight on the earth, pointing the feeble beam at the unlit doorway. "Can I see you now?" she whispered.

"Soon."

The voice was so close to her it seemed impossible that she couldn't locate the speaker. It was much closer than the pair of thuds that reverberated down the steps. The slab had been replaced. She knew she would never be able to raise it, and the resignation the knowledge brought with it felt like accepting her role at last, not that she'd had any other option since returning to Goodmanswood. She might have reflected on passages from Selcouth's journal—might even have tried to come to terms with its final revelation, which had disconcerted her so much that not only had she kept it from Sam, she'd done her best to hide it from herself—if her attention hadn't been trapped by the black rectangle of the doorway. Now and then her lips parted, but surely it was time for someone else to initiate a conversation. Nobody had spoken, and nothing had shown itself, when the beam that had grown so dim it barely touched the floor went out and all the subterranean blackness came to find her—at first, only the dark.

31

The Lucky Ones

WHAT else could I have done, Sam?"

He was watching the haze catch reflections of the traffic ahead on the bypass. It looked as though a medium was flooding out of the woods and struggling to transform into itself whatever it touched. He kept feeling it was about to cease to recede, having gained a hold on the world outside the forest, but he couldn't imagine how it would affect him if it lay in wait for the car. "When?" he scarcely knew he said.

"To make Sylvie stay." His mother gripped the steering wheel and peered nervously ahead as though she was sharing his thoughts about the haze, but of course she was searching for Margo. "Unless," she said even more wistfully, "it was something I did that made her leave."

"It wouldn't have been."

"It's kind of you to say so, but you can't be sure. I wish you could."

He was tempted to relieve her of her guilt, but how could he admit to having given Sylvia cause to leave? His mother would never be able to cope with it, nor he with her knowing. Nevertheless he muttered "I can."

"I keep meaning to tell you you're one of the kindest people I know. If Sylvie's gone on her travels again I suppose there's one good thing, however much we're going to worry about her." She glanced at him as she finished saying "You'll have one less reason to feel you have to stay."

"It wasn't her fault."

"I wasn't accusing her, Sam. There's been too much of that around lately for all of us." She seemed disappointed in his reply, however. "I hope you'll take the chance to have a word with Dr Lowe," she said, then leaned over the wheel as if she'd been jabbed in the stomach. "Is that . . ."

When he followed the direction of her gaze he wasn't immediately sure what he was seeing. It resembled the ghost of an accident: a car wobbling like red gelatin and throbbing with orange hazard lights as it watched over its victim, beside whom a figure knelt priest-like on the roadside. Then the tableau swam forward, and Margo's prone body appeared to float up as though the medium that had drowned it was returning it, however temporarily, to the familiar world. The kneeling man was Dr Lowe, and he was speaking to her. Behind the red Nissan hatchback with its guilty orange pulse was a police car, its roof lights imparting a lurid bluish twitch to the nearest trees while its driver interrogated an unhappy middle-aged man in the seat next to her. As Sam's mother sped in quest of a gap that would let her turn back, he hoped she had time to observe that Margo was conscious.

Beyond the Arbour, where several of the patients were watching the spectacle from their or someone else's windows, she found a place to turn. She parked rather less than expertly behind the police vehicle and ran past, leaving Sam to close the door she'd left ajar. Dr Lowe stood up, rubbing stiffness out of his legs, as Sam joined his mother. "Try not to move," she was advising Margo in a soft anxious voice, but Margo raised her head from the improvised pillow of a man's tweed jacket, apparently the doctor's. "Why, here's Sam now," she said with dreamy astonishment. "Look what your old grandmother's done to herself, Sam. What a family we are for falling off things and stepping in front of things."

Perhaps she felt that trivialised her husband's death. She frowned as if the pinching of her wrinkles might draw her thoughts together. "What I'm trying to say," she declared, though falling short of the forcefulness she was attempting to summon up, "is all these people put to trouble just because I forgot where I was for a moment."

Heather reached for her but withheld her hand. "Can you say where you're hurt?"

"Just my leg and the old hip where the car bumped into it, I think, and I suppose the shoulder where it hit the road." She blinked down herself but seemed unable to focus before letting her head sink back. "I'll be like you, Sam. We'll have to prop each other up, except you'll be somewhere else, won't you? You should be. You mustn't get the notion you have to hang around and help take care of me."

Heather rubbed the corners of her eyes as she turned to Dr Lowe. "Someone will have called an ambulance, will they?"

"Of course. It should be any minute."

"There's more people I'll be bothering," Margo complained, "as if the hospitals haven't enough incapable old wrecks to look after."

"You aren't one of those yet, mum. You won't ever be."

"I don't think I'm quite senile yet at any rate. I know I was distracted, so I can't be."

Sam felt a question stir within his lips, but his mother asked it. "What distracted you?"

"Maybe you'll think I still am. I know you won't like me saying this, Heather. I heard something and I nearly saw it as well. I thought it was Lennox."

"You mean you know it wasn't now."

"I don't, no. It had his voice."

Sam's mother glared over the tangle of fallen trees into the forest as if to dare her father to appear, and Sam felt as if the entire woods had leaned minutely forward to listen. "So what," she murmured with a pause that suggested she'd finished commenting, "did you think he said?"

"I wish I could tell you. It sounded like he couldn't find the words for it. Maybe there aren't any," Margo said and visibly lost patience with herself. "I can tell you how it felt to me if you think that'll be any use."

"You know you can tell me whatever you have to, mum."

"I got the impression he wanted to let me know something that's going to happen. Either that or what he's like now." With some defiance Margo added "Or both."

"Try and stay calm till someone's had a look at you."

"I'm as calm as I'm going to be." As though to demonstrate her self-control Margo said almost indifferently "My camera got smashed, you know, and I'd filmed things today I never imagined I'd see. I guess it's round here somewhere."

When she raised her head shakily Sam's mother supported it with one hand, though Sam could have told Margo that the camera was crushed under a rear wheel of the Nissan. "Well, here we still are at the woods. Do you know, when I did this to myself it felt like they were pulling me back in," Margo said, and then her gaze and her voice acquired some sharpness. "Where's Sylvia? Didn't she come?"

Sam's face grew hot with the question. When he turned towards the woods to hide however he was looking, they gave him the impression of pretending to be innocently still. "She's off on the research trail again," his mother said.

Margo slapped the clammy tarmac, either out of frustration or in an abortive attempt to sit up. "Where?" she protested.

"She only went this morning. Before we knew you were hurt, you understand. She hasn't been in touch yet to say where."

"Are you telling me she's gone away by herself in her state?"

"I'm sure she'll be fine, mum. She always has been, hasn't she?" Sam's mother sent a frown in search of the ambulance before insisting "She's old enough to know what she's doing."

"Maybe she doesn't. The closest I ever came to losing my mind was when I was pregnant. With her, not with you."

Presumably the distinction was intended to forestall any guilt Sam's mother might experience, but some part of Margo's response appeared to have given her pause. "I'm certain she'll be in touch," she said, "as soon as she knows where she's ended up."

Sam thought that had little chance of reassuring Margo but could summon up nothing to say that might help. His only thought was that since his aunt had managed to leave after having told him she couldn't, perhaps he could too. He was gazing into the forest as if to share an uninvited secret with the heart of the bristling labyrinth when Dr Lowe said "I think that's the ambulance."

Sam turned to see fierce lights throbbing like a storm as they swam up from the haze along the bypass and hauled their source after them. "Don't try to get up," his mother had to tell Margo as the ambulance swung onto the hard shoulder ahead. Sam could only feel redundant while the ambulance crew tenderly examined his grandmother and brought a stretcher. They were lifting her into the ambulance when she said through more than one grimace of pain "I hope the police believed me. I wasn't looking where I was going and the driver did his best to stop. I wouldn't like to think I was a trouble to him as well."

"You aren't to anyone," Sam's mother assured her, handing him the car keys. "You'll find us at the hospital, will you, Sam? I should take the chance to have that talk with Dr Lowe if he's free."

"I've half an hour if there's some way I can help," the doctor said.

"Poor Sam, are you having problems with your nerves as well?" Margo called from the ambulance. "Thank God we have your mother so there's at least one stable one among us. I don't know what Dr Lowe must have thought of the way I was carrying on just now. See if you can convince him the Prices aren't really mad."

Sam had less idea than ever what was required of him. He watched his mother climb into the rear of the ambulance with a brief anxious glance at him. The vehicle sped to the nearest gap and doubled back towards Brichester. As the haze melted it and swallowed it Dr Lowe said "Do you mind if we talk in my office?"

Sam found that no more unappealing than the prospect of the talk itself. "Will you drive us over?" the doctor suggested.

Sam walked to the Civic and opened the door for him. The doctor was silent as Sam manoeuvred the car across to the Arbour. Perhaps he was waiting for Sam to volunteer his problem or give some inadvertent sign of it, a thought that made Sam feel scrutinised, and not only by his passenger. As the car swung through the gates he saw the woods spring into the mirror while feigning stillness.

The reception desk and the pair of staircases that rose like outsize horns behind it were deserted. So was the stubby corridor that led to the doctor's office past framed landscapes that struck Sam less as abstract than on the point of transformation into some unimaginably fluid state. Dr Lowe hung on the back of the fat black chair behind his desk the tweed jacket he'd retrieved from the road, and moved to the window. "We'll have this open, shall we?"

Since Sam couldn't tell how loaded the question might be, he confined himself to a shrug. Surely the doctor wasn't raising the sash to enable the forest to listen in, though as he stepped from behind the desk and gestured at a chair opposite the one he took, he brushed a stray lock of hair away from his left ear as if readying it to receive instructions audible only to him. He placed his fingertips not quite together, short of praying, and advanced his gently quizzical face an inch. "Are you recovered enough to talk?" he enquired.

That made Sam feel worse than defensive. "What from?"

"Why, from your grandmother's accident. I thought you seemed the most upset of anyone."

If that was true, Sam wondered what else he mightn't realise about himself. "I can talk," he admitted. "I just . . ."

Dr Lowe gave an intent sympathetic look time to help before saying "Is it something to do with just yourself?"

If anyone besides Sylvia and Sam knew their secret, the woods and whatever they concealed did. It surely followed that if Dr Lowe was in league with them he wouldn't need to be told the secret. For a moment this felt like a profound insight, and then Sam became aware of the sly imprisoned unfamiliar way in which his mind was working. It frightened him so deeply that he blurted "Suppose I caught it from my grandfather?"

"What do you think you might have?"

"I can't go away and I'm afraid to stay here. My dad fixed me up with a job interview last week and I didn't even get as far as London."

"Your parents are divorced, aren't they?"

"So what if they are?"

"I understood from your grandfather that your mother felt she had to stay while your father needed to move because of his career."

Sam saw where this was leading, and it was wholly irrelevant. "Right," he muttered.

"This interview, would it have been the first one he's arranged for you?"

"Right."

"Do you think you may be afraid you'll estrange one of your parents whether you stay or leave? That kind of conflict can be paralysing if it's not faced."

Wasn't he meant to allow people to talk towards the truth? Sam was beginning to wonder if the doctor simply wanted to get rid of him— he wasn't a patient, after all. "It's worse than that," he said desperately. "If you knew how bad you might have me in here."

"What do you feel that would achieve?"

"Maybe you'd find out my grandfather, I don't know, infected me, passed something down to me."

"Could that be what you're most afraid of?"

"Suppose it is?"

"Then by all means admit it to yourself, because it isn't possible. What happened to your grandfather was the result of a drug he wasn't in contact with till after your mother was born."

"Unless they set off something that was already in him. If you've any chance of being schizophrenic that kind of drug can trigger it, can't it?"

"I don't believe that occurred in his case. There was nothing in his history to suggest any tendencies of the kind."

"Maybe you didn't go back far enough."

"I don't see how I could have gone back further."

Neither did Sam, nor indeed why he'd made the comment except to break any silence that would leave him alone with the knowledge of how little the doctor could help him. He was about to conclude that he'd done as much as he could to comply with his mother's request when Dr Lowe said "I should have thought there was a question you'd need to answer."

"What?" Sam felt forced to respond.

"If we're talking about problems that have to be triggered, what set them off in you? Have you been experimenting with drugs?"

"No." Sam was almost desperate enough to admit to his first encounter with Sylvia in the forest but found the disclosure too shameful to contemplate. "I wouldn't after what they did to my grandfather," he heard himself declare.

"I'm sure that's entirely wise, but I wonder if you're often afraid of following in his footsteps."

"Sometimes."

"Perhaps that fear exacerbates the conflict we've discussed and vice versa till you're unable to separate them in your mind."

Even if that was a possibility, it only made Sam realise how little of his experience he'd managed to communicate. He was seized by a dread that more of it was dormant, awaiting words or something else to rouse it—something that loomed at the edge of his perception like the woods brandishing their greenish antennae beyond the window. He was hardly aware that the doctor was saying "Do forgive me if I've covered all this too quickly. I hope I've given you some food for thought at least. Unfortunately with all the demands of this hospital I'm not available for consultation, but I'd be happy to refer you to one of my colleagues in Brichester if you feel the need."

"I'll let you know if I do," Sam said, which was the opposite of a promise.

"I'm hoping that means I've been some help, does it?"

"All you could have been."

"That's the most any of us can ask of ourselves." If Dr Lowe suspected any ambiguity on Sam's part, there was no hint on his face, which managed to appear steeped in concern and at the same time bland. "So I gather your aunt's on her travels again?" he said, standing up as Sam did.

In the midst of the released creaking of their chairs Sam thought he heard rapid stealthy footsteps retreating from outside the door. Dr Lowe either didn't notice or had trained himself not to react; he made no especial haste to open the door on the deserted corridor. By this time Sam had muttered "She went this morning."

"Do you think you might take that for an omen?"

Sam had to swallow a sour taste of guilt before he could demand "How do you mean?"

"Perhaps not the best choice of word. For an example, then. Do you think if she feels able to travel freely even in her condition you might see if you're up to it? Perhaps"—the doctor raised a hand towards his left ear as though he was receiving an inspiration—"you could go to your interview if it's still on and tell yourself it doesn't matter if you succeed or otherwise, only that you tried."

Sam had lost count of the points Dr Lowe was missing. "That sounds like an idea," he said as a way of making his escape.

He was bracing himself to be met at the stairs by whoever had been in the corridor, but the stairs were deserted. As he hurried down he saw the woods lowering themselves beyond the open front door to greet him as though they were sinking out of the sky. He'd almost reached the doorway when a woman came through it in what was meant to resemble a stroll, widening her already protuberant eyes in far too much surprise. "Mr Price," she cried.

"Hello," Sam said as conversationally as he was able, and dodged around her, fumbling his mother's keys out of his pocket so hastily that he almost dropped them. He was nearly at the Civic when the woman he'd last seen at his grandfather's funeral darted ahead of him to pat and stroke its roof. "Nice car," she said as she might have addressed a pet. "Doing well for yourself."

"It's my mother's."

"Ah," said the woman, and adopted a lopsidedly knowing look. "I'm Delia, you know."

"I didn't." That said, Sam could think of nothing to add except "Good."

Delia rolled her eyes upwards while she considered that, then fixed her gaze on him. "Pleased to make your acquaintance."

"And yours. Now I've really got to—"

It was her knowing look that made him falter before her words caught up with it. "We saw you in the woods."

The resurgent taste of guilt would have kept his lips shut if he hadn't needed to find out how much she knew. "When?"

"Just before the old lady, Lennox's wife was in the crash."

So she wasn't talking about Sam and his aunt. It was only to him that everything seemed to be about them, he reminded himself. "No you didn't," he said, trying to hide his relief. "I wasn't there till after it happened."

"It looked like you. The face did, anyway." Delia scrutinised him, tugging at her cheeks with her fingertips to let out more eye. "Maybe it wasn't," she granted at last. "You couldn't have been behind that many trees at once."

Sam's relief was dissipating, and he reached with the key for the door of the Civic. "Anyway—"

"How's the thin girl? Not so thin any more, eh?"

He mustn't take that as an accusation. Swallowing, he said "She's gone away."

"Can't be far."

Sam thrust the key into the lock. "Why not?"

"She's like us."

He felt as if there were increasingly fewer words he dared speak, and regretted demanding "Who?"

"You and me and the rest of us. All the ones who can't leave."

For a moment he wanted to accuse her of having eavesdropped outside Dr Lowe's office, but that would only delay the question he was afraid to ask. "Why can't we?"

At once her face looked about to crumple—whether with dismay or hysterical laughter he couldn't judge. "Don't you know yet?" she said in a voice driven high.

She was mentally ill, he found it necessary to point out to himself—never mind politeness, she was mad. Nevertheless he couldn't help almost pleading "Tell me."

She leaned towards him, and he fancied something vast and dark as a denial of the sunlight leaned with her. "The woods," she whispered, her gaze flickering from side to side. "Your grandfather's in there, and my mother."

Sam wondered why he'd thought she could be any help to him. He was twisting the key when she said "And lots that are older. Everyone who's been that close is part of them."

That needn't include him or be true, Sam attempted to convince himself. He snatched the car door open, and Delia lurched across the front of the vehicle at him. He felt as if something beyond darkness was descending towards him—as if it was about to part the pale blue sky. "We'll be like them. We'll all be the same," Delia said.

She was running her fingertips spider-like over her cheeks. Sam had an appalled notion that she was checking her face hadn't been somehow transformed. He was about to take refuge in the car when she looked abruptly sympathetic, which was yet more disturbing. "Don't worry," she said.

He had the impression of stepping over an edge into worse than blackness by asking "Why not?"

"We're the lucky ones."

"You think," Sam said, unable to laugh at the idea even inside himself.

"We are, because we're what people call mad or whatever they say we are these days. They don't know that means we'll be readier than they are. We're already on our way, so it won't be such a shock. Just imagine being Dr Lowe and the rest of them when it happens."

Sam's question was more an admission of despair at having to ask or at learning the answer. "What?"

"You should have asked Lennox. You still could. He knew the most of any of us." Delia smiled and stepped back, fingering her lips in case they'd changed. Sam had succeeded in starting the car when she waved her left hand and arm, stiff and contorted as a branch. He assumed she was bidding him adieu, though he would have made it a farewell, until he heard her belated answer to his question. "What called Lennox here in the first place," she said.

32

Sealed by the Past

HEATHER almost managed to refrain from saying any of the things she'd vowed she wouldn't say to Sam, but it surely couldn't hurt to accompany him as far as the front door and wish him good luck. The words earned her only a grimace, however. "What?" he said as if he didn't see how they applied to him.

"Try feeling lucky. No harm in that," Heather said, determined not to exert pressure on him and hearing herself continue to do so. "Sorry. Don't let me tell you how to feel. You feel whatever helps."

"Like what?"

She was beginning to wish they'd talked this through after all, though before it was time for him to leave. "Forget me," she said. "Forget your father. Just go because it's you that wants to. It still is, isn't it? You still want to try for the job."

"I've got to go where I'm going."

"You keep telling yourself that. And listen, I shouldn't think your father's friend would have rescheduled the interview if she wasn't biased in your favour, but there's no need to stake too much on it. If you don't get the job there'll be others, and the main thing is you'll have gone for it. You'll know you can."

"Dr Lowe said something like that."

"Well, there you are. What do they say about great minds?"

"Don't know."

She could have felt disparaged, but she was too concerned with his mental state while he was driving to London. "Are you worried about anything else, Sam?"

When his lips parted she tried to be prepared for whatever revelation he'd decided to entrust to her, but they closed again before releasing his apparently favourite word of the day. "What?"

"If it's your grandmother, the hospital would have called if there were any developments. I told you they said she has a pretty good chance of getting about on sticks when she comes home."

"She didn't seem that bad when they took her to the hospital."

"Her bones are old, Sam." Heather thought he sounded not unlike a child whose trust in the rightness of life had been betrayed. She reached to hug him, murmuring "Try not to have her on your mind too much. I'm sure they're doing everything they can for her at Mercy Hill."

She was disconcerted to find him unresponsive as a tree-trunk. It felt as if he'd formed himself into a barrier against some or all of her encouragement. "Isn't it just Margo?" she guessed.

He didn't answer until she let go of him and stepped back. Again she had the sense of an impending revelation, but couldn't be sure that wasn't to do with the gathering heat, which felt like the threat of a January storm. "Maybe," he muttered.

"Is it Sylvie?"

"Maybe."

His voice was well on the way to withdrawing into itself. He dropped his gaze as his bad leg gave a jerk that suggested it was eager to bear him away, but Heather didn't think she should abandon the subject now that she'd raised it in his mind. "She must be too busy to let us know where she is, that's all," she said, almost as much for her own benefit as his. "She's always been a bit like that. I know we'd expect her to keep us informed now there isn't only her to wonder about, but that's my sister, I suppose. I'm certain we'd have heard if anything was wrong."

His head appeared to be weighed down by her insistence or his thoughts. "Anyway," she said, and paused until he looked up. "Here I am using up oxygen when you should be on your way and make sure of having plenty of time."

She wouldn't have minded seeing agreement with that, but his thoughts were too deep in the dark of his eyes for her to read. "So long as I haven't made you feel worse," she risked saying.

He shook his head so rapidly he might have been attempting to dislodge a notion and nearly succeeded in hauling up the corners of his mouth. "Go on then," she said and restrained herself from delivering another hug. "You show the world."

It was simply a form of words, but as he limped to the Volkswagen she was left with the impression that she could have chosen better. She opened the gate for him and watched as the car, having elaborately cleared its throat, chugged away. He saw her waving in the mirror and raised one stiff hand without glancing back. She held back from stepping into the road to watch him as long as she could, and closed the gate. She heard him brake at the corner of Woodland Close as she returned to the house.

The interval until she next saw or heard from him was bound to feel stretched close to snapping, but she didn't mean to spend her day off work in worrying about him and her mother and sister. The house had stored up plenty of tasks—if she attacked them vigorously enough they might even leave her no spare energy for thoughts. She was making to release the vacuum cleaner from its cell beneath the stairs when she was halted by a smell so faint she was tempted to dismiss it as imagination. It was the secretively decayed odour of Selcouth's journal.

Heather didn't want the object in her house. It would be better kept at the university, available to anyone who needed to consult it— she couldn't imagine who or why. It could wait until tomorrow to be removed, even though now that she was aware of it she felt as if she'd been left alone in the house with it. She was about to open the cupboard under the stairs when she strode up them instead. Once she discovered what Sylvia had been reading aloud she would put the book out of her mind.

She pushed open the bedroom door and hesitated on the threshold. The room retained so little of Sylvia's presence that she might have fancied something had stolen every trace of their shared past, along with her sister. It seemed inhabited only by the journal in its binding black as a lump of night refusing to give way to the sun, and she caught herself wondering what Selcouth might have meant the blackness to recall. The book contained more than enough nonsense without her encouraging it, she thought fiercely. She sat at the desk and threw the volume open with a clunk like the fall of a dead branch.

Nat. Selcouth, his Journall.

She'd forgotten how much she instinctively disliked the thick angular handwriting that reminded her of twigs or of stains left on the page by rotten twigs. She wouldn't get far if she started off thinking like that, but the act of reading felt not unlike snagging her mind with the treetops that loomed at the upper edge of her vision.

I who am named for my Quallities shall here sette down the Historie of my Discoveries, that he who is to follow may carrie the Worke onwards. Let him understand that his Blood sets him as far above the Herd as my Powers have elevated me above the Flesh.

"Well, you did think a lot of yourself." She'd hoped to be objective—it was a piece of history, after all—but couldn't when she was aware that Sylvia had read from it to her own child, even if unborn.

Heather wasn't sure if that made it better or worse. So long as it didn't mean that Sylvia was losing control of her mind, surely it needn't matter. If Heather thought it did she would have to alert the police on behalf of Sylvia and her child, and her instincts suggested that her sister would never forgive her. She leafed onwards, trying to read no more than would show her the sentence she'd heard in the night, willing the phone to ring—to have Sylvia's voice.

Spirit calls to Spirit across the Gulphs of Space and Time, and thus my Spirit in its unflesh'd Journeyings was called to Goodman's Wood, which is a Site of great Powers forgotten by the Herd and a fit Setting for the Completion of my Experiments. Here have I caused to be builded an Habitation modelled on a Figure visible to me where once an antient Ring of Stone was raised to summon and containe the Daemon of this Place. The ignorant Invaders cast it down and planted Trees sacred to their feeble Gods but meerly constructed the Daemon a Lair wherein to brood and grow in Secret. Now my Tower shapes itself from the antient Circle and presents its one Halfe to the World while an equal Portion lies for ever in the Dark, as befitts the House of one whose Task it is to mate the Twain.

It occurred to Heather that much of this confirmed traditions Sylvia had wanted to believe were true of Goodmanswood—believe in the sense of adding them to her research. Just because Lennox had ended up convinced of the truth of local legends, it didn't mean Sylvia had followed him along that route. And yet she'd said she had felt summoned to the place as Selcouth apparently imagined he had. "It's not the same thing," Heather declared aloud and read on to drive the likeness out of her mind.

Some faintest Trace of Illumination must remaine to the gattering Minds of the Villagers that they keepe without the Wood and mumble

Prayers should they become sensible of its Proximity. Only the most aged Grandam of the Village remembers Tales told to affrighte her as a Child. Then would a very Cavalcade of Glimpses and Encounters be recount'd which I alone knew to betoken but one single Presence. So one Grey-Beard might speak of chancing upon Goodman in the Shape of a tall Man whose Shaddowe caused Insects to swarm within it where it fell, while another would whisper of a Mist with shifting Face, whose Passing thro' the Woods braught down Birdes like Fruit out of the Trees to rot in an Instant and loam the Forest. Againe a Grandfather would describe how, as he crossed the Common while a Boy, a great Arm reach'd forth from the Depths of the Forest to grope for him with many Fingers, and his with-ered Wife would prattle of her Girl-Hood, when beneath the Moone she saw the Trees perform an antient Dance from joining which her Prayers and Eyes closed tight could scarce protect her. Much else besides I learn'd upon a Mid-Night Visit to the quaking Grandam, whose Babblings con-firm'd my Belief that the Volatileness of the Forest Daemon fitts it to be shap'd to my Purpose, even as I have shap'd my House. Then, that she should not gossip of my Interest, I let the Grandam spy within my Eyes the meer Reflection of that outer Dark where my Spirit yearns to range at Will, at which the Blood flew from her Heart and sally'd forth from every Egress.

"Of course it did," Heather scoffed with distaste. Whatever beliefs might have been common in his lifetime, she was certain that the writer had been dangerously insane. Could anyone saner than Sel-couth find the book suitable for reading to even or perhaps especially an unborn child? Some of it had to be, otherwise Heather would be on the phone to the police.

So shall these forgotten Terrours, sunk too deepe in these dull Minds for sounding, keepe my Researches hid from prying Eyes. Even I, Nathaniel Selcouth, suffered that Feare which shrivells the Spirit as I kept the Vigill necessary to entice Goodman to me. Throughout the Whole of the first Night of my Vigill, as I watched without my House sans Lanthorn or Taper, I was circl'd about by Footfalls, now light as the Scurrying of many Insects, now ponderous as the Paces of a Colossus. Then from Dawn to renew'd Night the entire Forest held still as a great Cat waiting on its Prey. That second Night many Fingers or Bones touch'd and pluck'd at me, and the Trees were loud with many Whispers, despite there was no Wind. Againe a Stillness reign'd thro' the second Day, which I knew to be no more than a Pretence of Light amidst the veritable State of endless Dark. Thus arm'd with secret Knowledge, I had only to entrust my Vision to that Dark so as to observe Goodman when he appear'd in the Midst of the third Night. At first he shap'd himself into a Giant pale as any Toadstool, whose Face was but a Vapour, and then it was as if the very Ground opened a vast Mouth and Eyes and spake in a great Voice that set every Beast of the Village to imitating Babel in the Xtian Taradiddle. At the last Goodman sought to cow his Master by rearing higher than my House on many Legs like Trees and lowering his monstrous Face to me betwixt them, as it were a Moone should settle its decay'd Mask on the Earth. But I stood my Ground and spake the Words of Binding. So the awful Pact was seal'd, and I know that I have yield'd a Portion of my Spirit to this place in having striven with its Daemon. Yet my Spirit is greater than needs mourn the Loss.

Heather shook her head, mostly at herself. She was finding it hard not to be drawn into the imagery of the journal, which kept making her aware of the woods that loomed above the page, it seemed less distantly than they should. She glanced up to prove they had stayed where they ought to be, and caught herself fancying the treetops were upraised in search of the dark that lay in wait just beyond the sky. "Get on with it," she told both the book and its reader, and tried again to skim. Nevertheless she experienced some satisfaction when it became apparent that Selcouth had overreached himself.

Great and awful are the Perills even to my self of fathoming the Dark beyond the farthest Spheeres, for a Caprice of the Void may transmute the Spirit into Forms for which there are no Words and hence no Formula of Revocation. One such chang'd Horrour did I encounter that would have been a Magus, that now cry'd out sans Voice for it import'd not what Manner of Bodie in which to procure its own swift Death, and for a Month thereafter I feared the very Skies. No less grave are the Hazards of calling down a Messenger from that Dark, for that is to bring the antic Whims of the Void upon the Earth, to consume it as Rot consumes the Apple and make a Maggot even of my self. My Scheme was to send an Other as my Proxie, that I might observe the Transformations of its Essence and so learn how to wield those moderat'd Powers within and about my self. Thus I chose Goodman to voyage in my Stead, he being of more than human Power yet subject to my own.

What Agitation seiz'd the Forest whenever Goodman strove against my Sending! How the Trees groan'd and writh'd and cast up a very Blizzard of mournful Leaves, and how the Village Herd must have cower'd within their Pens! Thus was it borne upon me that as the Centuries transformed the Roman Grove into a Forest grown from Seedes pluck'd by Goodman from the Air, so he became besides the Daemon of the Wood, its Essence.

Thrice I sent Goodman forth to report upon the Dark that takes no Heede of Time. Thrice he rose up, his stretch'd Limbs trembling on the Earth they fear'd to quit, and vanish'd like thin Smoak between the Stars to return a-pace and crouch both like a Spider and a Dog before me. Well might I have thought he had fallen short of the Dark for Cravenness, had he not carry'd with him Traces of the Void that fasten'd on the Wood. Thus the Trees that surround my Tower, whose deepest Cellar is Goodman's Lair, became so altered as to found a new Genus that takes its Nourishment from such Life as may alight upon it, while the Shaddowes of the Forest acquired a Vigour which may yet outstrip that of their Source. Yet no

Formula was to be drawn from Observation of these Prodigies, nor any from interrogating Goodman about his Voyages, our Spirits lacking all Affinitie upon which to base a Discourse. Therefore I determin'd to contain within a Bodie of my own Begetting some Aspect of the Void that had company'd him to Earth, though the Process that had left one London Wench with Child had cast me downe with Wearyness and Loathing. To contain the Large within the Small is to concentrate its Power, and every Child must acknowledge its Father. In order to procure a Vessel to receive my Seede I shap'd Goodman into a scent'd naked Youth who would appear in a Maiden's Dream and at her Window also to escort her to my Bed, through the Forest that my Powers had render'd charming to every Sense.

It was a recluse's masturbatory fantasy, Heather told herself, and perhaps not even much more deranged than the average for all she knew. It made the oppressive heat and the woods that seemed poised at the edge of her vision feel closer, and she hardly knew why she was continuing to read the passage: she couldn't imagine Sylvia reading it aloud to anyone in the world.

On a Night of the full-belly'd Moone I performed my beastly Task upon a Village Wench and charged the Wood to snare her Memorie of our Encounter as Goodman shepherd'd her to her Cottage. When the Moone had fatten'd herself thrice upon the Dark I had the Trollop brought againe to me that I might bid her Inhabitant crawl forth from her and plant its hungry Root in the transformed and antic Earth of the lowest Cellar. Already its Essence was the outer Dark, for while I was at my Siring I had utter'd the Formula which I sette downe here for the Eyes and Understanding of my Follower.

Encompass us, o Daoloth, Lord of unveil'd Truth, that the Product of my Seede shall be endow'd with Vision that penetrates even to the Secrets of the farthest Dark . . .

Heather especially disliked the notion that Sylvia could have read this to the child inside her, but surely there was no reason to assume she had. There was a full page of it, much of it in some altogether less speakable language, from which Heather glanced up to dispel the notion that the trees at the edge of the common were imitating the letters on the page or otherwise responding to the written incantation. They hadn't moved that she could distinguish, but at least she didn't feel the need to recommence where she'd left off. She turned the page and immediately wished she hadn't, for it had concealed a drawing. *From life*, the caption said.

It wasn't the drawing from which she'd recoiled when Sylvia had shown her the journal, but it was as bad. It showed a small creature crouching on all fours beside a tower. Despite its lack of a mouth and its enormous eyes that looked trapped by an unnaturally lightless sky, it reminded her far too much of a toddler. She attempted to ignore it while she scanned the text opposite, then snatched at the page, only to reveal the drawing of a child with eyes swarming out of its honey-comb of a skull. The third and last was worse still; the figure grovel-ling in the shadow of the tower—a shadow, Heather was eager to realise, that wouldn't have existed given the blackness of the sky—had an almost perfect child's face except for the single huge eye perched on top like an egg in a cup. Fragments of the text caught at her mind:

> Though our Spirits were in Sympathie, no Intelligence could I gain from my benighted Offspring. I had thought to spy my Goal thro' its Eyes, but its Innocence did not protect its Wits from being blast'd to Idiocy by those Sights. Its solitary Meritt is to derive all its Nourishment from the Dark which was its Origin ...
>
> This second Creature and its vagrant Orbs also proved too puny to trawl the Secrets of the Dark ...
>
> So a third Bastard shows itself unworthy of my Goal, nor am I content with the Slavishness which besets the Embodiement of the Formula. There-

fore I must steel my self to undertake that Rite which none known to me has dared perform.

Part of Heather's mind was urging her to skip the rest, but she was suddenly enraged to feel daunted by a mere book, and one that smelled of its own senility at that. "So did you?" she said through her teeth.

The waken'd Dead have Strengths not grant'd to the Living, and I hold it to be more than Rumour that the Product of their Mating shall multiply their several Powers within it. Againe, it is an Axiom that Blood shall speak to Blood if generat'd by a Mage. On collecting a Package from London some Weeks past I learned that the Crone my Mother had quit her Prison of Flesh. This was of no greater Moment to me than had a Vessel of inferior Clay crack'd asunder of its Flawes, but now . . .

"That's all," Heather declared, and almost slammed the journal shut before she recalled why she was searching through it. Though she was increasingly reluctant to discover exactly what she'd overheard, she made herself continue skimming. "Do your worst," she said under her breath.

In London Wealth and less than Wealth will purchase Satisfaction of any Desire, and but little Payment was requir'd to coax a pair of Grave-diggers to reverse their Trade. Having buried the Casket afresh and borne its Contents to a Field yet strong in antient Magick, they were wonderful eager to leave me at my Task of summoning the Dark to restore Suppleness to the wither'd Limbs. Well short of the Hour at which I had bade a Coach-man to arrive, the Corse was a Puppet of my Will, prancing and curtseying however stiffly beneath the Moone. Once bath'd in Scents and conceel'd by Veils, it might have been mistook for a famous Courtesan, and I doubt not that the Coach-man fancy'd this of my Companion. Indeed, none Other shall its Function be, and thus the Grave shall be a Cradle.

Heather's father must have read this somewhere, she had to tell herself. Since this was the only copy, he must have read that. It followed that he must have left it for Sylvia to find—left it wherever she'd found it, at any rate. Recalling how Lennox had echoed the journal made Heather feel that she would catch him watching if she looked up, and when she did, that the woods were observing her with as many eyes as there were trees. If this was how having an active imagination felt, she didn't like it much. She skipped from paragraph to paragraph as though they were stepping-stones over a dark flood.

> Throughout the Ride to Goodman's Wood I suffer'd my Companion to keep its Peace, and so fail'd to mark the Renewal of its Stiffness. Upon gaining the Road beside the Forest it was my Task to assist the veil'd Lich forth from the Carriage. As the Coach-man whipp'd his Team towards the Village I summon'd Goodman to bear my Prize to my Tower . . .
>
> It is no great Labour to animate the Cadaver nor even to cause it to utter my Voice, but now I see that reviving some Porcion of its Essence and quickening its Venter may be an Affair of many Nights pass'd in its Company sans Illumination in the lowest Cellar. My Journall shall record the Process once it is braught to Fulfillment . . .
>
> The Rite has been interrupt'd meer Nights short of Success by the Interfeerence of the Herd . . .

Heather almost let out a murmur of relief. It wasn't that she would have been afraid to learn that Selcouth had believed he'd successfully completed his experiment all those centuries ago, but rather that she wouldn't be in danger of reading worse than she already had. In fact it seemed there was very little left to read.

> Whose Sport was it to betray me? The Coach-man, or some Village Dullard eager to advance his Cause by sucking up to the Magistrate? The

puny Minds of the Xtian Sheep can but persecute and seek to x-tinguish that which they lack Capacity to comprehend. A Mob of them has enter'd the Woods, bleating Prayers to ward off such Hosts as may greet them. But my Powers are sore enfeebl'd by my interrupt'd Vigil, and I lack the Vigour to direct Goodman upon the Intruders. Therefore I shall devote my last Moments with my Journall to setting down a Message to my Follower, then conceel the Booke where Goodman may at the appoint'd Time discover it to him.

I have no Feare of what shall come to pass. Two Visions have been afford'd me that I shall debase my self with no Show of Weakness such as the Xtians tattle of their Man-god. As from my Peak above the Flesh I have witness'd my own Execution, and I know that it is but an empty Husk that takes its Place upon the Scaffold while my Spirit regains the Conceelment of the Woods. A Scrying has shown me the Face of my Follower, so like unto my own that I might have mistook the Glass for a meer Mirror. Let him gaze upon his Likenesse and recognise his Destiny. He shall unite our Blood, and so shall my Powers be reawaken'd and marry'd to those that roam the Forest. At the Birth, all shall be contained withinne a single Form and give it Life. The Great gains Force when closed within the Small, and so shall I enter the Realm which is my Due.

The last third of the right-hand page was blank. At first Heather was bewildered by her own uneasy dissatisfaction—but she'd heard Sylvia continuing to read aloud the night before she'd left, and a good deal more than one sentence. Surely there had to be more to the journal; otherwise she must have been uttering for her child's supposed benefit some of the material Heather had read or had avoided reading. It was with something grotesquely like hope that she leafed through the rest of the book.

Blank page followed blank page, rustling like a nest of restless insects, offering her only an oppressive smell of papery decay that made her head swim. The binding twitched against the desk like a lid that was struggling to raise itself. She dug a fingernail into one corner to hold it still and resisted moistening a fingertip so as to turn the last few pages quicker; the notion that traces of the pages were gathering on her thumb and finger was disagreeable enough. Another yellowed sheet revealed itself to her, and another, and then one proved unexpectedly weighty. It was the last page—no, she'd taken hold of the last two. She let them fall against the binding with a muffled click that suggested they were composed of more than paper. She was about to separate them when she noticed what the unlikeliness had prevented her from seeing. The pages were stapled together.

All her understanding of time seemed to desert her as she tried to think how long ago the stapler could have been invented, and then she saw how indisputably new the staples were. One desk drawer contained a stapler. Why would Sylvia have sealed up the last page? By no means sure that she wanted to know, Heather nevertheless set about prising the staples open with a thumbnail.

Each margin was stapled. As she unfastened the third and refrained from sucking a twinge out of the quick of her thumb, both pages settled on the bulk of the journal, exposing a discoloured underside to her. A smell of more than age insinuated itself into her nostrils, and she leaned across the desk to heave the sash of the window up. It must have been her movement that stirred the page as if whatever it concealed was impatient to be seen. She almost tore the corner in a sudden fury at her reluctance to see.

The inscription on the left-hand sheet made her hesitate with the last page still held vertical. *My Follower as scry'd withinne the Glass*, it said. She had already glimpsed the ink drawing it described, and she was scarcely aware that her fingers were losing their hold on the page. As it fell open, the woods at the edge of her vision appeared to crane forward to watch. She hadn't time to argue herself out of that impression; she was too desperate to find some evidence that the drawing had been added recently, no matter why. Although the face that was the whole of it somewhat resembled her father, it looked far more like Sam.

33

The Last Descent

WHEN she'd finished peering at the last page in a vain attempt to identify some evidence of tampering, Heather let the book slump shut. She might have sat there staring at the cover if its blackness hadn't too closely resembled the way the inside of her head felt. She had a sudden notion that the book was offering its blackness to the woods. As she leaned across the desk to close the window, her body shrank away from the lump of dark and all its contents. She pushed the chair back and retreated to the door, leaving the smell of centuries to take possession of the room. She was going to rid her house of the book, but not until she'd decided whether to confront Sam with the drawing or destroy it if she learned he hadn't seen it. Just now she was desperate to talk to someone, perhaps only to convince herself that not every aspect of life she had taken for granted was keeping secrets from her.

She was hardly conscious of descending the stairs and laying a hand on the phone. She would have picked up the receiver if she'd been able to think of anyone who could help. She wasn't about to bother her mother in hospital, and she mustn't trouble Sam at his interview, not that he was likely to be there yet, though Selcouth's journal had absorbed more of her time than she'd realised. When she began to contemplate calling Sam's father or even Randall if she could manufacture some pretext that wouldn't betray she was close to panic, she did her best to seize control of her thoughts. She rang Mercy Hill to learn that Margo had been restless during the night, though her injuries were healing well, and was now asleep. While Heather was glad of her mother's progress she found she would have liked to speak to her, however briefly and inconsequentially. Relinquishing the phone, which was no more of a lifeline than it felt like, she wandered out of the house.

The thud of the door behind her sounded unnervingly final, a conclusion for which there were no words to some part of her life. As she trudged out of the gate she couldn't tell whether she was being hindered more by her own mind or by the oppressively humid air, which felt heavy with undeclared thunder beneath the pallid clotted sky. At the far end of Woodland Close the tarmac was quivering as though invaded by a swathe of energy. Around her the houses kept stonily still, and she felt as though they were isolating her with the prospect of an instability the quaking haze only symbolised. The haze slithered backwards as she advanced, and when she turned the corner it was lurking beyond J's and J's, reshaping cars parked on either side of the road.

Jessica was alone in the shop. She turned from unloading a carton of packs of American cigarettes onto a shelf behind the counter as the bell above the door sprang its brassy note. She ran a hand through her haphazard curls as if they mightn't be sufficiently dishevelled, then spread wide a finger and thumb to raise her spectacles on her small nose. Her eyes grew large in the thick lenses to no especially welcoming effect. "Oh, hello, Heather," she said.

The step Heather took across the threshold felt as tentative as her greeting. "Hello, Jessica."

"What's it about now?"

"I wish I knew."

A further hint of sympathy found its way into Jessica's voice. "Is it all getting to be a pain?"

"All . . ." The problems Jessica might be expected to know about came to a kind of rescue. "Did you hear mother was in an accident?" Heather said.

"Wandered out in front of a car near the Arbour, somebody was saying."

"I hope that doesn't mean you think she ought to be in that kind of hospital."

"Not unless she's a lot different from all the times I've seen her recently, and I wouldn't go round saying it if I did."

"You're making me wonder if someone else has been."

"A few."

"Do I have to ask who?"

"I'd rather you didn't, Heather, to tell you the truth."

"Maybe you could let them know next time you see them," Heather said with a fierceness mostly aimed past Jessica, "that her attention was distracted for a moment. That can be all it takes."

"I will."

"Dr Lowe at the Arbour didn't seem to think she needed his kind of help."

"I'm glad," Jessica said, and less uncomfortably "How is she?"

"On the mend when I spoke to Mercy Hill a few minutes ago."

"That must be a weight off your mind."

It felt more to Heather as though her mind was a weight in itself. "You'd imagine so," she said.

"Oh dear, poor Heather. More's wrong, I know."

Jessica let her hands stray onto the counter, where they remained face down on the day's newspapers, not having quite reached for Heather. Heather felt as if the array of headlines about politics and crime and stardom was a barrier between herself and Jessica, an indication of how remote her unvoiced problems were from the everyday. She couldn't begin to discuss Selcouth's journal and its implications; it was more to fend those off that she admitted "If anyone's wandering, it's my sister."

Jessica met this with a look as careful as her words. "How would that be?"

"I don't know where she is."

"That's . . ." Rather than define it, Jessica said "Since when?"

"Since before mother was hurt. I'm sure if Sylvie knew she'd come back."

"I'm sure," said Jessica, blinking at the newspapers as if they might display some trace of Sylvia. She kept her gaze on them even after she murmured "Is it because of how she is?"

Heather felt detected on her sister's behalf. "How's that supposed to be?"

"You know." Jessica frowned and glanced streetward to confirm that nobody was in earshot. "Having a little one."

Heather saw how befuddled she must be to have suspected Jessica of guessing that Sylvia had needed mental treatment. "She's researching another book. That's what the note she left me said," she explained, and instantly realised it mightn't have meant that at all.

"Then she's bound to be in touch once she's settled wherever, isn't she?"

"I'd have hoped so." Heather was scarcely aware of thinking aloud as she said "I can't believe nobody saw her going and mentioned it to me. I mean, a pregnant woman with three suitcases . . ."

"I expect she took a taxi, did she?"

Heather thought of phoning all the taxi firms in Goodmanswood and Brichester to ask if anyone remembered Sylvia, but what could that achieve? Amid the snarl of her thoughts she found nothing to say beyond "Even so . . ."

"Can I say something as a friend?"

"I'm glad if you're still one."

"Forgive me for saying, then, but maybe they didn't want to see her."

"I do. Why wouldn't they?"

"You have to understand there's been talk."

"There always is. About what now?"

"Some friend of your sister's. Some strange American who was asking the way to your house. The people she spoke to think she was on drugs."

The truth rose to Heather's lips before retreating, having found no reason to declare itself. "Did you meet her?" Jessica said.

"I may have."

"Then you'll understand why people don't want anyone like her having an excuse to hang around anywhere near here."

Heather was feeling unable to argue, given her own reaction to Merilee, when Jessica added "You mustn't think I'd ever mean you or your family."

"You're saying others would."

"I don't think I can be telling you anything you haven't already noticed."

Heather was struggling to grasp what else she should have when Jessica said "By the way, you weren't looking for Sam."

"I wasn't, no. Should I be?"

"Not if you know where he is, I suppose."

"He's gone for a job in London. I don't mind telling you I'll be happy to see him leave Goodmanswood."

What she saw just then was the drawing in the journal. She was willing Sam to put as much distance between it, not to mention whatever it implied, and himself as he could when Jessica gave her a blink beneath a frown. "I don't believe so, Heather."

"What don't you believe?"

"He hasn't gone that far."

"Why not?" As Heather tried to clarify her question it came out harsher too. "Why do you say that?"

"Because I saw him."

Heather found herself ready, however irrationally, to blurt that it might only have been someone who resembled him, but the idea was as dismaying as the situation it was meant to resolve. "You saw what?"

"Sam going where he keeps going."

Heather tried to tell herself that he'd assured her he was bound for London, but couldn't recall his having said anything so unambiguous. "Where's that?" she said, a last despairing attempt to put off the truth.

"Across the common, and you know where that leads."

"How long ago?"

"I'd say at least an hour."

Heather was distressed to think she might have seen him crossing the common if she hadn't been so reluctantly engrossed in Selcouth's journal. "I don't understand how you could have seen him from here," she said.

"I saw him walk past and I went out to ask how Margo was. I called after him but he couldn't have heard me."

"But he wasn't walking when he left the house," said Heather, and tramped out of J's and J's to stare along the street. At the far end, its base wallowing in a pool of haze, she saw a green hump that appeared to resemble an overgrown mound at least as much as a Volkswagen— a mound that quaked as though its contents were struggling to emerge. When she strode towards it the number plate dredged itself up and quivered into focus. Once she'd identified it she kept walking towards it until she made herself swing round and hurry back past the shop. "Thanks, Jessica," she called, and marched down an alley between houses to the common.

The forest stretched itself wide as though to acknowledge her, and so did the pale overgrown sky; she could have thought one was a symbol or a version of the other. Clammy grass dragged at her ankles as she strode towards the woods. The grass in their shadow appeared restless, though the rest of the common lay inert, and she saw the shadows behind the outermost trees begin to grope about the forest floor despite the utter stillness of the woods. It must be an effect of the heat, since it continued to withdraw as she advanced, and she couldn't let it trouble her. All that mattered was that Sam was in whatever state had prevented him from leaving Goodmanswood.

She glanced back at Woodland Close in the faint hope that he might have returned to the house, but his window was blank. Some trick of the light made it look almost as black as the cover of Selcouth's journal. Feeling as if the massed ranks of houses had cast out both her and Sam, she grasped a creaking scaly branch to help her step over a fallen tree into the woods. For the briefest instant her hand tingled as her skin used to after an April shower, though last year Sam had suggested that was the fault of chemicals in the rain. Across the common several dogs started to bark, but fell silent once she was past the barrier. As soon as she thought she was beyond earshot of the houses she began to call Sam's name.

Her calls seemed incapable of travelling far. It sounded as if much of her voice was being walled in by the multitude of tree-trunks or absorbed by the canopy of branches. She had apparently never noticed how soon the branches closed overhead, nor how few places among the trees offered a sight of the open sky, although today the sky resembled whitish fungus caught in the net of wood. When she raised her voice she felt it scarcely left her, as though the forest had pressed imperceptibly around her to compensate. She was almost certain she knew where Sam was: at the remains of Selcouth's tower, the location that had so obsessed Lennox and then Sylvia. If Sam didn't prove to be there, at least it was the middle of the woods, from which Heather would be more likely to make herself heard throughout them.

She wasn't going to let anything remind her of the contents of Selcouth's journal. There were a good few hours between her and nightfall. The shapes and patterns of the foliage around her and above her weren't relevant to her search, nor were the objects in the treetops— greenish bulges that could be nests or growths, with a tendency to resemble faceless heads—let alone the impression that a shape as wide as the forest was keeping pace with her above the trees, using them or shapes that they concealed for limbs. "Sam," she shouted with growing anger. "Answer me. I know you're here."

Her sense that he was failed to encourage her. She kept feeling she was about to blunder past a tree and come face to face with him—

with someone who was close to her, at any rate. That was the kind of prank Sylvia might play, though surely not in her present condition. "Sam," Heather called at the top of her voice, "will you show yourself," as she dodged around a fallen tree that formed with its neighbours a shape like an enormous hieroglyph. She wasn't aware of disturbing the roots that were matted with upheaved soil, but she thought she heard a pattering of earth; perhaps it was somewhere ahead. She opened her mouth to shout again, but instead cupped both ears, to be met by a silence that challenged her to believe she'd heard anything. She was pacing forward, leaves cracking like beetles under her feet, when the woods produced another sound—a thump like a single giant heartbeat muffled by the earth.

It was ahead of her. She couldn't judge how far—how distance might have minimised it and its source. She made herself keep moving, though before long she grew reluctant to call out, not for fear of an impression that the presence above the trees had halted to await her but because she'd identified the cause of the impression: the patch of toadstool sky that was visible between the trees. She was coming to the space in the middle of the woods, and there was no sign of Sam.

Then what had made the sound? Perhaps a branch or a nest had fallen. It was absurd of her to be nervous in broad daylight of entering the largest open space the woods contained. There was nothing to be seen in it except the mound encircled by brick—nothing that need remind her of Selcouth's journal. She stalked forward, furious with herself for being wary when her concern should be for Sam. She tramped into the clearing between a pair of trees shaped no more oddly than their neighbours and tipped with half-revealed green objects that had to be leaves. She was striding to the centre of the space, less interested in identifying what she'd heard than in locating Sam, when she faltered. Someone had dug up the mound.

A squarish hole surrounded by moist earth and more than wide enough to admit or release a man was gaping at the low pale fat sky. Heather was infuriated to feel sweat pricking her hands as she ventured closer. For a moment she thought she wouldn't be able to step over the mouldering bricks to see into the hole. "Sam," she yelled, almost as much from frustration as in the hope of summoning him. When there was no response from among the host of trees, she planted a foot on the yielding upturned earth and followed it with the other.

The digging had exposed a curve of steps slippery with earth. At the top of the steps two unequal pieces of a stone slab had been levered up with a spade whose head was bent half out of shape by the task. At first she thought the realisation that the passage led to Selcouth's cellars was allowing her to distinguish the lowest steps more clearly, if her eyes weren't adjusting unusually swiftly to the dimness into which the steps descended, and then she wondered if the sun had managed to break through the clouds. When she glanced at the sky it was as coated as ever. She peered down and immediately saw why the steps were growing more visible. Someone was climbing out of the dark.

The light that came crawling up the passage seemed reluctant to reveal itself or its bearer, and she found she had to make herself breathe and swallow. The lowest steps began to shiver with the glow, and a flashlight wavered into view, followed by a hand, an arm, a shoulder, the top of a bowed head. They were Sam's, and his posture made her nervous of seeing his face.

He was halfway up the curve of steps when he raised his head. It was obvious that he hoped nobody was awaiting him. As he met her eyes he did his best to hide any expression, but looked guilty enough to retreat if something below him hadn't daunted him. His gaze flickered, both desperate for a way of escape and unable to leave her, so that she was almost too apprehensive to ask "What have you been doing, Sam?"

He took hold of the shaft of the damaged spade as if he meant to claim he had only been digging. "Looking for Sylvia," he said.

"And did you find her?"

The solitary nod that was his response looked like another unsuccessful attempt to drag his gaze away from Heather's. "Where?" she prompted impatiently. "Not down there."

Some seconds elapsed before he delivered another trapped nod, and she felt as if the heat was making them both sluggish. "Come out before that falls on you," she said, reaching an urgent hand down to him.

He didn't take it—his face suggested that he felt she mightn't want him to touch her—but she refused to step back until he was past the threat of the heavy slab. He retreated to the far side of the hole from her and stared unhappily into it. "What's down there?" Heather said loudly enough to deny there was anything to fear.

"I told you."

"You've told me nothing yet, and I think it's about time you did. Why aren't you in London?"

"Same reason."

"As what?"

He was looking more cornered than ever. "Sylvia," he muttered.

"Where are you trying to tell me she is?"

One corner of his mouth winced, and it was with some difficulty that he said "She's gone."

"I'm sorry, Sam, you're not making yourself remotely clear. Have I got to go down and see for myself what's there? In that case give me the flashlight."

He clutched it with his free hand, covering the lens as though to deprive her of the illumination. "Don't," he mumbled.

"I can assure you I don't want to, but I will unless you tell me why you were down there. Is it something to do with that wretched old book of my sister's?"

"Have you read it?"

"I've read enough to know what this place is and the kinds of things the sad case who wrote it imagined about it. If you're thinking of that picture, someone else could have drawn it, must have. I know what it says, but I shouldn't think that kind of writing would take much to forge. Don't ask me why anyone would have done all that."

Nevertheless she was ready to wonder aloud whether Sylvia had—whether she wasn't as stable as she had pretended to be—if that would relieve Sam of the notion that he was at the mercy of any aspect of the journal. She wasn't expecting to hear him ask "What picture?"

"Never mind if you don't know," Heather said, willing him to forget she'd mentioned it. "You still haven't told me why you're here."

"Yes I did."

She was about to lose all patience when she glimpsed the guilt that was trying to hide behind his eyes. A surge of panic made her blurt "What have you done, Sam?"

"I wouldn't hurt her. I'd never have done that."

"I know you wouldn't." Heather took a deep breath to say or to delay saying "Has someone . . ."

"I told you, she's gone. It's gone."

"Do you mean her baby?"

She saw him glance downwards under the imperfect cover of a nod, and had the sudden awful notion that she understood the shame he was trying to conceal. "Sam, you haven't . . ."

"What?" he said with a fierceness that might have been exhorting her to speak or the reverse.

"Did she turn against having the baby? Did you—did you help?"

She couldn't have been prepared for his reaction. He'd scarcely pressed his lips together when they started writhing with a violence that made it impossible for her to guess the expression he was struggling to withhold. She snatched the flashlight from his slackened grasp and jabbed the beam into the hole. She had taken one step down, so angrily that it bruised her heel, when he mumbled "Don't. You don't want to see."

"Why don't I? I will unless you tell me what you've done."

At first it seemed the threat was insufficient to gain her an answer. She had exhausted staring at him and was descending another step when he managed to pronounce "Wait. I . . ."

Heather looked up to find him gazing at her in something like anguish. That was enough to dispel an impression that not only he was watching her—that they were being spied upon from between all the trees or behind the sky. "Go on, Sam," she urged. "Go on."

"I'd be the last person to harm it."

"I knew you couldn't really have. It's our baby too."

"No," he said, and she saw the hope that he'd implied enough desert him. "It's mine."

She felt everything close in—the audience of trees, the heavy bloated secretive sky, the dark beyond the shaky flashlight beam—to dwarf her voice. "How do you mean?"

"How do you think?"

"I'm not thinking anything," Heather said, her mind having turned into an inert lump. "You've got to say."

A shiver passed through him, perhaps only with the effort of drawing a harsh breath that emerged as harsher words. "I'm the father."

He might have been shouting it to the woods. If she hadn't been trying to calm him, she could have imagined that the echoes the last word awakened were in a succession of voices quite unlike his. "You can't be really, can you, Sam?" she said. "Whatever gave you that idea?"

"It's true. Christ," he snarled in disgust at her or himself.

"What would Sylvia say if she could hear you?"

"She knew it was before I did."

"You mean she put it into your head? Sam, I wish I didn't have to tell you this, because I promised I'd keep it to myself, but she's had some mental problems."

"Just like me."

That had the sound of a question or even a denial, but Heather did her best to use it. "I know you have, and we'll find someone who can help. It needn't be Dr Lowe if you don't think he's much use. But this idea has to be part of what's wrong, hasn't it?"

"Because it's true."

"All right then, tell me how."

"We met here the day she came home, before we knew who we were. It's all to do with this place, everything is. That's why we came back."

No, Heather thought: it was all the fault of Selcouth's journal. There was no knowing what Sam and Sylvia might have imagined together based on it while both their minds were less than balanced. She was at the disadvantage of not knowing what he'd unearthed or thought he'd unearthed. "Wait here for me or come down with me, whichever you prefer," she said. "I have to look."

She was below the surface of the mound when she thought she heard him mutter "I can't." "You can," she said, not lingering to make sure he'd heard. She hurried down the steps as fast as she could bear the swaying of the light in the narrow spiral passage, and slowed only whenever she came abreast of a room. There were several, all of them seared black and bare. If they'd had anything to do with Selcouth, she was glad of the damage. They contained nothing but tangles of old bones and in one case a lumpy heap of burned books—nothing worth a second glance. All she wanted to find was Sylvia. Her lips kept parting to call to her but managing no more than to whisper her name. She found her in the lowest room.

Sylvia lay on a heap of rotting vegetation, her knees drawn up towards her chest, her arms pressing her legs together, her hands clenched on the hem of her dress to tug it down to her feet. She was no longer pregnant; indeed, very little remained of her. She looked thinner than the oldest person Heather had ever seen, as though she had been almost entirely consumed. Even her face was hardly more than skin and bone, and yet it seemed to Heather that it had reverted to being her little sister's, perhaps because the eyes and mouth were as wide as a child's. There was no telling whether they expressed wonder or terror or some emotion beyond those—no knowing what she might have seen or thought she'd seen in her final moments.

Heather felt as though time had grown pointless. She had no idea how long she stood in the doorway, adding her free hand to her grip on the flashlight when the beam began to droop towards the floor. If there was a faint trail across the bare earth from Sylvia's body, Heather was unable to care. She was seeing how a solitary toe exposed by a sandal was peeking from beneath Sylvia's dress. All at once Heather lurched across the room as if her grief had dealt her a violent shove, and bent to close her sister's eyes.

The gesture seemed to fall short of any meaning, because there was nobody to respond to it. Heather stepped back, avoiding a flashlight that was trained on the doorway, its lens as blank as Sylvia's vacated eyes had been. It brought home to Heather that her sister might have died not just in the depths of Selcouth's cellars but in the blind dark. She couldn't think past that idea, which overwhelmed her mind with dismay and rage. Some of that found her voice. "Sam, come down," she shouted. "We aren't leaving her here. Come and help me carry her."

She heard no answer. Perhaps her shout was muffled by the passage. Though it distressed her to take herself and the light away from Sylvia even for a moment, she backed fast if less than steadily out of the room. For an instant, on the threshold, she thought something was at her back. It could only be the dark, because she sensed its presence whichever way she turned, and then not at all. "Come down. Come here," she called as she climbed to find Sam.

34

The Revelation of the Forest

HEATHER had barely lost sight of the lowest room when, in the midst of her shock, she grasped what was most important and real. She shouldn't upset Sam more than he already had to be. Whatever his mental state had been, finding his aunt's body must have made it worse. He must be blaming himself for her death—for not finding her in time—and so confused that he was taking the blame for her having been pregnant. He needed help and understanding, not to feel even more accused. He needed his mother's support as much as she would welcome any that he could provide. "Sam, are you there?" she called more gently. "Can you hear me? Wait there if you don't want to come down."

She wouldn't have minded hearing a response. She felt awaited before she came abreast of the next highest room, and couldn't help turning the light aside through the doorway. Shadows—only shadows—flexed themselves as if the charred bones just inside were preparing to scuttle towards her. They were only bones, and bones couldn't move, which meant she needn't waste another glance on them. They returned to the dark behind her, and she kept the flashlight beam firmly on the steps above her until she had almost reached the next gaping entrance. This showed her the remains of books, and however much she deplored any damage to rarities, if these had led to Selcouth's activities she was happy they'd been destroyed. If the contents of the other rooms were also related to his journal she preferred not to think about that, not down here in the dark, not while she had more immediate anxieties. "Sam, can't you answer?" she would rather not have had to call, but there was silence apart from the flat trapped sound of her footsteps. At least that meant there was no sound from the rooms she had passed or still had to pass, and certainly no reason for her to send the light into the two she had yet to encounter. She managed to restrain herself from doing so, though as the dim edge of the light trailed into the rooms it almost made her glimpse shapes trying shakily to raise themselves where she remembered the bones had been huddled. She was nearly in sight of the outer world—she would have heard if the slab had fallen in the way. The beginnings of panic sent her stumbling upwards, thrusting the flashlight beam ahead as though it might be capable of moving stone. It found the top of the steps, beyond which the opening appeared to be filled with darkness as solid as earth. She lurched at it and saw a cloudless lucid blue sky overhead. She grabbed the shaft of the spade to help her onto the mound, and for the briefest instant felt as if she'd seized a weapon to defend herself against something behind or above her. Then the sense of a presence left her, and she murmured "Sam."

Perhaps she had spoken too softly. The nearest to a response she heard was a creak of branches and a fluttering of wings. As her head emerged above the surface of the mound the forest rose to its full height around her. Sam was nowhere to be seen.

He had to be within earshot, she promised herself. "Sam," she called as she stepped over the ring of brick, off the mound. The bright horde of trees and their intricate dense web of shadow held themselves still as though to help her listen, and then a blackbird—it was black, at any rate—clattered out of the highest branches of a tree about a hundred yards beyond the edge of the clearing nearest Goodmanswood. Its shadow raced across the leaf-strewn ground like a denizen of the web, and as the shadow vanished she glimpsed Sam's face peering around the tree where the creature had made itself apparent. "Wait there," she called. "Let's talk."

She wanted to believe he hadn't heard. Before she'd finished speaking she couldn't see him, and had to tell herself she hadn't imagined doing so. As she hurried across the grass, which was so elaborately patched with unfamiliar weeds she might have thought the glade was determined to represent every species it could bring to mind, she brandished the flashlight as though it would help her see. "Don't go any further, Sam," she called at the top of her voice.

He was the one she was anxious about, but she didn't mind if he thought she was pleading on her own behalf, if that would halt him. She heard a movement that must have been the scraping of twigs beneath his feet while he risked another glance at her from behind a tree half as distant again as the place she'd last seen him. She hadn't realised there was sufficient cover to let him move that far unobserved. "Stay there," she pleaded rather than try to decree. Working her shoulders, which felt burdened by nerves, she hurried forward. She had barely left the clearing when she lost sight of him.

"Don't keep doing that," she cried, though she was in no doubt that she understood his behaviour: he didn't want to face her now that he'd admitted what he thought he'd done. He should know it would take more than that to turn her against him, especially since she'd done her best to let him know that he hadn't begun to persuade her. "Nothing's changed," she called, "nothing's changed between us," and tried a question. "Has it, Sam?"

She was hoping this would coax an answer out of him even if he didn't show himself, but the only sound the woods produced was a single piercing note of birdsong. As she ran towards his ambush, a bird that she'd taken for a bunch of fallen leaves darted across her shadowy path and took cover behind an elm tree scaled by ivy. Was Sam beyond one of the elms? It seemed unlikely, since all the thick trunks were canted as though to indicate or reach for Goodmanswood. Perhaps she would find him behind the walnut tree whose branches were raised almost vertical in a gesture suggestive of a blessing or of some more occult sign, or the sycamore encircled by concentric patterns of its own withered wings, or the birches patched with silver she remembered taking as a child to be a sign that a hidden treasure was coming to light, or the low secretive masses of box, although to use those for concealment he would need to crouch. Never before had the woods seemed so intensely present to her; it must be an effect of her scrutinising them for any trace of him. A sudden notion that he'd doubled back towards the ruins of Selcouth's tower made her twist around, but she could see neither Sam nor the clearing. She faced forward just in time to catch sight of a movement dodging behind an oak.

Its lowest branches were rooted in the ground as if the tree was bent on uniting earth and sky, and it was more than broad enough to hide Sam, even if those weren't his fingers on the edge of the trunk, which bore several excrescences like knobbly wrinkled hands, their nails painted with moss. When she rounded the oak, her lips parting to emit a murmur of relief, it proved to be harbouring only a contorted tangle of branches as tall as a man. She could only think she must have glimpsed the squirrel that was leaping from treetop to treetop. As she watched the thin grey shape vanish like windblown mist across the canopy of greenish branches, she was struck afresh by how few places in the forest offered a clear view of the sky; perhaps only the space around the ruins did. That wasn't important now, only Sam was, and he surely couldn't be far—could be hidden by one of the hawthorns, their trunks split like ancient bones and rearing their spiky branches to claw the sky down. "Sam, don't keep going away from me," she begged, "not now," but her shout only sent up a virtually silent flight of birds from high in the trees, as though the sky enmeshed by branches had splintered to reveal its underlying blackness. Some aspect of the forest seemed oddly wrong, but she couldn't spare it any of her attention while she had yet to find Sam. He wasn't behind any of the gathering of willows—each of their boles was split into three, rather too reminiscent of the fingers of half-buried malformed hands—nor beyond the fir trees lined up like skeletons of Christmas. She remembered the tree Sam had brought home, and immediately knew where he had found it. She had never noticed fir trees in the woods.

Then, with a lurch of her consciousness that felt as if every tree had taken an unseen pace towards her, she realised there was more to it. Her search wasn't just showing her the woods in greater detail than she had ever seen in her life. She was unable to recall having seen them clearly even once.

A bird the colours of several dead leaves flew out of the cage of the roots of an oak with a single chirp. It might almost have been responding to her thoughts, but it was the wrong response, because it reminded her that she had never seen a bird find a perch in the woods. Until today she had only observed birds flying over, and her memory of any birds or other creatures she'd encountered was very approximate, just convincing and detailed enough not to arouse her suspicions and yet so vague it might have been designed to forestall examination. Before she could consider this, she caught a glimpse of Sam.

He was peering through a rank of beeches whose grey trunks she'd taken for a mist. She might have continued in the error, since they were so much more distant than she would have expected him to be, if his face hadn't made clear the spaces between them. "I can see you," she cried, which immediately ceased to be the truth. If nothing she said would persuade him to wait for her, she could only strive to catch up with him. At least he seemed to be leading her out of the forest, and she didn't mind admitting to herself that wasn't entirely unwelcome. When she came back for Sylvia she hoped to be with more people, though not Sam.

A wind must have entered the forest. As she dodged between the trees, hurrying faster than she would have thought Sam could limp, she grew aware of movements overhead. Perhaps they were only the shadows of clouds, even if they appeared to be passing through the treetops rather than over them, but it had certainly turned colder, and she could hear more sounds among the trees than Sam was capable of making by himself. Indeed, she couldn't hear him—didn't know when she last had—and wished he would abandon his stealth. She thought she was hearing a nearby stream until the sound ceased, so that it must have been twigs rattling like pebbles and a liquid rush of foliage, though all around her the trees had stayed quite still. A sudden chorus of crows broke out as if to convince her she had often heard them in the forest, but the croaking was only a violent spasm of the treetops to her left. She'd begun to shiver and shiver again, because now it was apparent that the shadows were the source of the chill; each one felt like a stripe of ice penetrating her skin. An outburst of birdsong all around her failed to raise her spirits, not just because she could see no birds but since the various birdcalls sounded a little too sharp and thin, a little too similar. She opened her mouth to shout to Sam in the hope that would make him show himself, but her breath shrank from the task. She thought she might be close to the outer world, because surely she was hearing more than one cyclist race through the forest, even if it would be the first time she had ever heard one there. No, the noise was caused by restlessness in a mass of low bare bushes like a patch of fibrous ground mist ahead and to her left, although the trees around them held themselves quite still, or were their shadows hinting otherwise? She might have imagined her confusion was being mocked by hysterical laughter if she hadn't identified the uproar as a shrill flapping in the treetops. Her attention had no business up there while she needed to find Sam—and that must be his face peering around a fir, even if the distance made the trunk appear too scrawny to conceal him. "Just be sure you know where you're going," she shouted, but her nerves wouldn't leave it at that. "If you were a gentleman you'd wait for your mother."

She thought she had managed to reach him at last. He didn't vanish until she advanced half a dozen steps towards him. At least there were only small areas of cover for several hundred yards beyond his hiding place. She ought to be able to see where he dodged, and she concentrated on trying as she sprinted across the slippery treacherous ground, dislodging fragments of its intricate decoration and a sweetish earthy scent that she found less alluring than it seemed designed to be—concentrated on ignoring the clamour of birdsong that sounded about to converge on a solitary note to reveal that its source was as singular, and the vast slow darkness that paced her through the highest branches, and the shadows rippling like disturbed water at the edge of her vision, although the trees owned up to no movement. Were the shadows betraying that pretence? The notion wasn't quite enough to stop her in her tracks, not when she was both desperate to catch up with Sam and anxious to ignore a stack of bracket fungi on an oak she had to pass, fungi unpleasantly reminiscent of a gathering of at least a dozen pallid lips—and then a further realisation seized her. "Sam," she cried, and faltered to a standstill only a moment before the shadows grew motionless. Their stillness might have been challenging her to believe they had ever moved, but her suspicion went deeper than that. If there was darkness overhead, how could the trees cast shadows at all?

Not until she raised the flashlight as though it could somehow illuminate the problem did she notice that she hadn't switched it off, because she could see its beam climbing a pair of trees, etching blackness into cracks within bright patches of bark and throwing two elongated shadows ahead. At once those were the only visible shadows. Apprehension clenched her neck and shoulders, which felt as if a burden was riding them. She jerked the flashlight higher in a panicky attempt to locate Sam. Then everything she'd imagined she was seeing was extinguished, and a blackness vaster than the woods fell on her.

For a moment she thought she was back under the mound—that she had never left the lowest room—and then she managed to distinguish through the branches that looked blacker than the sky a feeble star. By the time she succeeded in drawing a breath, another tiny point of light had shown itself, though its unsteadiness suggested that it was in danger of failing. The stars gave no illumination; only her flashlight did while shivering with the cold that was no longer confined to the shadows, or with panic, or both. Had she been searching the woods for so long that night had somehow fallen unnoticed, concealed by a pretence kept up by the woods, or was the darkness their true state? All she knew was that it had made her lose Sam.

She gripped the flashlight so hard it bruised her hands and tried to level the wavering beam. Trees appeared to lean towards it to hint at their shapes and absorb a portion of it while fallen leaves used shadows to help raise their insect heads, and she told herself she hadn't glimpsed the stack of fungoid mouths begin to part their lips with a dismaying randomness. Then, at the ill-defined limit of the beam, a figure stepped forward just enough for its face to be dimly recognisable. It was Sam.

"You'll have to wait for me now," she called, struggling to hold her voice steady, "or you won't be able to see." Whatever the truth about the darkness might be, she had to bear it if it brought Sam back to her. She took a shaky pace towards him. She didn't see him retreat, but the beam swayed so wildly that she'd advanced less than a yard before it lost him.

"Stay in the light, Sam," she pleaded, doing her utmost to stabilise it so that he could, even though the effort slowed her down when she was frantic to escape the woods. As she strained her eyes, which felt as though the dark was massing on them, she tried to see only him, not the trees that kept appearing to lean hungrily towards the light. That must surely be a consequence of the swaying of the beam, and the oppressive blackness had to be the reason why the trees seemed composed so nearly of the dark that they consumed more of her light than they should, or was she suffering the effects of some trace of the substance that had overcome her father? Of course, that would explain the tingle she'd experienced on handling the tree at the edge of the common—it would explain the movements she glimpsed here and there as if the light was awakening fragments of the woods. They were threatening to grow altogether too clearly defined by the time the beam relocated Sam.

Before she could call out to him he limped away from the edge of the dimness into the dark. He must be watching her over his shoulder, for his face appeared to vanish an instant later than the rest of him. "Wait for the light," she cried. "Look where you're going. You'll fall over something. You'll hurt yourself."

Her voice was wobbling as much as the light from trying to catch up with him. She tried to concern herself only with that, not with the sights that the beam persisted in rousing—a rounded variously gaping stump that nodded to itself as it returned to the dark, a whitish log that set about using the remains of a dozen or more branches to inch caterpillar-like towards her, a fallen tree split into fragments that resembled eyeless reptiles with deformed legs, especially once they began to lumber after her, splintering twigs and rustling dead leaves. They were the kinds of thing her father would have imagined he saw and heard, she made herself think as she watched an object she had taken for a fir-cone extend spindly legs covered with scales and scuttle away from the flashlight beam, although a child might fancy she was seeing faces in the lumps the size of heads the beam found on some of the tree-trunks. What sort of mind would have the notion that the forest had grown carnivorous, if insects and birds and small animals weren't sprouting partially formed from branches? At the edge of her vision, articles were scrabbling up and down the trees, a process that involved considerable alterations in size and shape, of which those that resembled giant spiders were the least alarming. She was beginning to feel like a child abandoned in the dark, and didn't know what kind of appeal she might have made to Sam if the beam hadn't offered her a glimpse of him. Even though it left her with the impression that he was limping forward away from her while continuing to face her, she dared to feel reassured. Through the trees beyond him she was just able to distinguish the lights of Goodmanswood.

So he'd found the way out, and nothing else need matter. She wasn't certain if the beam had grown dimmer or only more diffuse because she'd raised it higher to greet the lights, but surely enough power was left in the flashlight to see her and Sam to the edge of the woods. The apprehension underlying that thought had to be sufficient reason for her to feel paced by a companion behind all the trees at once. She could ignore it if she concentrated on catching up with Sam—ignore the vast presence that loomed behind the trees from which she'd begun to think the frantic shapes were hatching or otherwise emerging, though some of the tree-trunks seemed content to display swollen wrinkled growths that peered and mouthed at her. She wasn't compelled to look at any of this, not when she could see lit windows, however distant, through the trees and better still, Sam limping while the flashlight beam staggered around him as if they were competing at unsteadiness. She was yet more relieved to hear his voice until she realised her mistake. "Mum," she imagined she heard. "Mum, is that you?"

Even if that had made any sense, she seemed to be hearing him somewhere at her back. It had to be as much of a hallucination as the rest of the misperceptions her mind was struggling to exclude. That was Sam ahead of her, imitating the unbalanced flashlight beam, and only Sam need be real. She was chasing him as fast as the trees and the slithery ground would allow—she'd abandoned trying to hold the flashlight any steadier than was required to keep him visible, however dimly—when she seemed to hear his voice again, more separate than ever from the sight of him. "Is the light you?" it said.

It wasn't just its tone that succeeded in making her hesitate, though it sounded more desperately hopeful than she thought she could have borne to imagine; it was the notion of his being lost in the dark dreadful woods because she'd taken the light away from him. His voice had to be a product of her state, which must be worse than she was able to admit, but nevertheless she stumbled to a halt. As the flashlight beam steadied, so did the figure that was leading her towards the town. Only the swaying of the light had caused its gait to appear lopsided. As she realised that, she saw the figure remember to limp.

She was jabbing the light towards it in a vain attempt to discern it and its reversed face more clearly when Sam's voice grew despairing. "Is it you? Can't you speak?"

Tightness renewed itself on her neck and shoulders as though to fix her where she was, but she swung herself and the light in the direction of the blackness that had seemed to produce his voice. "Sam?"

"I'm here. Can't you see me?"

She couldn't deny him the light any longer, and yet she felt compelled to glance over her shoulder. Though it blocked more of her vision than she found reasonable, she was virtually certain that nobody was on the move between her and the town; indeed, the woods had become oppressively, intently still. "Not yet," she called as directly towards his voice as she could, and began to trail the flashlight beam across the waiting trees. "Am I pointing at you yet? Tell me when I am."

Nothing moved except the net of dim shadows that she or the dark might have been casting for him. Whatever had been ranging up and down the trees had disappeared as though absorbed by the tree-trunks. Only swellings and the faces trapped in them remained on the scaly wood, faces that refused to own up to being hallucinations, however passionately she felt they should. She dragged the light across them, unable to move it faster in case she missed Sam, and then it shuddered to a halt on a growth as high as but larger than a man's head on a trunk that bore at best a token resemblance to a cypress. Though the excrescence was patched with glistening lichen and starting to collapse, it had her father's face.

The bulging eyes were no more than pale knots in the wood. The mouth that looked paralysed in the act of uttering a cry was only one of several holes in the face, and just as full of restless insects. It was all too recognisable, however, and so was its absolute helplessness. That seemed to gather on her, adding to the pressure on her neck and shoulders. Perhaps nothing could have jerked her out of her appalled trance except Sam's plea. "Why have you stopped? I'm over here."

She forced herself to swing the beam towards his voice, and the night closed like black water over the ruins of her father's face. "Stay there. I'll find you," she had to swallow in order to call, and made herself walk away from the lights of Goodmanswood. She'd taken just one step when she felt the woods change.

At first she wasn't sure how. She sensed only that the transformation was or was about to be immense and terrible. The air had thickened with the imminence of some event far larger than a storm, so that she was barely able to draw breath. The trees seemed poised to execute some movement—to cut her off from Sam. Whatever surrounded her in the dark didn't want her to reach him. She yearned to continue doubting its existence, but she couldn't if that entailed leaving him at its mercy. She managed a breath that aggravated her shivering, and pressed the heels of her hands together in case that might reduce the shaking of the flashlight beam, and pushed one foot in front of the other. "I'm still coming," she declared in not much of a voice.

Shadows twitched ahead of her as if they were determined to find him before she did. As she told herself that was merely an effect of the light, they moved more than they should. They reared up in unison behind the trees that cast them, and each shadow merged with its source. At once it was apparent how much darkness was involved in the composition of the trees, which began to soak up the flashlight beam with a thirst so voracious Heather felt it in her shrinking fingertips. In a second the beam was twice as dim and reached scarcely half as far.

"That won't stop me," she whispered, unless she simply thought it. If there were no longer any shadows, however insane that seemed, and the woods maintained their intimidating stillness, then any movement would surely have to be Sam. It took her a moment to gain enough control of her mind to realise she needn't rely on her sight. "Talk to me, Sam. Don't stop," she pleaded, and lurched forward a step.

The trees fastened on the light as if they didn't need to move in order to pounce. As her foot found the earth, whose decaying surface felt ready to slither apart beneath her, every visible tree vanished into blackness, or it welled out of them. Nothing was visible except the filament of the flashlight bulb, a shrivelled reddish ember—not even any stars or the difference between the sky and the branches she sensed looming overhead, if they were only branches. "Where are you?" Sam called, his voice giving way. "Where's the light?"

"Here. I'm here."

She was afraid of alerting the dark by telling him. She had so little idea where she was that she felt in danger of losing her balance, of sprawling into whatever the darkness hid. She risked planting her feet wider apart but found herself retreating a step, to be where she could be certain she'd already stood. The next moment the bulb flared up.

Though the beam had by no means regained all its strength, she was able to make out the nearest trees. "Can you see that?" she did her best to shout.

"I'm not sure."

She heard him struggling to sound his age. She mustn't worsen his panic, she mustn't panic herself, but it felt as though she might have to when she yielded to the only idea she could find in her aching brittle skull. As she stepped back a pace the action felt like an unspoken prayer. It was answered; the flashlight brightened, hinting at dozens of trees. "I can now," Sam told her as if his voice had drawn power from the beam.

She scarcely heard him. If the darkness hadn't come close to extinguishing the flashlight in order to keep her and Sam apart, what had its purpose been? She paced backwards and saw the beam stretch dimly further in what was unquestionably a response—and then she became aware that she was backing towards Goodmanswood. In that moment she didn't just understand: she sensed the thirst of whatever was intent on urging her in that direction, a thirst more profound and awful than the voraciousness that had consumed her light. Perhaps everything she'd glimpsed in the woods had been designed to lead or drive her out of them. Something wanted her to carry it or its influence beyond them, into the world.

"Where are you going?" Sam protested, but his words were dwarfed into insignificance. She was unable to halt her insight, which was letting her perceive far too much. She was beginning to glimpse the essence of the woods—the presence they had grown both to summon and conceal.

At first it seemed that her surroundings had been reversed—that the woods were rooted less in the earth than in the darkness the familiar sky would have masked. This left her utterly disoriented, in the grip of a vertigo that let more of the truth come for her. Her mouth opened as her mind did, but she no longer knew if she was desperate to cry out or to breathe. The entity whose thirst she'd sensed was using the forest to reach for her and the world. The forest was a member with as many claws or digits or tendrils as there were trees. It was the end of a gigantic limb that stretched into a blackness she was terrified to contemplate. However insubstantial the limb might be in terms of the reality she had taken for granted, it was gaining some kind of substance. The body to which the limb belonged was drawing itself along it like a spider down a thread of web. The prospect of looking up appalled her, and yet her head was tilting helplessly skywards as if her neck was being manipulated like a puppet's. Any moment she might see more than blackness overhead. She might see what its inhabitant had for a face.

"What's wrong?" Sam called, which struck her as almost, though dreadfully, comical. She heard his footfalls pounding towards her, muffled by leaves, if only leaves. She was suddenly afraid that he would be prevented from reaching her—afraid of how he might be prevented—but apparently all concentration was on her. She felt frozen by the notion that she and Sam were less than insects trapped beneath a great cat's paw. Her gaze edged upward, dragged towards the blackness that was no longer merely night. She was peripherally aware

that Sam was close to her; he'd halted a few feet away and was muttering "Oh Jesus." Had her perception somehow rendered her unrecog-
nisable? When he came at her and thrust his hands around her neck,
she thought he meant to strangle her. Even this seemed negligible
under the blackness that was lowering itself to settle on her or to crush
her in its grasp. Then she realised that he was trying to remove some
object from her neck.

At once the sense of hugeness grew unfocused, and there was only
the weight on her shoulders. She felt thin limbs clinging to her neck
an instant before Sam broke their grip and flung away the creature that
had been riding her ever since she'd crossed the threshold of Selcouth's lowest room. As it struck the ground it began to squirm feebly
on its back and grope at the air with its rudimentary limbs as though
searching for Heather. It was pallid and half-formed, very obviously
premature, except for its oversized head. That was all Heather
glimpsed—she hadn't even time to turn the beam on it—before Sam
grabbed the flashlight. "Sam," she gasped.

She'd realised what he meant to do, but it was too late to stop him,
even if she should. As he swung the flashlight, the beam lit up the
creature's face. It was by no means unlike Sam's, but dauntingly
ancient, and transformed into a mask of flesh by the eyes, which were
filled to their brims by a blackness deeper than any night. Was it grinning or baring its toothless gums in some other kind of anticipation?
In a moment Heather might have known, but two blows with the
flashlight made sure of crushing its fragile skull.

A cry was rising to her lips when an indrawn breath cut it off.
Every visible tree was straining towards the sky, an agonised convulsion that she heard seizing the entire forest, while the creature lost its
substance. In an instant it was skinless, in another shapeless, and then
there was only a trace like a glistening mist or a haze that seeped into
the shrouded earth. A faint sweetish scent lingered in the air for a
heartbeat before she sensed the withdrawal of a presence, how far and
in what direction she was unable to judge. When she dared to glance

up, having heard the trees creak back into their everyday form, she saw stars pretending there was nothing besides them in or beyond the sky. "Gone," Sam muttered, and stood fingering his forehead as if something had vanished from within it. Heather found she couldn't stop writhing her shoulders as she turned to urge him to light the way out of the woods.

EPILOGUE:

The Watcher

S AM."

"Did it have to be me?"

"No, but I hoped it was. How are you this week?"

"Pretty good. How about you?"

"Never better. I'm the last person you should worry about. Only pretty good?"

"No, fine."

"Now, Sam, the last person you should try that on is your mother. What's wrong?"

"Just the job."

"You aren't enjoying it as much."

"Yes I am, and there's none I'd rather be doing. None I can think of that would be more worthwhile either, but it can get frustrating."

"For example?"

"We've a family where I'm sure the father is abusing all his daughters, but the hard part is getting anyone to say so."

"I can imagine how you must feel about that."

"I don't want you to think I wish I didn't have to handle it. It's my kind of case."

"I've gathered that. Why, do you think?"

"Because it's the worst kind, the kind that most needs somebody to intervene."

"That's it, of course. That must be it. Sam . . ."

"I'm still here."

"I keep meaning to ask you, that's if you feel like talking about it, how much you remember."

"What about?"

"Before you made the move to London."

"Not being able to, you mean? I expect half of that was really knowing the job dad wanted to fix me up with wasn't right for me."

"I hadn't thought of that. I know he's proud of the one you're doing. Anything else you recall?"

"You're thinking of Sylvia."

"I could be."

"How we found her after she got rid of the baby and then we somehow got lost in the woods all night. I still wish you'd gone for counselling like me."

"The important thing is you did. Otherwise you mightn't have realised you wanted to do social work, you said so yourself."

"But if you'd gone . . ."

"Seriously, don't waste any worrying on me. I'm like you. I'm exactly where I want to be and need to be."

"Mum."

"And don't sound like that either."

"Then can I ask you something?"

"You always can, and you should."

"Why were you so anxious to make sure they filled in the place we found Sylvia?"

"We wouldn't want children wandering down there and hurting themselves, would we? Nothing and nobody's going to get through all that concrete."

"Fair enough, if that's all."

"What else were you thinking it could be?"

"I wondered if it had anything to do with the book you said Sylvia found."

"You're still telling me you never saw it. You don't have to go that far, Sam."

"It's the truth."

"Well, you're never going to see it now. It's no great loss if it made Sylvie go where she ended up, you'll agree."

"I never understood how you thought it could have influenced her so much."

"Then don't let it bother you. It's just your mother being strange."

"I wish you wouldn't keep on saying that about yourself. Listen, I have to go in a moment. I'm meeting someone for dinner."

"Someone I'd like, I hope."

"I think you would. Maybe I'll bring her to meet you."

"You don't want to do that, Sam."

"Of course I do. Why wouldn't I?"

"No point in coming back here now you've made the break. There's nothing for you here, it would only depress you, and I'd be worrying about you driving here. I'd get even less sleep. I can't help that, being your mother."

"You sound as if you don't want me ever to come."

"Suppose you found you couldn't leave when all your clients need you?"

"That isn't going to happen, not now I've figured out why it did."

"You mustn't be too sure, Sam. I know what we can do instead. We'd like to see where he's living, wouldn't we, mummy? Let's go soon."

"Is Margo there? Say hello for me."

"Sam says hello."

"Hi, Sam."

"And tell her congratulations that her work's popular again."

"I will. Why do you think that's happened?"

"Things go in and out of fashion. What else could it be?"

"You don't think the world's changed somehow."

"Only like always. Listen, I really have to go, but don't have Margo driving all this way unless she's absolutely certainly up to it."

"She's a better driver than ever now she's had her car altered. Custom Car Margo, that's my mother. Do you want a word with her?"

"I better had another time. I'll speak to you both again soon."

"Sleep well tonight and every night, then. Sam says he's sorry but he has to run."

"I ought to as well, Heather. Lucinda was supposed to call about taking more of my work. Don't say it, I won't be running, even less than Sam will."

"I think you're a phenomenon. I'd be nowhere near as sprightly if I'd had to survive what you have."

"And at my age, you're too gracious to say. You've been through plenty, and I know you'll get over it."

"That's the attitude. Looking to the future, that's how the Prices operate. Anyway, someone's after you. Just Lucinda, that's right. Thanks for all the news."

"You know me, always up for a gossip."

"Was there anything else I should know?"

"I can't think what."

"Any new babies in town lately?"

"Not that I've heard. Heather, you're not starting that again, are you?"

"I wasn't aware that I'd stopped. I haven't been visiting, if that's what you mean."

"I hope you won't. You know how people felt about that."

"I expect they feel safe from me now."

"You don't have to tell me nobody was ever anything but safe with you, but you know the kind of stories people have made up about us. I still don't understand why you feel you have to stay so close."

"So long as you don't let it worry you."

"I won't if I know you're getting better."

"Every day I'm more myself."

Margo released a toneless sigh that might have been a comment or a hint of the effort involved in standing up. Once she was on her feet, however, she made no fuss about hobbling four-legged to her car. As Heather held the lightweight crutches while Margo lowered herself into the driver's seat, she risked saying "So you're still going in the woods."

"Wouldn't you want me to?"

"I don't know how I could stop you."

"Not when I'm trying to make a tribute to your sister."

"How are you?"

"By finding traces of her in the woods. The way she'd put her head on one side when she was thinking of a secret. The way she'd hold her hands out when she was going to tell us one."

"You're saying she's there."

"I'm saying nobody but me might notice these things, but that's the point of what I do, isn't it, to make others see? If the shape's growing I paint it, if it's dead and I can carry it on my little trolley I carve it." Margo gestured her closer before murmuring "I keep looking for signs of her baby. I just feel there ought to be some when he or maybe she was never found."

She blinked at Heather's reaction and seemed unhappy with it, especially since she was quick to pretend not to be affected. She reached for her crutches and stored them beside her, then made a parting effort to be positive. "I think I've been rediscovered because I'm sharing what I feel about Sylvia."

Heather managed to conceal her unease for her mother's sake. "Goodbye but not for long," she said, dealing her a kiss on the forehead, and watched her drive out of the gate. Surely nothing much was liable to gain a hold yet—surely the sowing of Margo's vision was less dangerous than any seeds that might have strayed out of the forest, though didn't that mean it was still another reason for Heather to be watchful?

She was making for her father's room when she was accosted. "Heather."

"Yes."

"I heard you with your mother. We can help."

"Tell me how."

"Parents put births in our paper, don't they? We can ask for it to be delivered. We needn't say it's you wanting it or why."

"That would be a start, but . . ."

"Then you'd know where to go and look, or you could tell us what to look for. They can't watch all of us all the time. And there's something better."

"Let me hear it, then."

"We've got them to agree to take a couple of us walking in the woods each day. That's including you, and we'll tell you everything we see when you aren't there. You're the leader now, remember. You've seen the most. You've got more people in the woods than anyone, as well."

"Thanks, Delia," said Heather, and left her tugging at her cheeks as if to help herself survey more of the forest at once. Heather was careful to smile at the receptionist on the way up to her room—her father's room. Even if she oughtn't to be there—even if nothing except gossip made it best for her to be—she couldn't refuse the help of her father's circle now that she'd taken his place. She mustn't underestimate the woods as Selcouth had, never realising that he'd been lured to them to increase their power. Perhaps that had been dissipated for a while, but she knew it would gather itself afresh for its next attempt to enter the world.

The trees rose drowsily to meet her gaze as she crossed the room, her shoulders continuing to squirm. As she lifted the sash the few inches it would travel, a faint sweetish smell drifted in. Though the woods looked paralysed by the August afternoon, the smell suggestive of decay betrayed the activity they hid. At least there were birds in the treetops now, or were they black fragments of some far larger restlessness? "You'll have to show yourself sometime," she whispered, and settled down to watch.